VOLUME 2: **BLACK CLOUD**™ **NO RETURN**

Story	**JASON LATOUR AND IVÁN BRANDON**	
Script	**IVÁN BRANDON**	
Art	**GREG HINKLE**	ISSUES 7,8,10
	SAUMIN PATEL	ISSUES 9,10
	PAUL REINWAND	ISSUE 6
Color	**MATT WILSON**	
Lettering	**ADITYA BIDIKAR**	
Logo and design	**TOM MULLER**	
Cover	**GREG HINKLE AND MATT WILSON**	
Production artist	**DEANNA PHELPS**	
Color flats	**DEE CUNNIFFE**	

Chapter 6

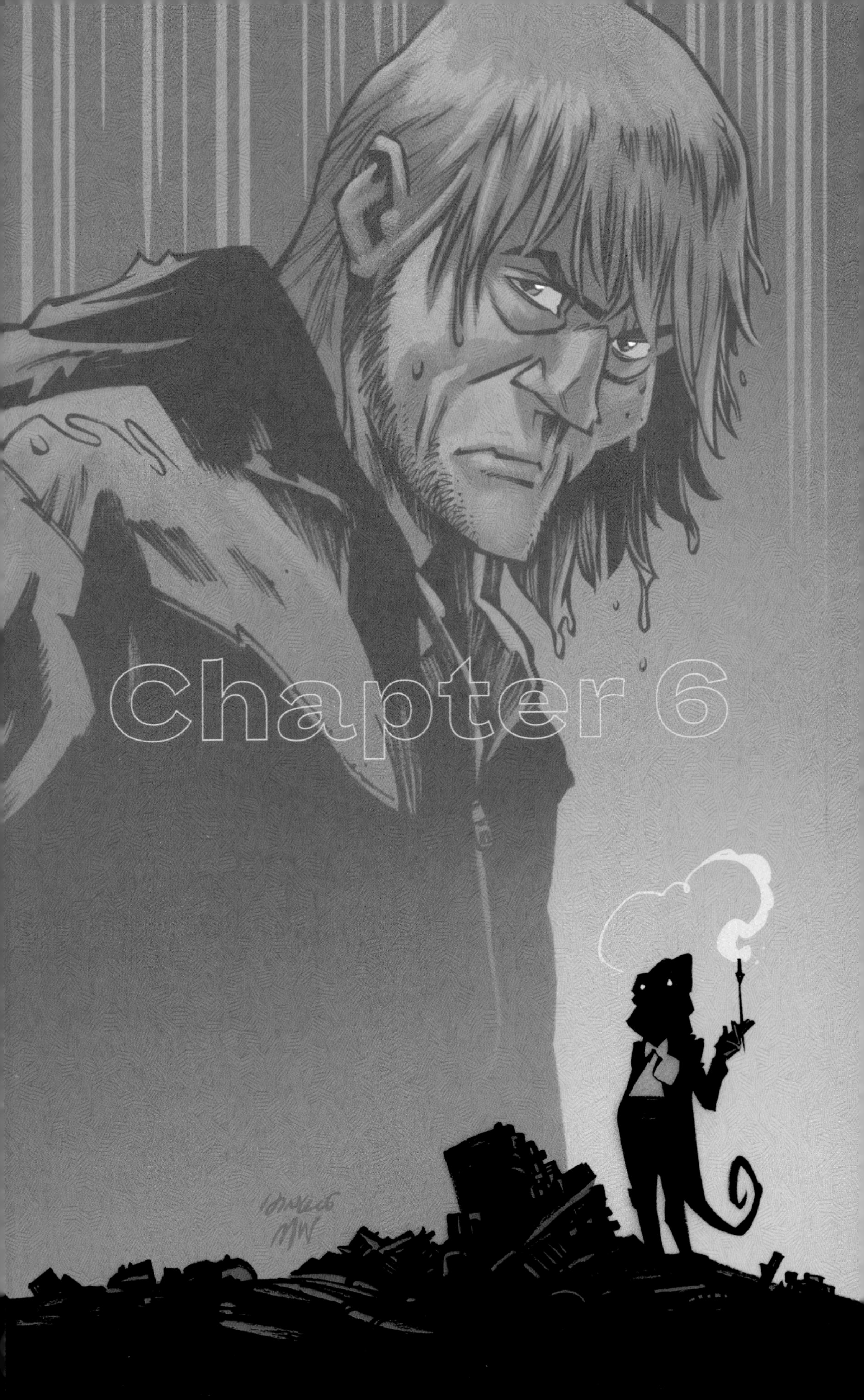

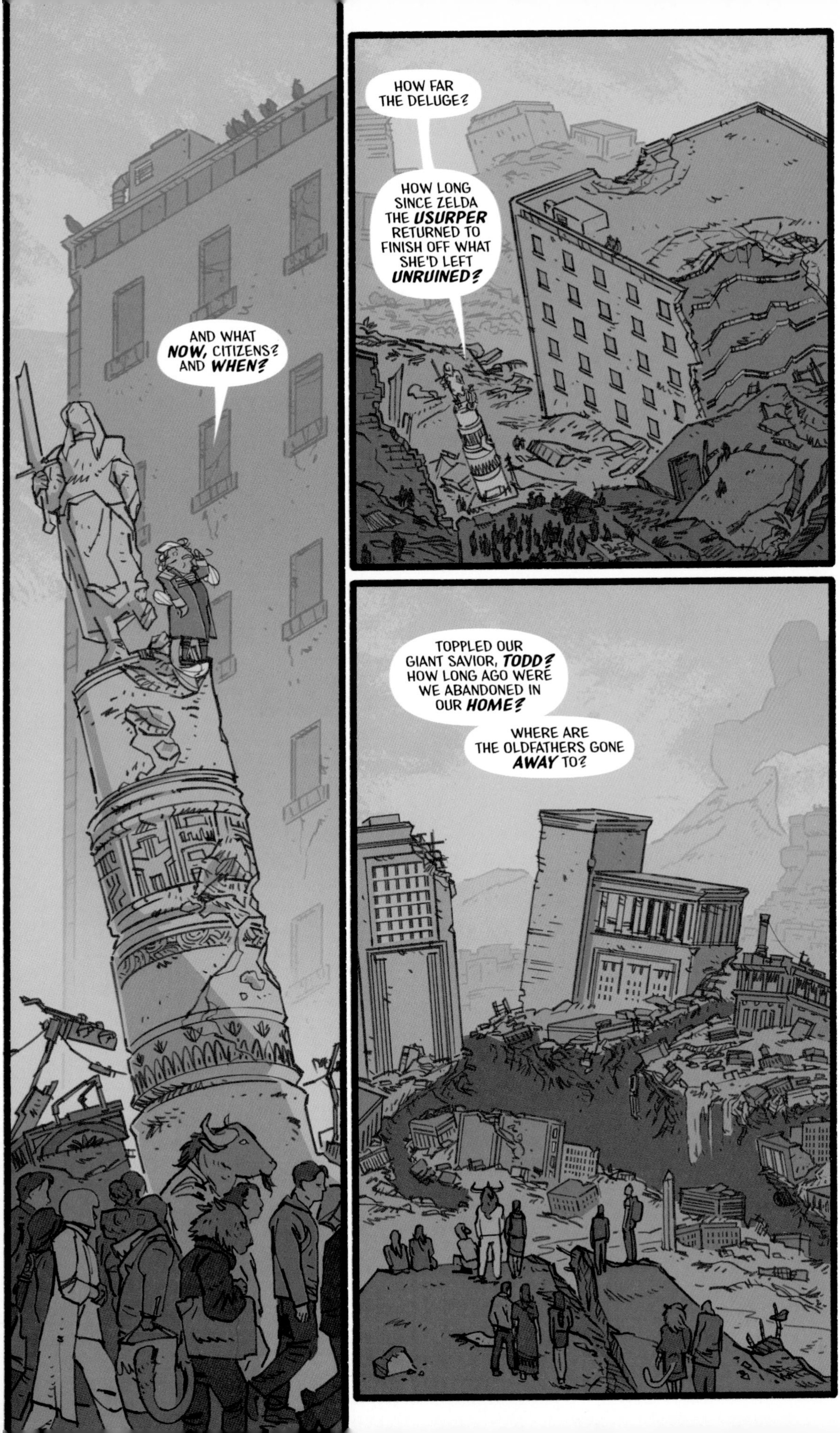
AND WHAT NOW, CITIZENS? AND WHEN?
HOW FAR THE DELUGE?
HOW LONG SINCE ZELDA THE USURPER RETURNED TO FINISH OFF WHAT SHE'D LEFT UNRUINED?
TOPPLED OUR GIANT SAVIOR, TODD? HOW LONG AGO WERE WE ABANDONED IN OUR HOME?
WHERE ARE THE OLDFATHERS GONE AWAY TO?

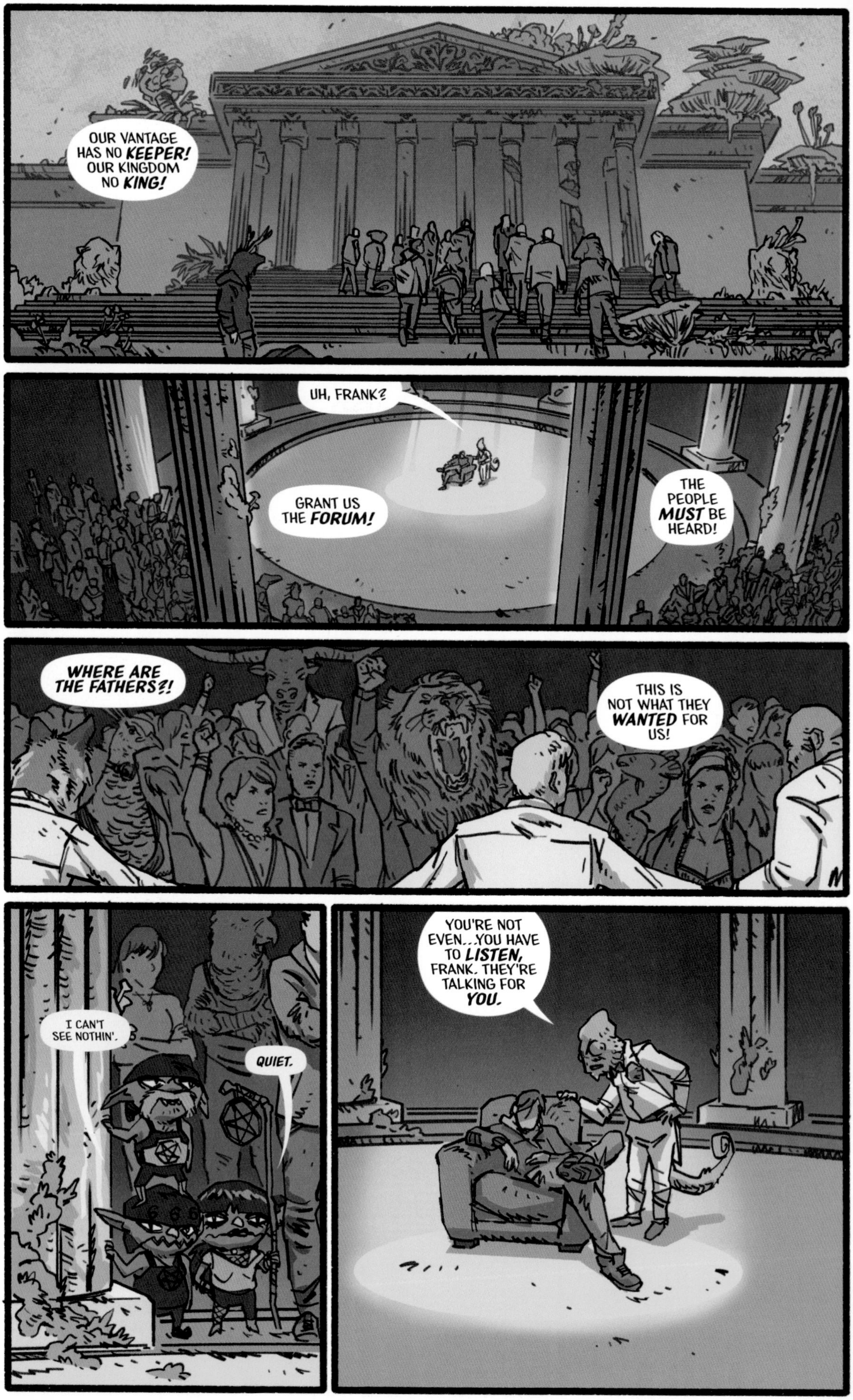
OUR VANTAGE HAS NO KEEPER! OUR KINGDOM NO KING!
UH, FRANK?
GRANT US THE FORUM!
THE PEOPLE MUST BE HEARD!
WHERE ARE THE FATHERS?!
THIS IS NOT WHAT THEY WANTED FOR US!
I CAN'T SEE NOTHIN'.
QUIET.
YOU'RE NOT EVEN...YOU HAVE TO LISTEN, FRANK. THEY'RE TALKING FOR YOU.

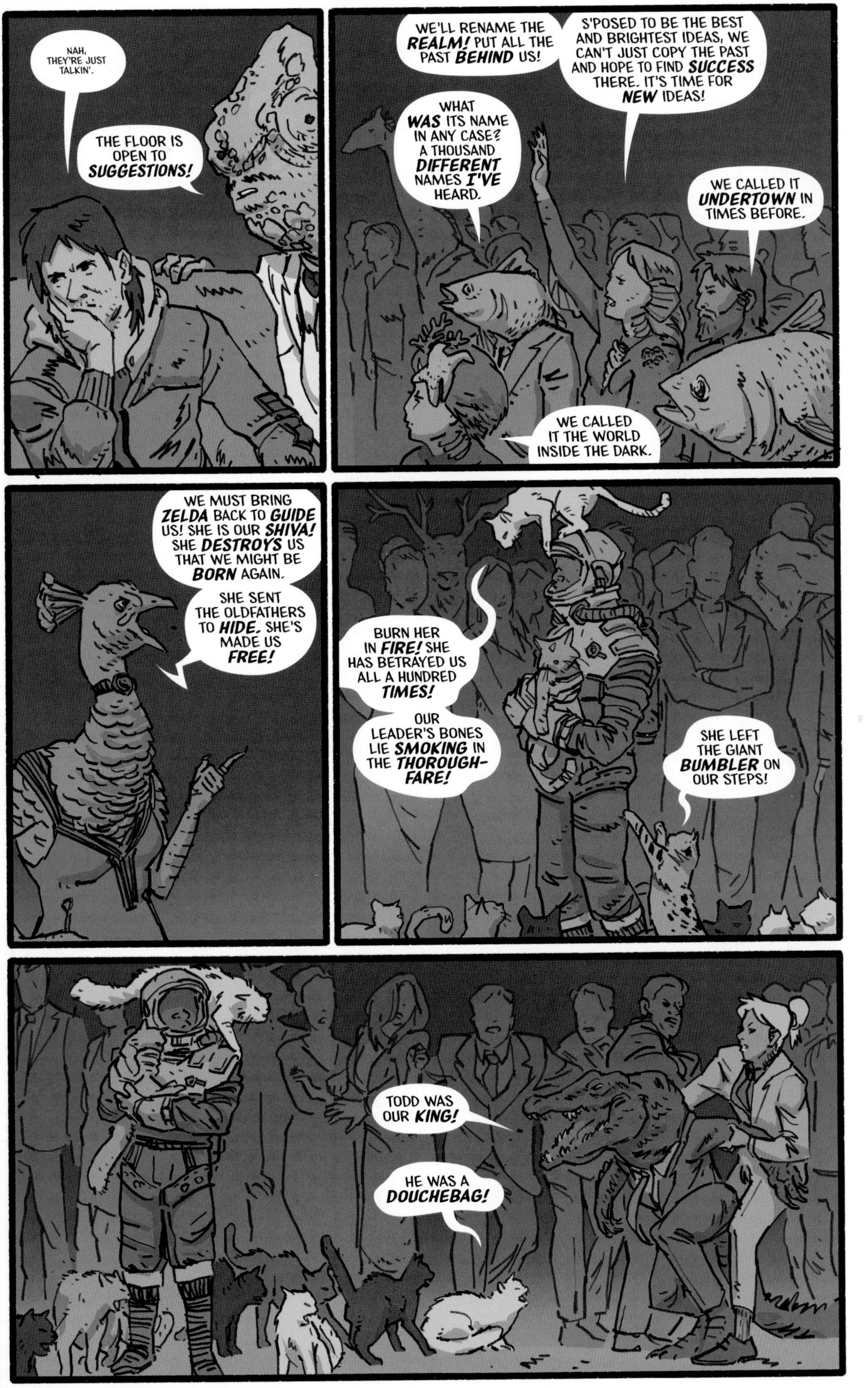

NAH, THEY'RE JUST TALKIN'.
THE FLOOR IS OPEN TO SUGGESTIONS!
WE'LL RENAME THE REALM! PUT ALL THE PAST BEHIND US!
S'POSED TO BE THE BEST AND BRIGHTEST IDEAS, WE CAN'T JUST COPY THE PAST AND HOPE TO FIND SUCCESS THERE. IT'S TIME FOR NEW IDEAS!
WHAT WAS ITS NAME IN ANY CASE? A THOUSAND DIFFERENT NAMES I'VE HEARD.
WE CALLED IT UNDERTOWN IN TIMES BEFORE.
WE CALLED IT THE WORLD INSIDE THE DARK.
WE MUST BRING ZELDA BACK TO GUIDE US! SHE IS OUR SHIVA! SHE DESTROYS US THAT WE MIGHT BE BORN AGAIN.
SHE SENT THE OLDFATHERS TO HIDE. SHE'S MADE US FREE!
BURN HER IN FIRE! SHE HAS BETRAYED US ALL A HUNDRED TIMES!
OUR LEADER'S BONES LIE SMOKING IN THE THOROUGH-FARE!
SHE LEFT THE GIANT BUMBLER ON OUR STEPS!
TODD WAS OUR KING!
HE WAS A DOUCHEBAG!

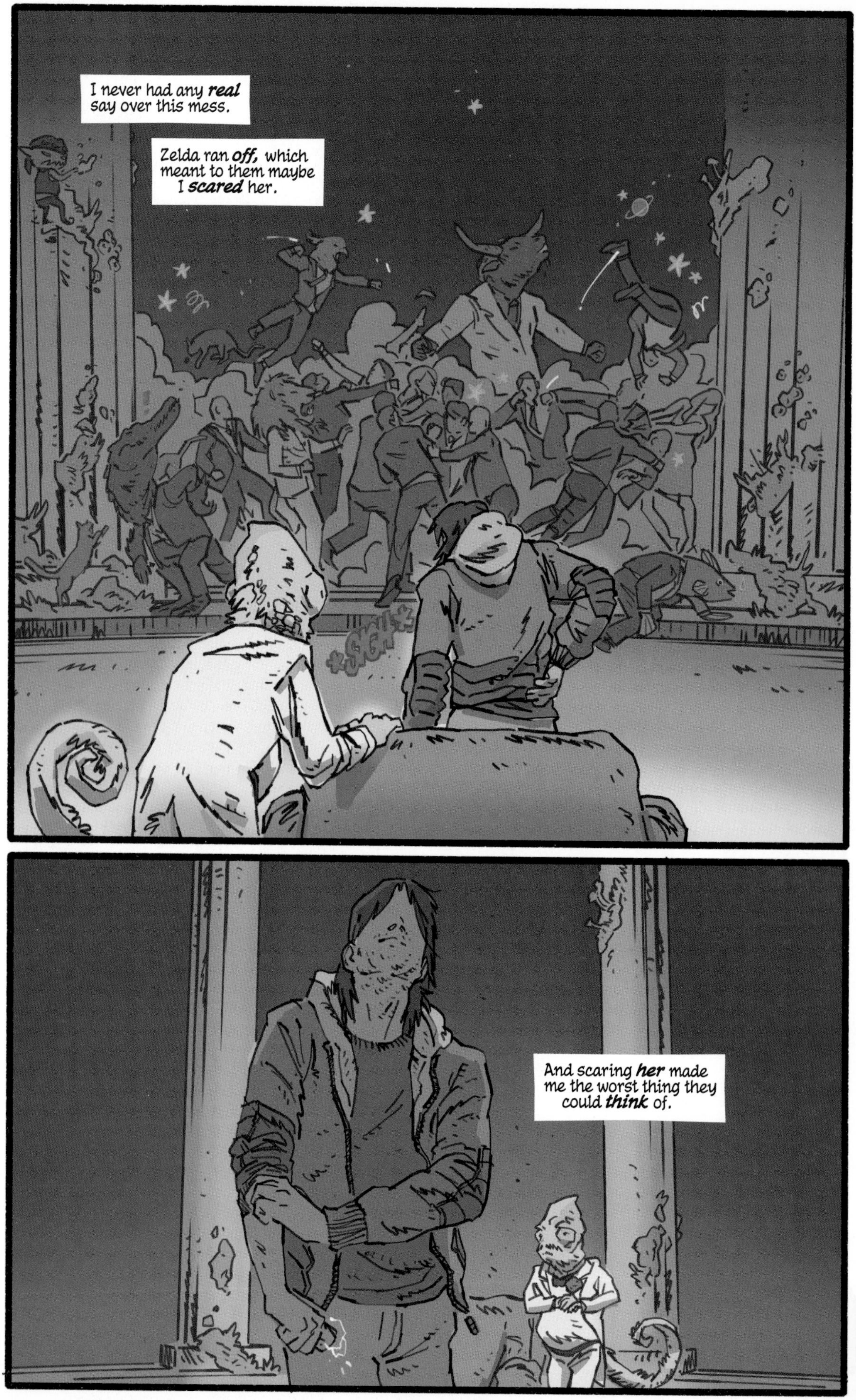

I never had any ***real*** say over this mess.
Zelda ran ***off,*** which meant to them maybe I ***scared*** her.
SIGH
And scaring ***her*** made me the worst thing they could ***think*** of.

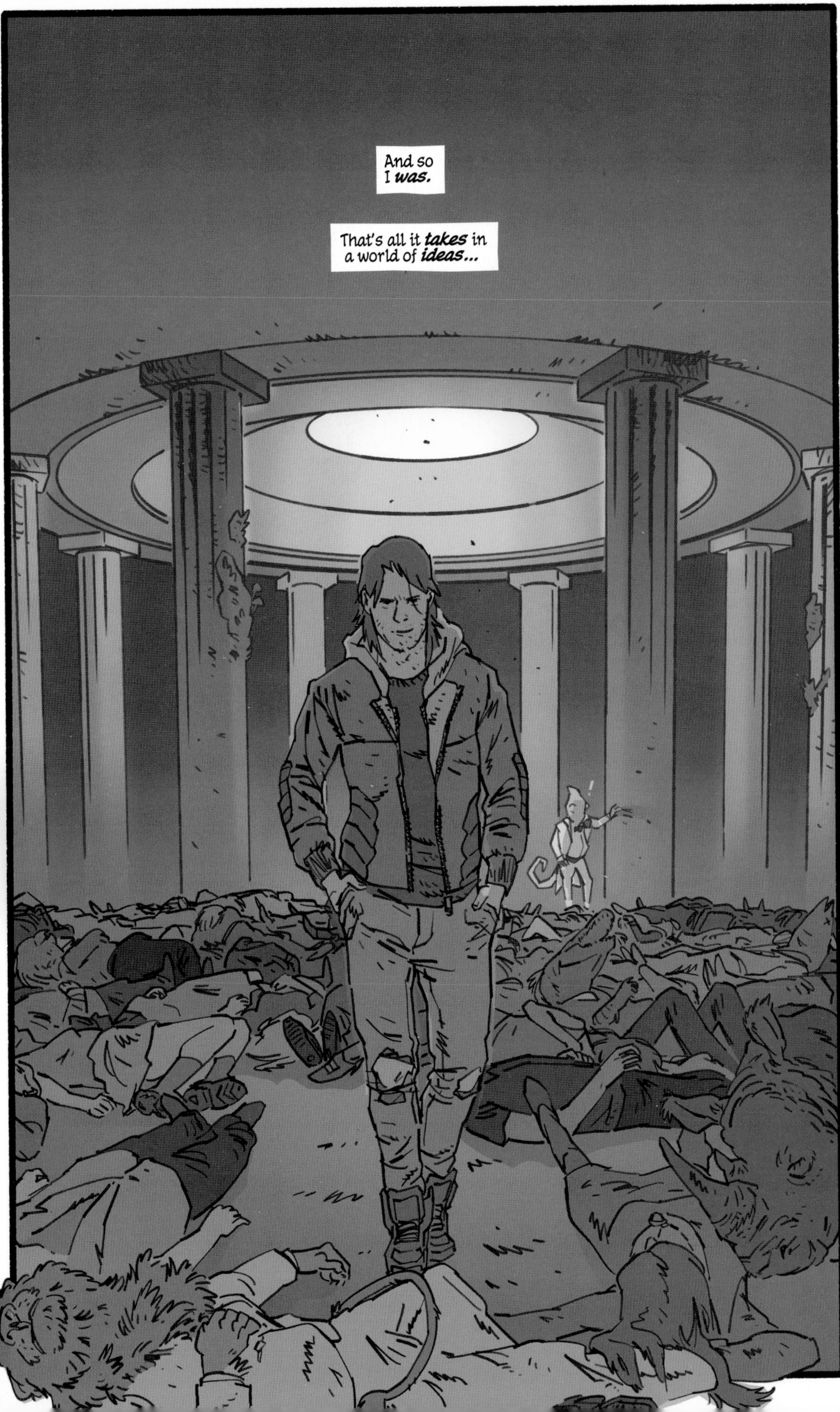
And so I *was.*
That's all it *takes* in a world of *ideas...*

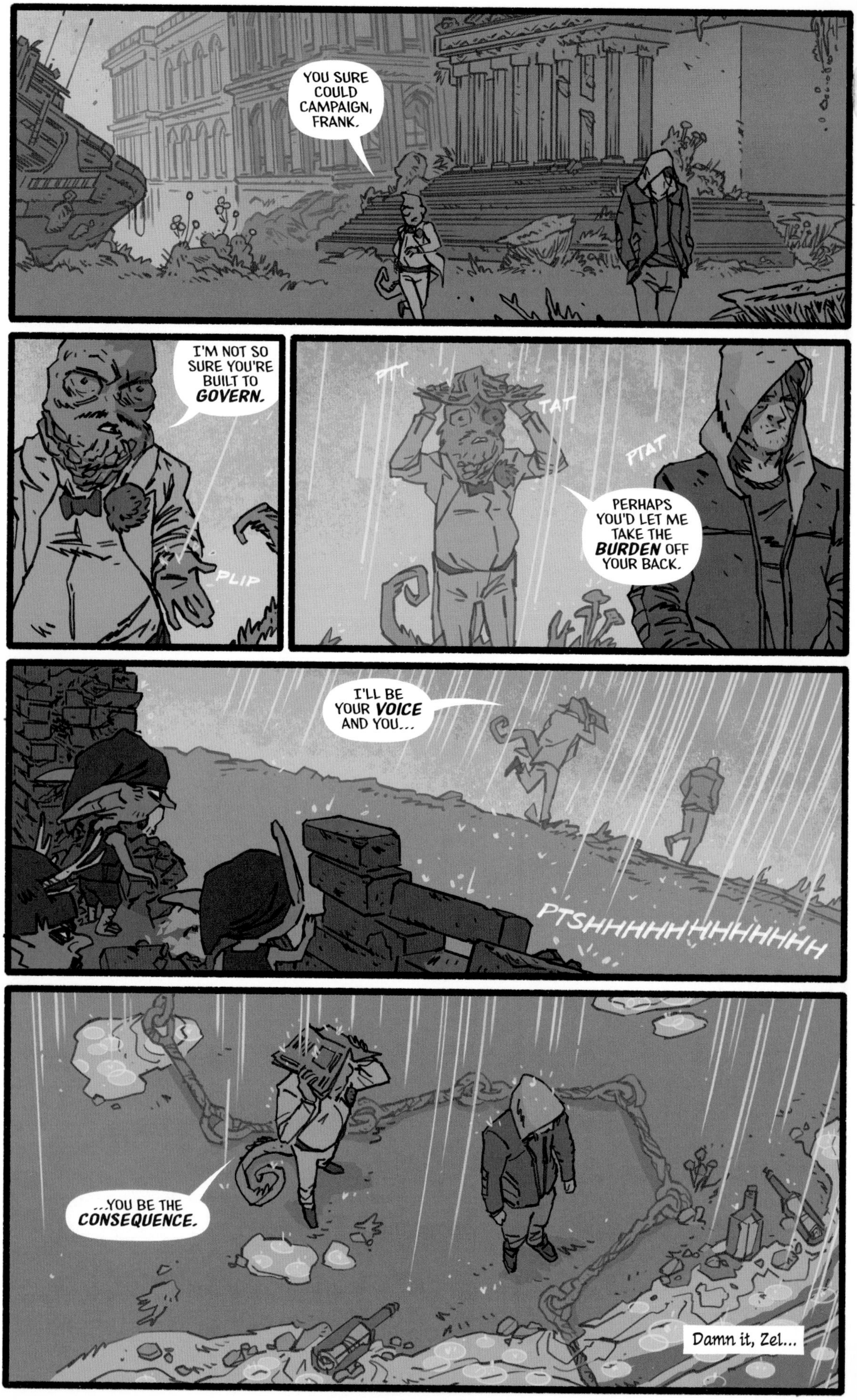
YOU SURE COULD CAMPAIGN, FRANK.
I'M NOT SO SURE YOU'RE BUILT TO GOVERN.
PLIP
PTT
TAT
PTAT
PERHAPS YOU'D LET ME TAKE THE BURDEN OFF YOUR BACK.
I'LL BE YOUR VOICE AND YOU...
PTSHHHHHHHHHHHHH
...YOU BE THE CONSEQUENCE.
Damn it, Zel...

...Why do you always leave me such a *mess?*

Then.

ZEL, CAN YOU JUST...

THIS IS *HEAVY,* I CAN'T *MOVE* AS FAST AS...

ALL THESE HALF-BAKED IDEAS, TOSSED ASIDE...

SOME OF THIS IS *DEPRESSING.* FORGOT THAT *ANY* OF THIS WAS A THING. OR MOST OF IT.

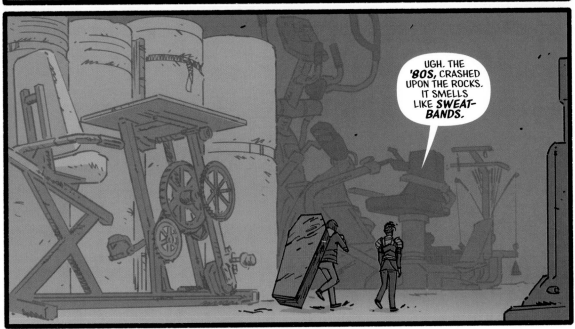

UGH. THE *'80S,* CRASHED UPON THE ROCKS. IT SMELLS LIKE *SWEAT-BANDS.*

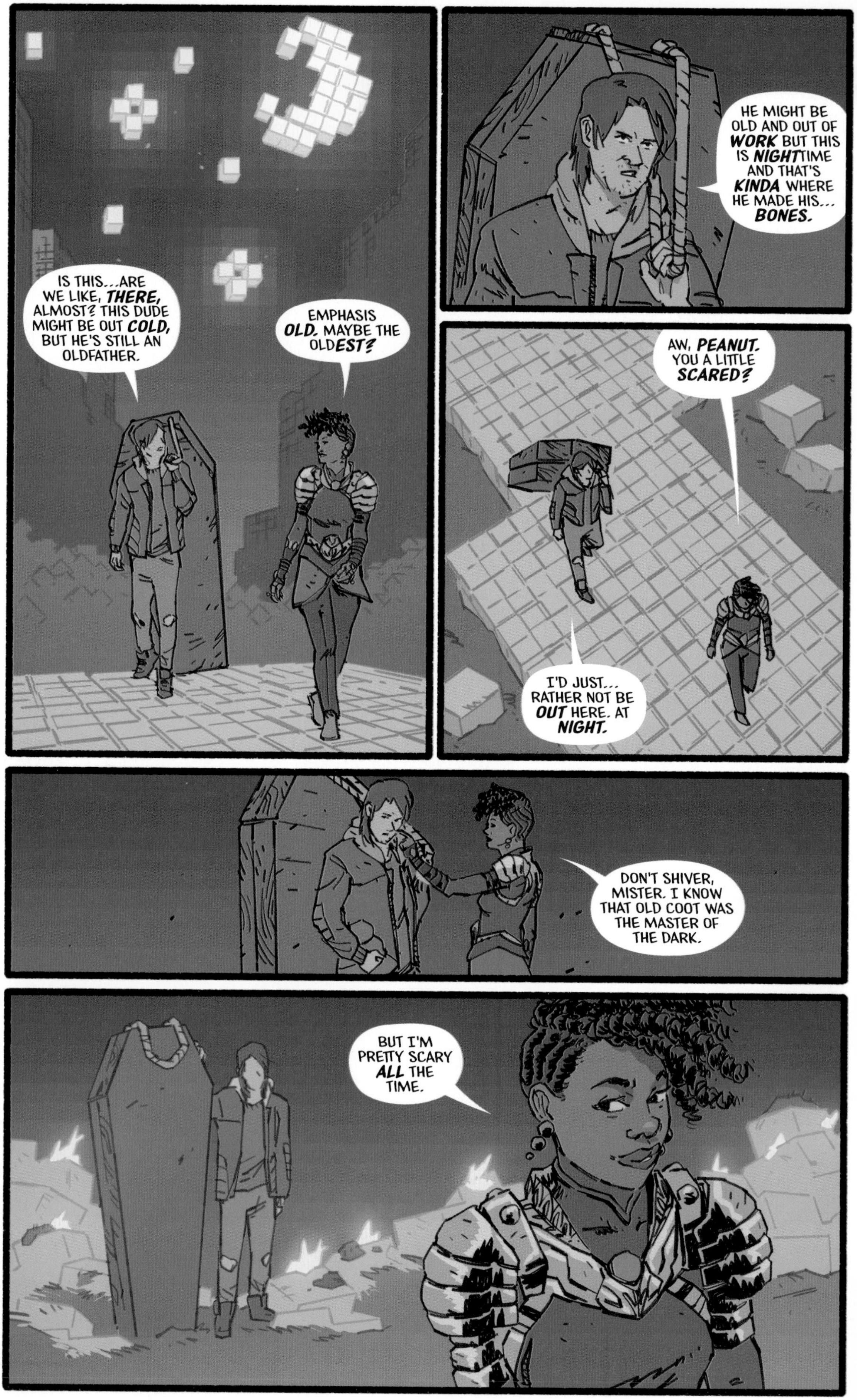
IS THIS...ARE WE LIKE, THERE, ALMOST? THIS DUDE MIGHT BE OUT COLD, BUT HE'S STILL AN OLDFATHER.
EMPHASIS OLD. MAYBE THE OLDEST?
HE MIGHT BE OLD AND OUT OF WORK BUT THIS IS NIGHTTIME AND THAT'S KINDA WHERE HE MADE HIS... BONES.
AW, PEANUT. YOU A LITTLE SCARED?
I'D JUST... RATHER NOT BE OUT HERE. AT NIGHT.
DON'T SHIVER, MISTER. I KNOW THAT OLD COOT WAS THE MASTER OF THE DARK.
BUT I'M PRETTY SCARY ALL THE TIME.

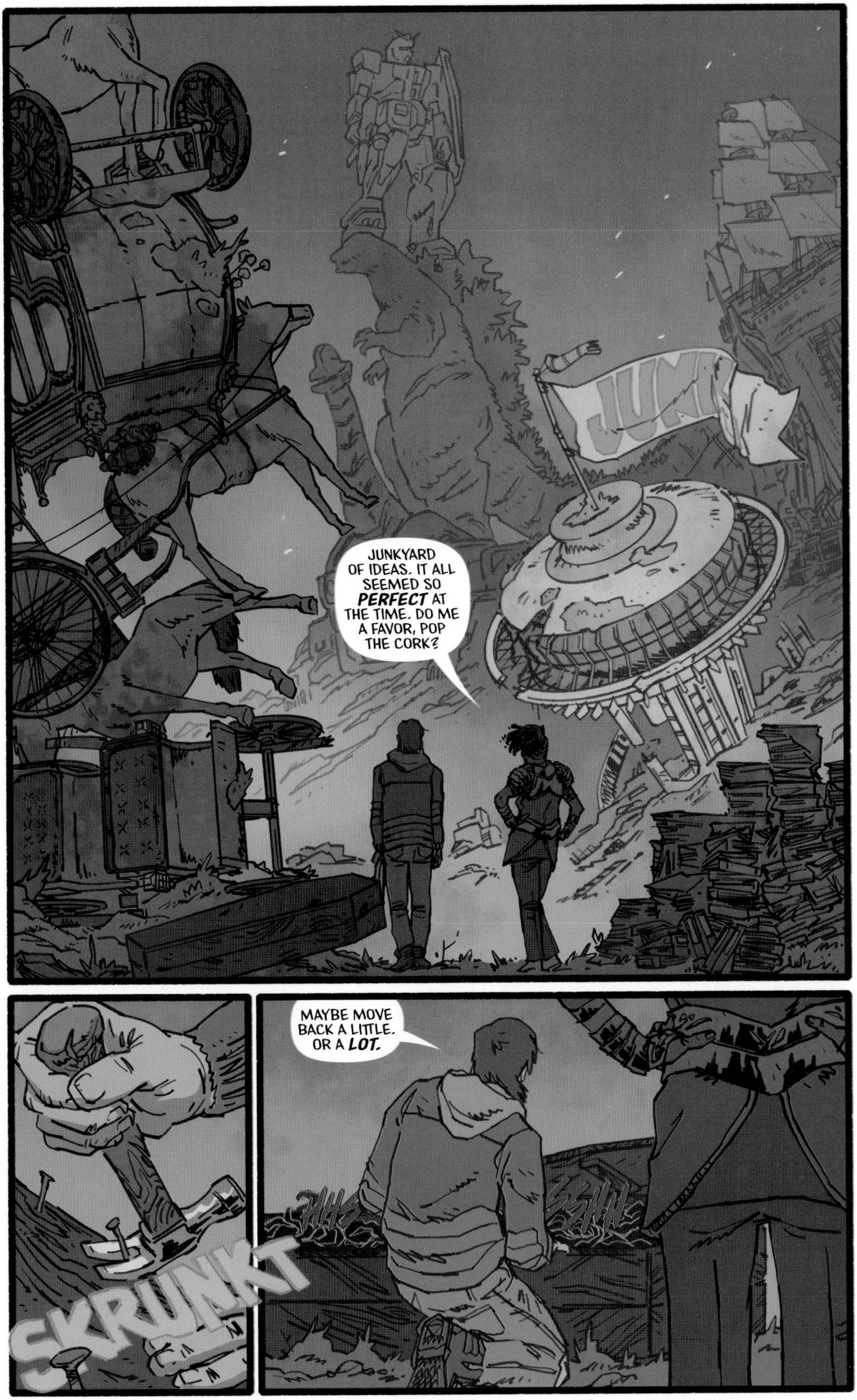
JUNKYARD OF IDEAS. IT ALL SEEMED SO PERFECT AT THE TIME. DO ME A FAVOR, POP THE CORK?
SKRUNKT
MAYBE MOVE BACK A LITTLE. OR A LOT.

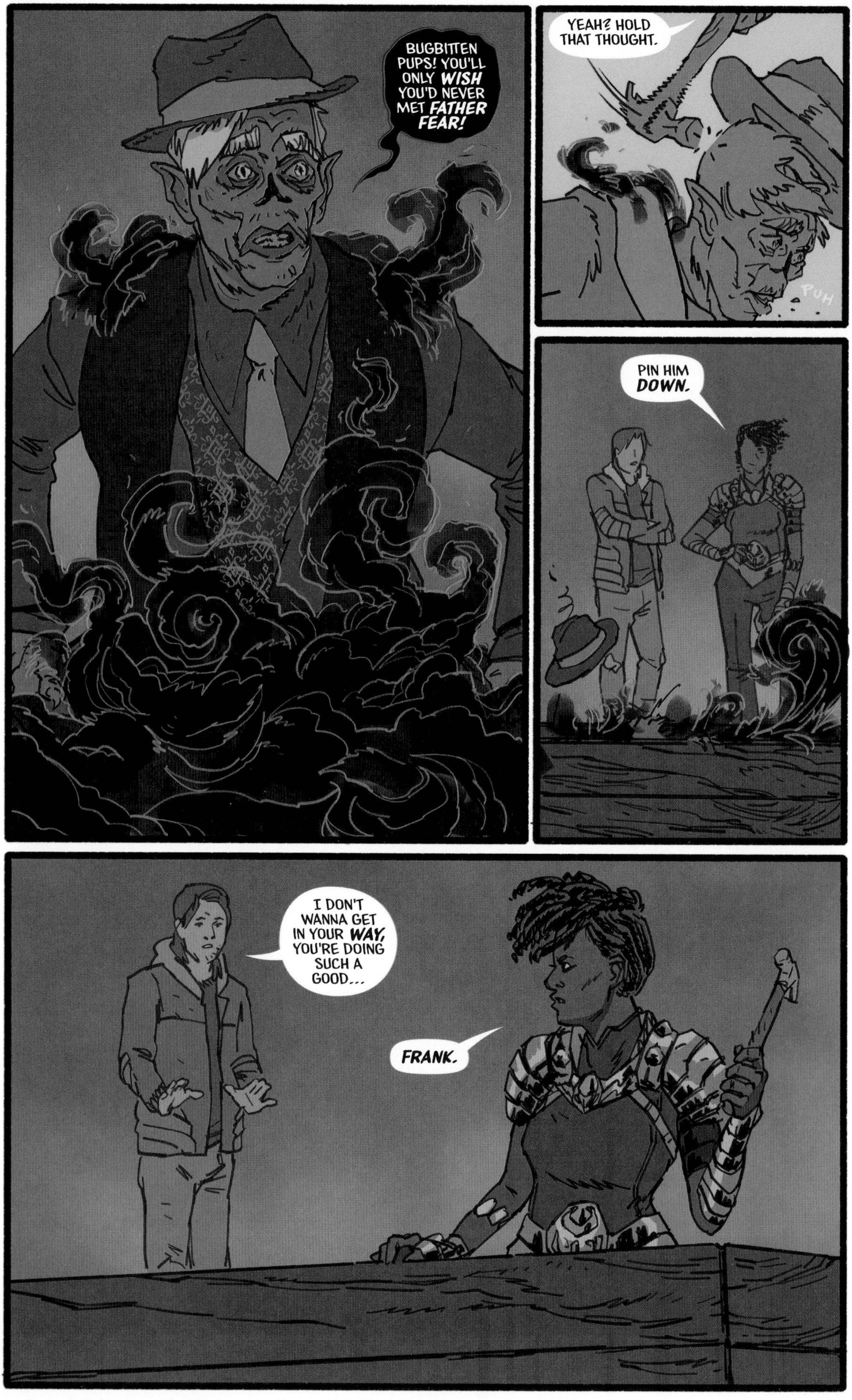
BUGBITTEN PUPS! YOU'LL ONLY WISH YOU'D NEVER MET FATHER FEAR!
YEAH? HOLD THAT THOUGHT.
PUH
PIN HIM DOWN.
I DON'T WANNA GET IN YOUR WAY, YOU'RE DOING SUCH A GOOD...
FRANK.

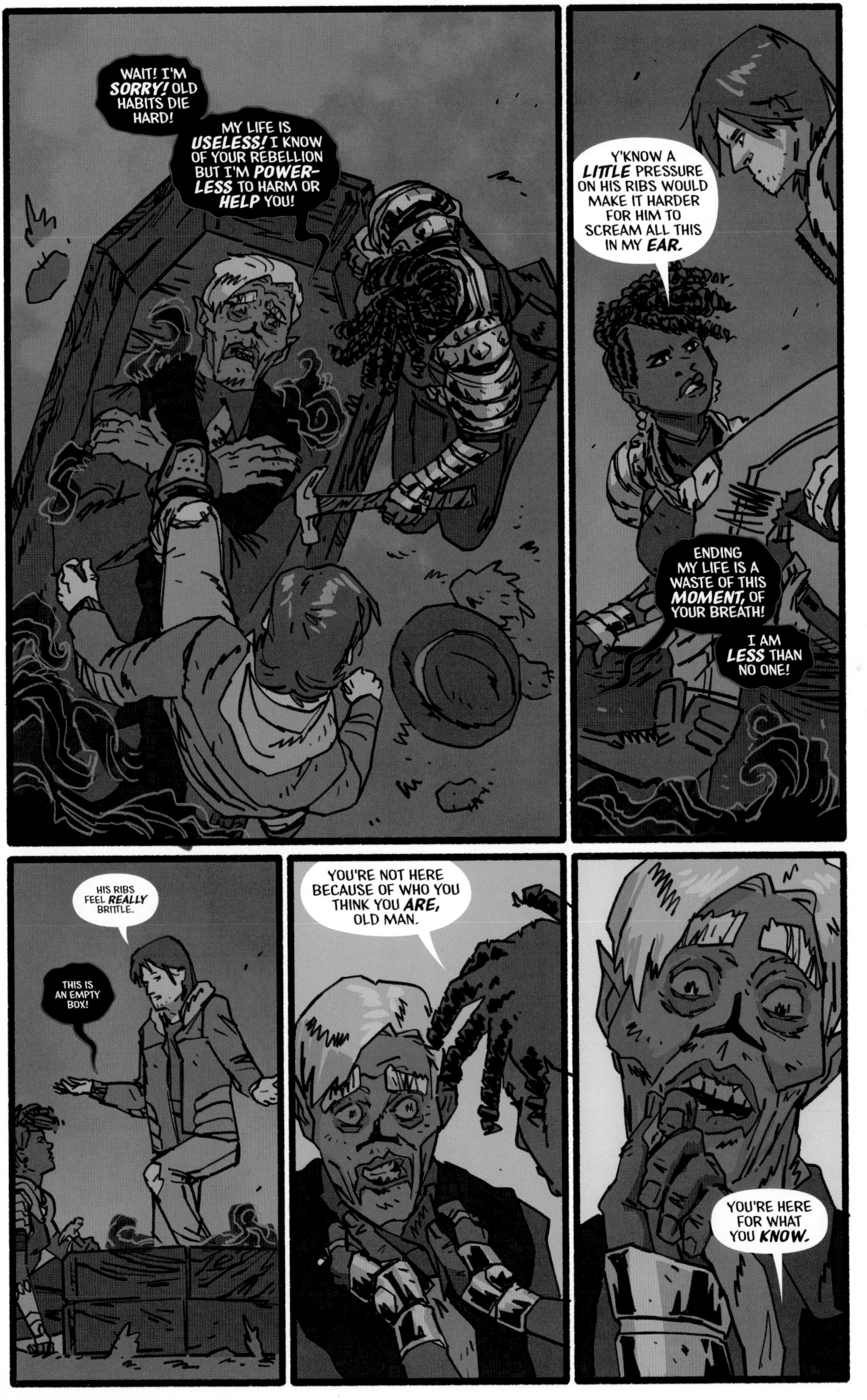
WAIT! I'M SORRY! OLD HABITS DIE HARD!
MY LIFE IS USELESS! I KNOW OF YOUR REBELLION BUT I'M POWER-LESS TO HARM OR HELP YOU!
Y'KNOW A LITTLE PRESSURE ON HIS RIBS WOULD MAKE IT HARDER FOR HIM TO SCREAM ALL THIS IN MY EAR.
ENDING MY LIFE IS A WASTE OF THIS MOMENT, OF YOUR BREATH!
I AM LESS THAN NO ONE!
HIS RIBS FEEL REALLY BRITTLE.
THIS IS AN EMPTY BOX!
YOU'RE NOT HERE BECAUSE OF WHO YOU THINK YOU ARE, OLD MAN.
YOU'RE HERE FOR WHAT YOU KNOW.

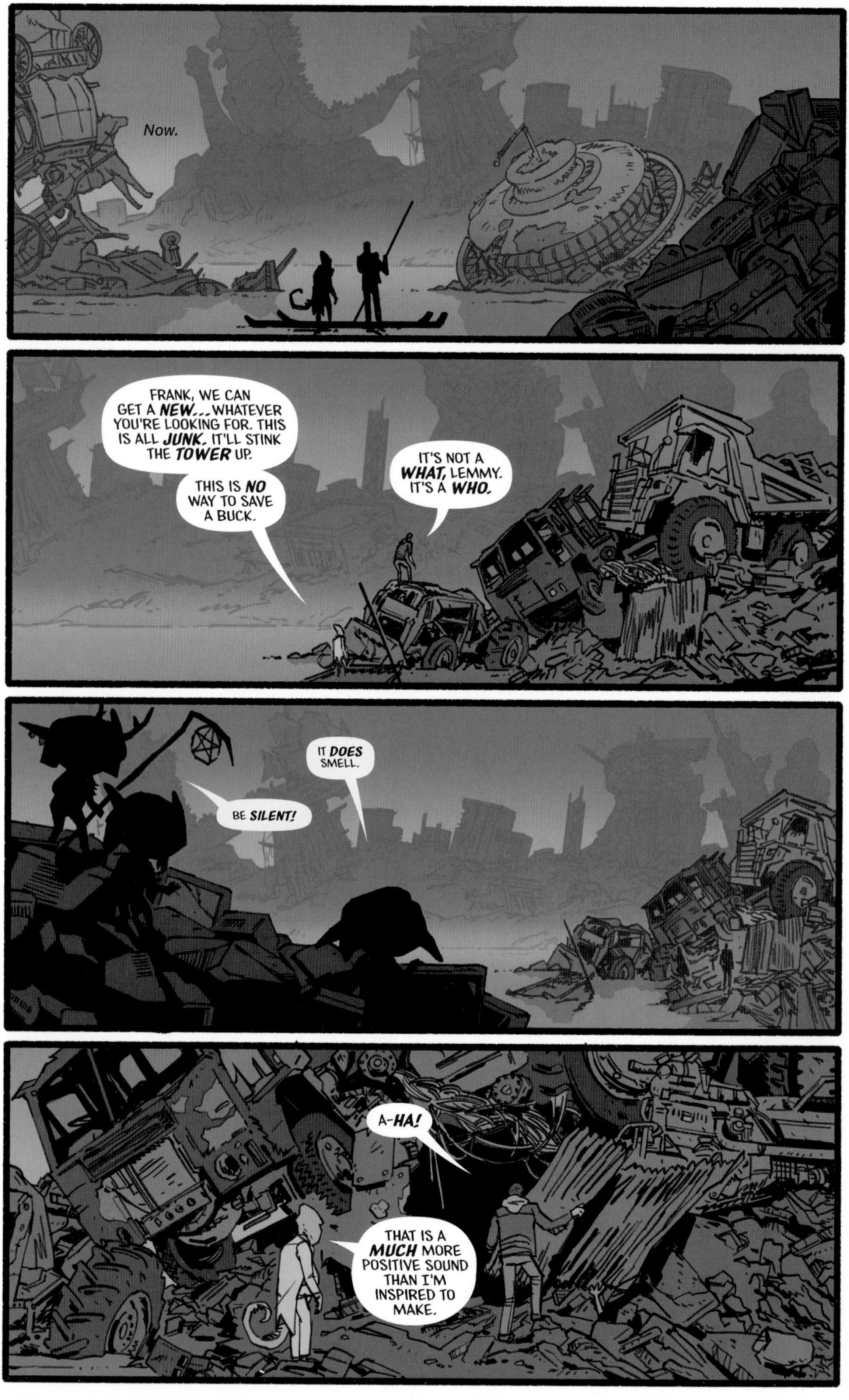
Now.
FRANK, WE CAN GET A NEW... WHATEVER YOU'RE LOOKING FOR. THIS IS ALL JUNK. IT'LL STINK THE TOWER UP.
THIS IS NO WAY TO SAVE A BUCK.
IT'S NOT A WHAT, LEMMY. IT'S A WHO.
BE SILENT!
IT DOES SMELL.
A-HA!
THAT IS A MUCH MORE POSITIVE SOUND THAN I'M INSPIRED TO MAKE.

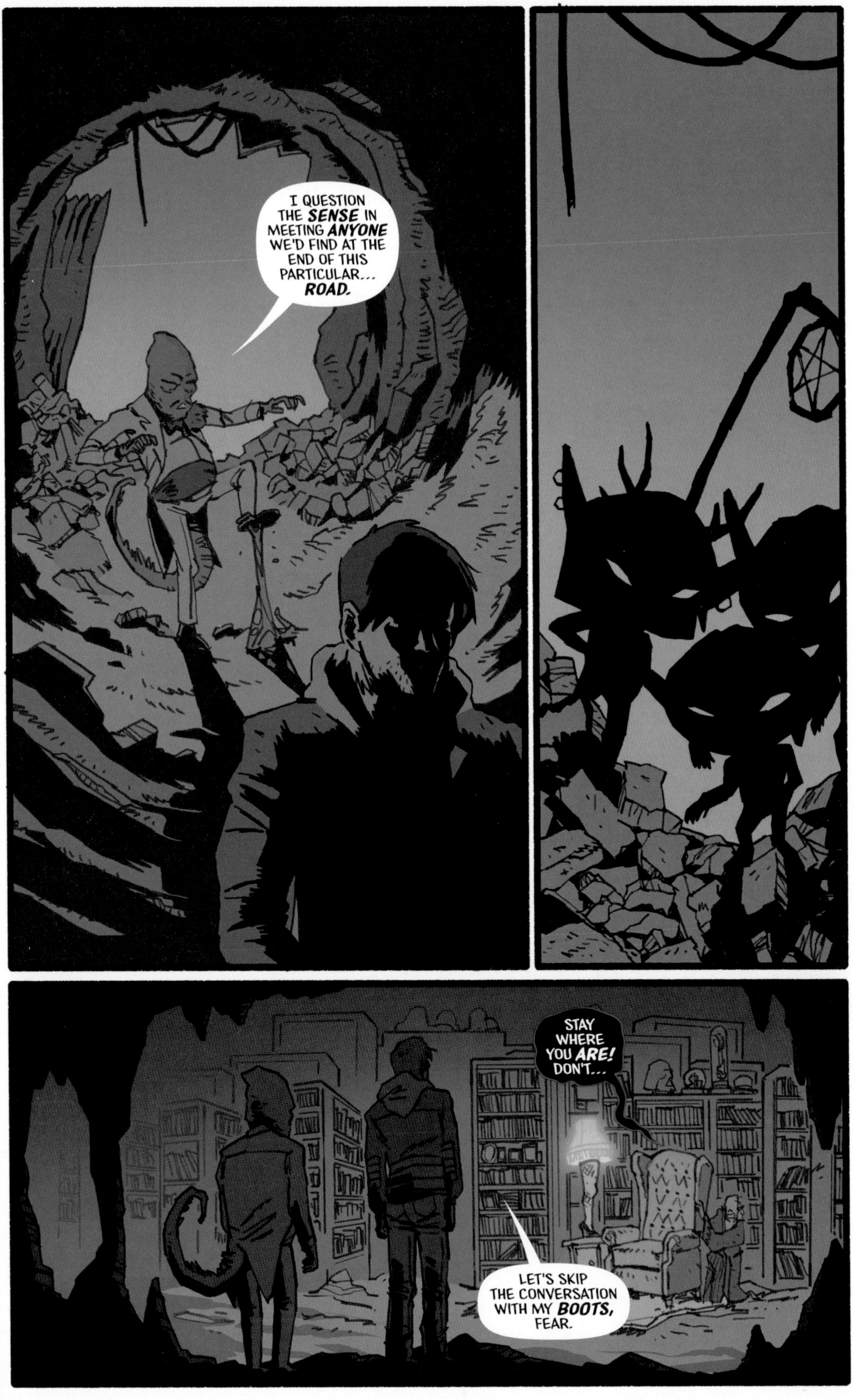
I QUESTION THE SENSE IN MEETING ANYONE WE'D FIND AT THE END OF THIS PARTICULAR... ROAD.
STAY WHERE YOU ARE! DON'T...
LET'S SKIP THE CONVERSATION WITH MY BOOTS, FEAR.

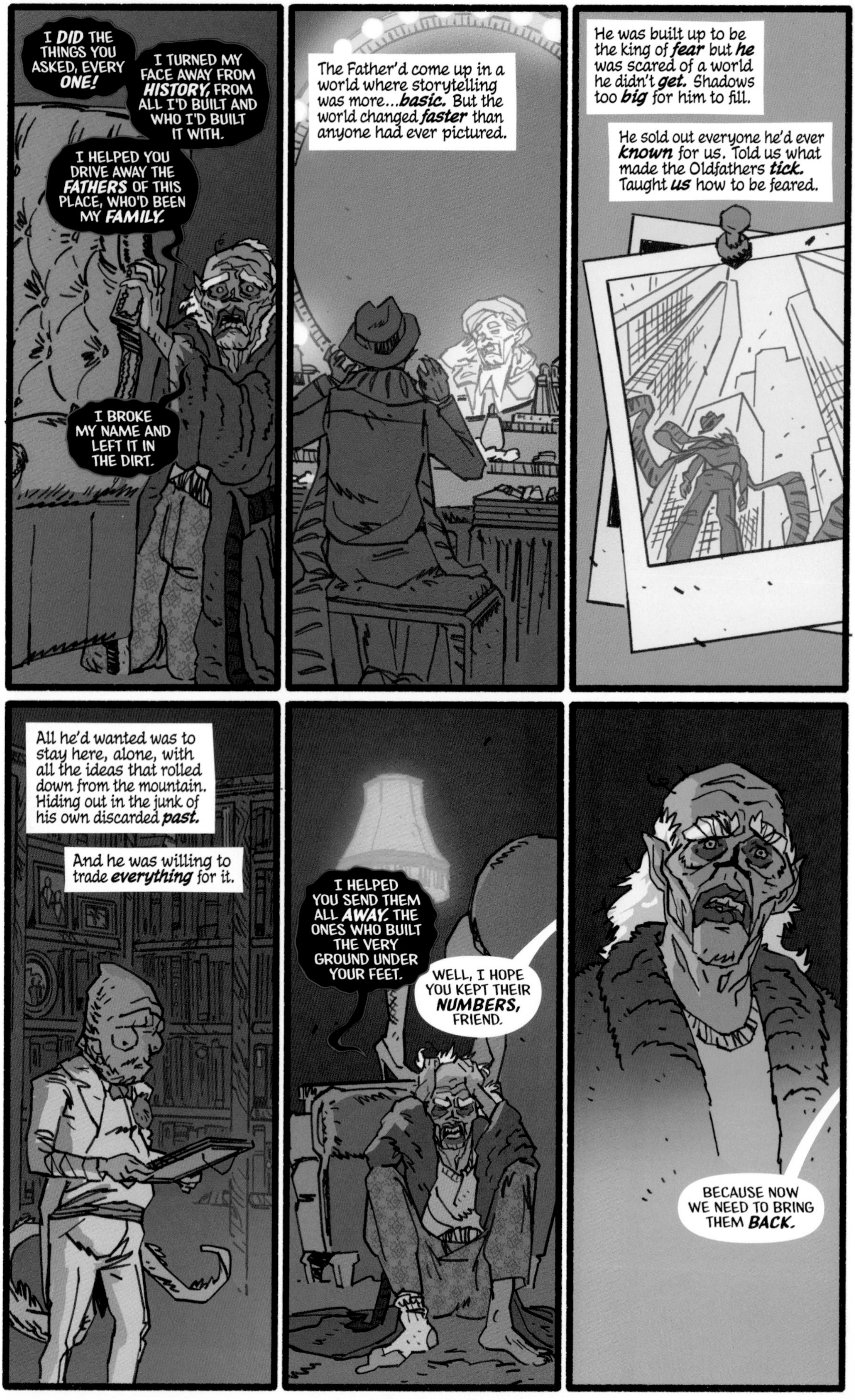

I DID THE THINGS YOU ASKED, EVERY ONE!
I TURNED MY FACE AWAY FROM HISTORY, FROM ALL I'D BUILT AND WHO I'D BUILT IT WITH.
I HELPED YOU DRIVE AWAY THE FATHERS OF THIS PLACE, WHO'D BEEN MY FAMILY.
I BROKE MY NAME AND LEFT IT IN THE DIRT.
The Father'd come up in a world where storytelling was more...basic. But the world changed faster than anyone had ever pictured.
He was built up to be the king of fear but he was scared of a world he didn't get. Shadows too big for him to fill.
He sold out everyone he'd ever known for us. Told us what made the Oldfathers tick. Taught us how to be feared.
All he'd wanted was to stay here, alone, with all the ideas that rolled down from the mountain. Hiding out in the junk of his own discarded past.
And he was willing to trade everything for it.
I HELPED YOU SEND THEM ALL AWAY. THE ONES WHO BUILT THE VERY GROUND UNDER YOUR FEET.
WELL, I HOPE YOU KEPT THEIR NUMBERS, FRIEND.
BECAUSE NOW WE NEED TO BRING THEM BACK.

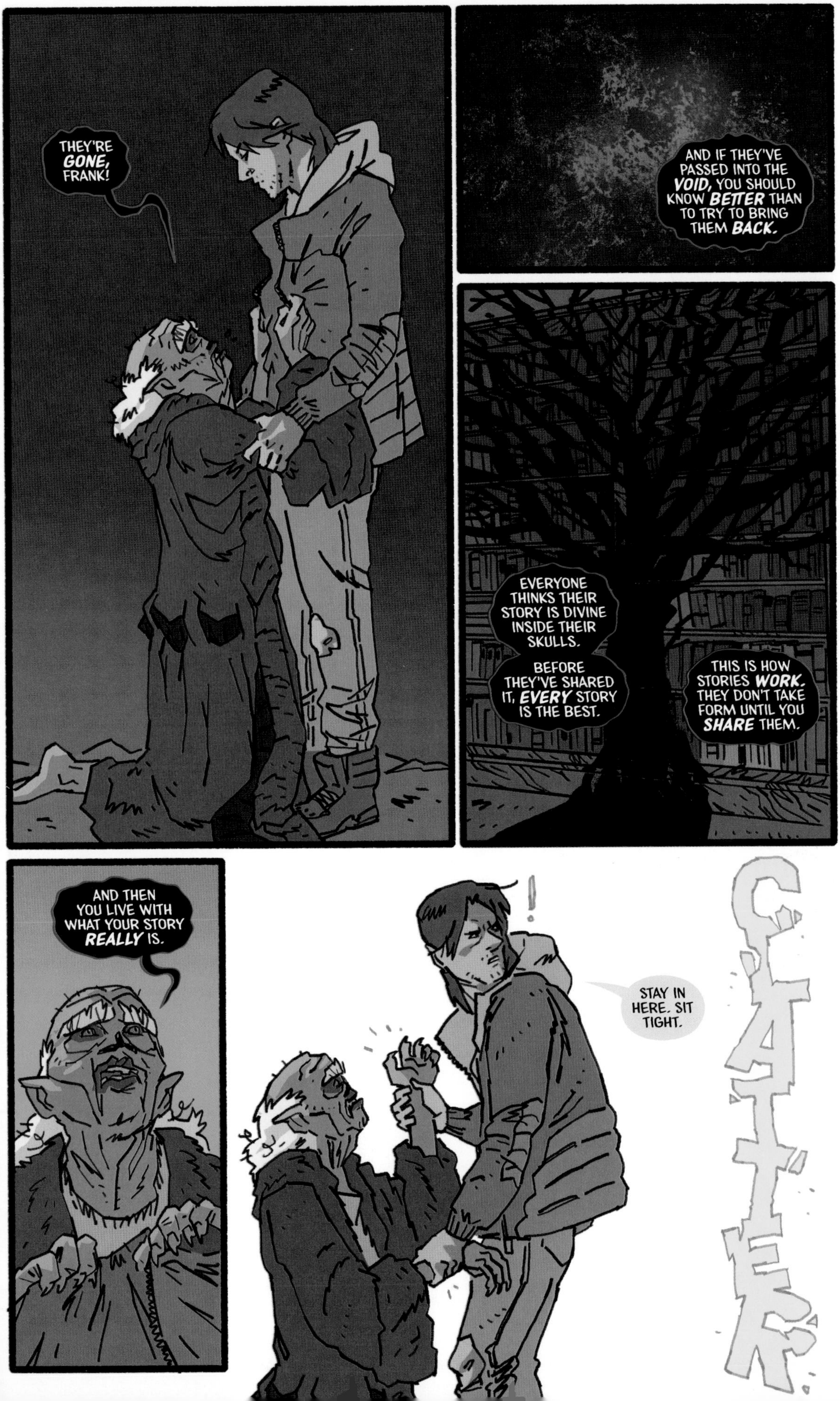
THEY'RE GONE, FRANK!
AND IF THEY'VE PASSED INTO THE VOID, YOU SHOULD KNOW BETTER THAN TO TRY TO BRING THEM BACK.
EVERYONE THINKS THEIR STORY IS DIVINE INSIDE THEIR SKULLS.
BEFORE THEY'VE SHARED IT, EVERY STORY IS THE BEST.
THIS IS HOW STORIES WORK. THEY DON'T TAKE FORM UNTIL YOU SHARE THEM.
AND THEN YOU LIVE WITH WHAT YOUR STORY REALLY IS.
!
STAY IN HERE. SIT TIGHT.
CLATTER

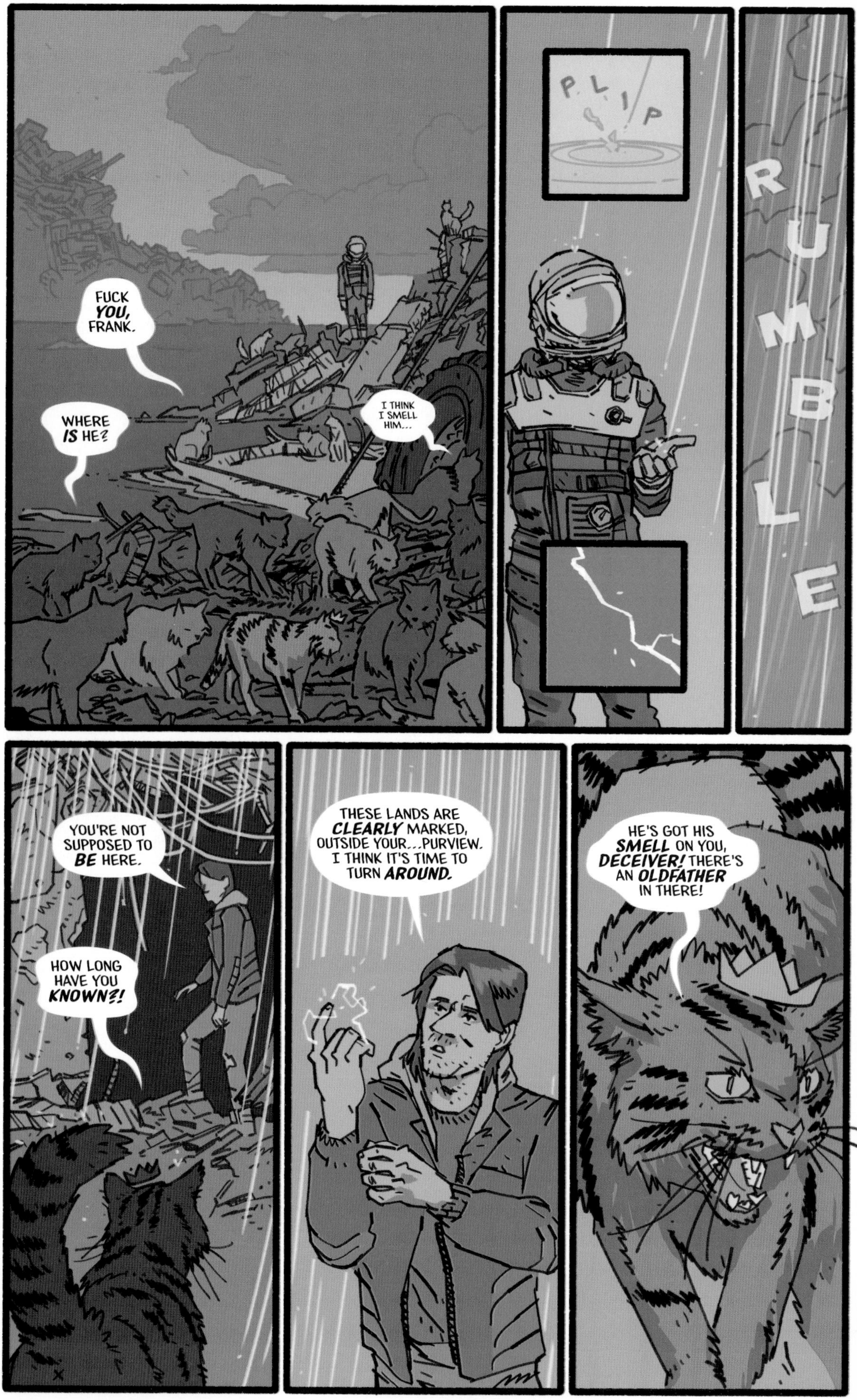
FUCK YOU, FRANK.
WHERE IS HE?
I THINK I SMELL HIM...
P.L.I.P
RUMBLE
YOU'RE NOT SUPPOSED TO BE HERE.
HOW LONG HAVE YOU KNOWN?!
THESE LANDS ARE CLEARLY MARKED, OUTSIDE YOUR...PURVIEW. I THINK IT'S TIME TO TURN AROUND.
HE'S GOT HIS SMELL ON YOU, DECEIVER! THERE'S AN OLDFATHER IN THERE!

DUNNO WHAT YOU'RE TALKING ABOUT. I THINK YOU'RE HITTING THE SPOILED MILK.
GO ON AND SLEEP IT **OFF.**
AIN'T IT A **GAS,** FRIENDS? THE WAY HE NEVER **KNOWS?** WHERE ARE THE OLDFATHERS? WHERE IS THAT SAVAGE OLD-BLOOD **MESS** HE USED TO RUN WITH?
THERE'S ONLY **ONE** OF YOU. AND WHEN WE'RE DONE WE WILL **EXPOSE** YOU.
WELL, YOU'RE INVITED TO TRY ME OUT.
BUT YOU MUST BE FULL FROM BITING MORE THAN YOU CAN CHEW.
SFFVVT SWFFVT
HOW'D THINGS GO FOR YOU WITH ZELDA?
BLOOP
LET'S CHECK THE INSTANT REPLAY.

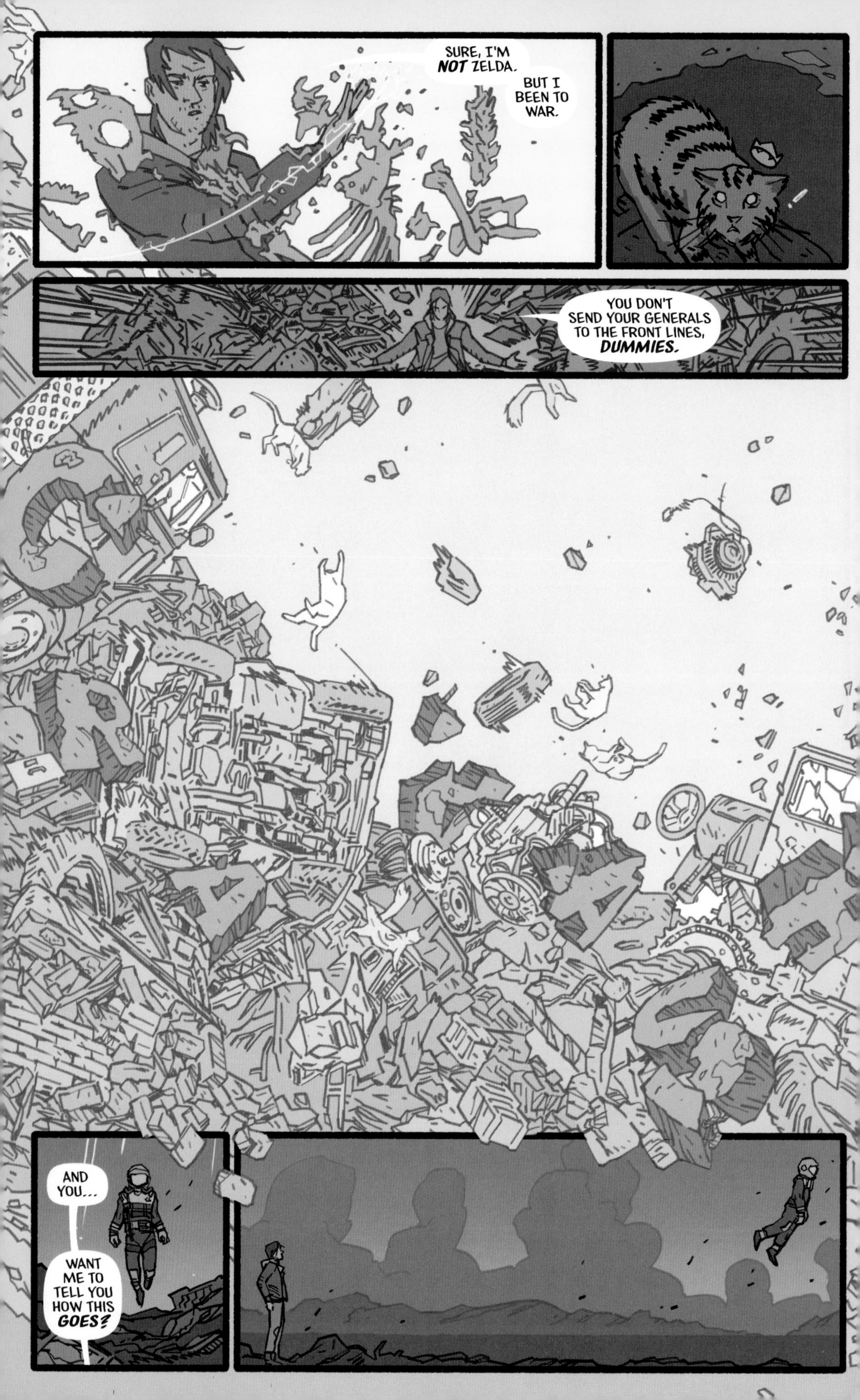
SURE, I'M *NOT* ZELDA.
BUT I BEEN TO WAR.
YOU DON'T SEND YOUR GENERALS TO THE FRONT LINES, *DUMMIES.*
AND YOU...
WANT ME TO TELL YOU HOW THIS *GOES?*

THAT WAS A BAD *MOVE.* A *BIG* ONE. YOU'VE GOT YOUR BIG TOE DIPPED IN *WAR.*

YEAH, *WELL.* ZELDA'S THE ONE WHO TAUGHT ME HOW TO DANCE.

BAD MOVES ARE ALL I EVER *LEARNED.*

AH, *SCREW* IT. COME ON, WE'RE *LEAVING.*

YOU BETTER FIND A PLACE TO *HIDE,* FEAR! WHERE THEY CAN'T *FIND* YOU!

AND WHERE *I* CAN'T, EITHER.

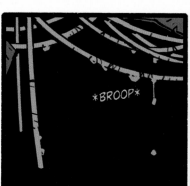
BROOP

PLIT

CROOAAK!

THIS IS YOUR PERFECT WORLD.

COWERING ON THE FLOOR.

YOU KNOW MORE THAN *ANY* WHAT'S AT *STAKE.*

HEELLP! FRAAAANK!

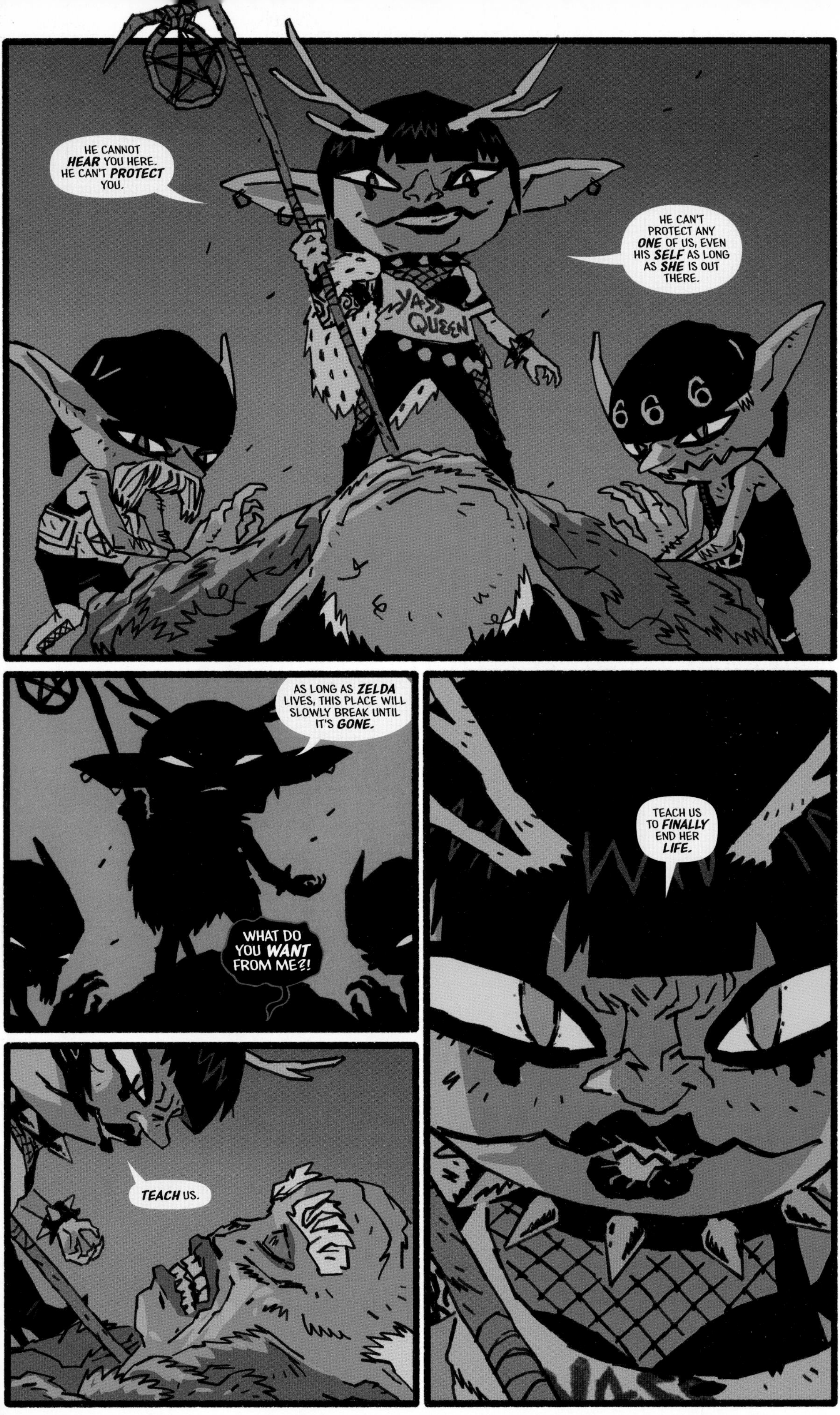
HE CANNOT HEAR YOU HERE. HE CAN'T PROTECT YOU.
HE CAN'T PROTECT ANY ONE OF US, EVEN HIS SELF AS LONG AS SHE IS OUT THERE.
YASS QUEEN
666
AS LONG AS ZELDA LIVES, THIS PLACE WILL SLOWLY BREAK UNTIL IT'S GONE.
WHAT DO YOU WANT FROM ME?!
TEACH US.
TEACH US TO FINALLY END HER LIFE.

Chapter 7

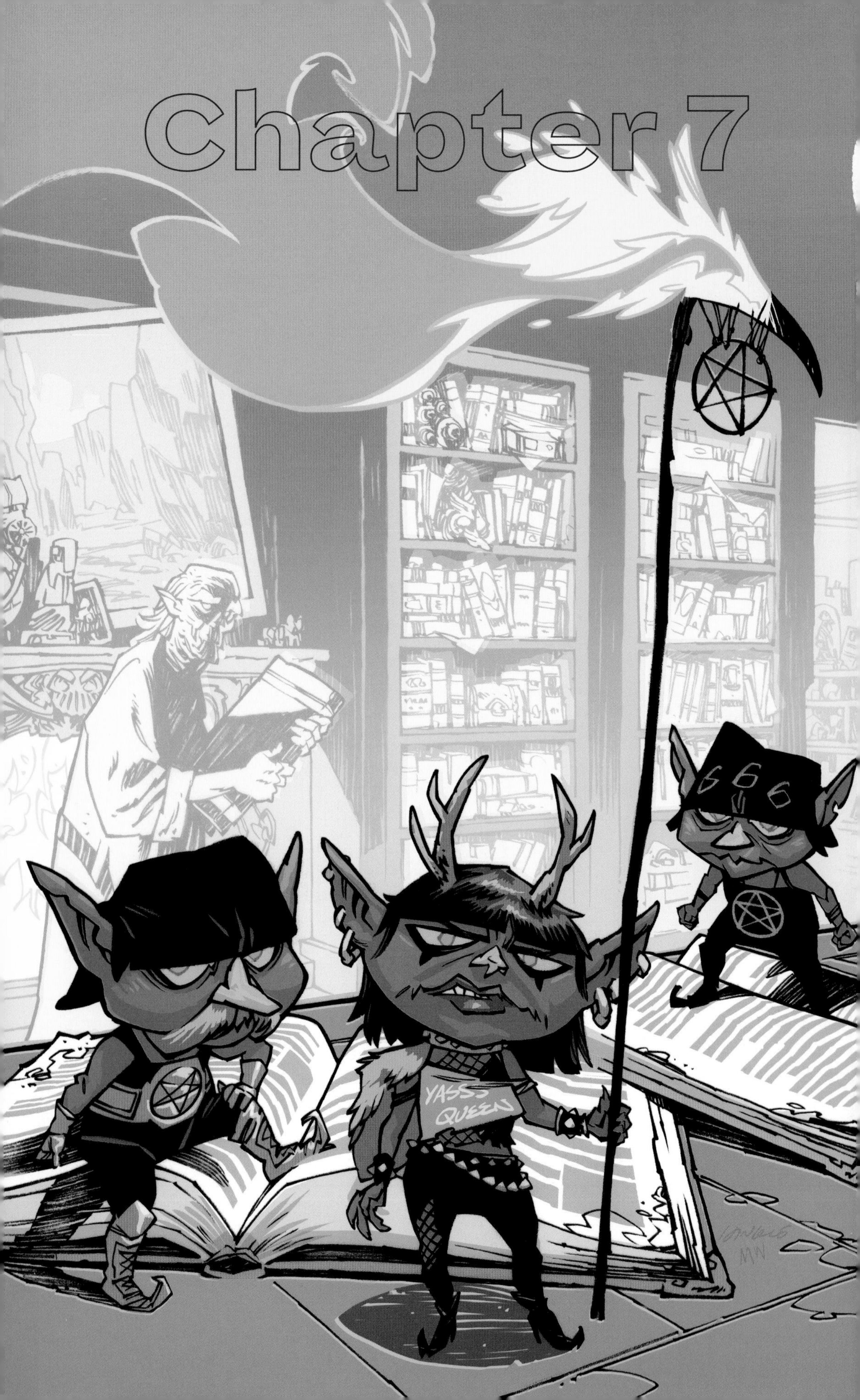
666
YASSS QUEEN

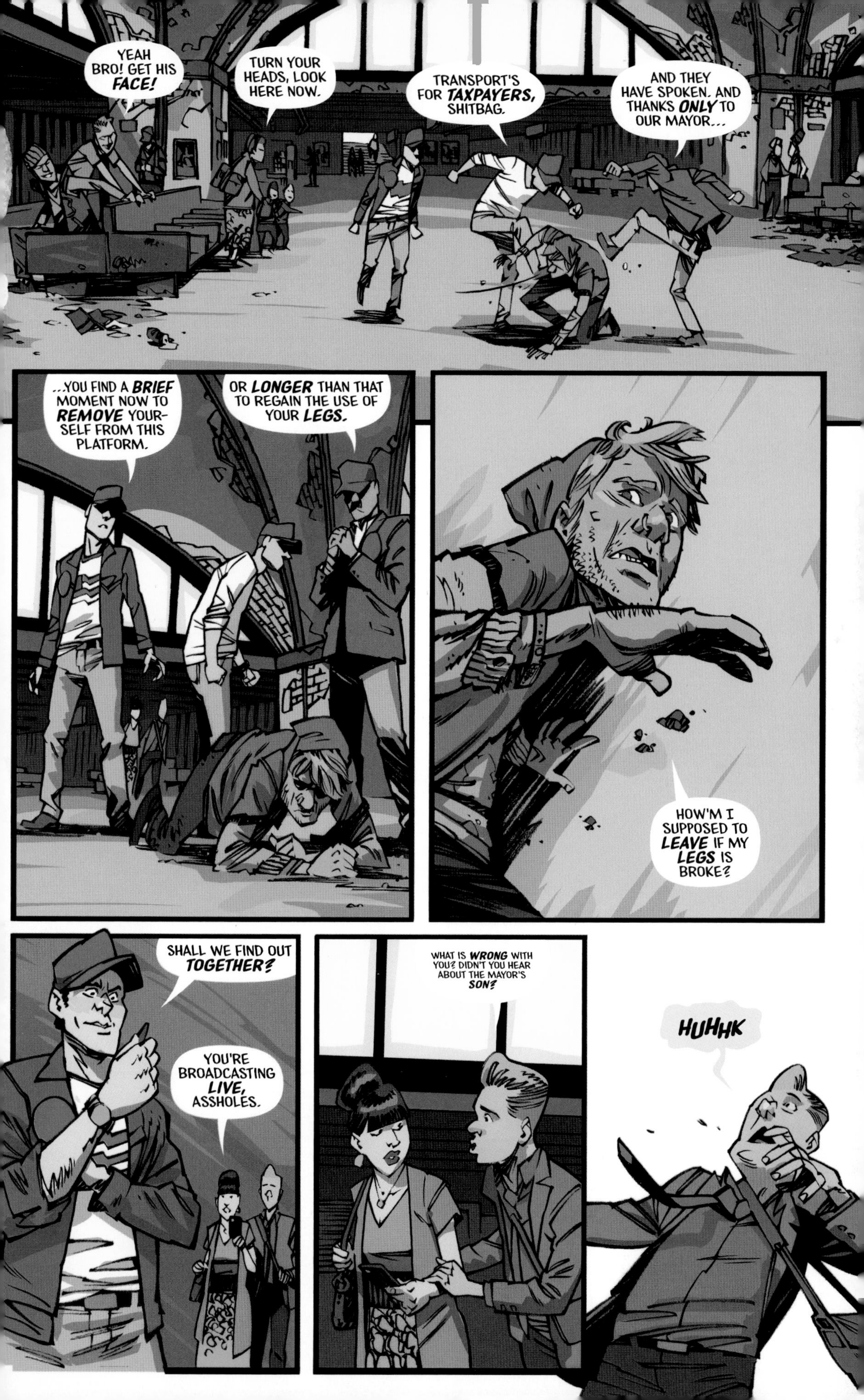
YEAH BRO! GET HIS FACE!
TURN YOUR HEADS, LOOK HERE NOW.
TRANSPORT'S FOR TAXPAYERS, SHITBAG.
AND THEY HAVE SPOKEN. AND THANKS ONLY TO OUR MAYOR...
...YOU FIND A BRIEF MOMENT NOW TO REMOVE YOURSELF FROM THIS PLATFORM.
OR LONGER THAN THAT TO REGAIN THE USE OF YOUR LEGS.
HOW'M I SUPPOSED TO LEAVE IF MY LEGS IS BROKE?
SHALL WE FIND OUT TOGETHER?
YOU'RE BROADCASTING LIVE, ASSHOLES.
WHAT IS WRONG WITH YOU? DIDN'T YOU HEAR ABOUT THE MAYOR'S SON?
HUHHK

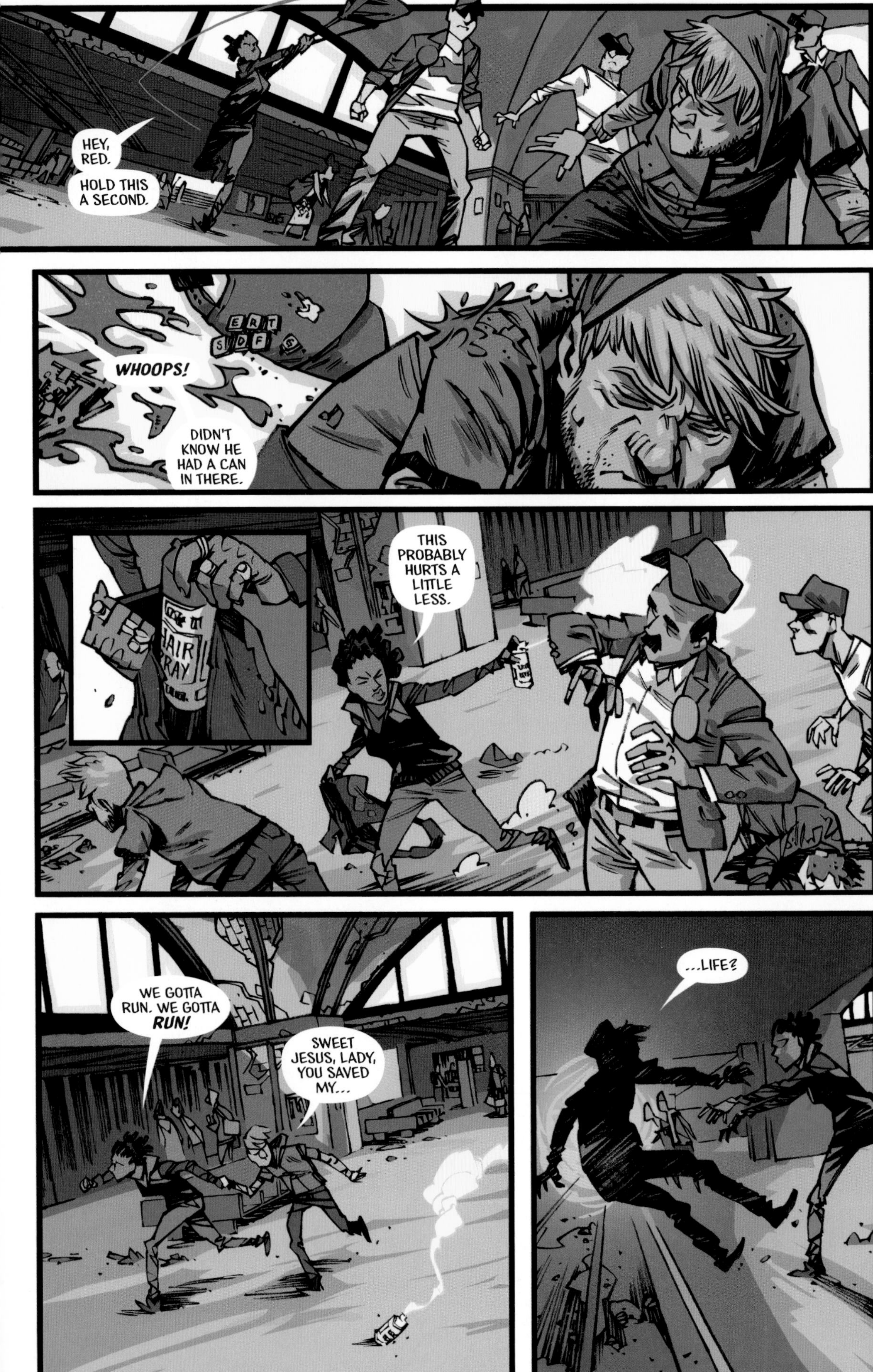
HEY, RED.
HOLD THIS A SECOND.
WHOOPS!
DIDN'T KNOW HE HAD A CAN IN THERE.
THIS PROBABLY HURTS A LITTLE LESS.
HAIR SPRAY
WE GOTTA RUN. WE GOTTA RUN!
SWEET JESUS, LADY, YOU SAVED MY...
...LIFE?

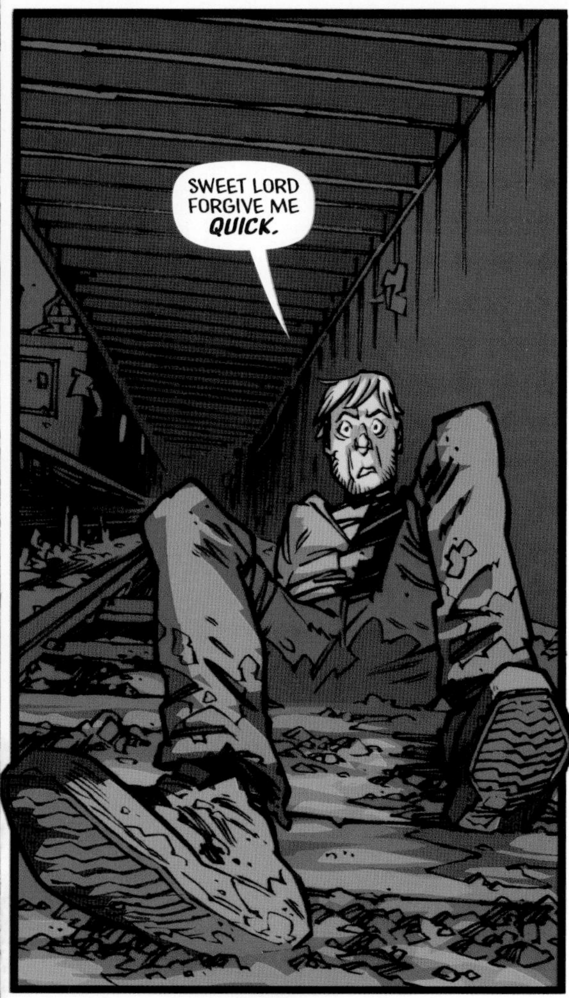
SWEET LORD FORGIVE ME QUICK.

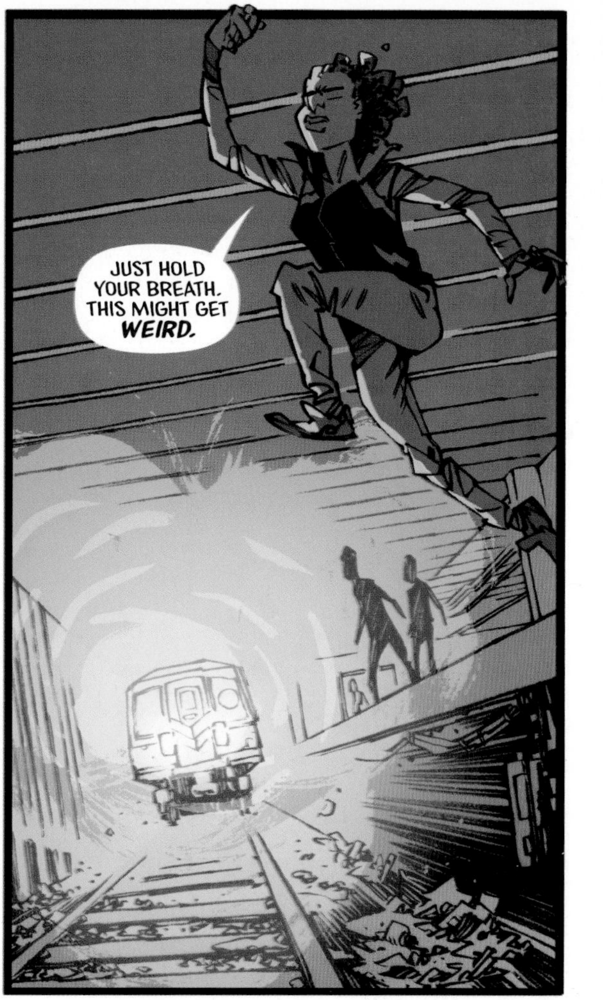
JUST HOLD YOUR BREATH. THIS MIGHT GET WEIRD.

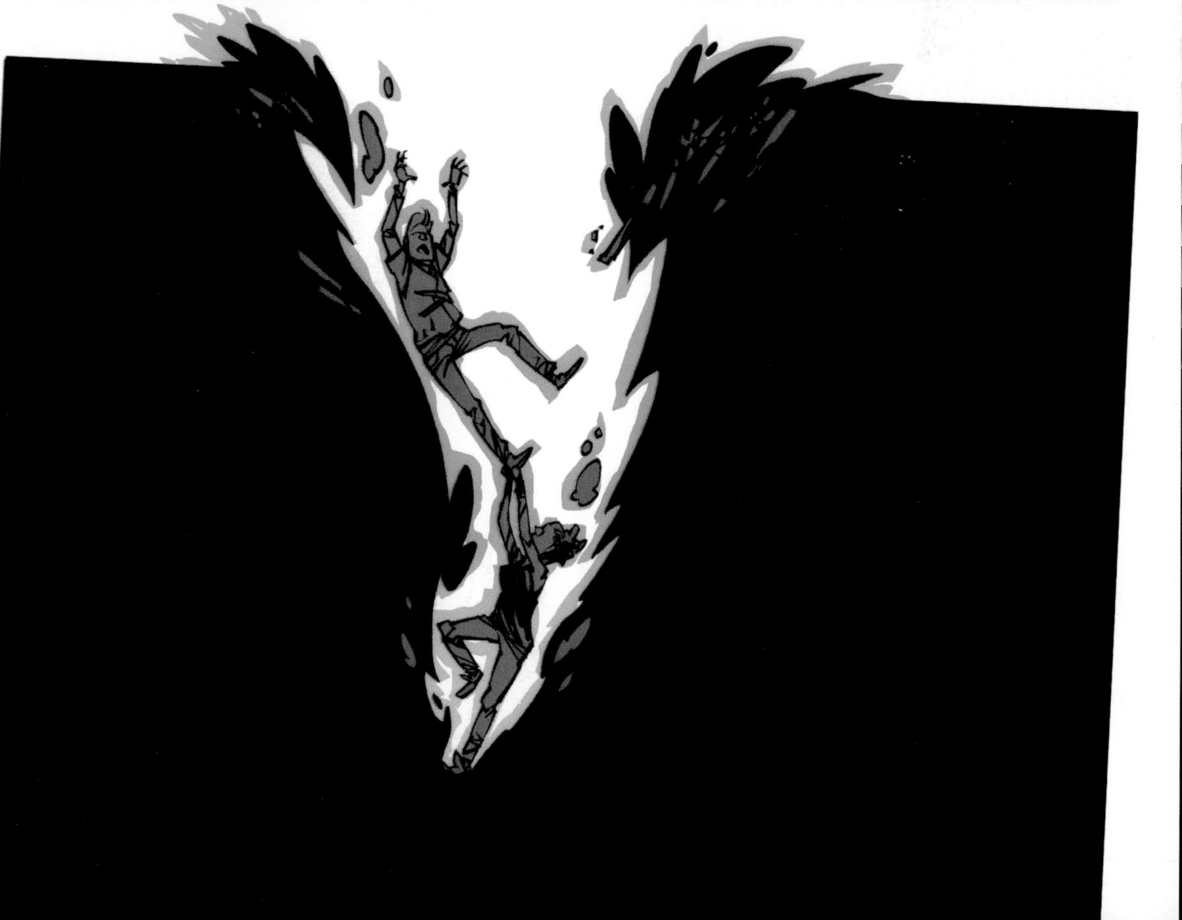

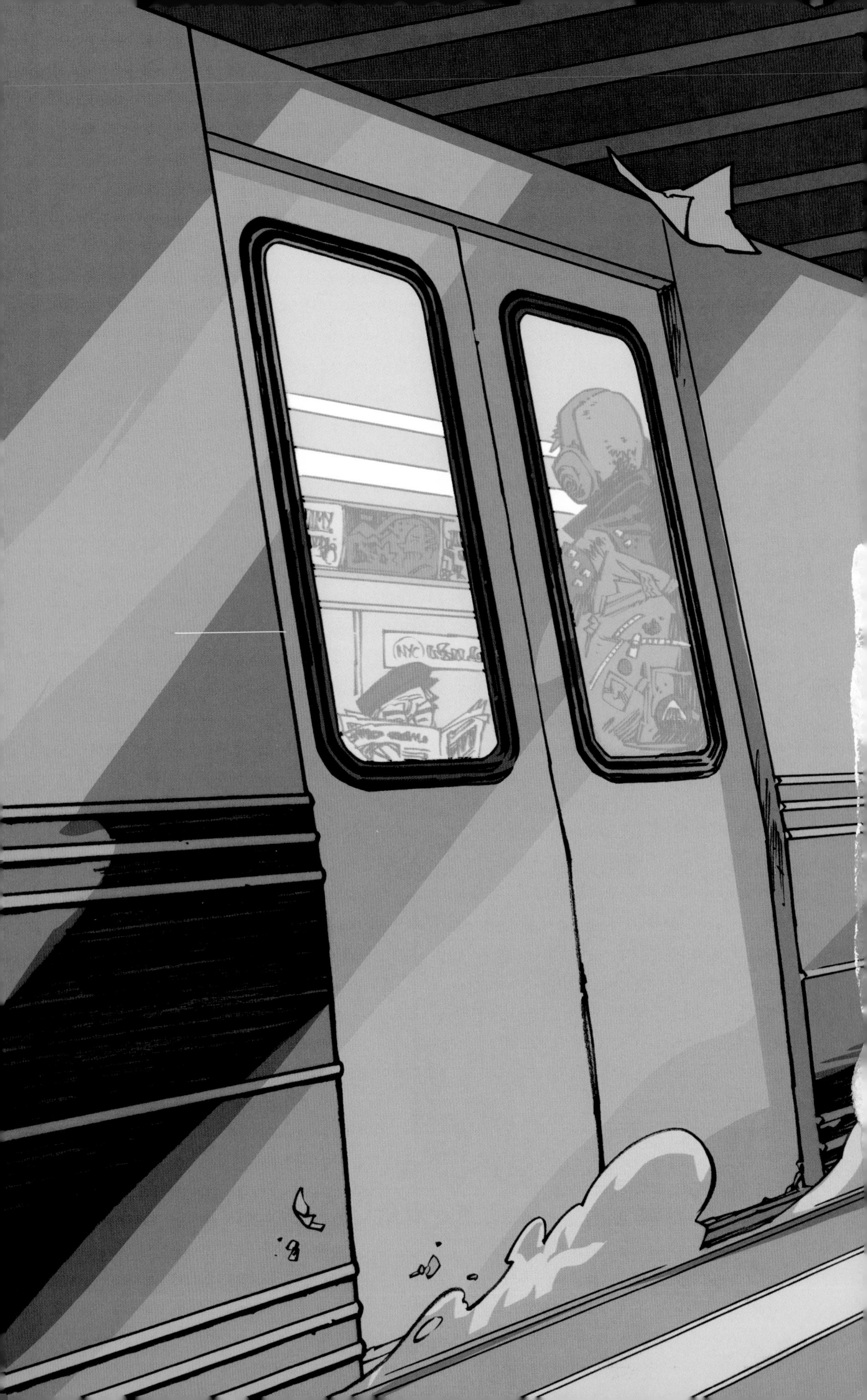

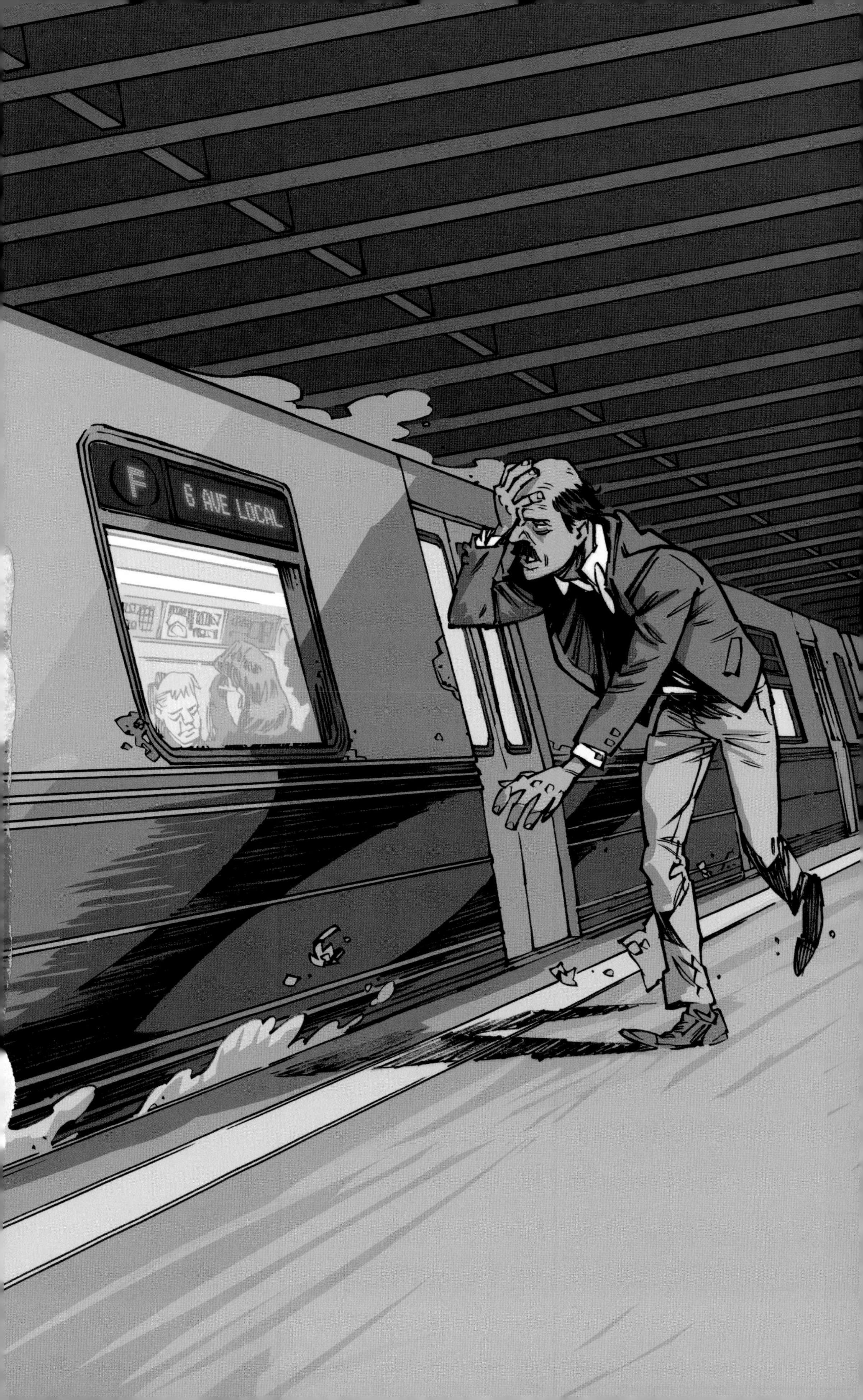
F
6 AVE LOCAL

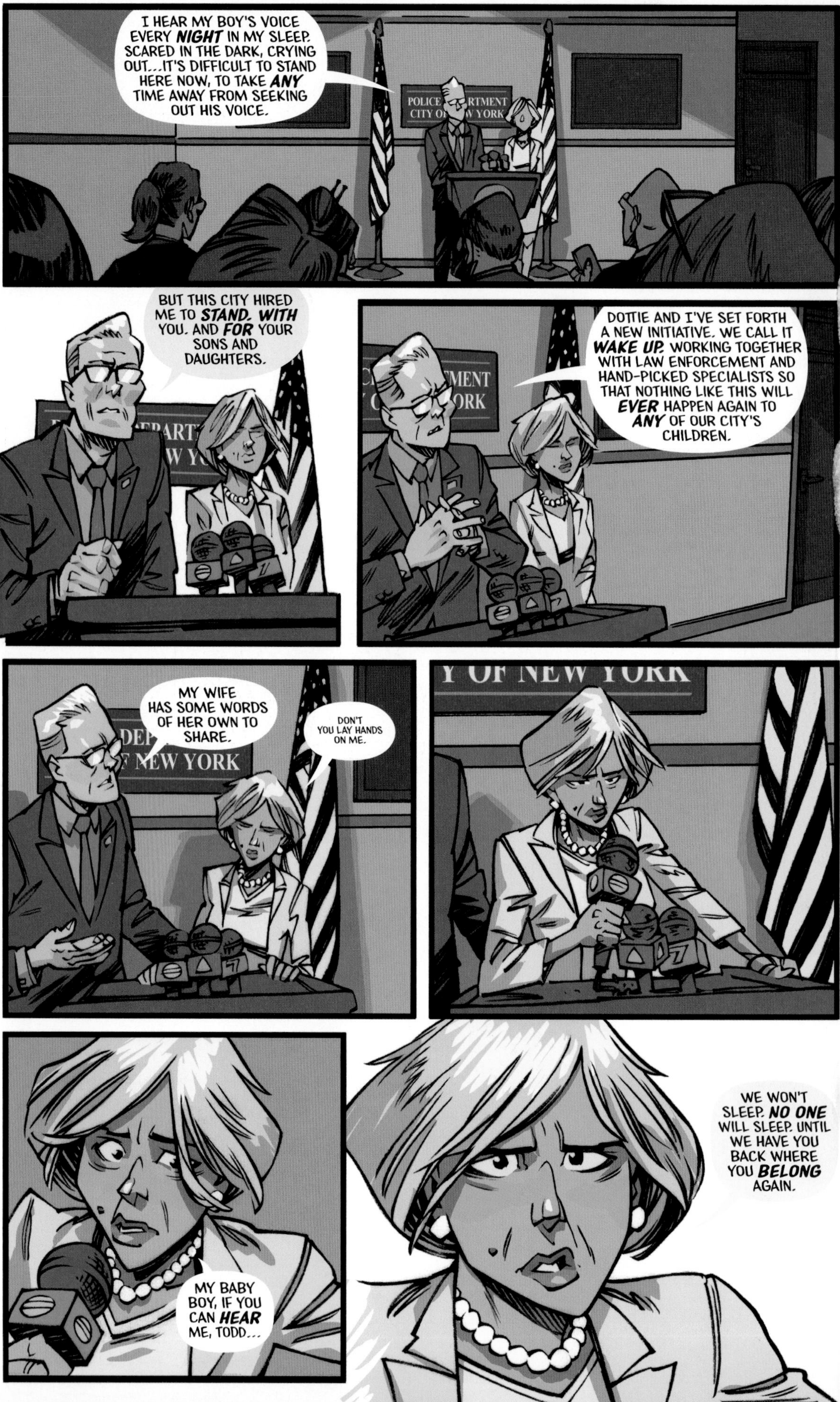
I HEAR MY BOY'S VOICE EVERY NIGHT IN MY SLEEP. SCARED IN THE DARK, CRYING OUT...IT'S DIFFICULT TO STAND HERE NOW, TO TAKE ANY TIME AWAY FROM SEEKING OUT HIS VOICE.
POLICE DEPARTMENT CITY OF NEW YORK
BUT THIS CITY HIRED ME TO STAND. WITH YOU. AND FOR YOUR SONS AND DAUGHTERS.
DOTTIE AND I'VE SET FORTH A NEW INITIATIVE. WE CALL IT WAKE UP. WORKING TOGETHER WITH LAW ENFORCEMENT AND HAND-PICKED SPECIALISTS SO THAT NOTHING LIKE THIS WILL EVER HAPPEN AGAIN TO ANY OF OUR CITY'S CHILDREN.
MY WIFE HAS SOME WORDS OF HER OWN TO SHARE.
DON'T YOU LAY HANDS ON ME.
MY BABY BOY, IF YOU CAN HEAR ME, TODD...
WE WON'T SLEEP. NO ONE WILL SLEEP. UNTIL WE HAVE YOU BACK WHERE YOU BELONG AGAIN.

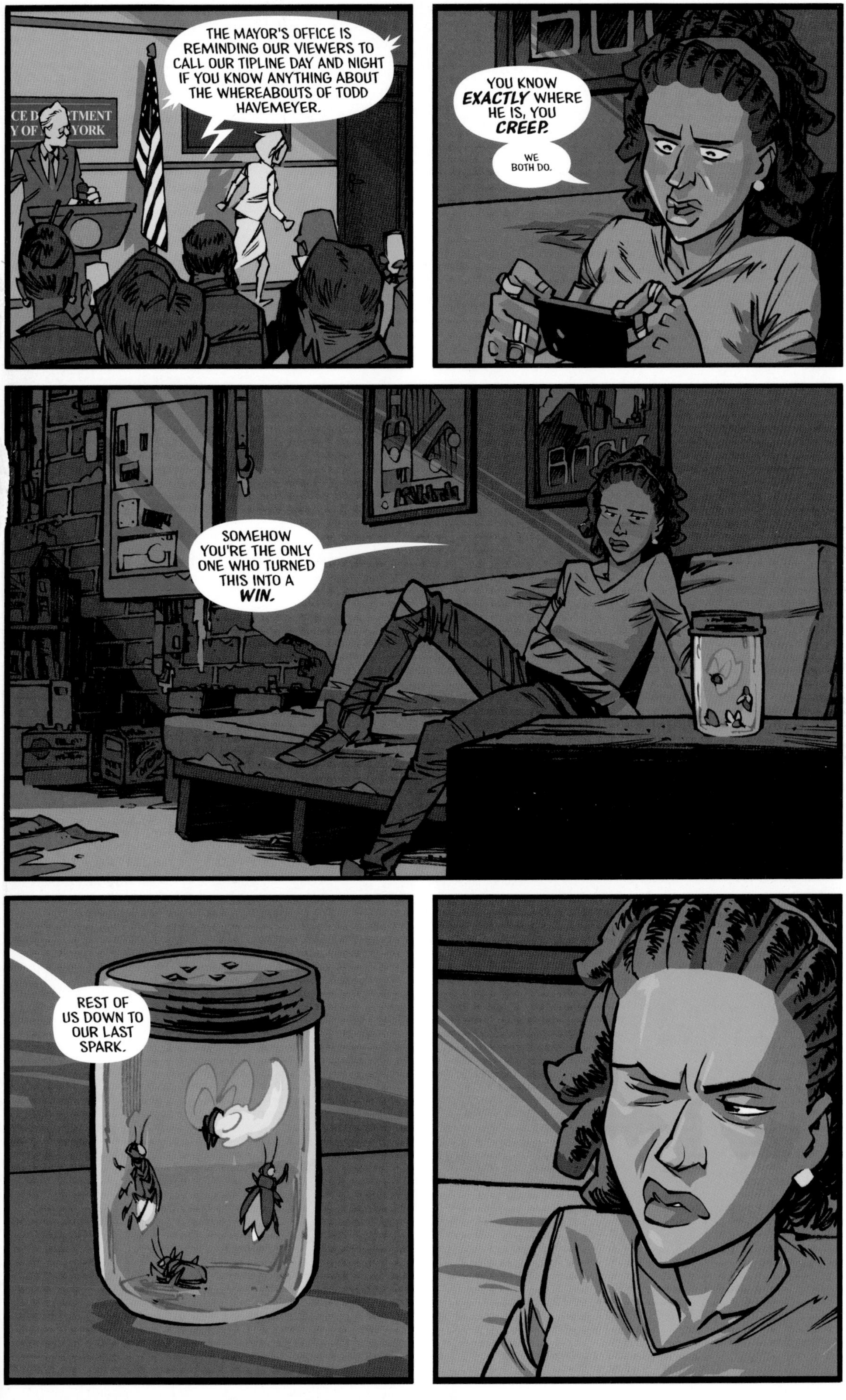
THE MAYOR'S OFFICE IS REMINDING OUR VIEWERS TO CALL OUR TIPLINE DAY AND NIGHT IF YOU KNOW ANYTHING ABOUT THE WHEREABOUTS OF TODD HAVEMEYER.
YOU KNOW EXACTLY WHERE HE IS, YOU CREEP.
WE BOTH DO.
SOMEHOW YOU'RE THE ONLY ONE WHO TURNED THIS INTO A WIN.
REST OF US DOWN TO OUR LAST SPARK.

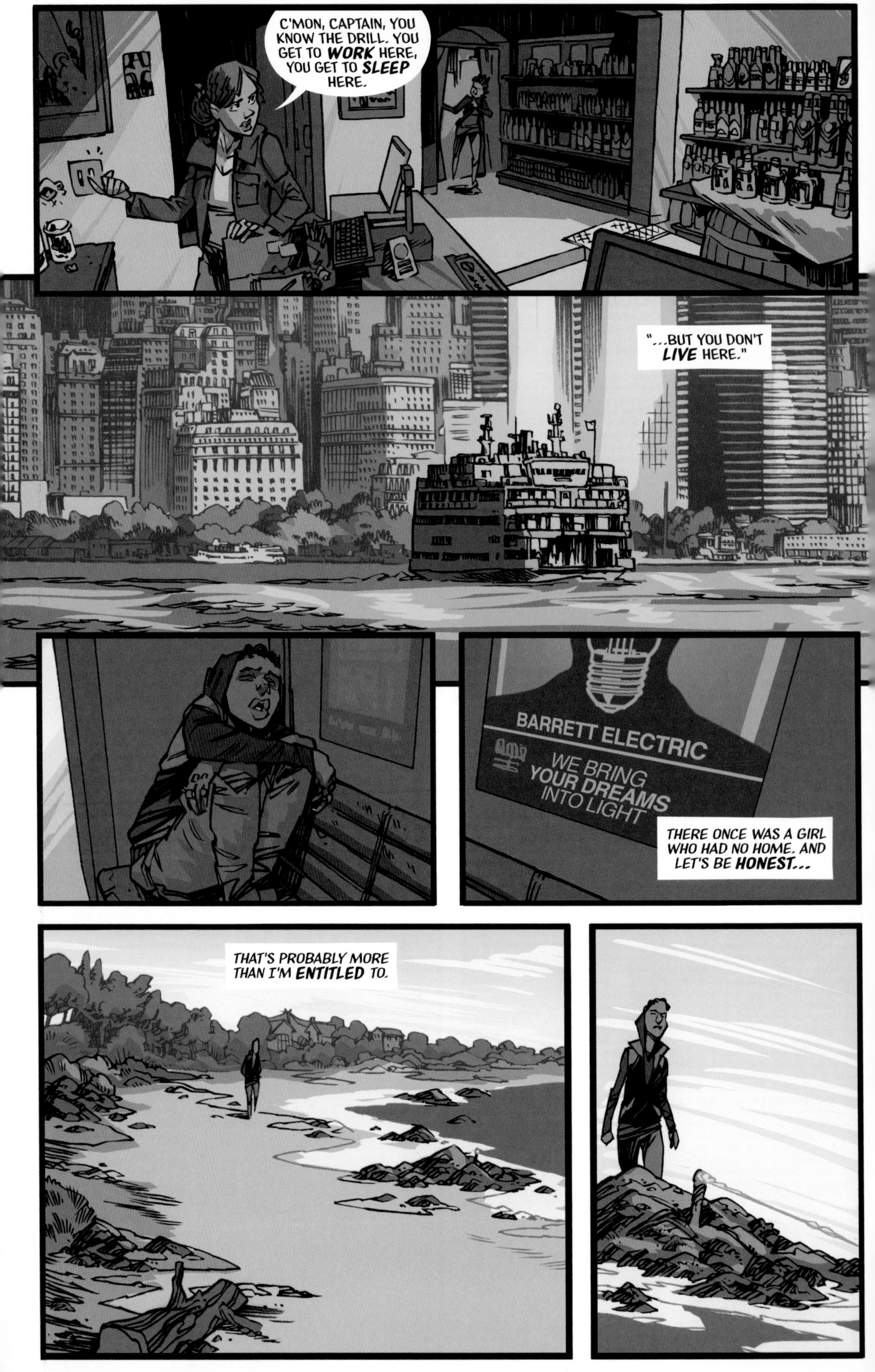
C'MON, CAPTAIN, YOU KNOW THE DRILL. YOU GET TO **WORK** HERE, YOU GET TO **SLEEP** HERE.
"...BUT YOU DON'T **LIVE** HERE."
BARRETT ELECTRIC
WE BRING **YOUR DREAMS** INTO LIGHT
THERE ONCE WAS A GIRL WHO HAD NO HOME. AND LET'S BE **HONEST...**
THAT'S PROBABLY MORE THAN I'M **ENTITLED** TO.

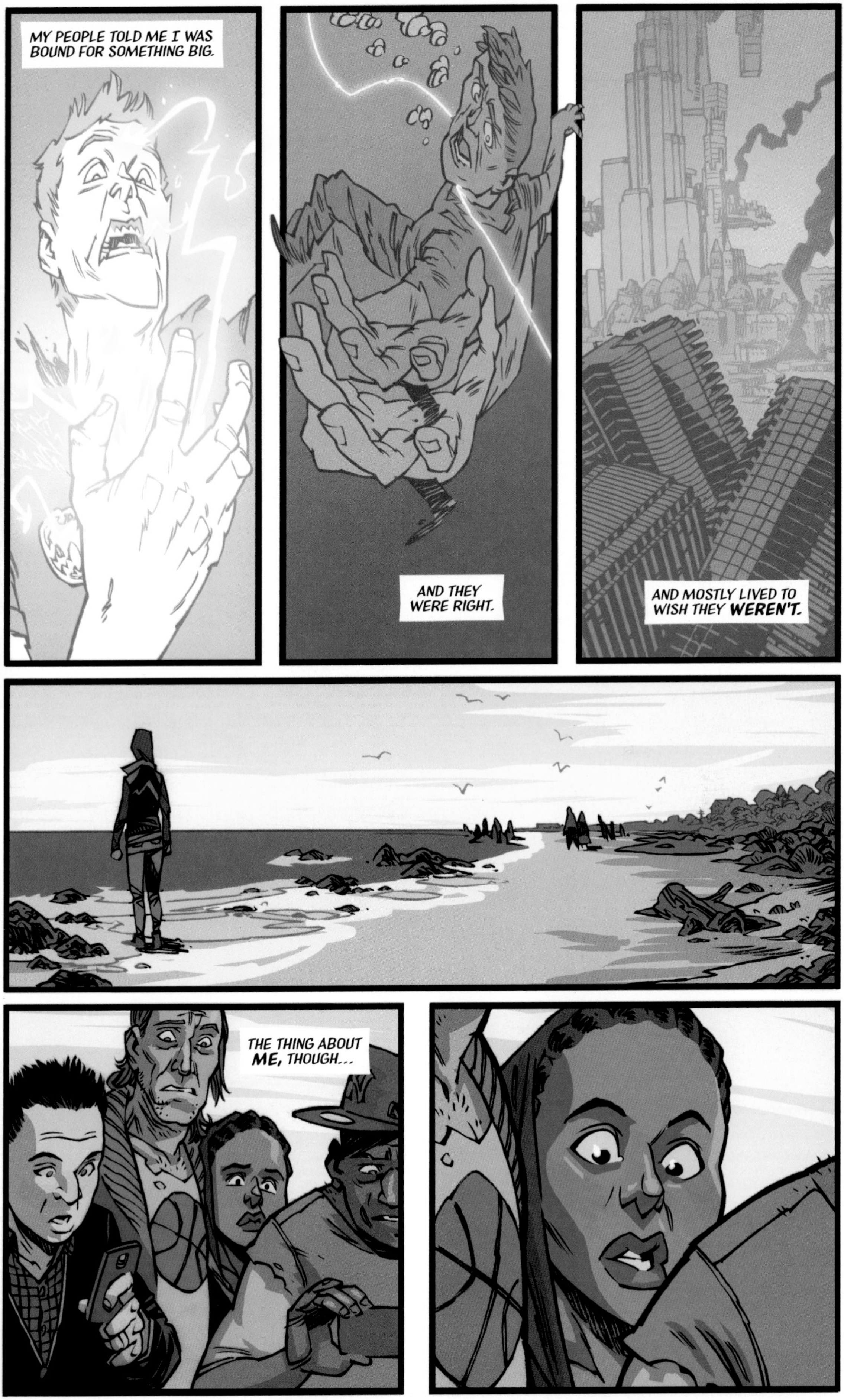
MY PEOPLE TOLD ME I WAS BOUND FOR SOMETHING BIG.
AND THEY WERE RIGHT.
AND MOSTLY LIVED TO WISH THEY WEREN'T.
THE THING ABOUT ME, THOUGH...

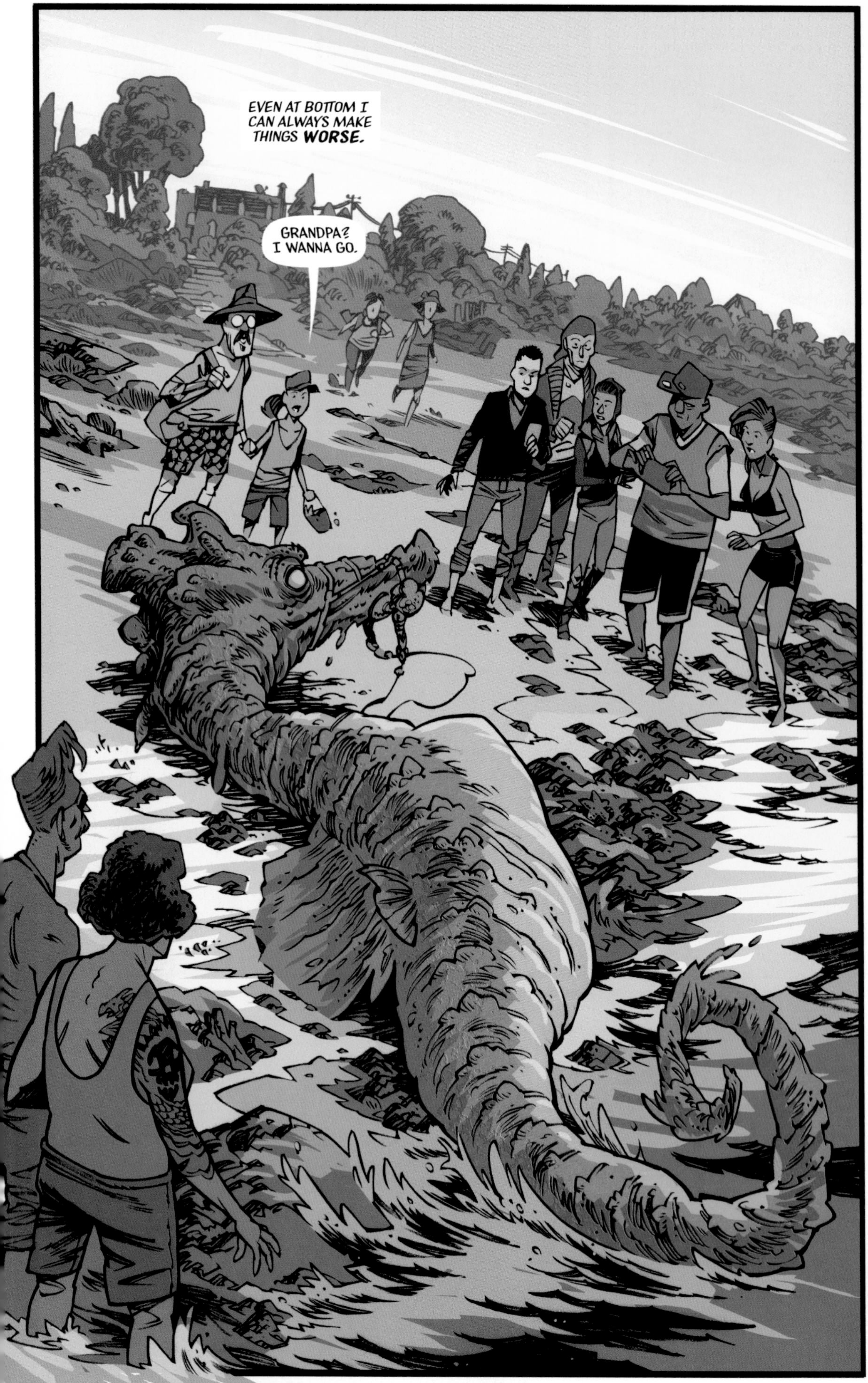
EVEN AT BOTTOM I CAN ALWAYS MAKE THINGS WORSE.
GRANDPA? I WANNA GO.

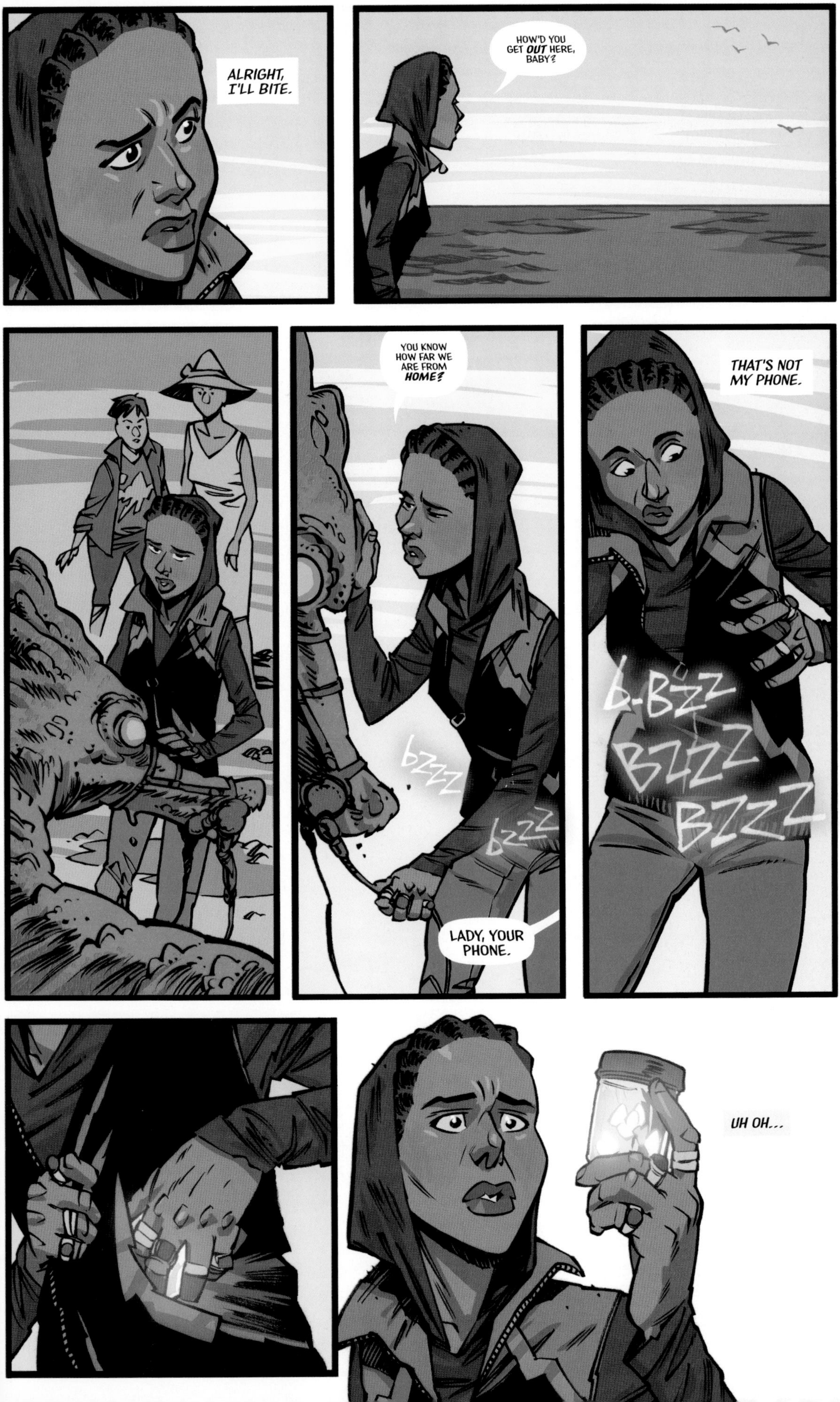
ALRIGHT, I'LL BITE.
HOW'D YOU GET OUT HERE, BABY?
YOU KNOW HOW FAR WE ARE FROM HOME?
bzzz
bzzz
LADY, YOUR PHONE.
THAT'S NOT MY PHONE.
b-BZZZ
BZZZZ
BZZZ
UH OH...

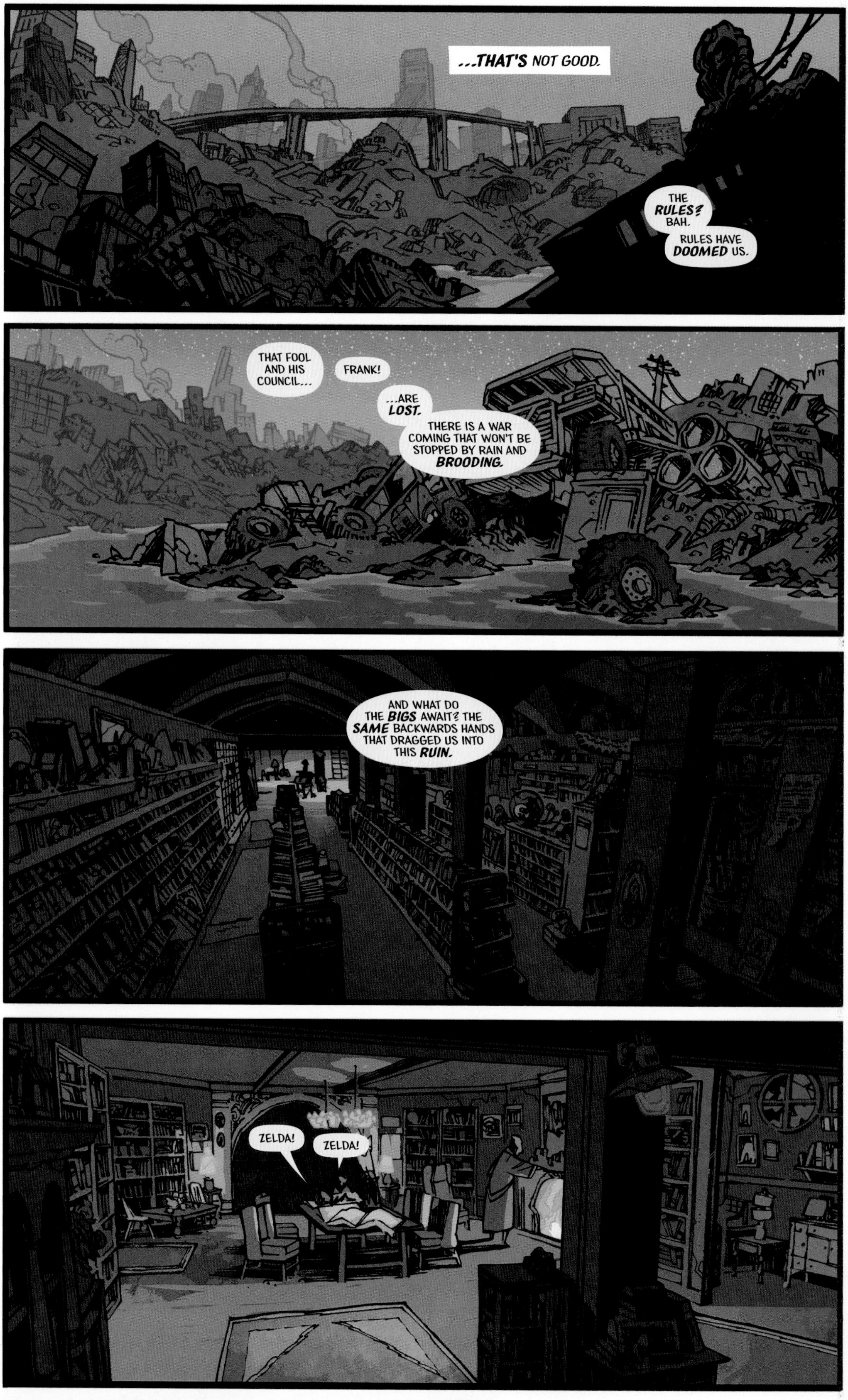
...THAT'S NOT GOOD.
THE RULES? BAH.
RULES HAVE DOOMED US.
THAT FOOL AND HIS COUNCIL...
FRANK!
...ARE LOST.
THERE IS A WAR COMING THAT WON'T BE STOPPED BY RAIN AND BROODING.
AND WHAT DO THE BIGS AWAIT? THE SAME BACKWARDS HANDS THAT DRAGGED US INTO THIS RUIN.
ZELDA!
ZELDA!

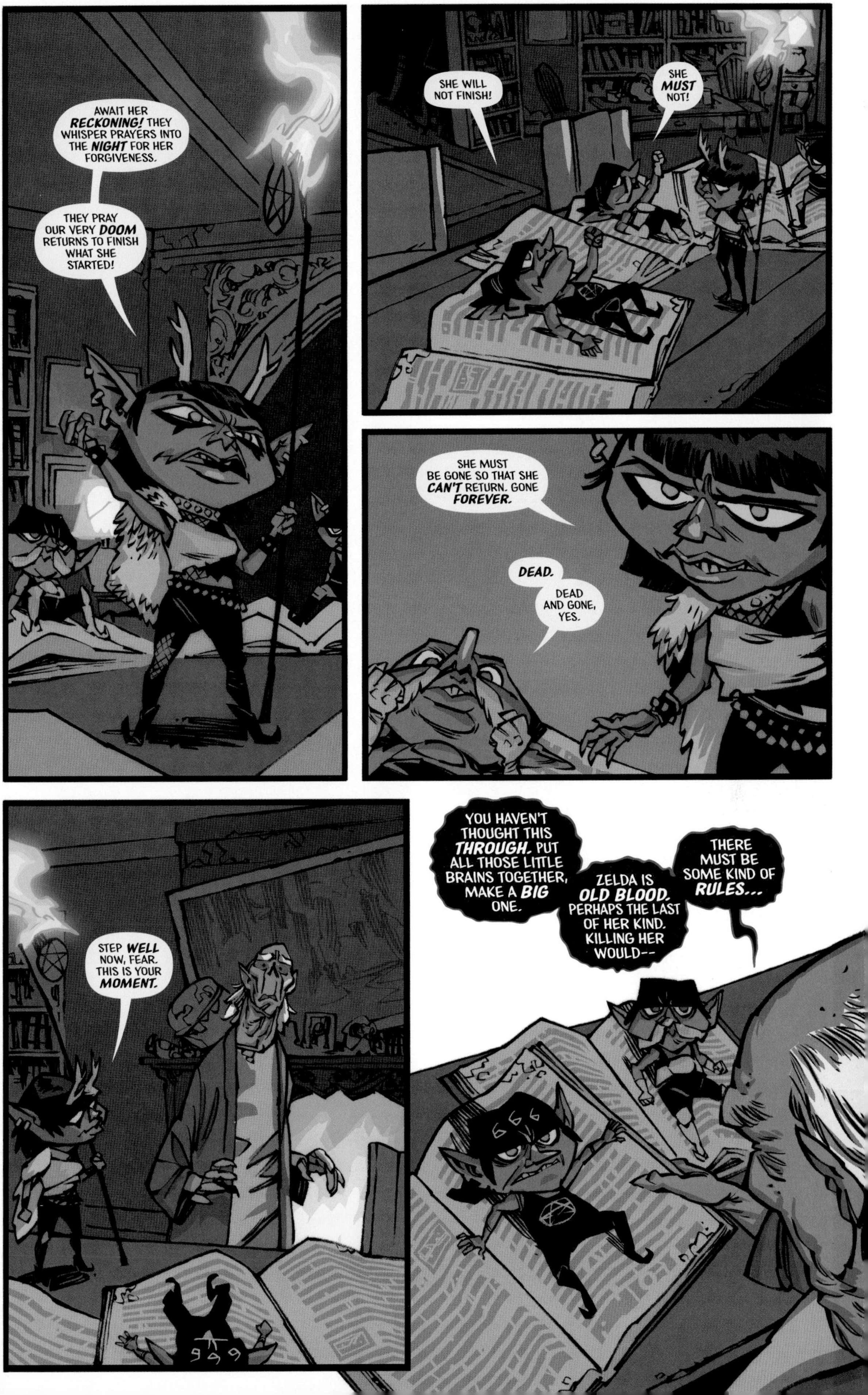
AWAIT HER RECKONING! THEY WHISPER PRAYERS INTO THE NIGHT FOR HER FORGIVENESS.
THEY PRAY OUR VERY DOOM RETURNS TO FINISH WHAT SHE STARTED!
SHE WILL NOT FINISH!
SHE MUST NOT!
SHE MUST BE GONE SO THAT SHE CAN'T RETURN. GONE FOREVER.
DEAD.
DEAD AND GONE, YES.
STEP WELL NOW, FEAR. THIS IS YOUR MOMENT.
YOU HAVEN'T THOUGHT THIS THROUGH. PUT ALL THOSE LITTLE BRAINS TOGETHER, MAKE A BIG ONE.
ZELDA IS OLD BLOOD. PERHAPS THE LAST OF HER KIND. KILLING HER WOULD--
THERE MUST BE SOME KIND OF RULES...

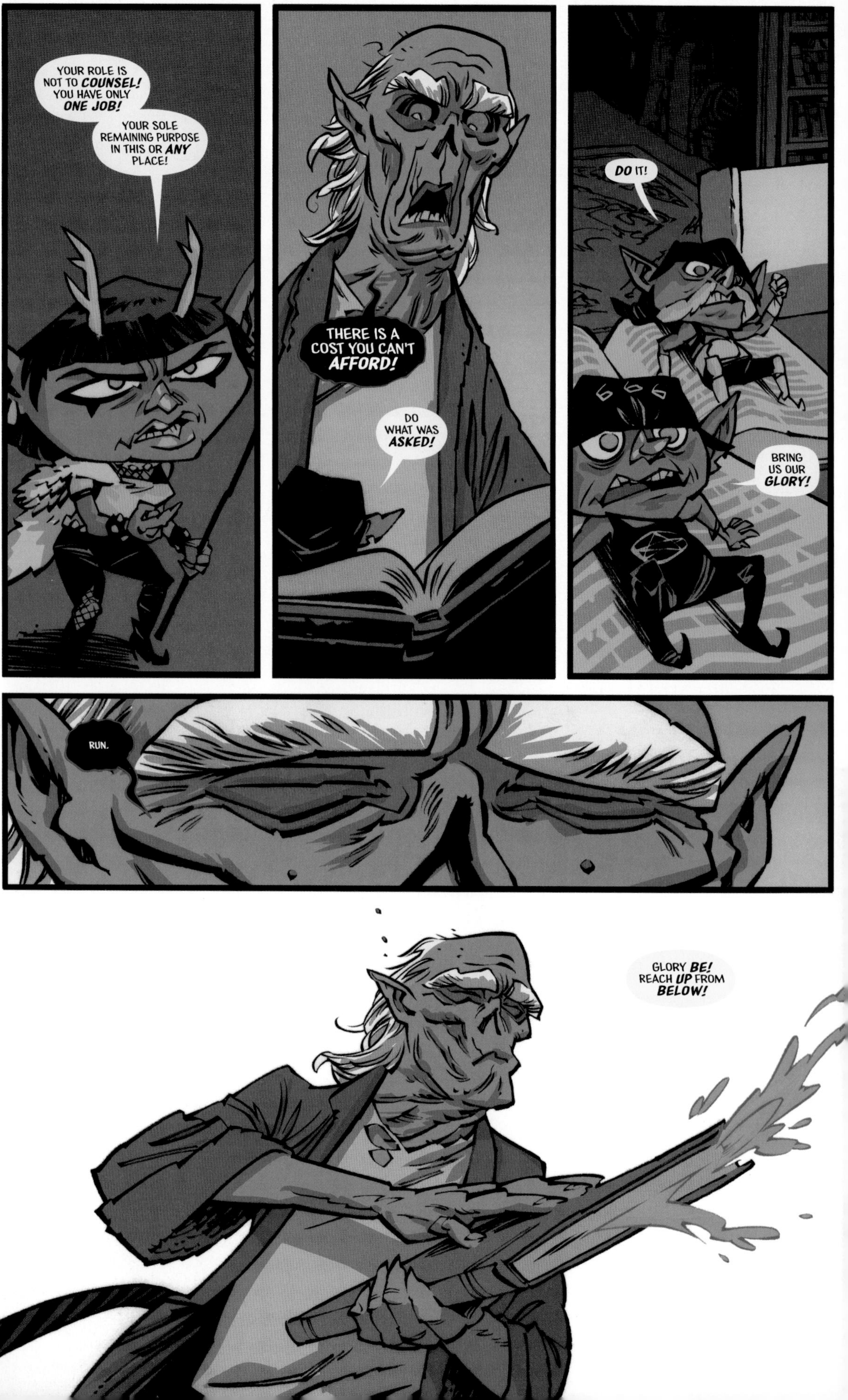
YOUR ROLE IS NOT TO COUNSEL! YOU HAVE ONLY ONE JOB!
YOUR SOLE REMAINING PURPOSE IN THIS OR ANY PLACE!
THERE IS A COST YOU CAN'T AFFORD!
DO WHAT WAS ASKED!
DO IT!
BRING US OUR GLORY!
RUN.
GLORY BE! REACH UP FROM BELOW!

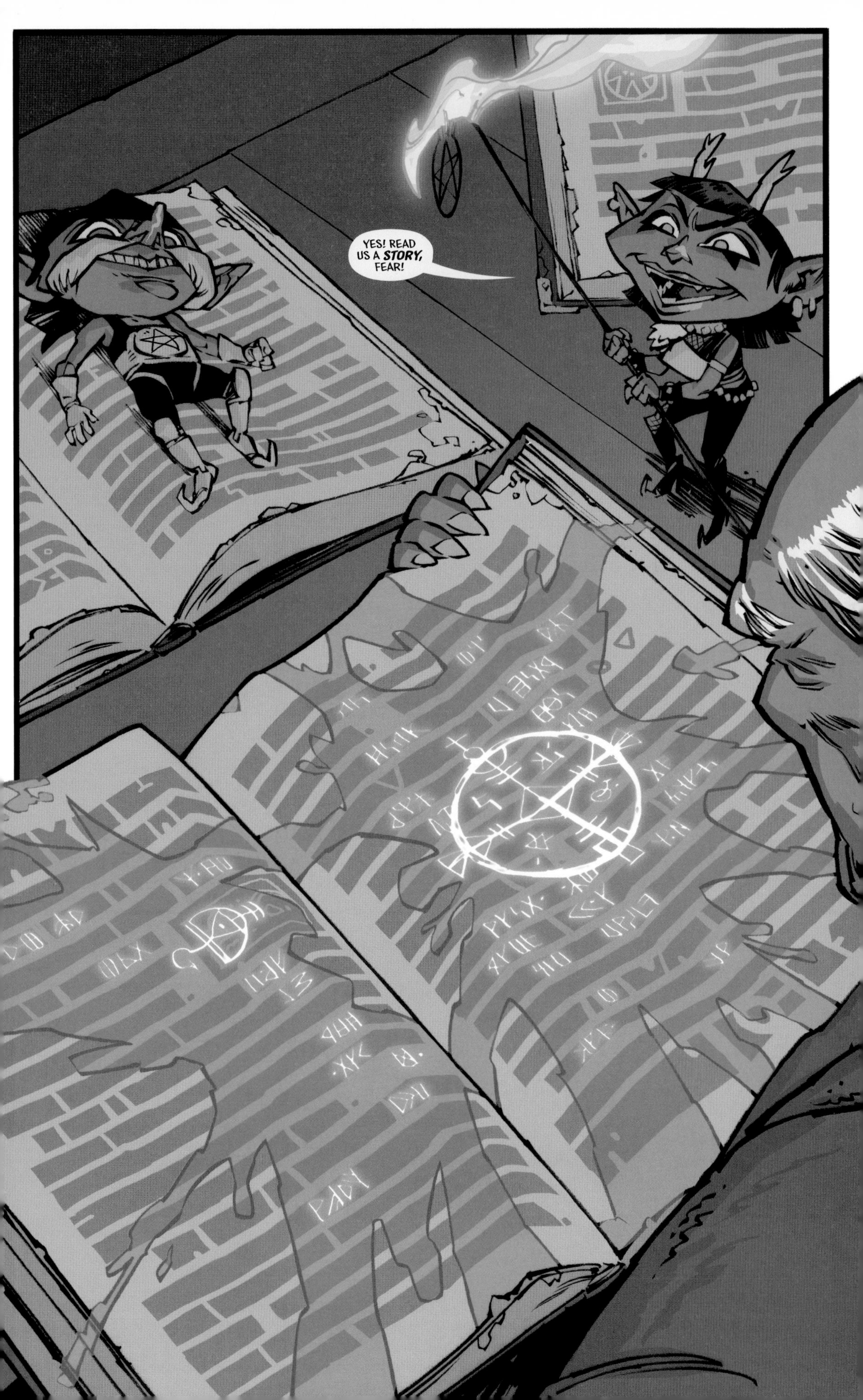
YES! READ US A STORY, FEAR!

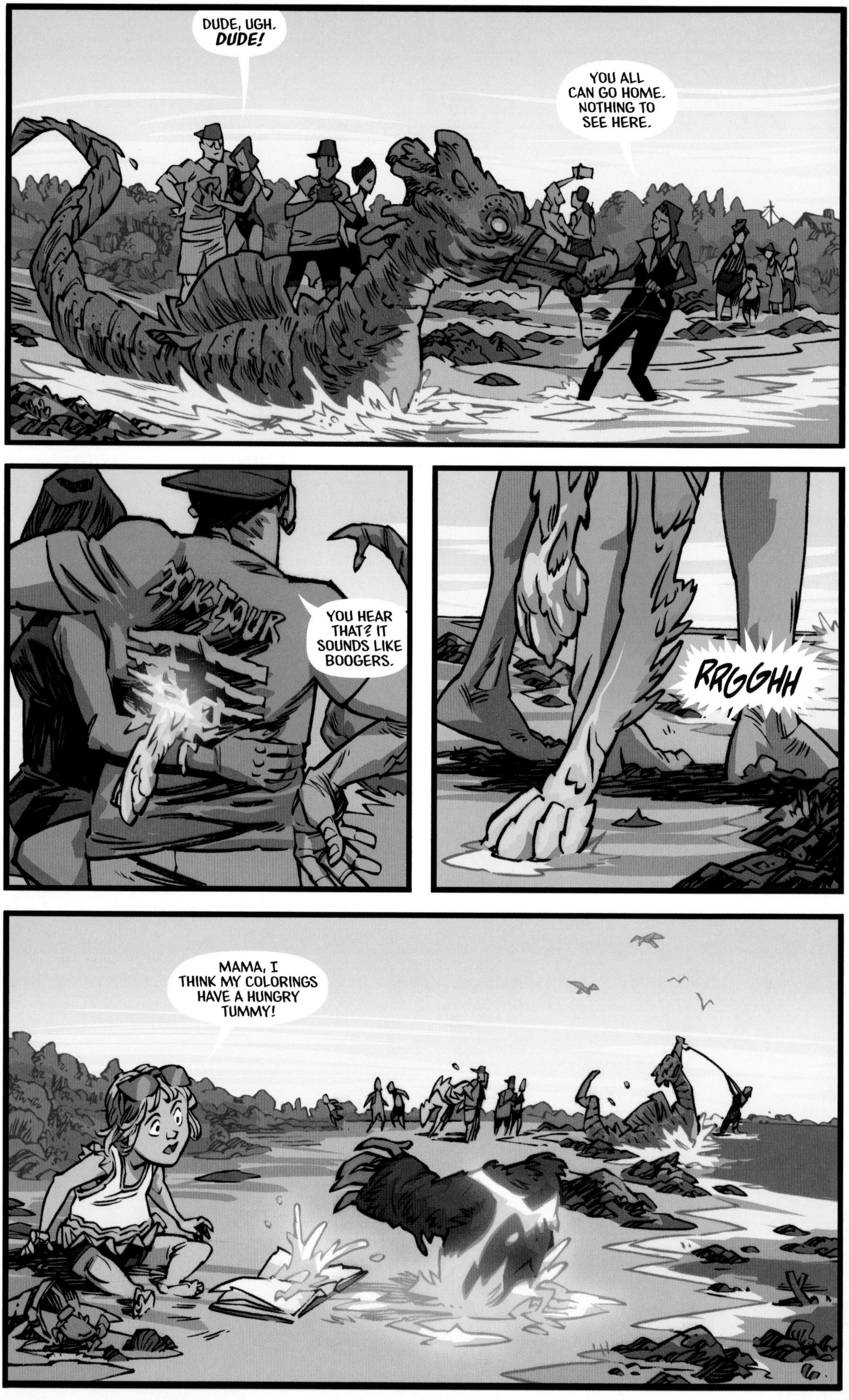
DUDE, UGH. *DUDE!*
YOU ALL CAN GO HOME. NOTHING TO SEE HERE.
YOU HEAR THAT? IT SOUNDS LIKE BOOGERS.
RRGGHH
MAMA, I THINK MY COLORINGS HAVE A HUNGRY TUMMY!

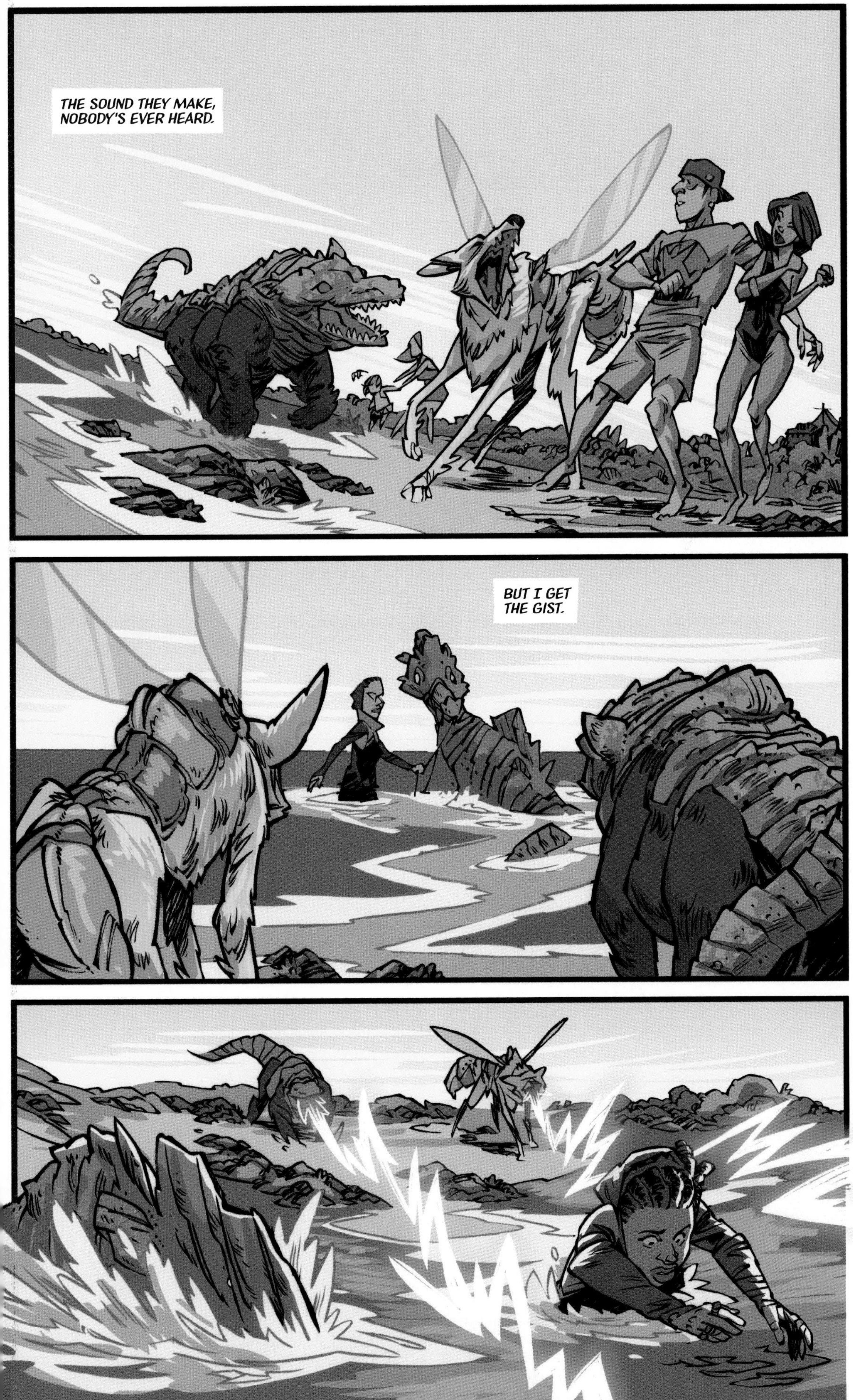
THE SOUND THEY MAKE, NOBODY'S EVER HEARD.
BUT I GET THE GIST.

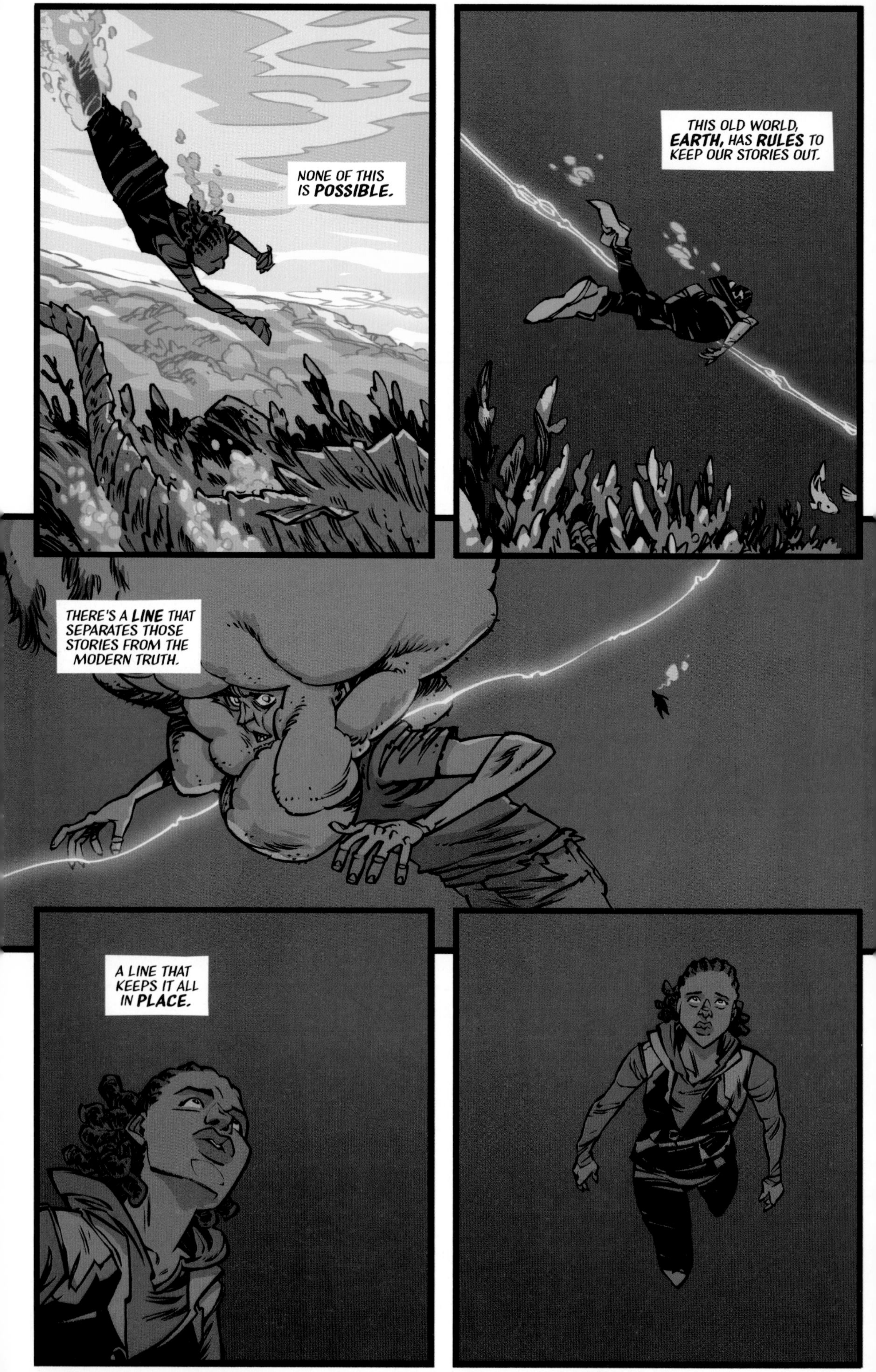
NONE OF THIS IS POSSIBLE.
THIS OLD WORLD, EARTH, HAS RULES TO KEEP OUR STORIES OUT.
THERE'S A LINE THAT SEPARATES THOSE STORIES FROM THE MODERN TRUTH.
A LINE THAT KEEPS IT ALL IN PLACE.

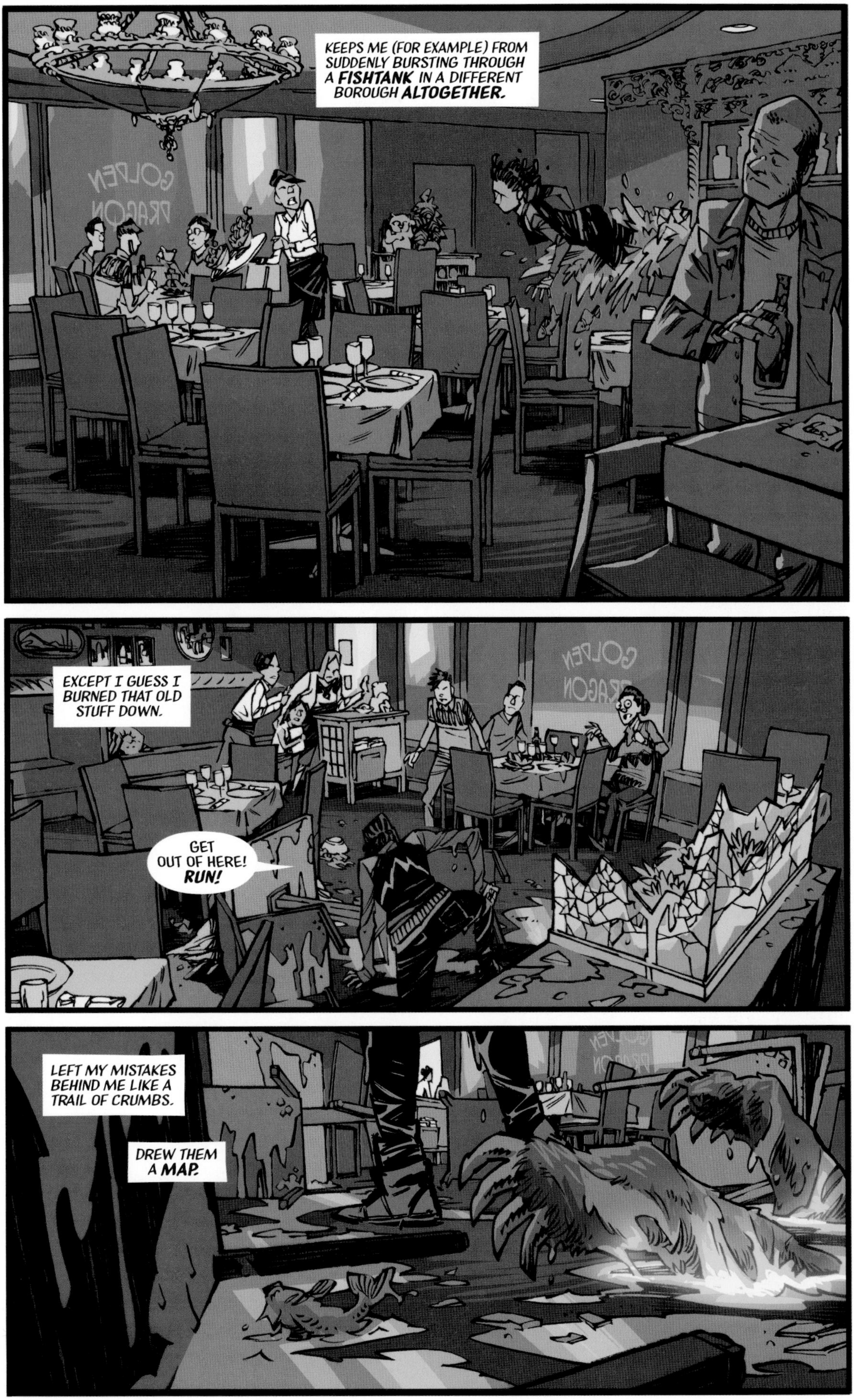
KEEPS ME (FOR EXAMPLE) FROM SUDDENLY BURSTING THROUGH A **FISHTANK** IN A DIFFERENT BOROUGH **ALTOGETHER.**
EXCEPT I GUESS I BURNED THAT OLD STUFF DOWN.
GET OUT OF HERE! ***RUN!***
LEFT MY MISTAKES BEHIND ME LIKE A TRAIL OF CRUMBS.
DREW THEM A **MAP.**

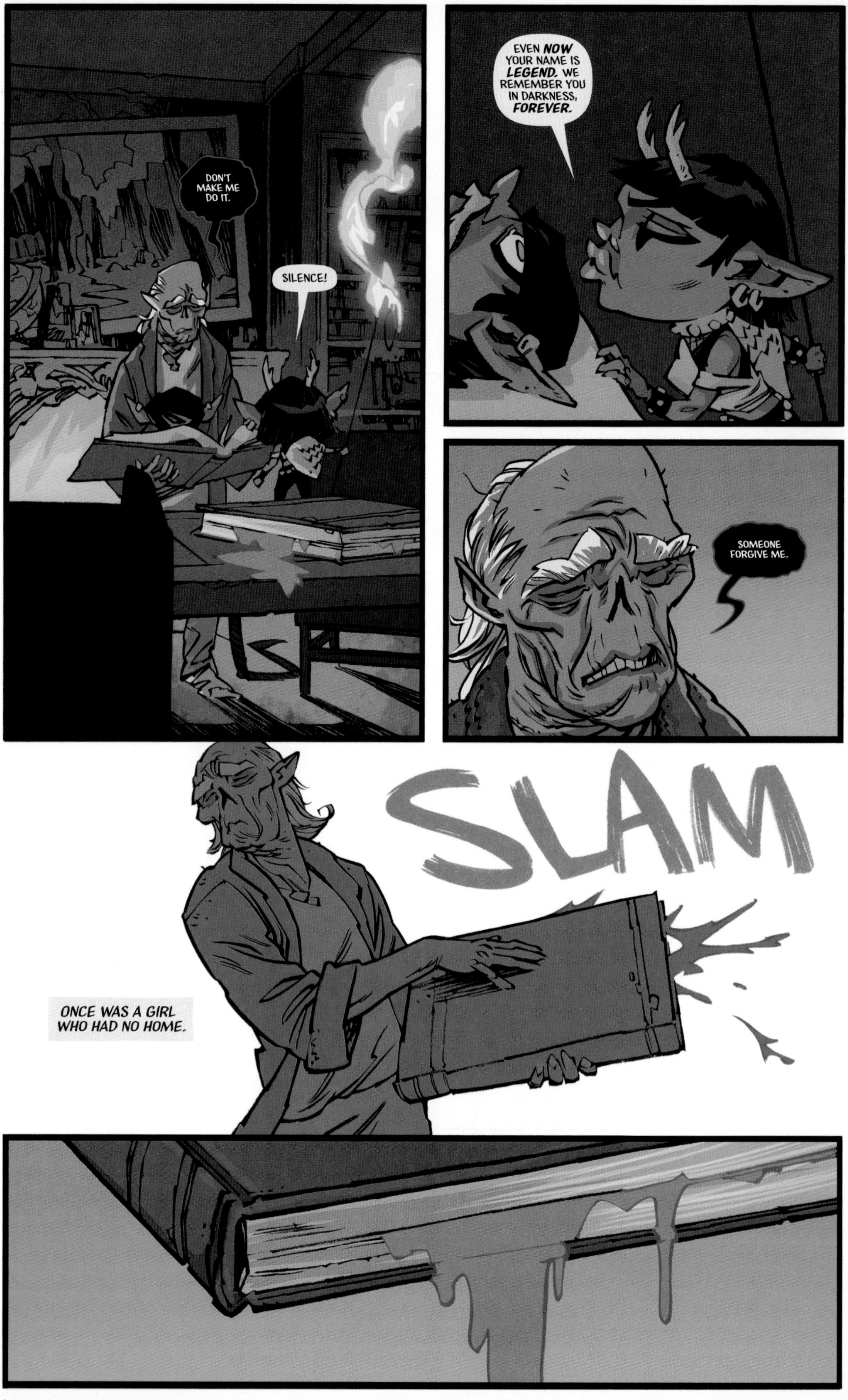
DON'T MAKE ME DO IT.
SILENCE!
EVEN NOW YOUR NAME IS LEGEND. WE REMEMBER YOU IN DARKNESS, FOREVER.
SOMEONE FORGIVE ME.
SLAM
ONCE WAS A GIRL WHO HAD NO HOME.

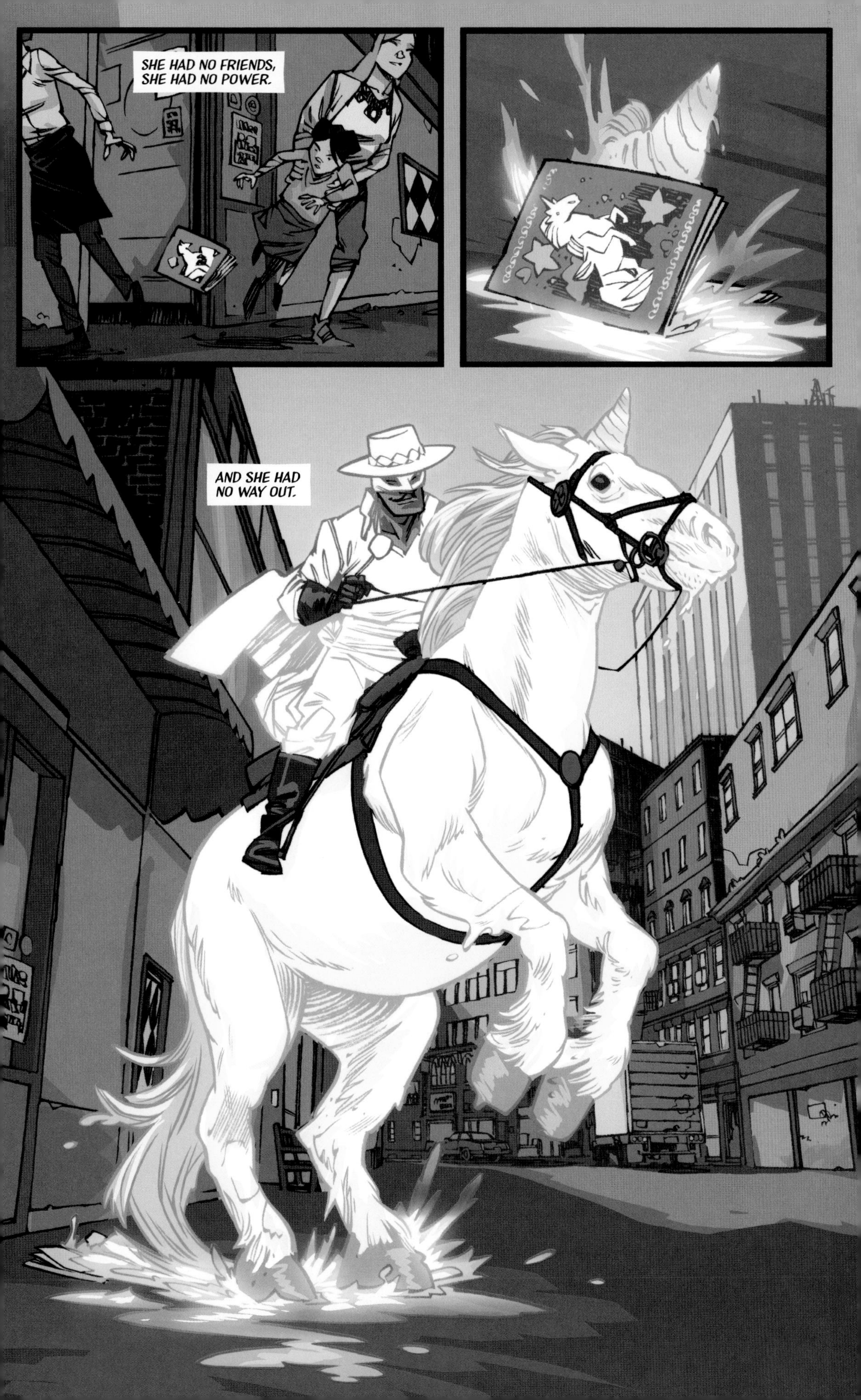
SHE HAD NO FRIENDS, SHE HAD NO POWER.
AND SHE HAD NO WAY OUT.

Chapter 8

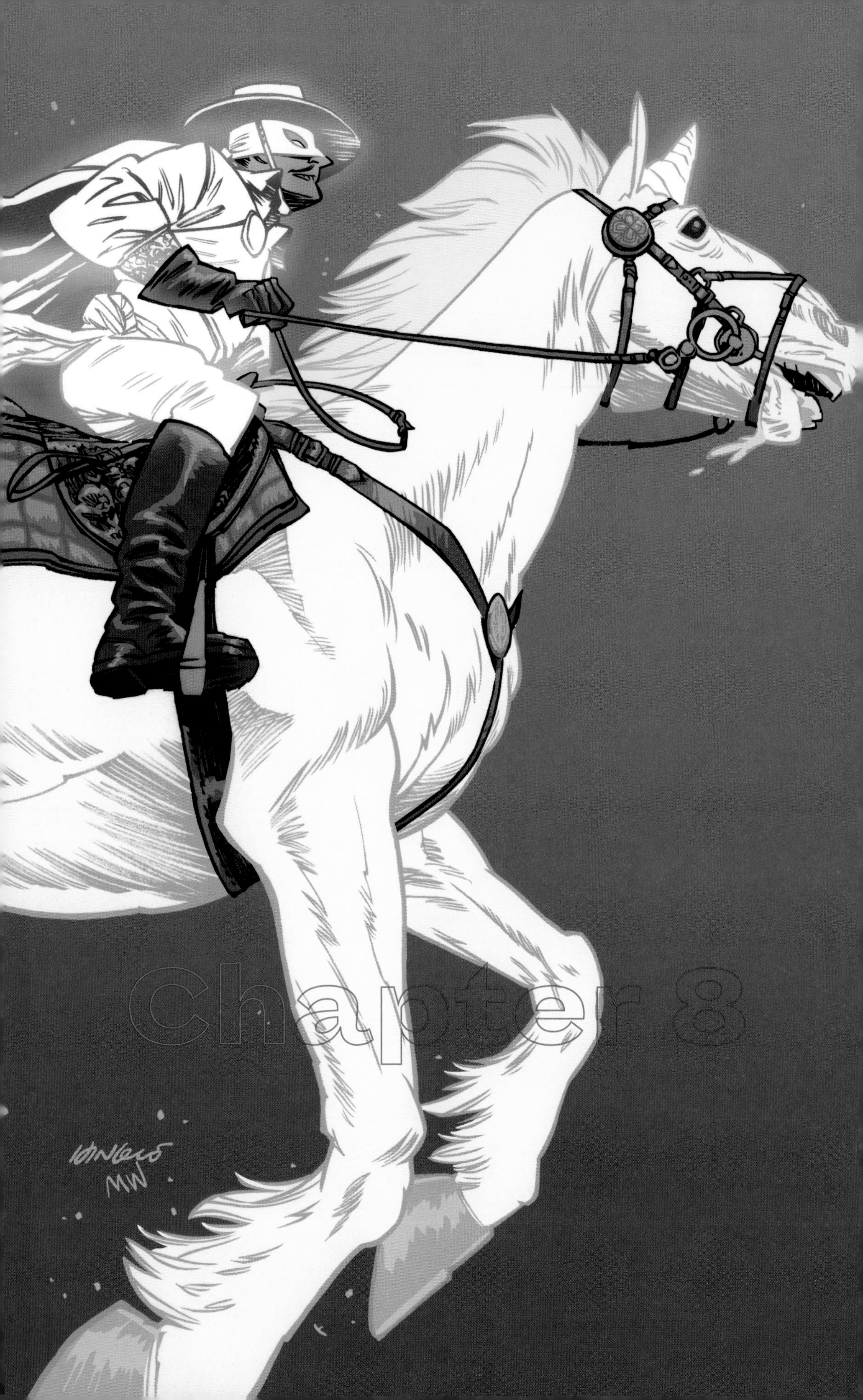

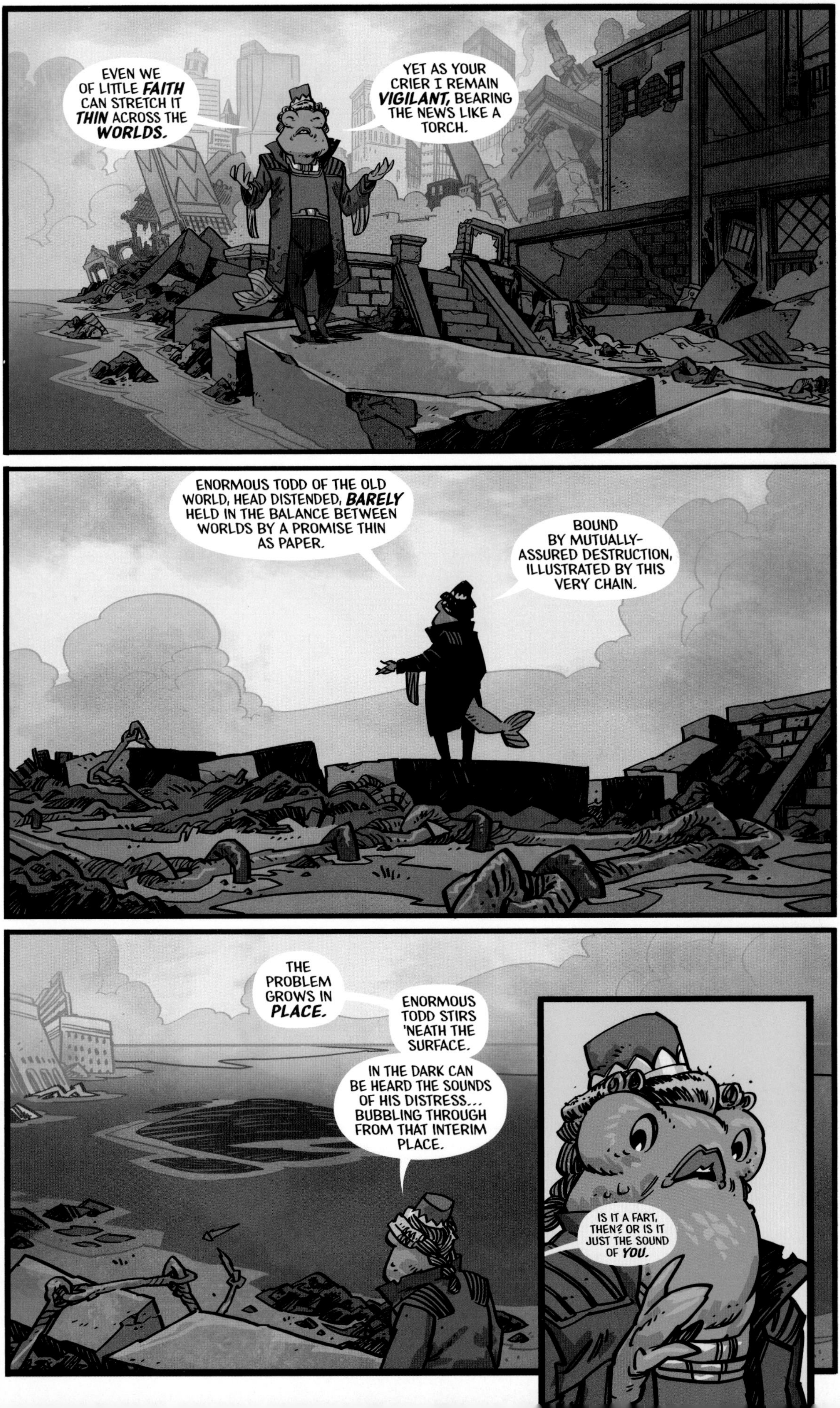
EVEN WE OF LITTLE FAITH CAN STRETCH IT THIN ACROSS THE WORLDS.
YET AS YOUR CRIER I REMAIN VIGILANT, BEARING THE NEWS LIKE A TORCH.
ENORMOUS TODD OF THE OLD WORLD, HEAD DISTENDED, BARELY HELD IN THE BALANCE BETWEEN WORLDS BY A PROMISE THIN AS PAPER.
BOUND BY MUTUALLY-ASSURED DESTRUCTION, ILLUSTRATED BY THIS VERY CHAIN.
THE PROBLEM GROWS IN PLACE.
ENORMOUS TODD STIRS 'NEATH THE SURFACE.
IN THE DARK CAN BE HEARD THE SOUNDS OF HIS DISTRESS... BUBBLING THROUGH FROM THAT INTERIM PLACE.
IS IT A FART, THEN? OR IS IT JUST THE SOUND OF YOU.

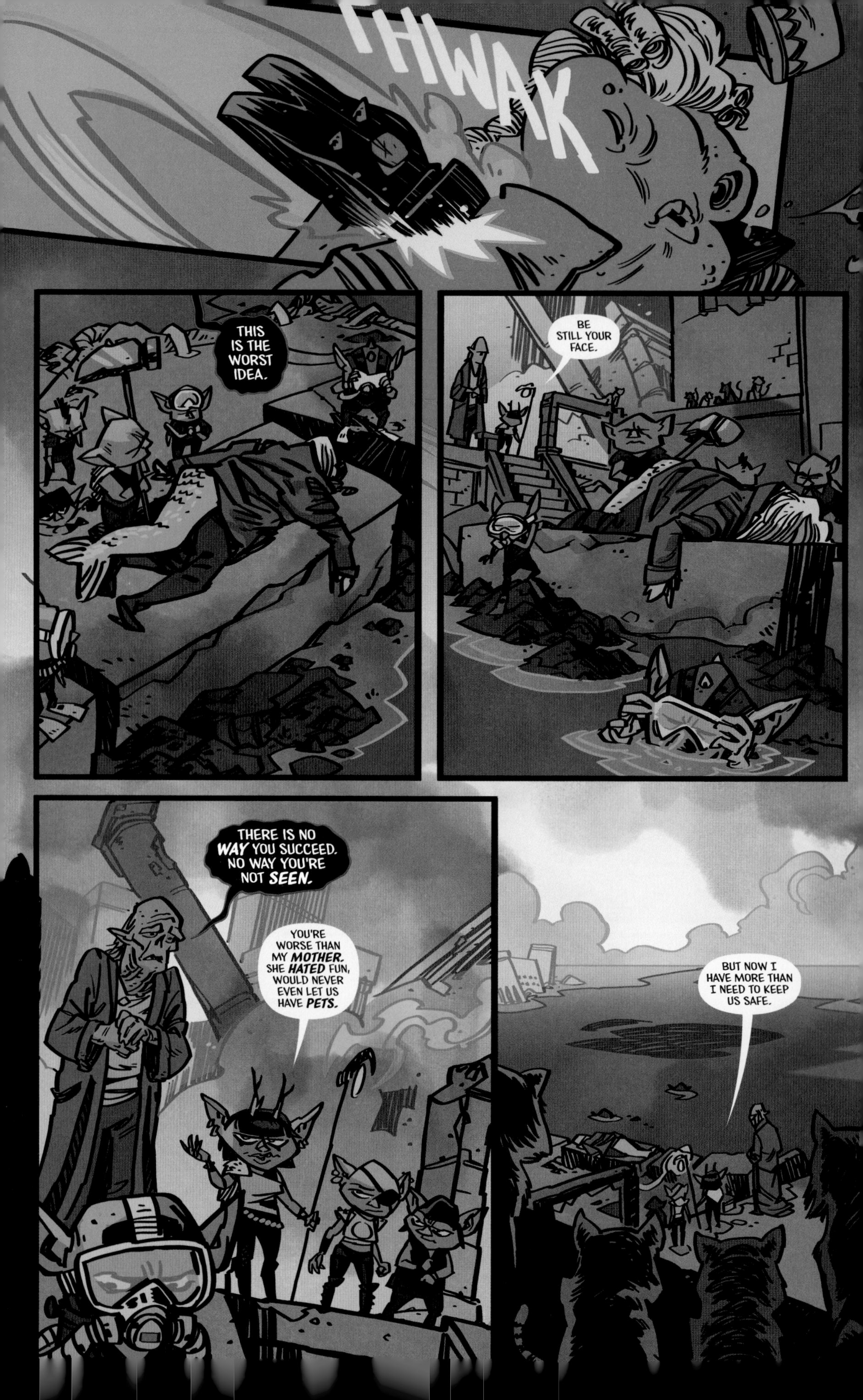

THWAK
THIS IS THE WORST IDEA.
BE STILL YOUR FACE.
THERE IS NO WAY YOU SUCCEED. NO WAY YOU'RE NOT SEEN.
YOU'RE WORSE THAN MY MOTHER. SHE HATED FUN, WOULD NEVER EVEN LET US HAVE PETS.
BUT NOW I HAVE MORE THAN I NEED TO KEEP US SAFE.

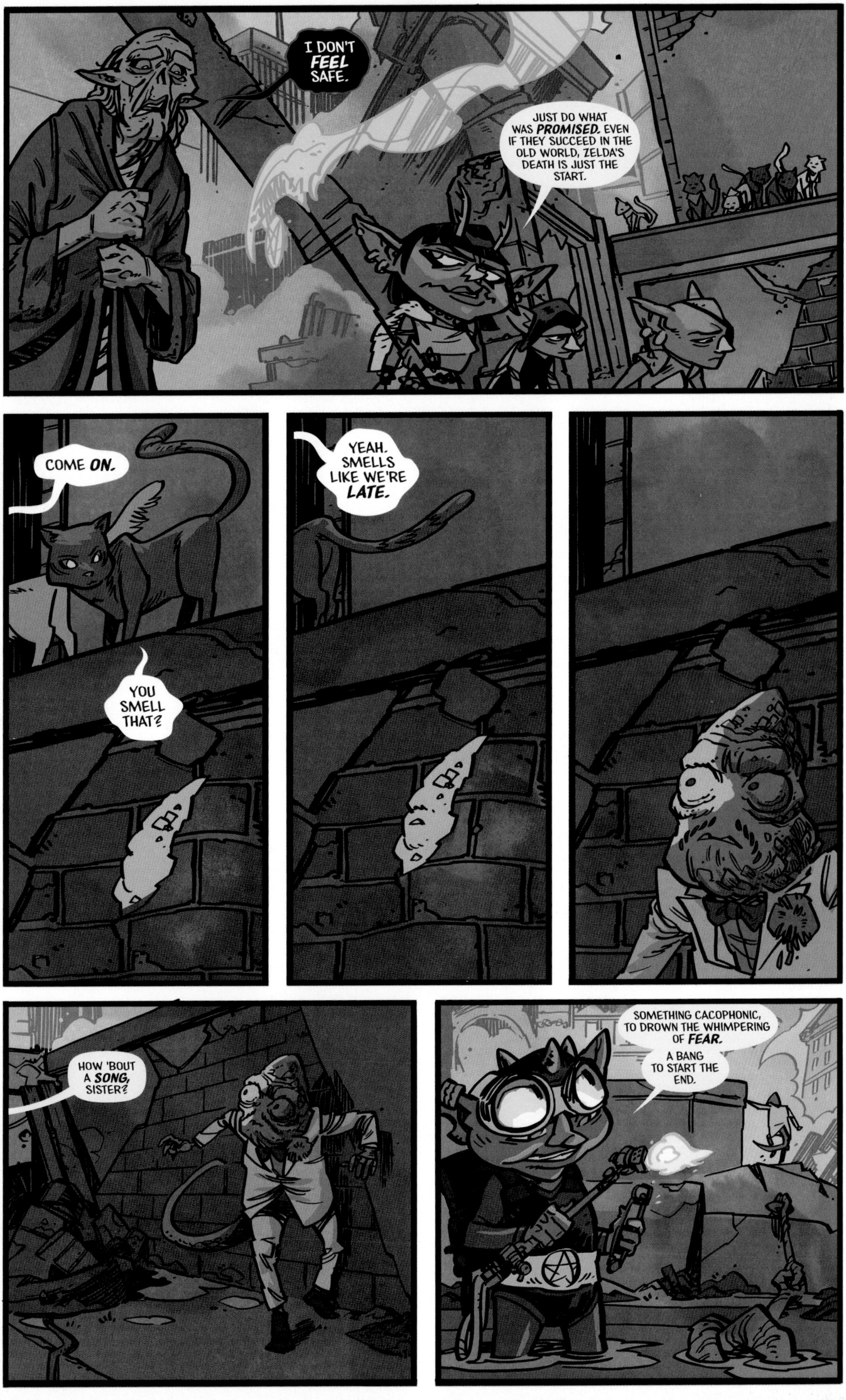
I DON'T FEEL SAFE.
JUST DO WHAT WAS PROMISED. EVEN IF THEY SUCCEED IN THE OLD WORLD, ZELDA'S DEATH IS JUST THE START.
COME ON.
YOU SMELL THAT?
YEAH. SMELLS LIKE WE'RE LATE.
HOW 'BOUT A SONG, SISTER?
SOMETHING CACOPHONIC, TO DROWN THE WHIMPERING OF FEAR.
A BANG TO START THE END.

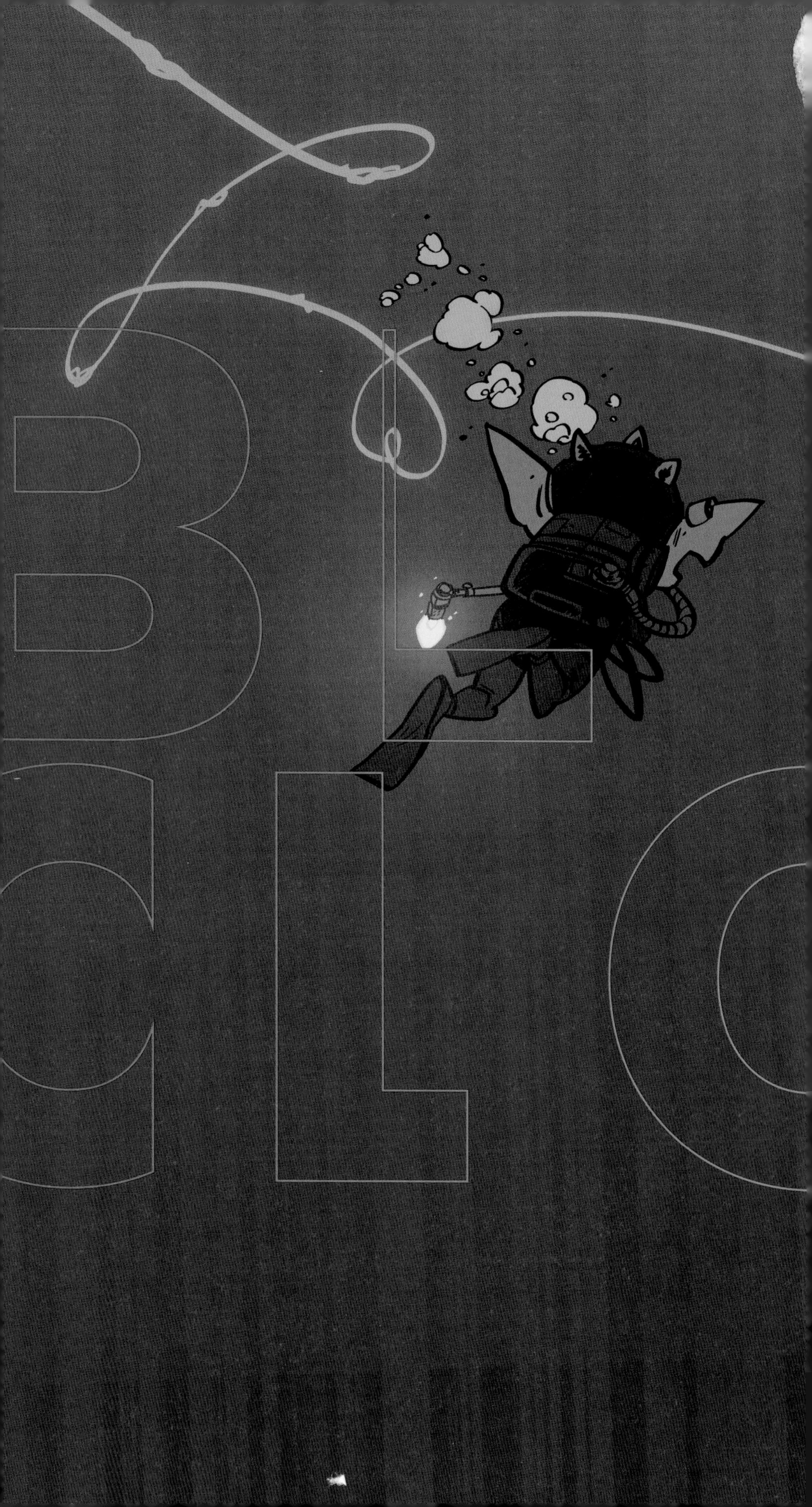

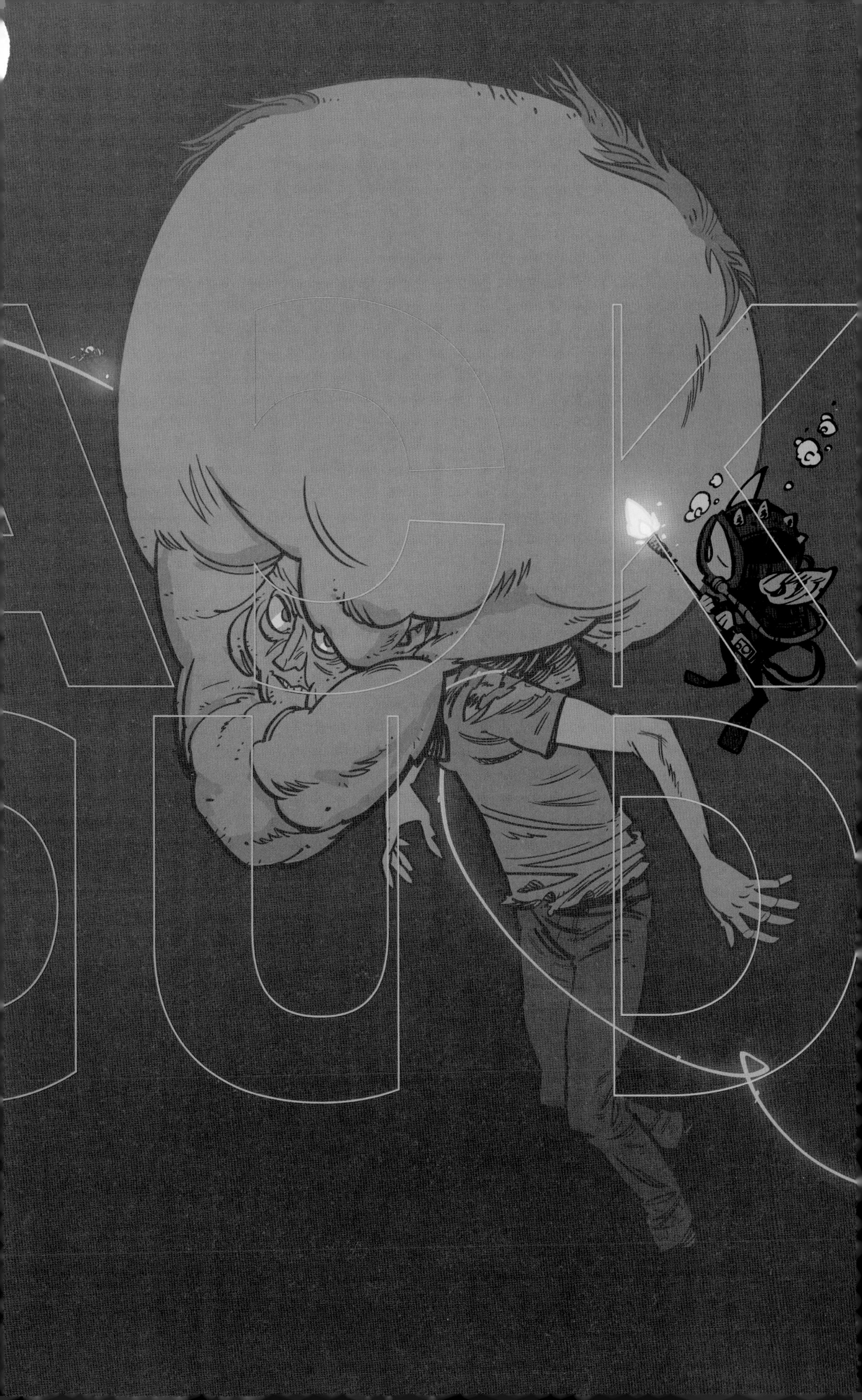

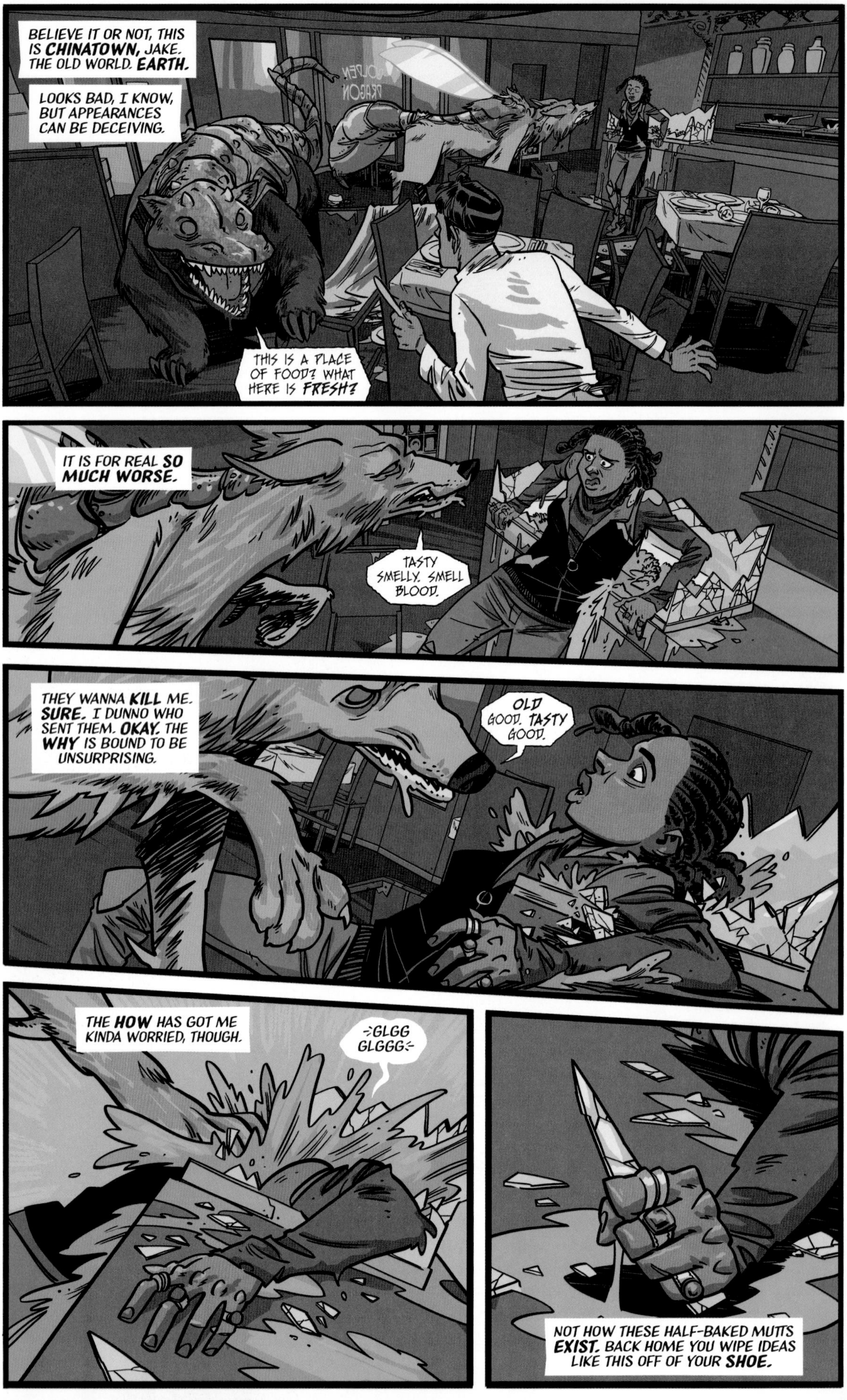
BELIEVE IT OR NOT, THIS IS CHINATOWN, JAKE. THE OLD WORLD. EARTH.
LOOKS BAD, I KNOW, BUT APPEARANCES CAN BE DECEIVING.
THIS IS A PLACE OF FOOD? WHAT HERE IS FRESH?
IT IS FOR REAL SO MUCH WORSE.
TASTY SMELLY. SMELL BLOOD.
THEY WANNA KILL ME. SURE. I DUNNO WHO SENT THEM. OKAY. THE WHY IS BOUND TO BE UNSURPRISING.
OLD GOOD. TASTY GOOD.
THE HOW HAS GOT ME KINDA WORRIED, THOUGH.
GLGG GLGGG
NOT HOW THESE HALF-BAKED MUTTS EXIST. BACK HOME YOU WIPE IDEAS LIKE THIS OFF OF YOUR SHOE.

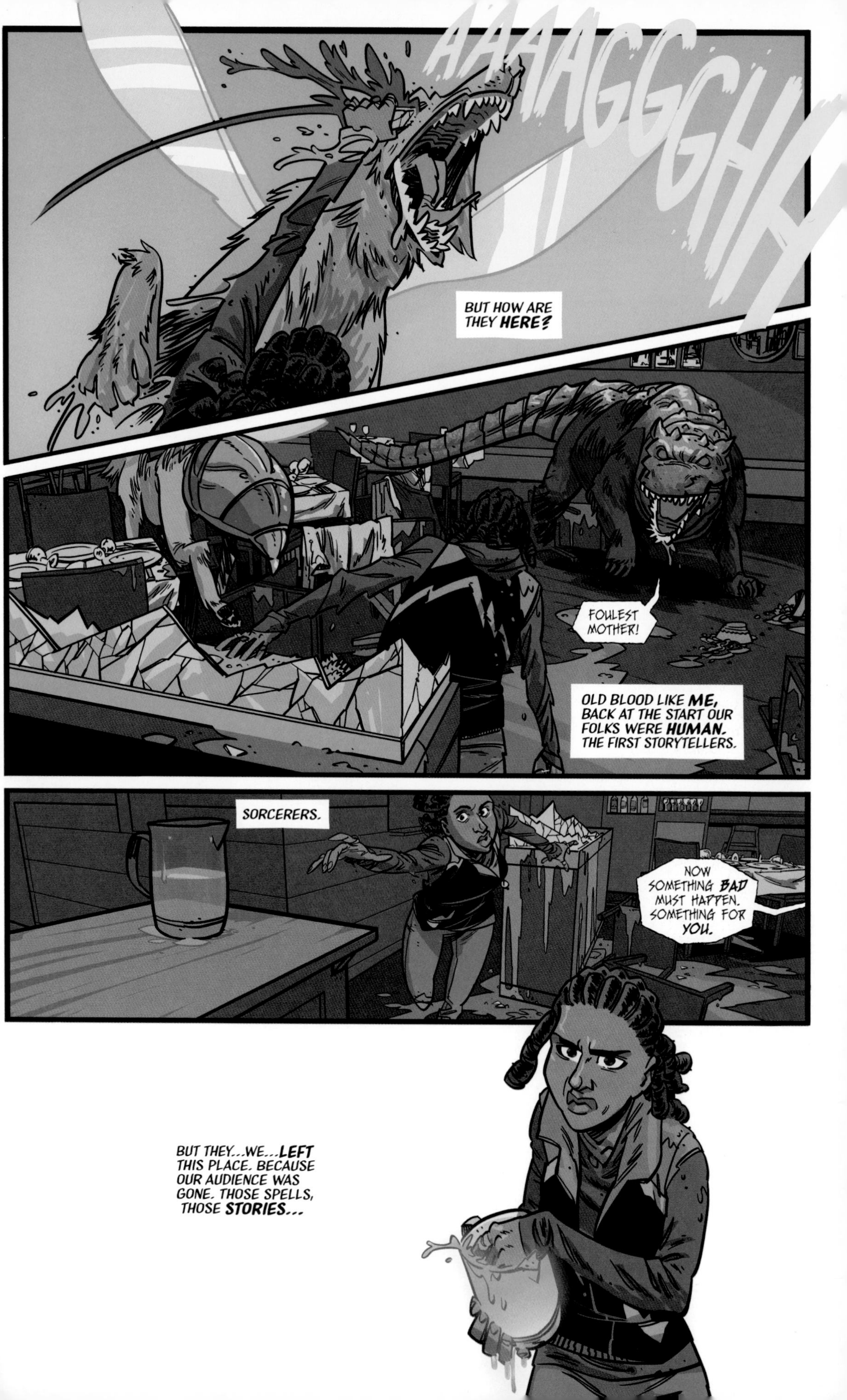
AAAAGGGHH
BUT HOW ARE THEY HERE?
FOULEST MOTHER!
OLD BLOOD LIKE ME, BACK AT THE START OUR FOLKS WERE HUMAN. THE FIRST STORYTELLERS.
SORCERERS.
NOW SOMETHING BAD MUST HAPPEN. SOMETHING FOR YOU.
BUT THEY...WE...LEFT THIS PLACE. BECAUSE OUR AUDIENCE WAS GONE. THOSE SPELLS, THOSE STORIES...

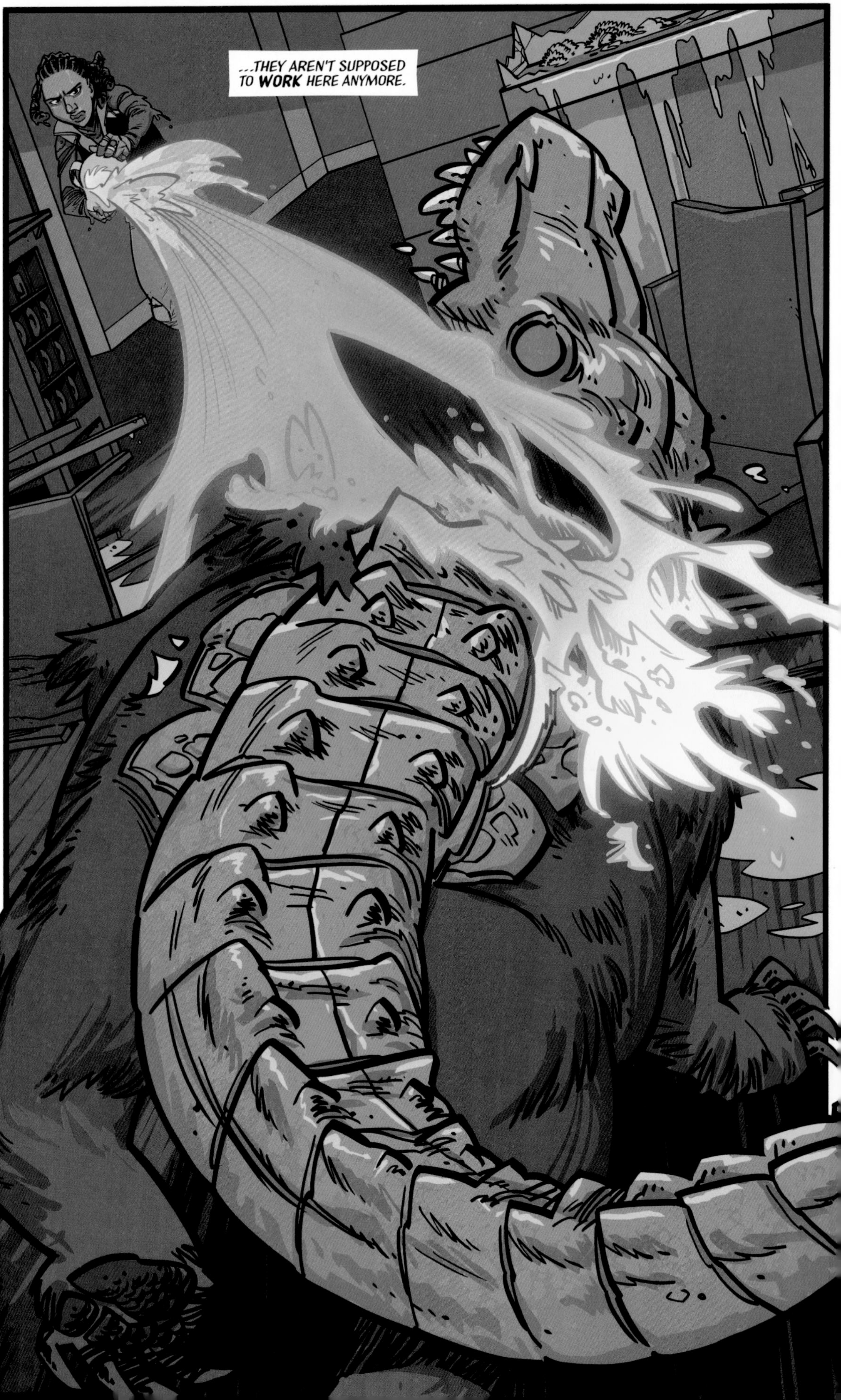
...THEY AREN'T SUPPOSED TO WORK HERE ANYMORE.

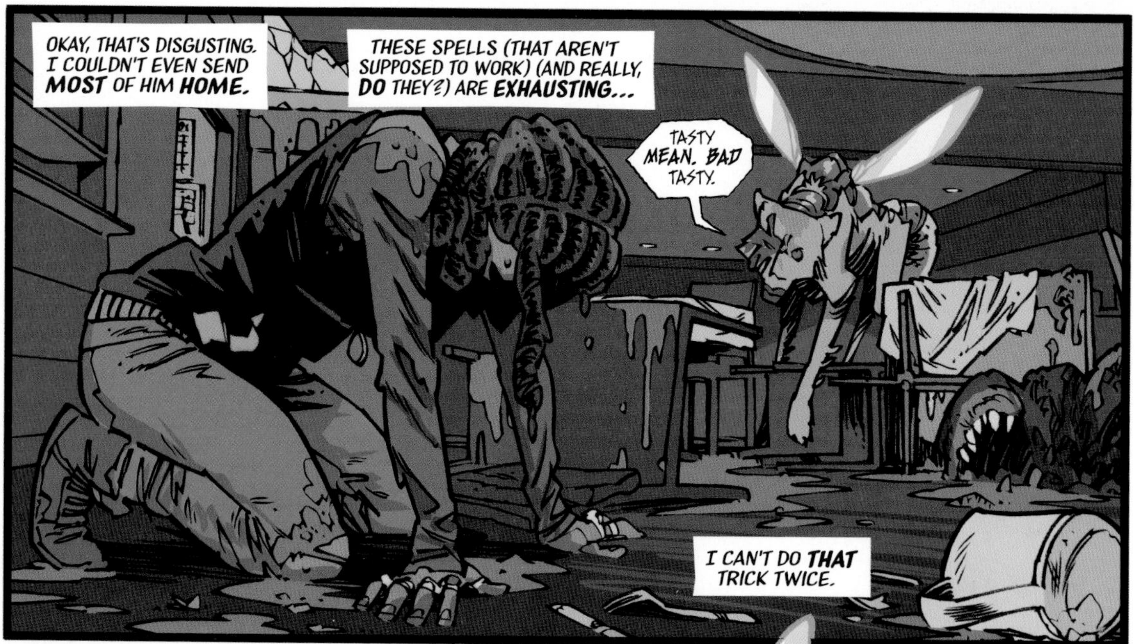
OKAY, THAT'S DISGUSTING. I COULDN'T EVEN SEND MOST OF HIM HOME.
THESE SPELLS (THAT AREN'T SUPPOSED TO WORK) (AND REALLY, DO THEY?) ARE EXHAUSTING...
TASTY MEAN. BAD TASTY.
I CAN'T DO THAT TRICK TWICE.

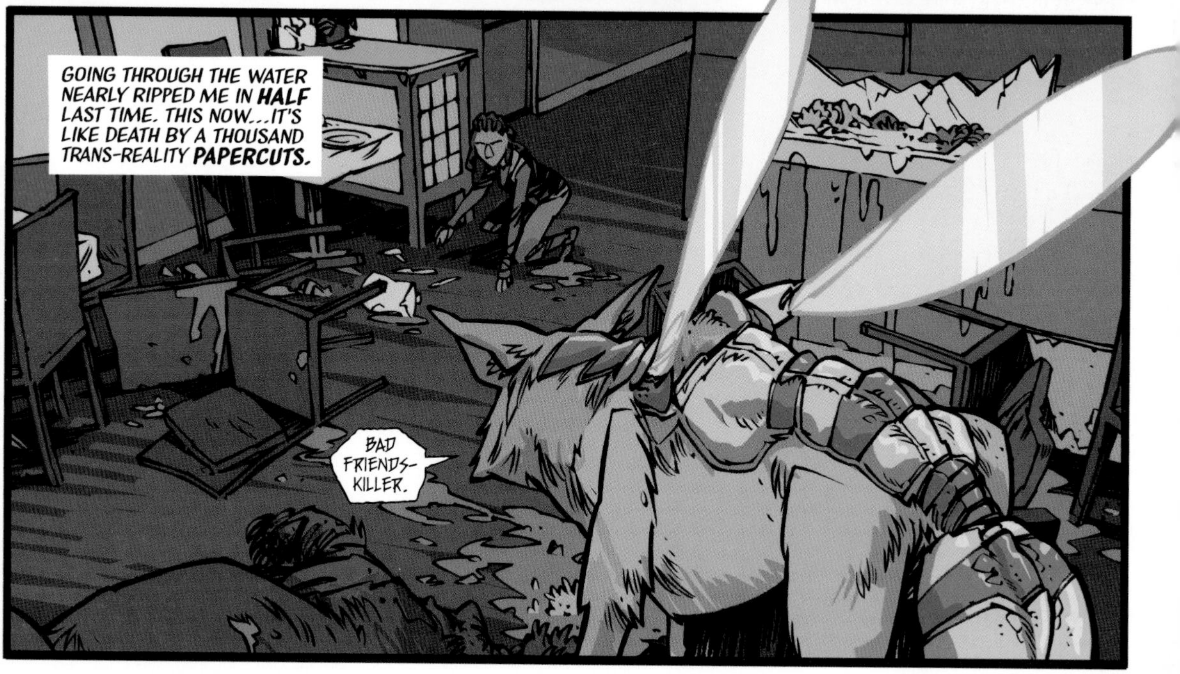
GOING THROUGH THE WATER NEARLY RIPPED ME IN HALF LAST TIME. THIS NOW...IT'S LIKE DEATH BY A THOUSAND TRANS-REALITY PAPERCUTS.
BAD FRIENDS-KILLER.

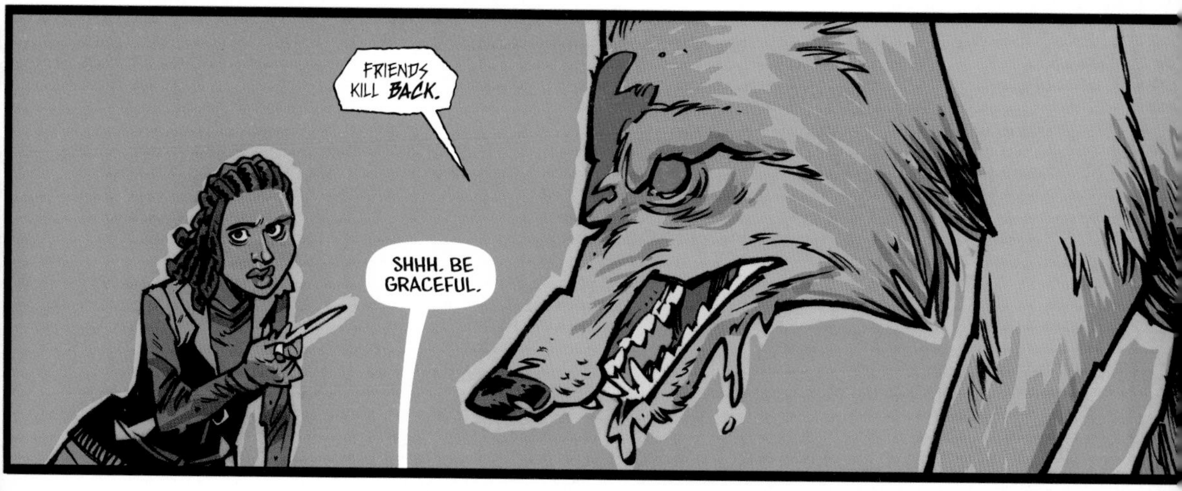
FRIENDS KILL BACK.
SHHH. BE GRACEFUL.

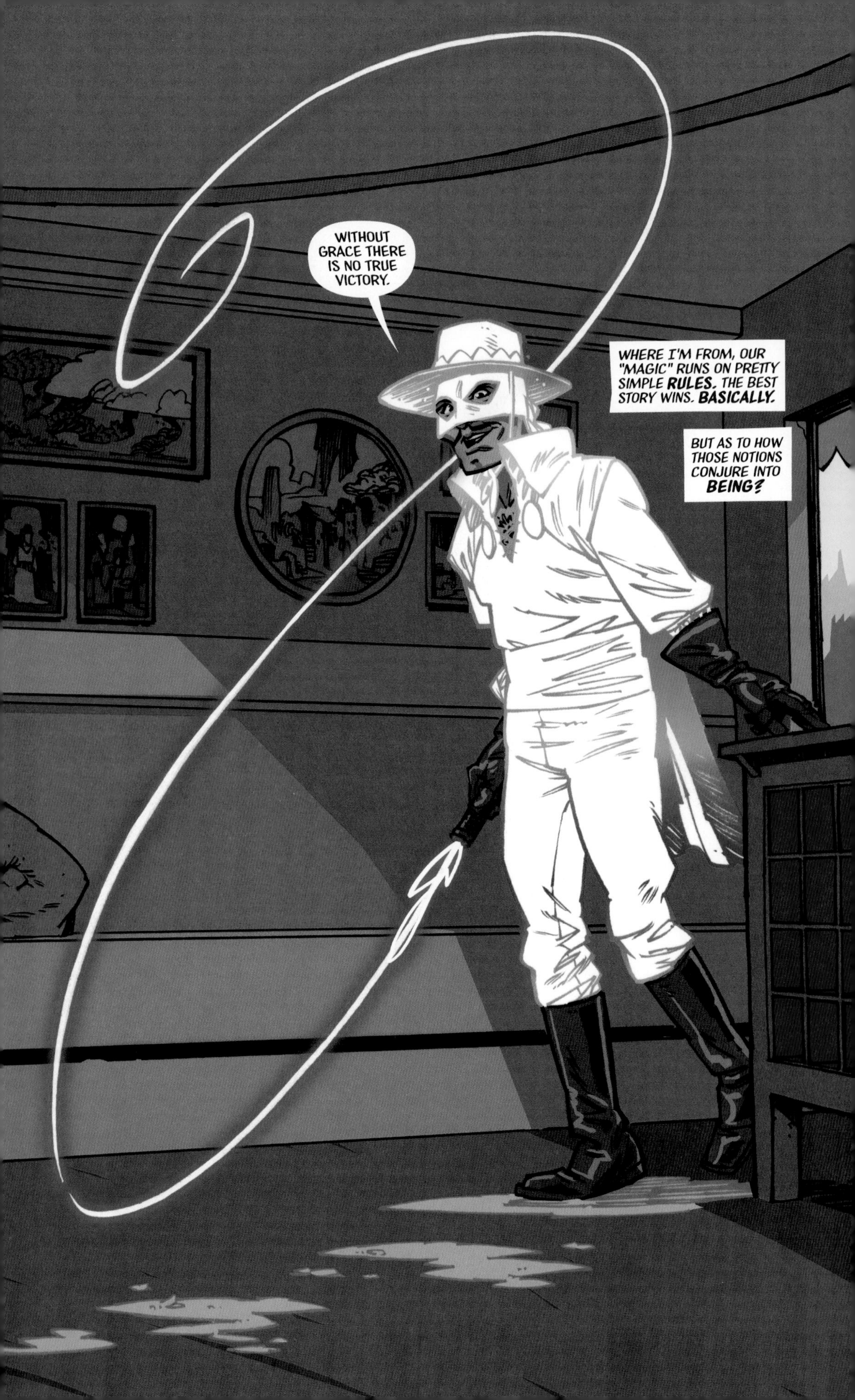
WITHOUT GRACE THERE IS NO TRUE VICTORY.
WHERE I'M FROM, OUR "MAGIC" RUNS ON PRETTY SIMPLE **RULES.** THE BEST STORY WINS. **BASICALLY.**
BUT AS TO HOW THOSE NOTIONS CONJURE INTO **BEING?**

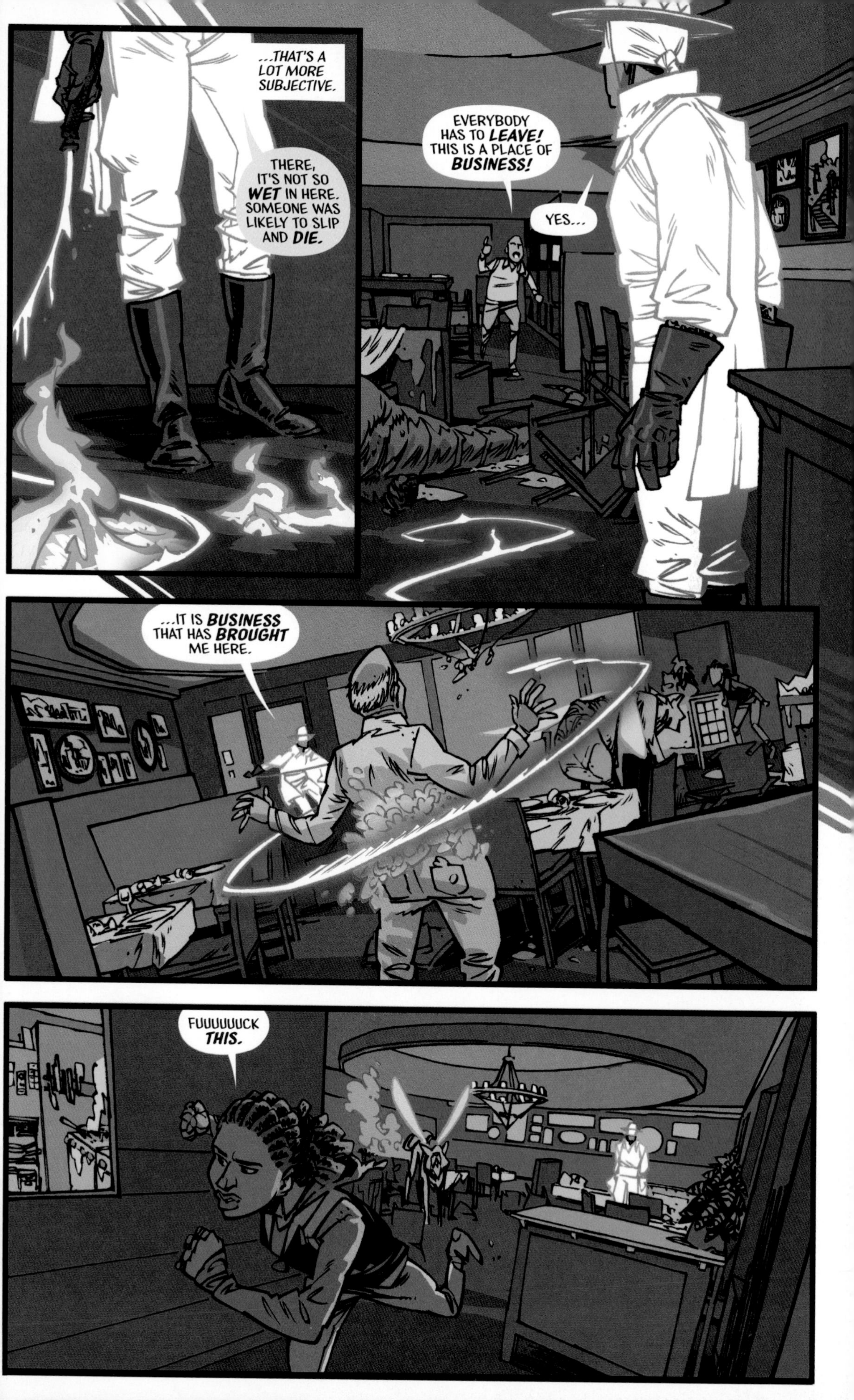
...THAT'S A LOT MORE SUBJECTIVE.
THERE, IT'S NOT SO WET IN HERE. SOMEONE WAS LIKELY TO SLIP AND DIE.
EVERYBODY HAS TO LEAVE! THIS IS A PLACE OF BUSINESS!
YES...
...IT IS BUSINESS THAT HAS BROUGHT ME HERE.
FUUUUUUCK THIS.

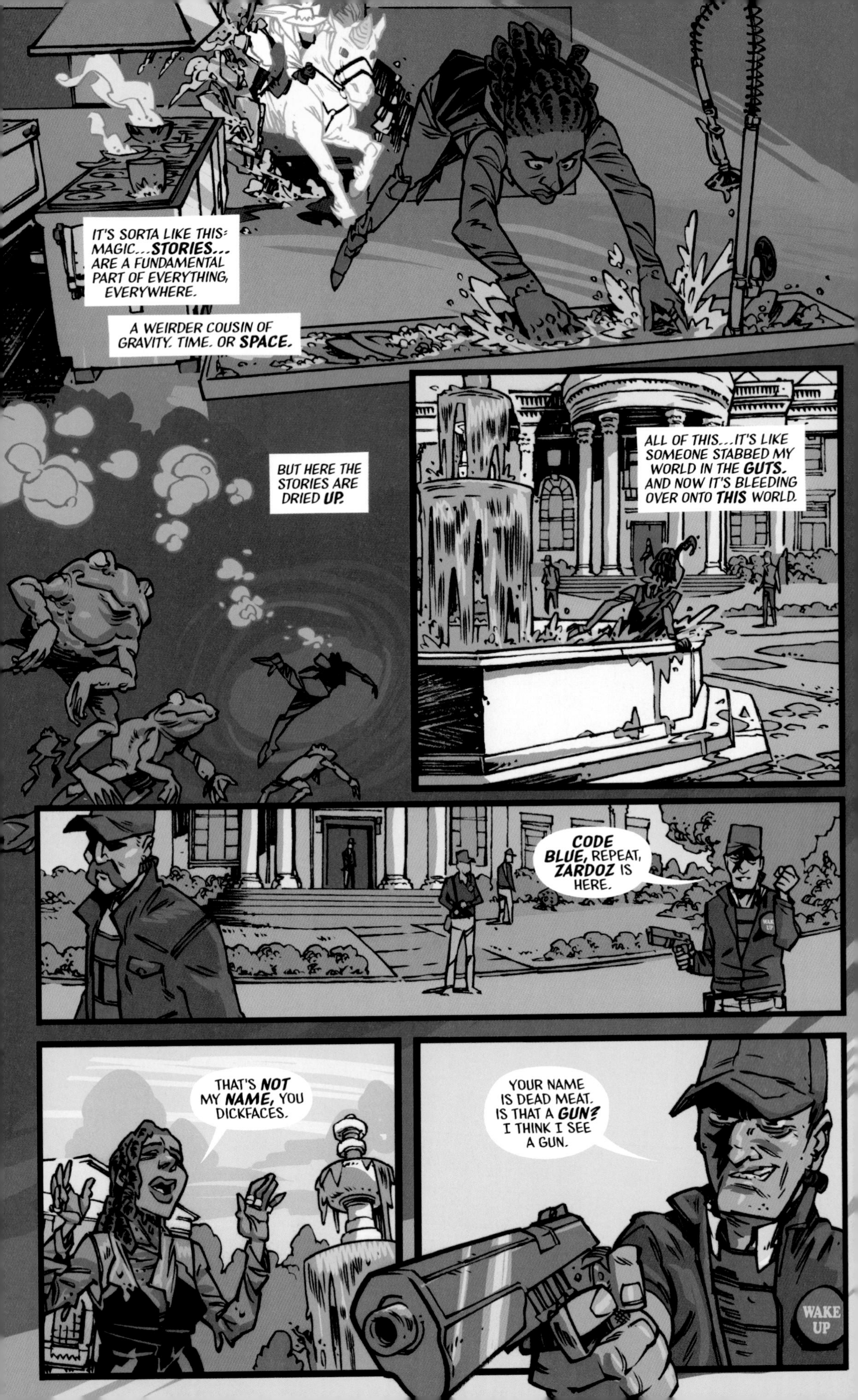
IT'S SORTA LIKE THIS: MAGIC... STORIES... ARE A FUNDAMENTAL PART OF EVERYTHING, EVERYWHERE.
A WEIRDER COUSIN OF GRAVITY. TIME. OR SPACE.
BUT HERE THE STORIES ARE DRIED UP.
ALL OF THIS... IT'S LIKE SOMEONE STABBED MY WORLD IN THE GUTS. AND NOW IT'S BLEEDING OVER ONTO THIS WORLD.
CODE BLUE, REPEAT, ZARDOZ IS HERE.
WAKE UP
THAT'S NOT MY NAME, YOU DICKFACES.
YOUR NAME IS DEAD MEAT. IS THAT A GUN? I THINK I SEE A GUN.
WAKE UP

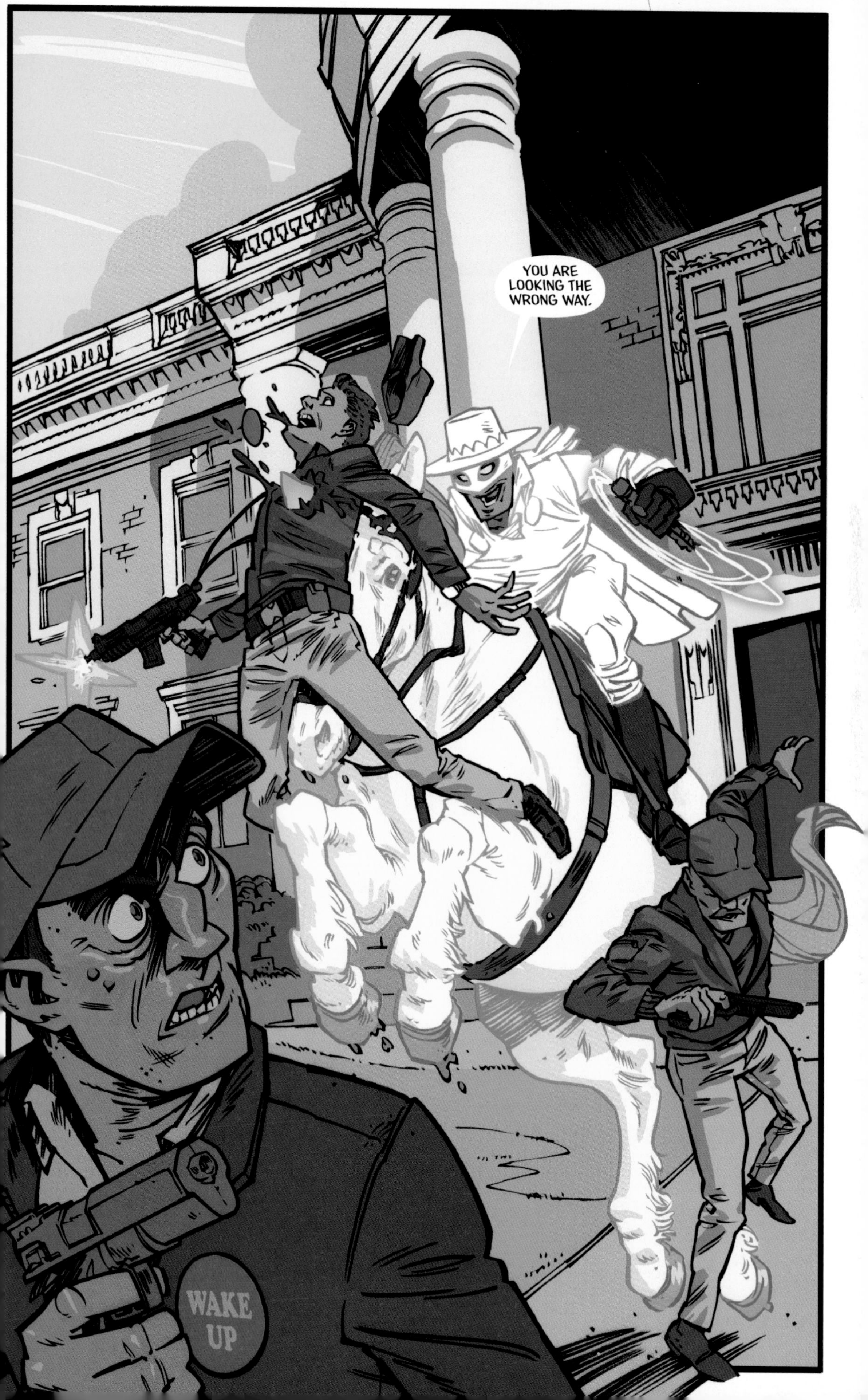
YOU ARE LOOKING THE WRONG WAY.
WAKE UP

RUN, YOU IDIOTS!

MAYOR'S GOONS CLEARLY TRYING TO SEE ME DEAD.

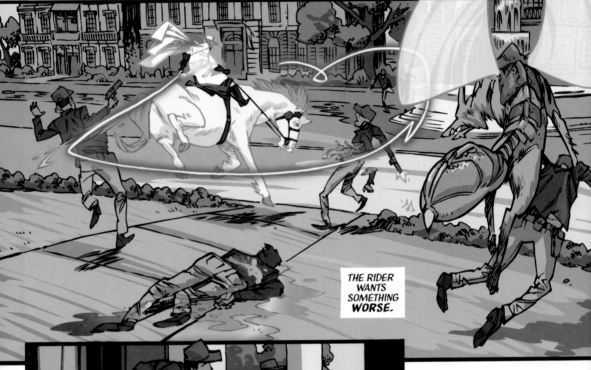

THE RIDER WANTS SOMETHING **WORSE.**

BUT THE SCREAMS ARE LIKE A **STORM.**

THIS IS THE RIGHT MOVE. THE **ONLY** MOVE. THEY CAN TEAR EACH **OTHER** DOWN.

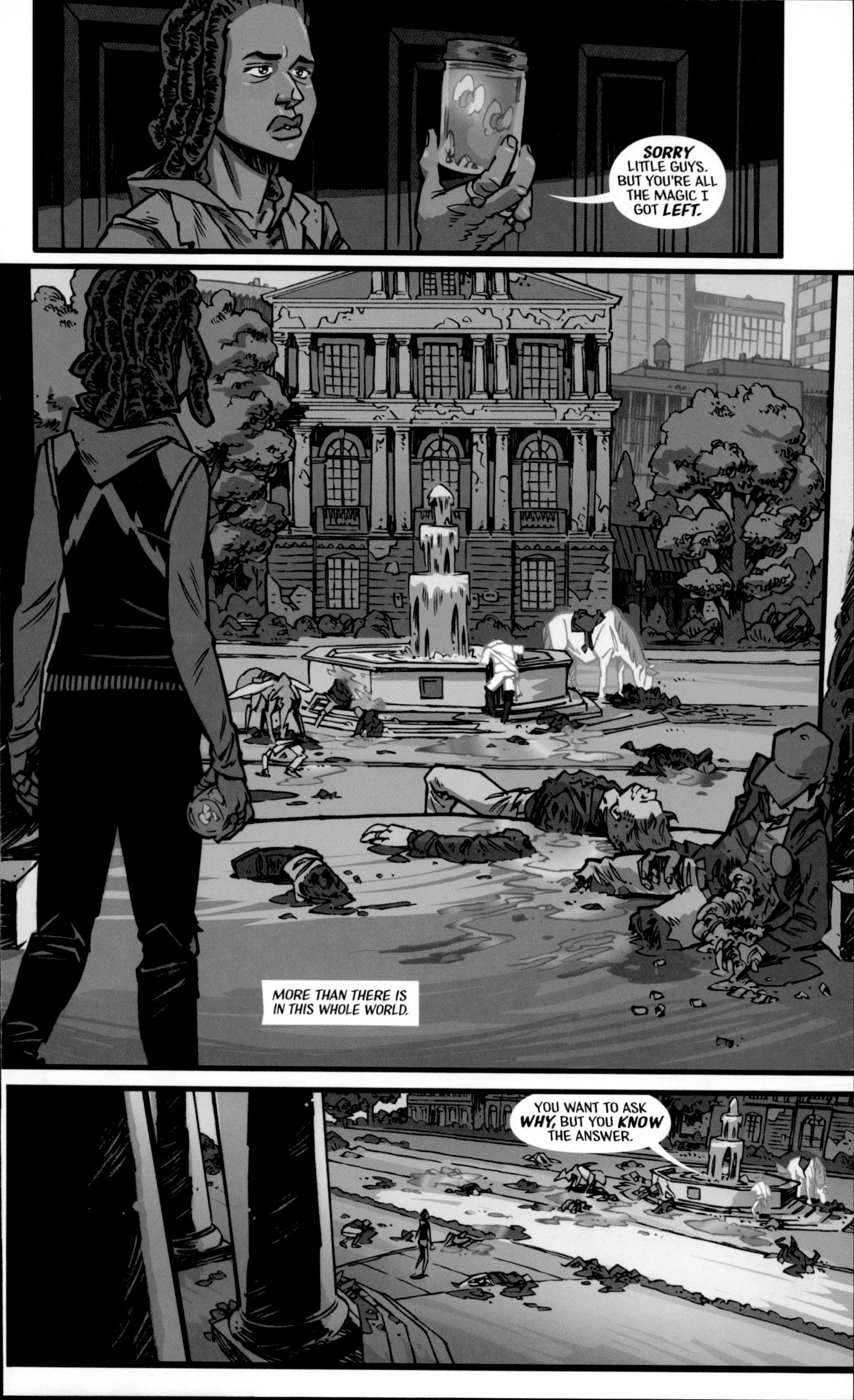
SORRY LITTLE GUYS. BUT YOU'RE ALL THE MAGIC I GOT LEFT.
MORE THAN THERE IS IN THIS WHOLE WORLD.
YOU WANT TO ASK WHY, BUT YOU KNOW THE ANSWER.

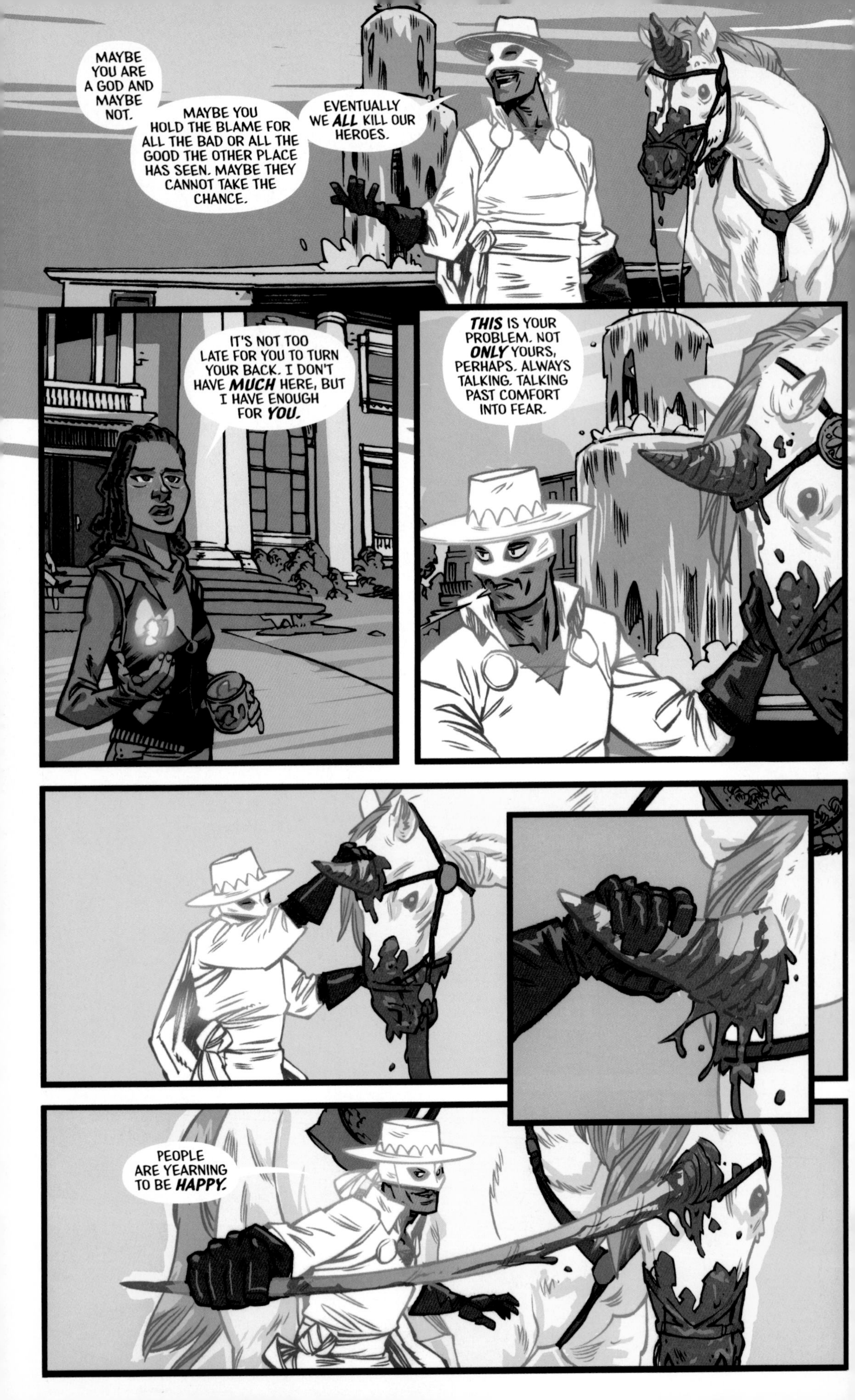
MAYBE YOU ARE A GOD AND MAYBE NOT.
MAYBE YOU HOLD THE BLAME FOR ALL THE BAD OR ALL THE GOOD THE OTHER PLACE HAS SEEN. MAYBE THEY CANNOT TAKE THE CHANCE.
EVENTUALLY WE ALL KILL OUR HEROES.
IT'S NOT TOO LATE FOR YOU TO TURN YOUR BACK. I DON'T HAVE MUCH HERE, BUT I HAVE ENOUGH FOR YOU.
THIS IS YOUR PROBLEM. NOT ONLY YOURS, PERHAPS. ALWAYS TALKING. TALKING PAST COMFORT INTO FEAR.
PEOPLE ARE YEARNING TO BE HAPPY.

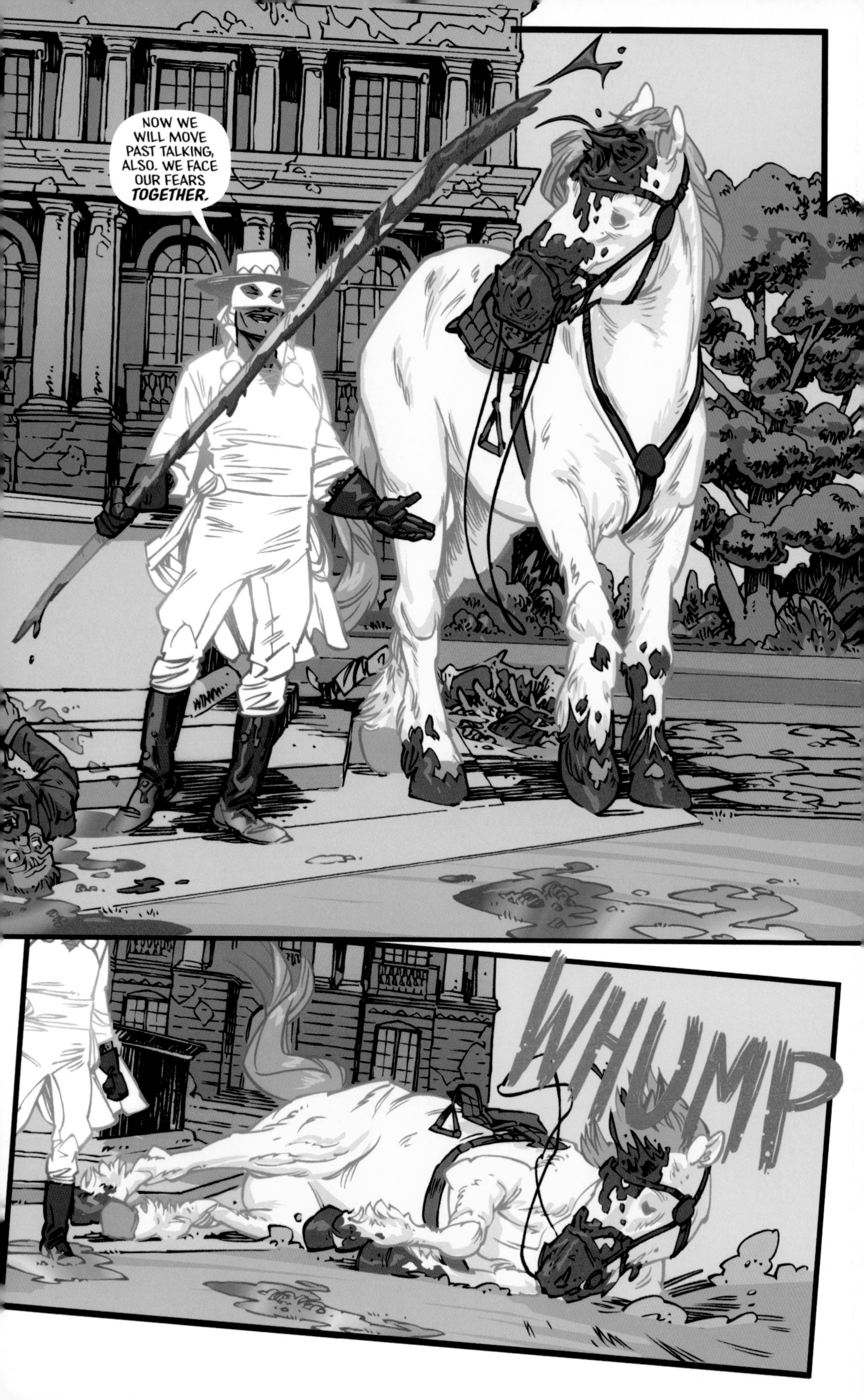
NOW WE WILL MOVE PAST TALKING, ALSO. WE FACE OUR FEARS *TOGETHER.*
WHUMP

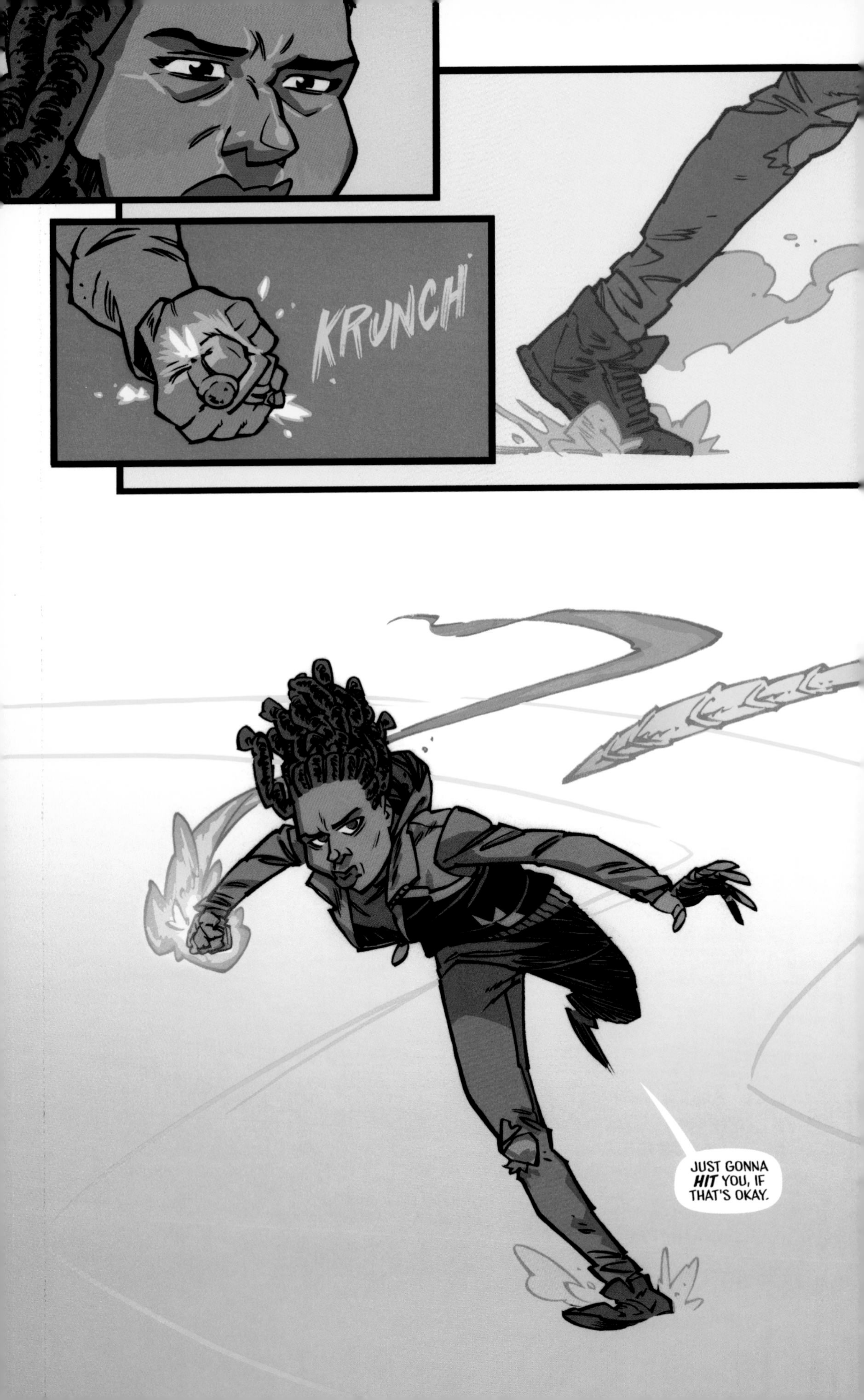
KRUNCH
JUST GONNA HIT YOU, IF THAT'S OKAY.

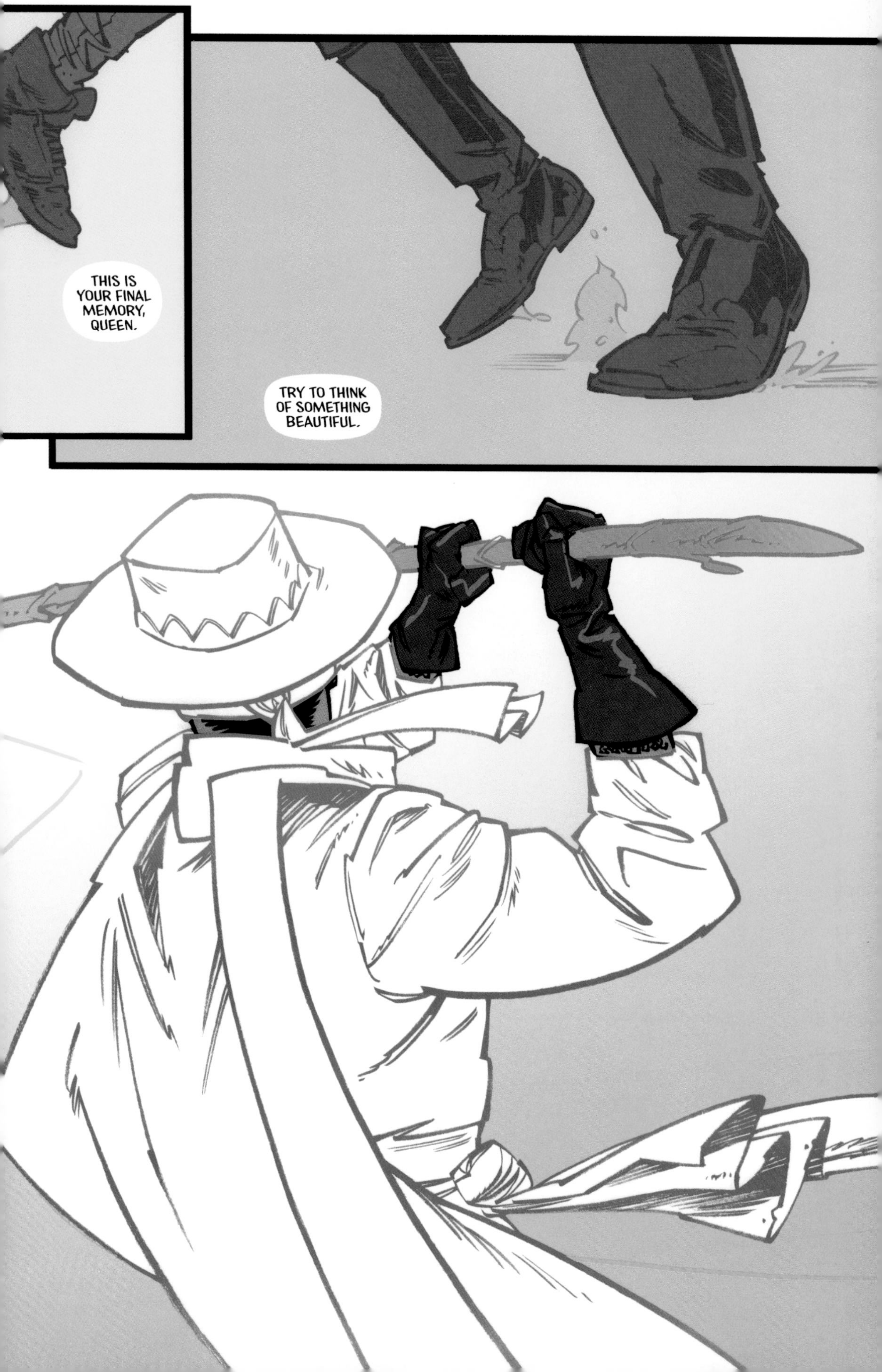
THIS IS YOUR FINAL MEMORY, QUEEN.
TRY TO THINK OF SOMETHING BEAUTIFUL.

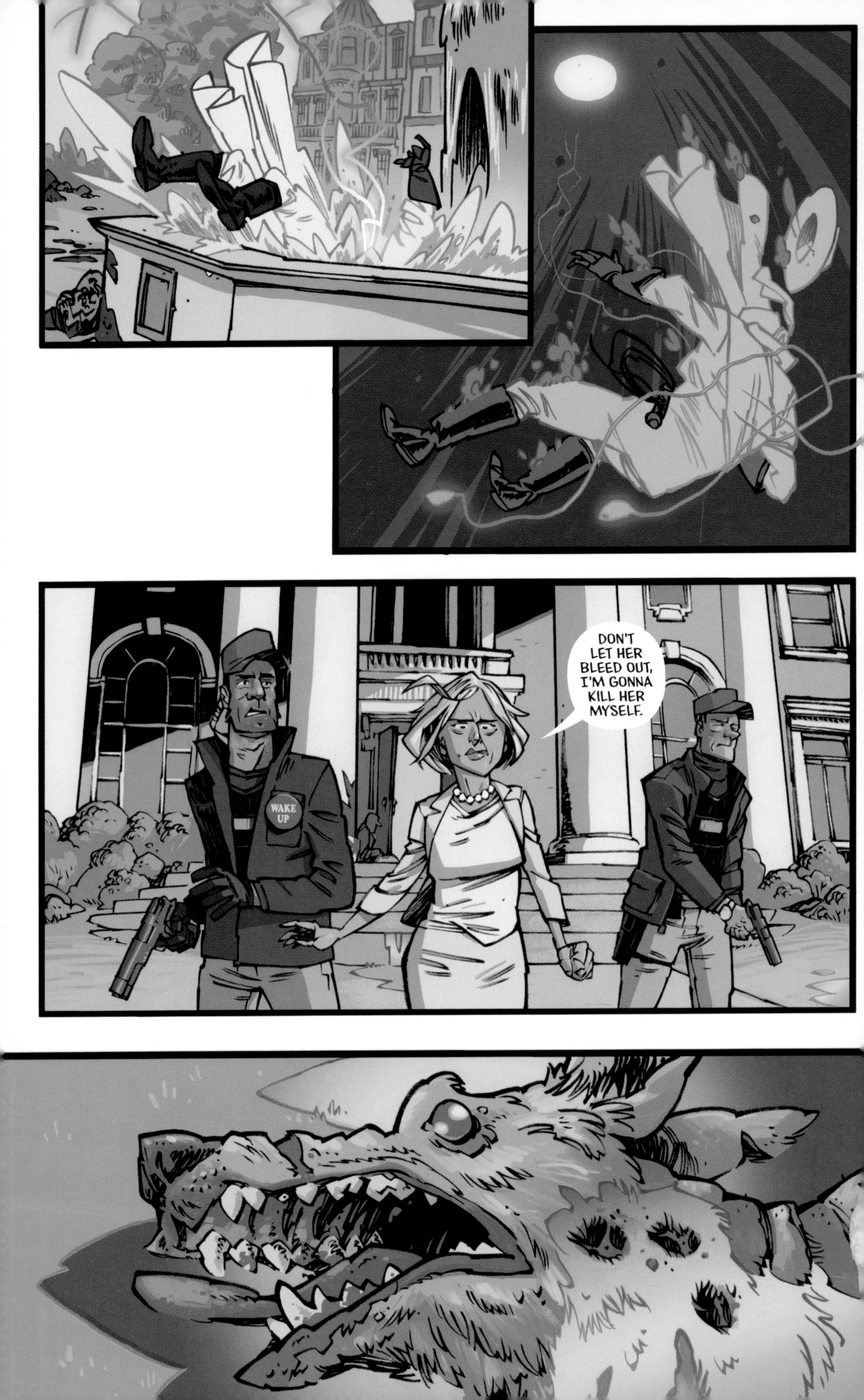
DON'T LET HER BLEED OUT, I'M GONNA KILL HER MYSELF.
WAKE UP

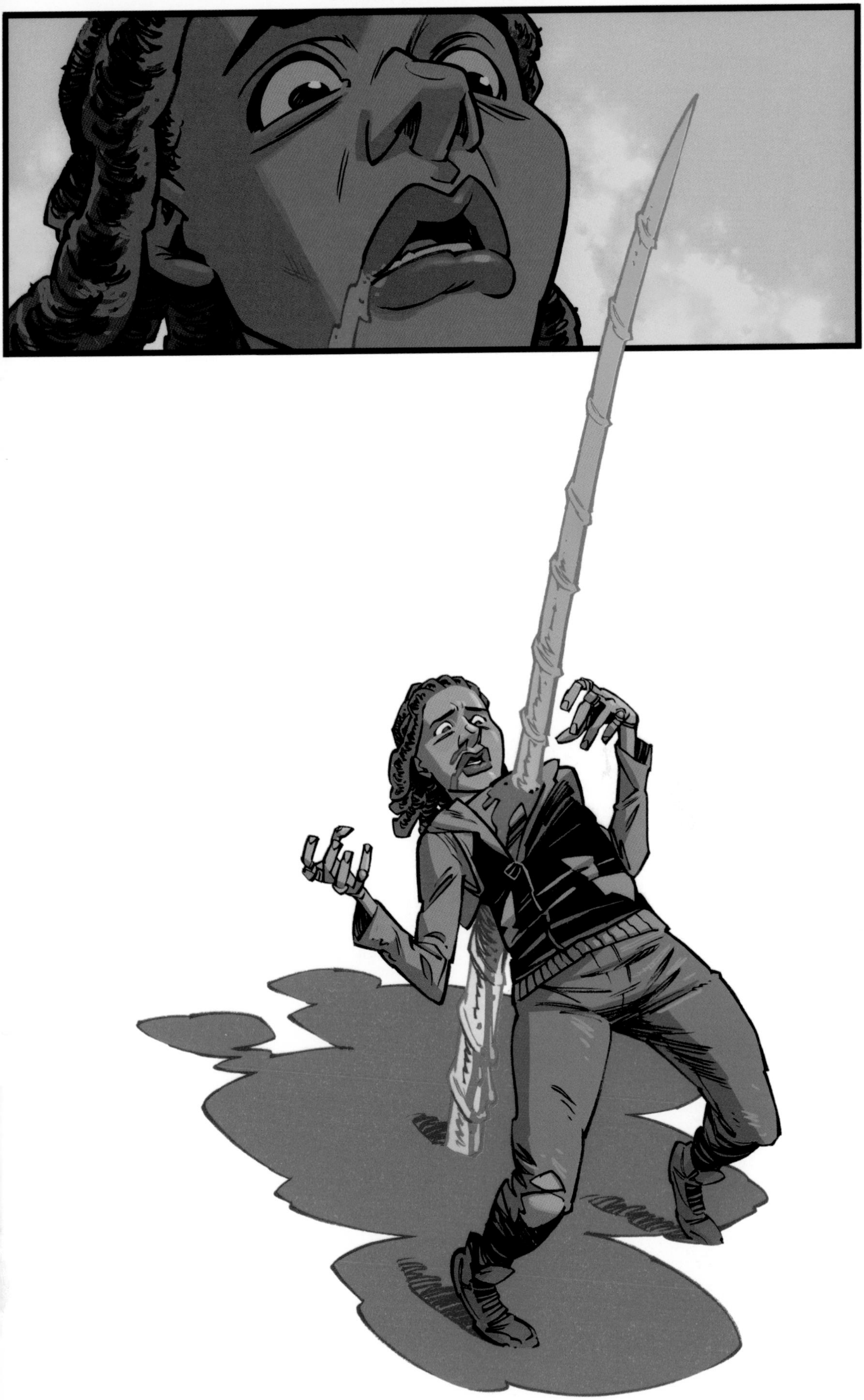

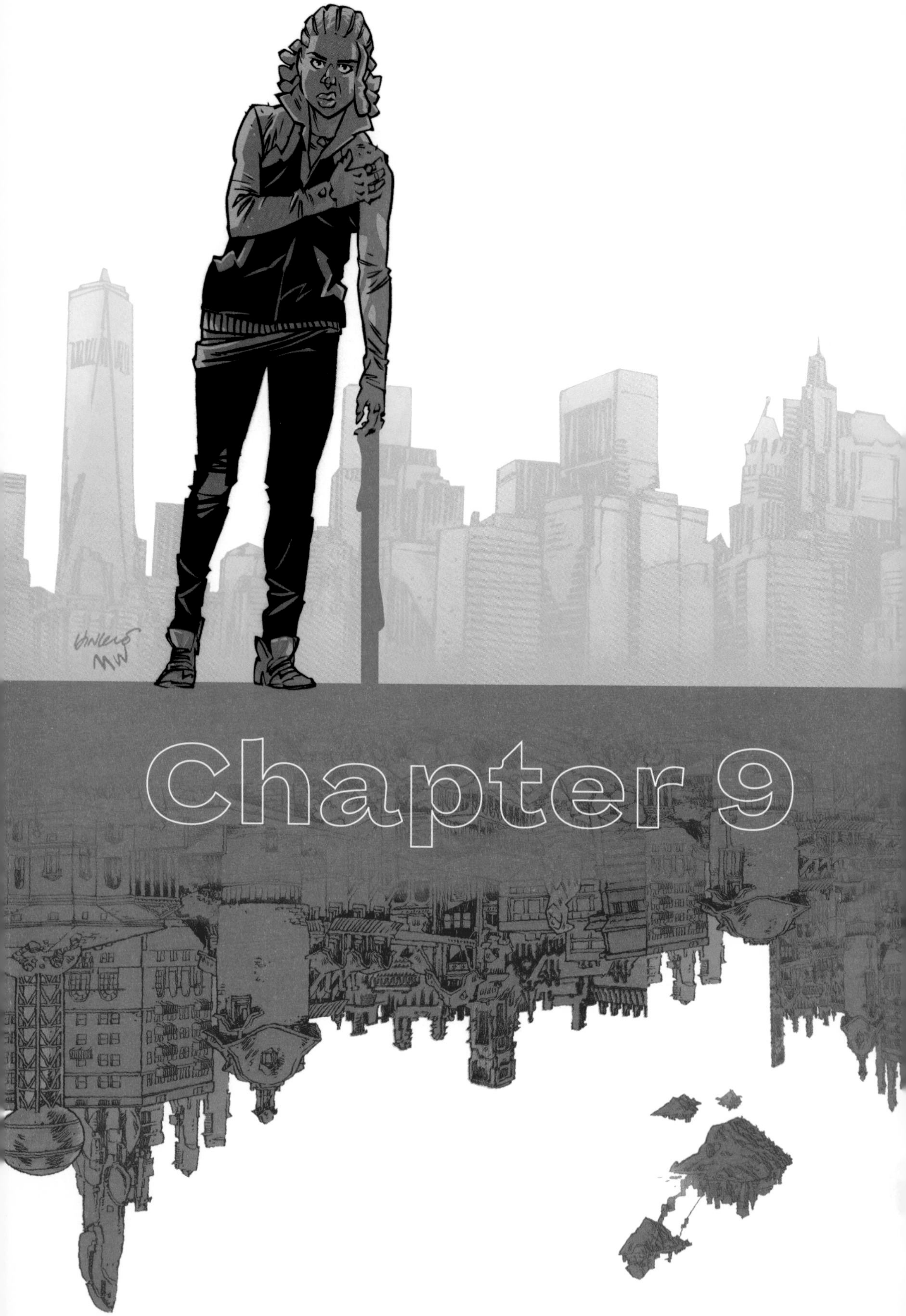

Chapter 9

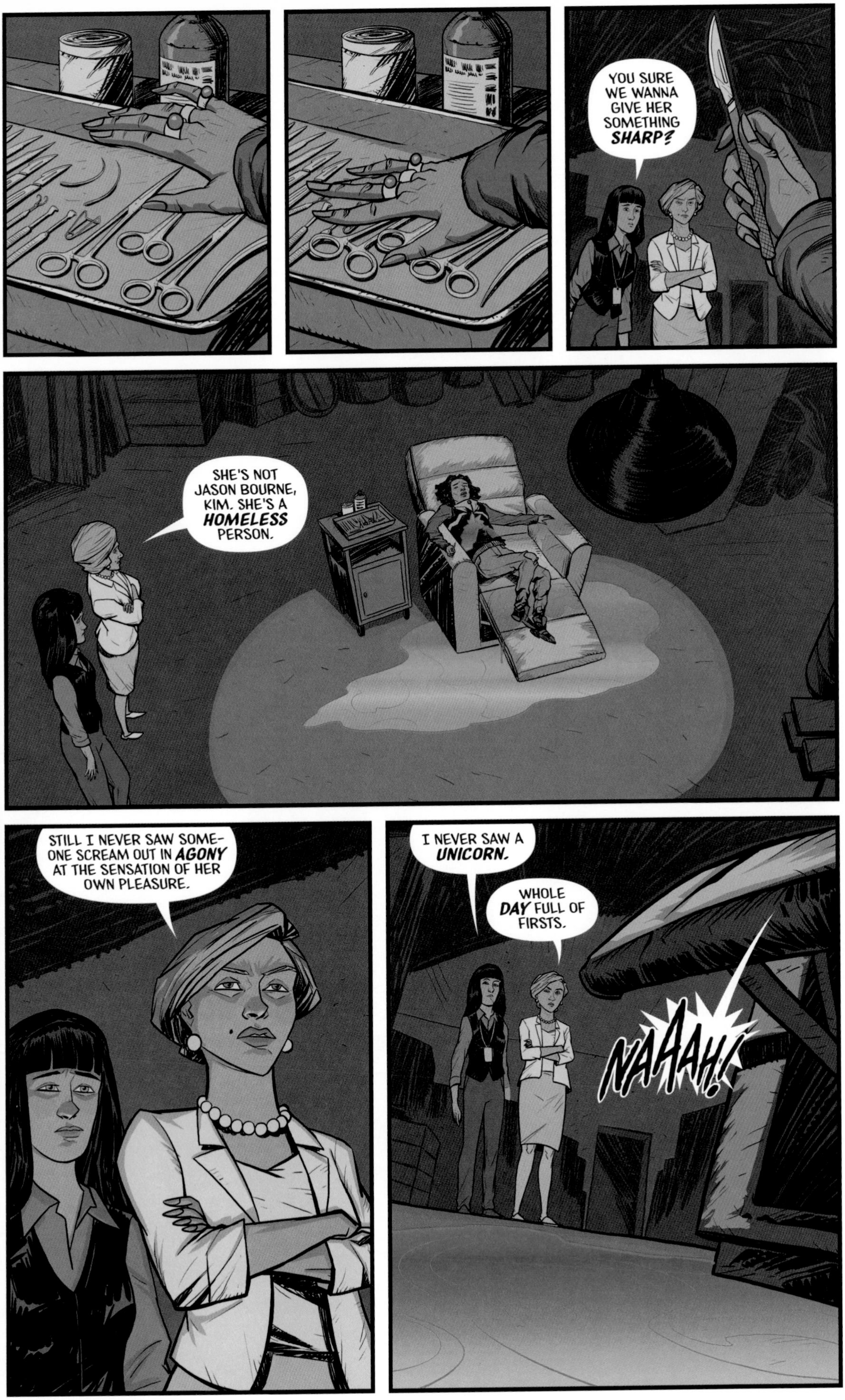
YOU SURE WE WANNA GIVE HER SOMETHING SHARP?
SHE'S NOT JASON BOURNE, KIM. SHE'S A HOMELESS PERSON.
STILL I NEVER SAW SOME-ONE SCREAM OUT IN AGONY AT THE SENSATION OF HER OWN PLEASURE.
I NEVER SAW A UNICORN.
WHOLE DAY FULL OF FIRSTS.
NAAAH!

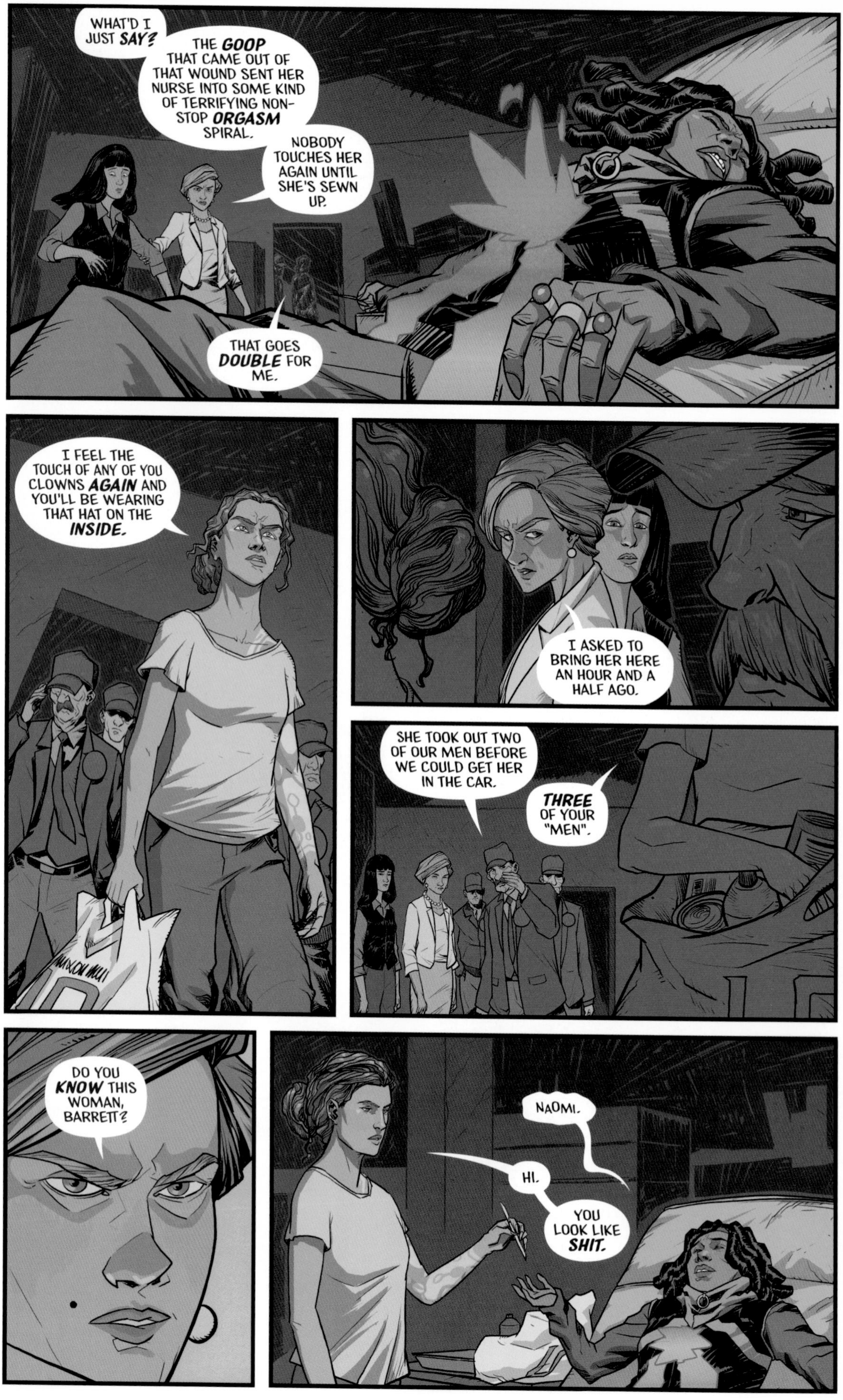
WHAT'D I JUST SAY?
THE GOOP THAT CAME OUT OF THAT WOUND SENT HER NURSE INTO SOME KIND OF TERRIFYING NON-STOP ORGASM SPIRAL.
NOBODY TOUCHES HER AGAIN UNTIL SHE'S SEWN UP.
THAT GOES DOUBLE FOR ME.
I FEEL THE TOUCH OF ANY OF YOU CLOWNS AGAIN AND YOU'LL BE WEARING THAT HAT ON THE INSIDE.
I ASKED TO BRING HER HERE AN HOUR AND A HALF AGO.
SHE TOOK OUT TWO OF OUR MEN BEFORE WE COULD GET HER IN THE CAR.
THREE OF YOUR "MEN".
DO YOU KNOW THIS WOMAN, BARRETT?
NAOMI.
HI.
YOU LOOK LIKE SHIT.

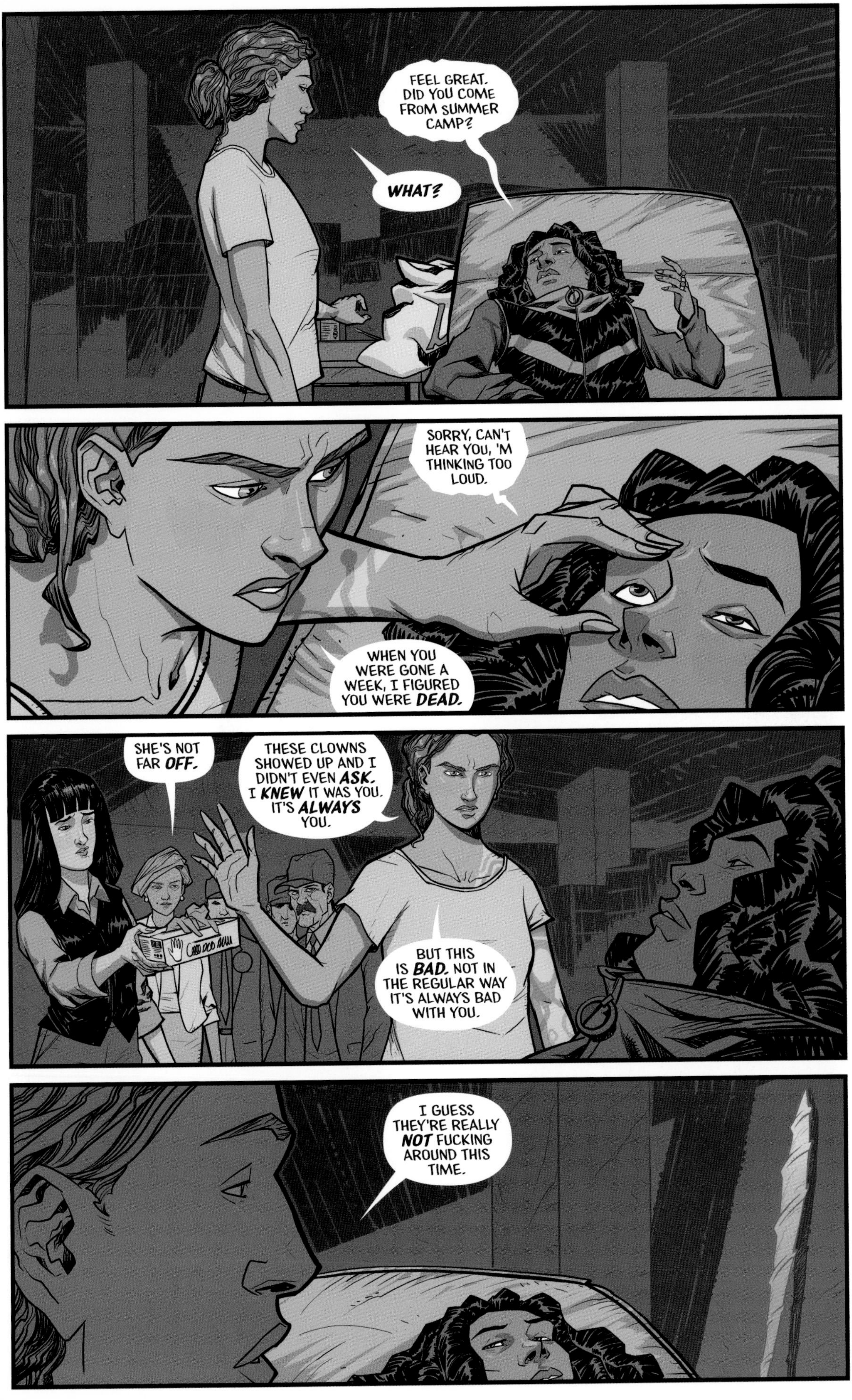
FEEL GREAT. DID YOU COME FROM SUMMER CAMP?
WHAT?
SORRY, CAN'T HEAR YOU, 'M THINKING TOO LOUD.
WHEN YOU WERE GONE A WEEK, I FIGURED YOU WERE DEAD.
SHE'S NOT FAR OFF.
THESE CLOWNS SHOWED UP AND I DIDN'T EVEN ASK. I KNEW IT WAS YOU. IT'S ALWAYS YOU.
BUT THIS IS BAD. NOT IN THE REGULAR WAY IT'S ALWAYS BAD WITH YOU.
I GUESS THEY'RE REALLY NOT FUCKING AROUND THIS TIME.

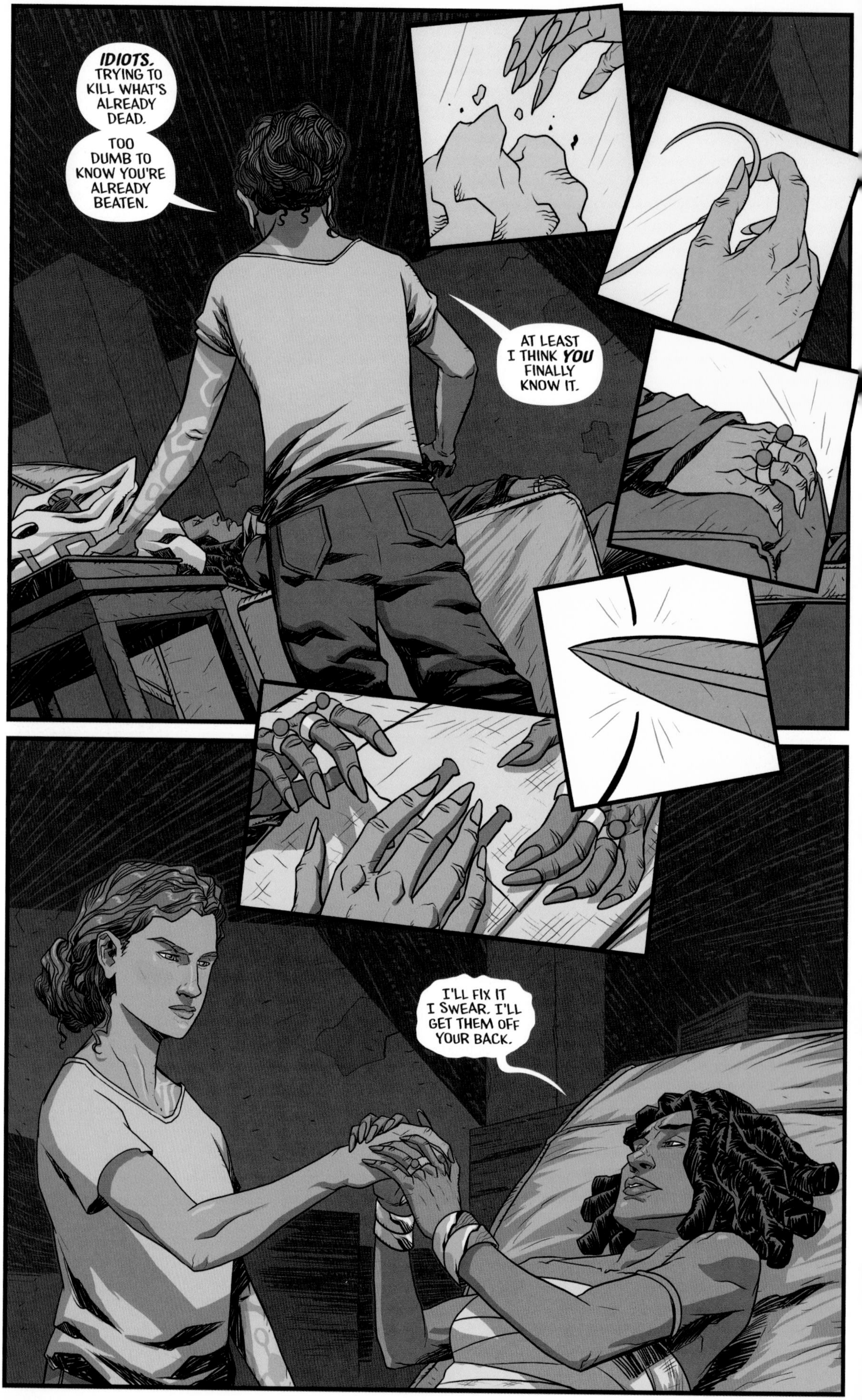
IDIOTS. TRYING TO KILL WHAT'S ALREADY DEAD.
TOO DUMB TO KNOW YOU'RE ALREADY BEATEN.
AT LEAST I THINK YOU FINALLY KNOW IT.
I'LL FIX IT I SWEAR. I'LL GET THEM OFF YOUR BACK.

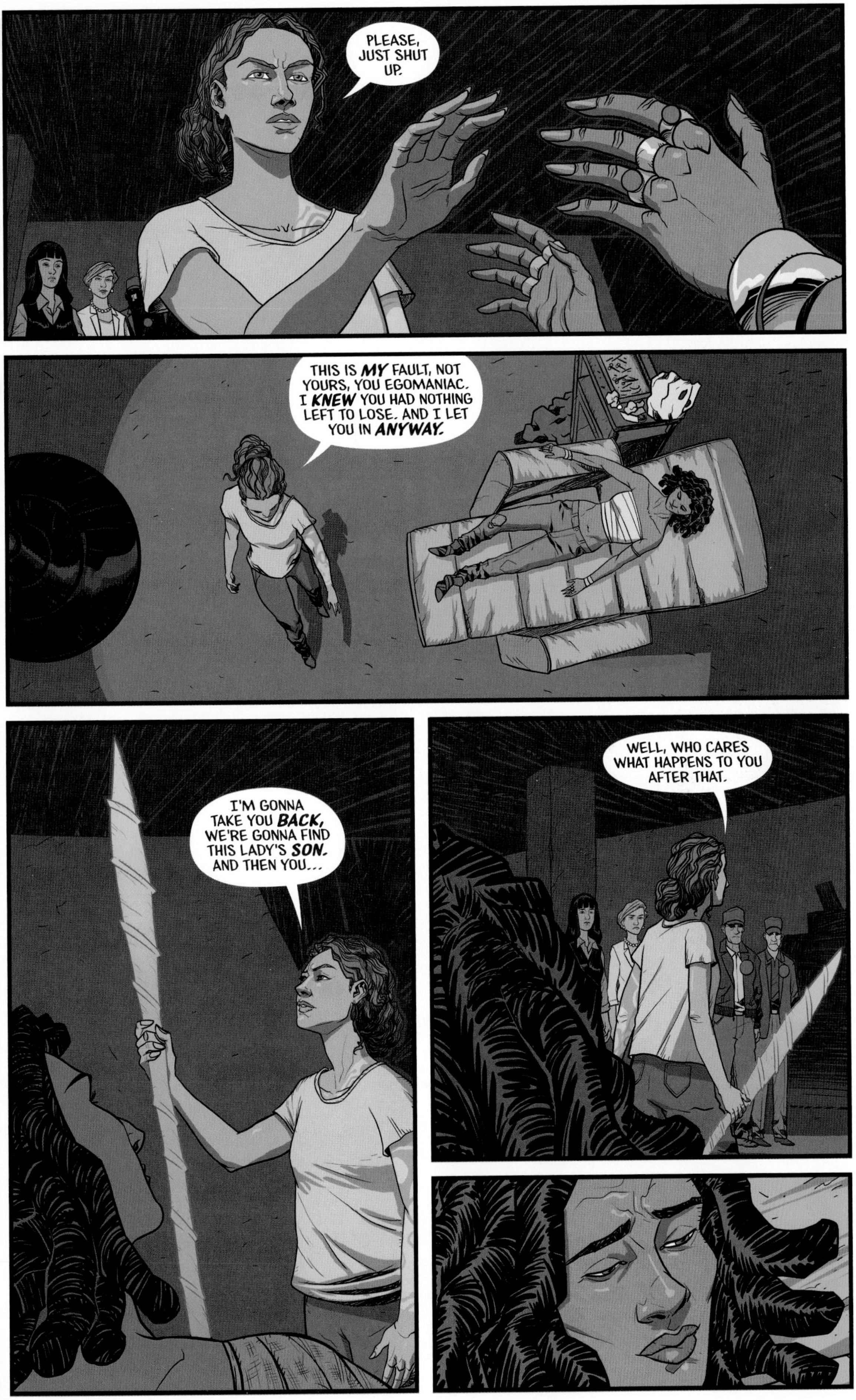
PLEASE, JUST SHUT UP.
THIS IS MY FAULT, NOT YOURS, YOU EGOMANIAC. I KNEW YOU HAD NOTHING LEFT TO LOSE. AND I LET YOU IN ANYWAY.
I'M GONNA TAKE YOU BACK, WE'RE GONNA FIND THIS LADY'S SON. AND THEN YOU...
WELL, WHO CARES WHAT HAPPENS TO YOU AFTER THAT.

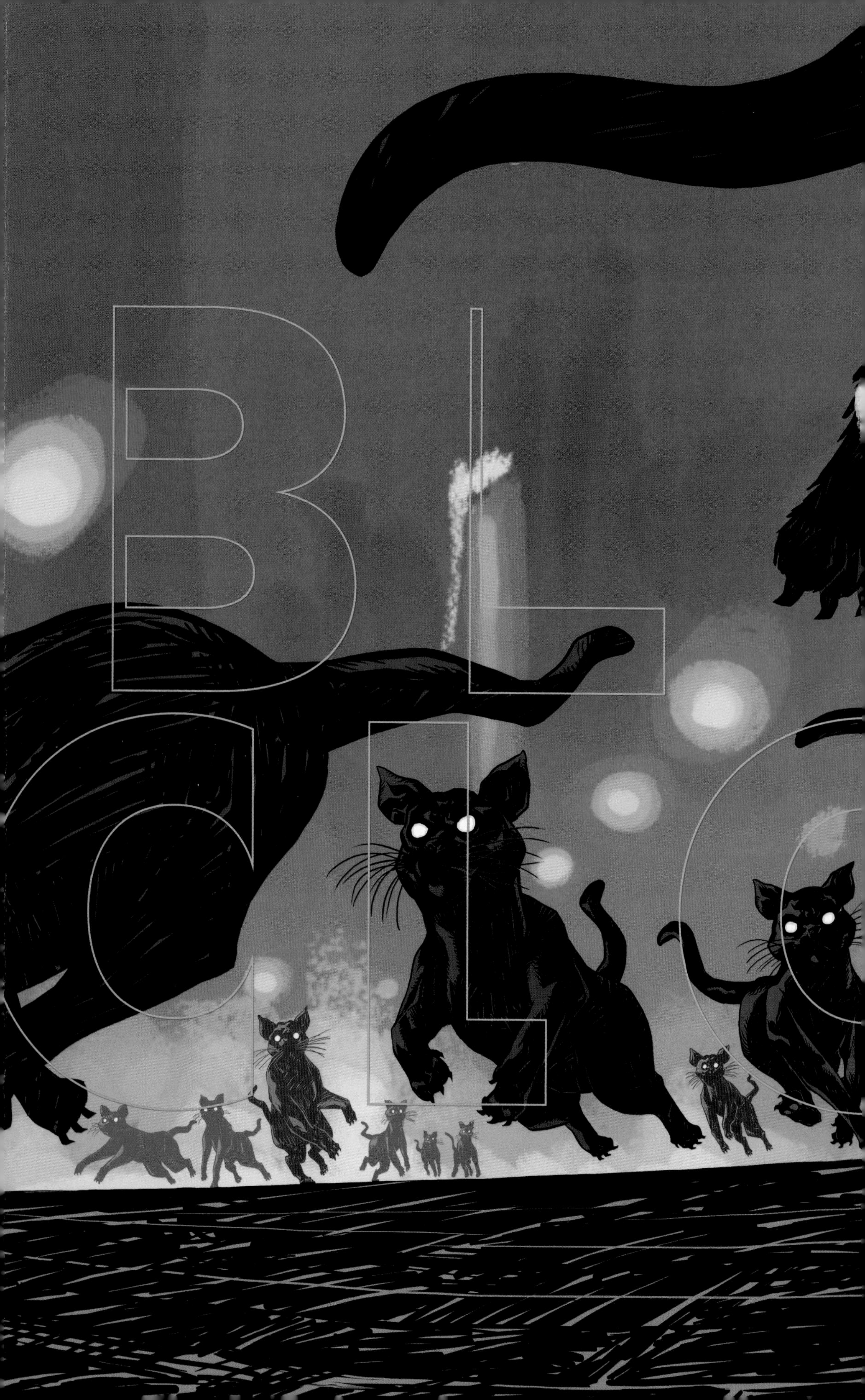
BL
CL

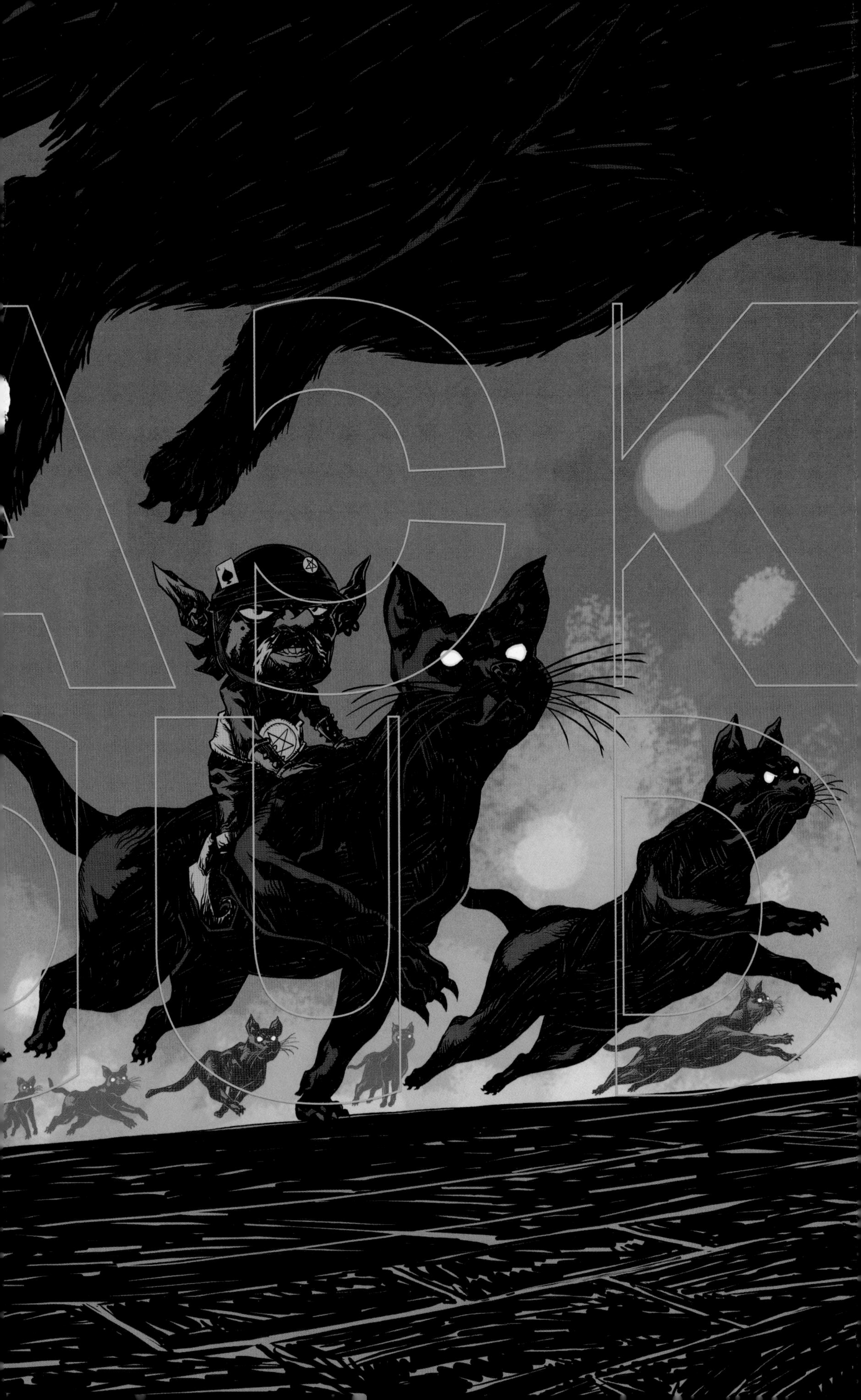

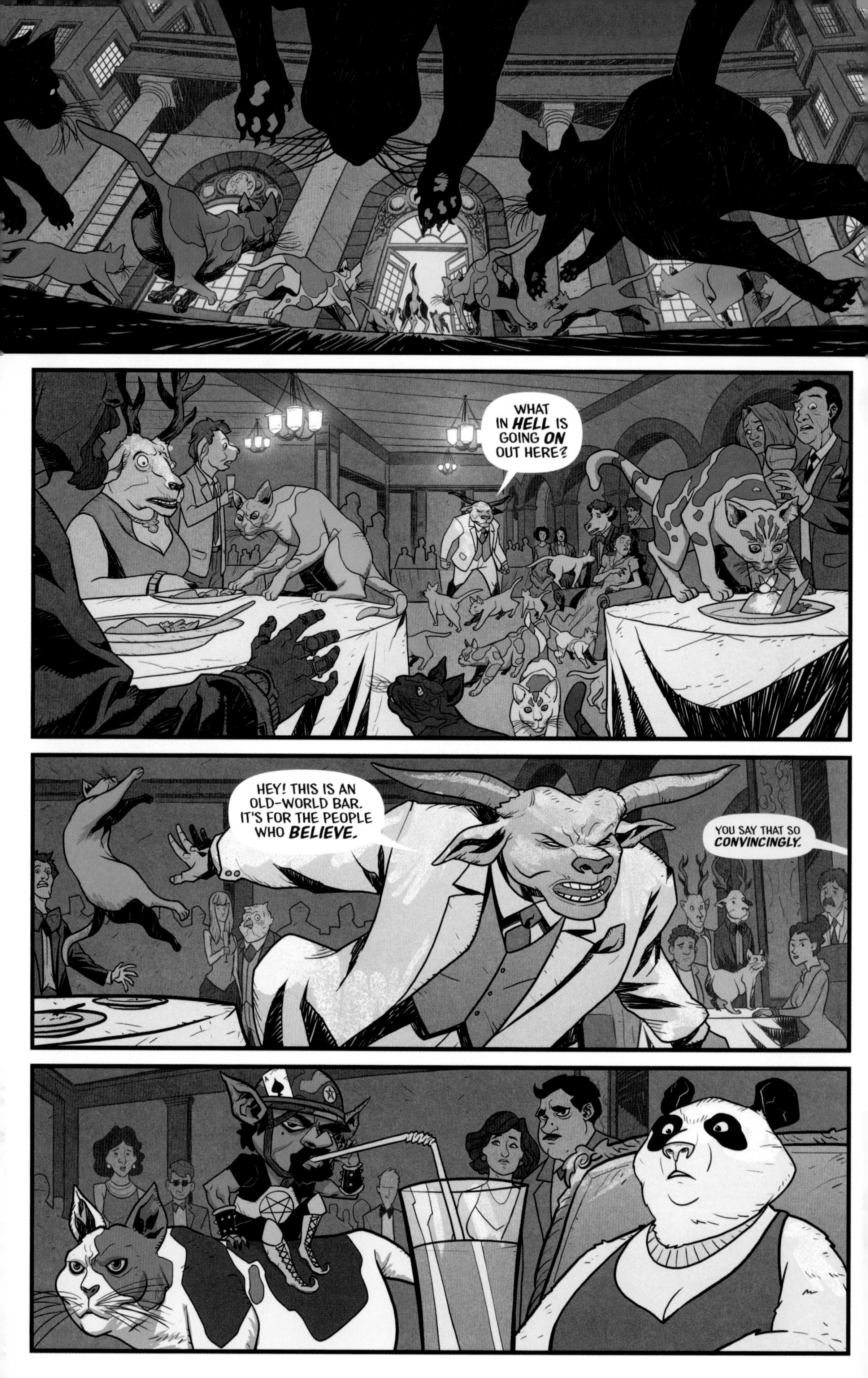
WHAT IN HELL IS GOING ON OUT HERE?
HEY! THIS IS AN OLD-WORLD BAR. IT'S FOR THE PEOPLE WHO BELIEVE.
YOU SAY THAT SO CONVINCINGLY.

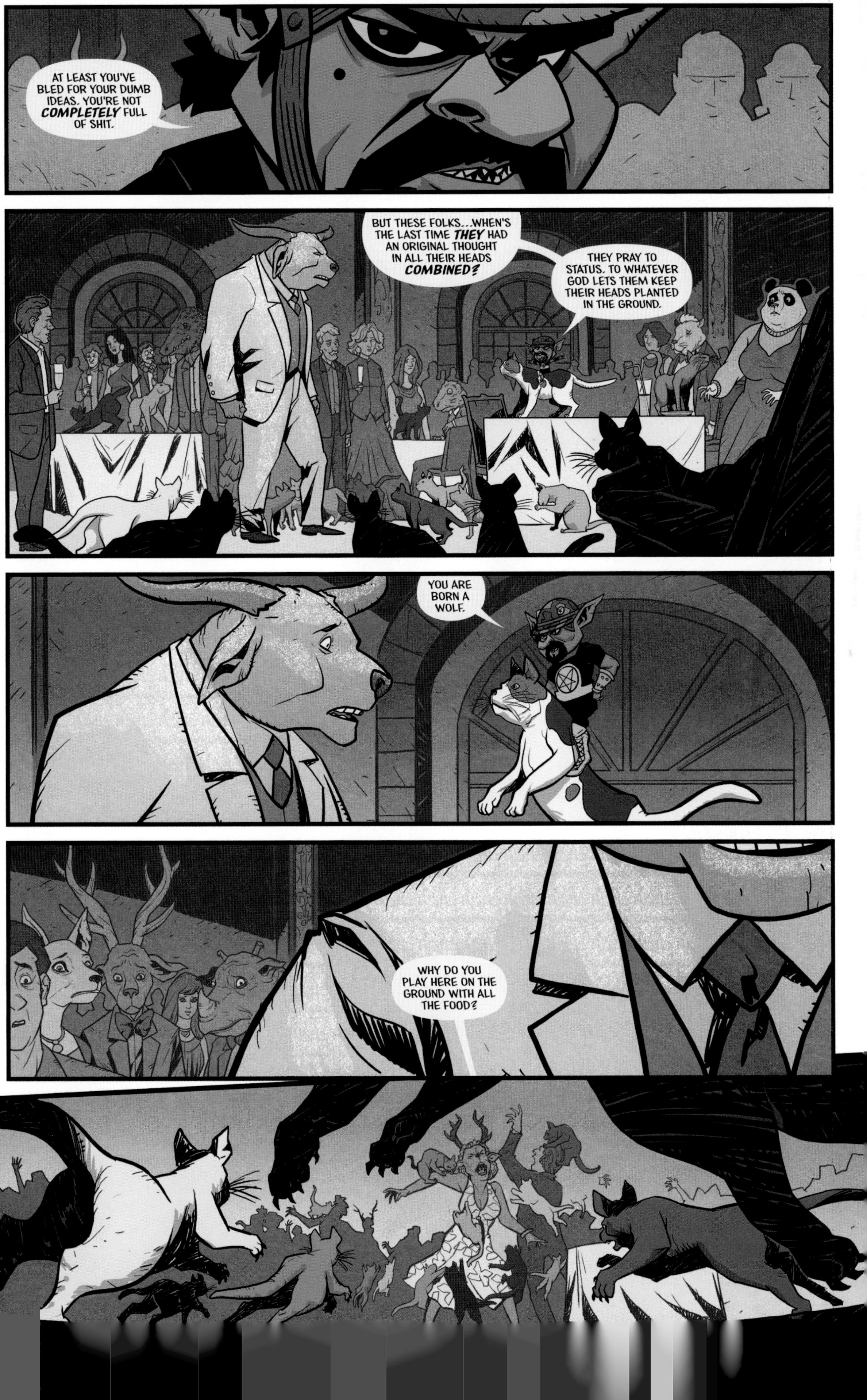
AT LEAST YOU'VE BLED FOR YOUR DUMB IDEAS. YOU'RE NOT COMPLETELY FULL OF SHIT.
BUT THESE FOLKS... WHEN'S THE LAST TIME THEY HAD AN ORIGINAL THOUGHT IN ALL THEIR HEADS COMBINED?
THEY PRAY TO STATUS. TO WHATEVER GOD LETS THEM KEEP THEIR HEADS PLANTED IN THE GROUND.
YOU ARE BORN A WOLF.
WHY DO YOU PLAY HERE ON THE GROUND WITH ALL THE FOOD?

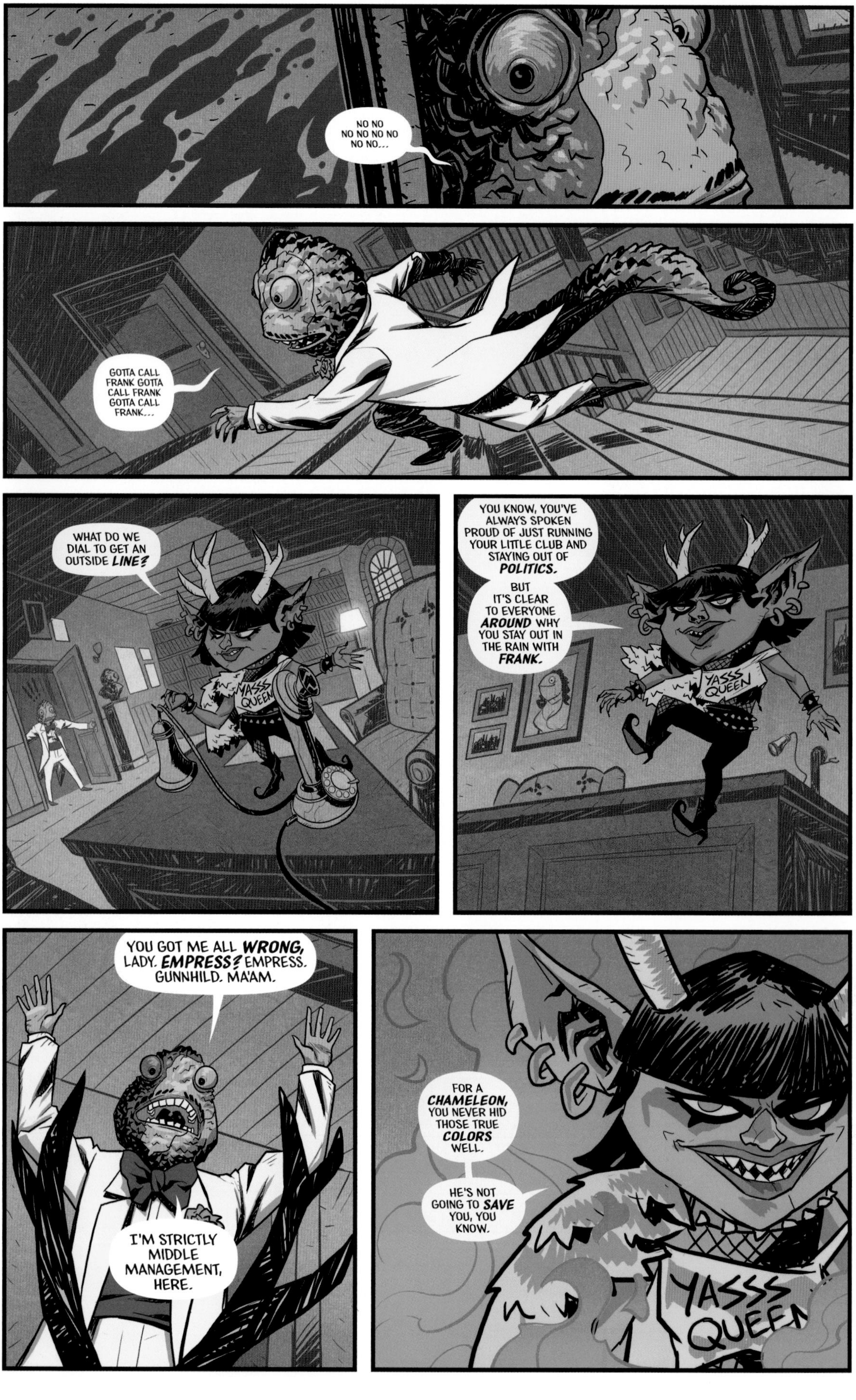
NO NO
NO NO NO NO
NO NO...
GOTTA CALL FRANK GOTTA CALL FRANK GOTTA CALL FRANK...
WHAT DO WE DIAL TO GET AN OUTSIDE LINE?
YASSS QUEEN
YOU KNOW, YOU'VE ALWAYS SPOKEN PROUD OF JUST RUNNING YOUR LITTLE CLUB AND STAYING OUT OF POLITICS.
BUT IT'S CLEAR TO EVERYONE AROUND WHY YOU STAY OUT IN THE RAIN WITH FRANK.
YASSS QUEEN
YOU GOT ME ALL WRONG, LADY. EMPRESS? EMPRESS. GUNNHILD. MA'AM.
I'M STRICTLY MIDDLE MANAGEMENT, HERE.
FOR A CHAMELEON, YOU NEVER HID THOSE TRUE COLORS WELL.
HE'S NOT GOING TO SAVE YOU, YOU KNOW.
YASSS QUEE

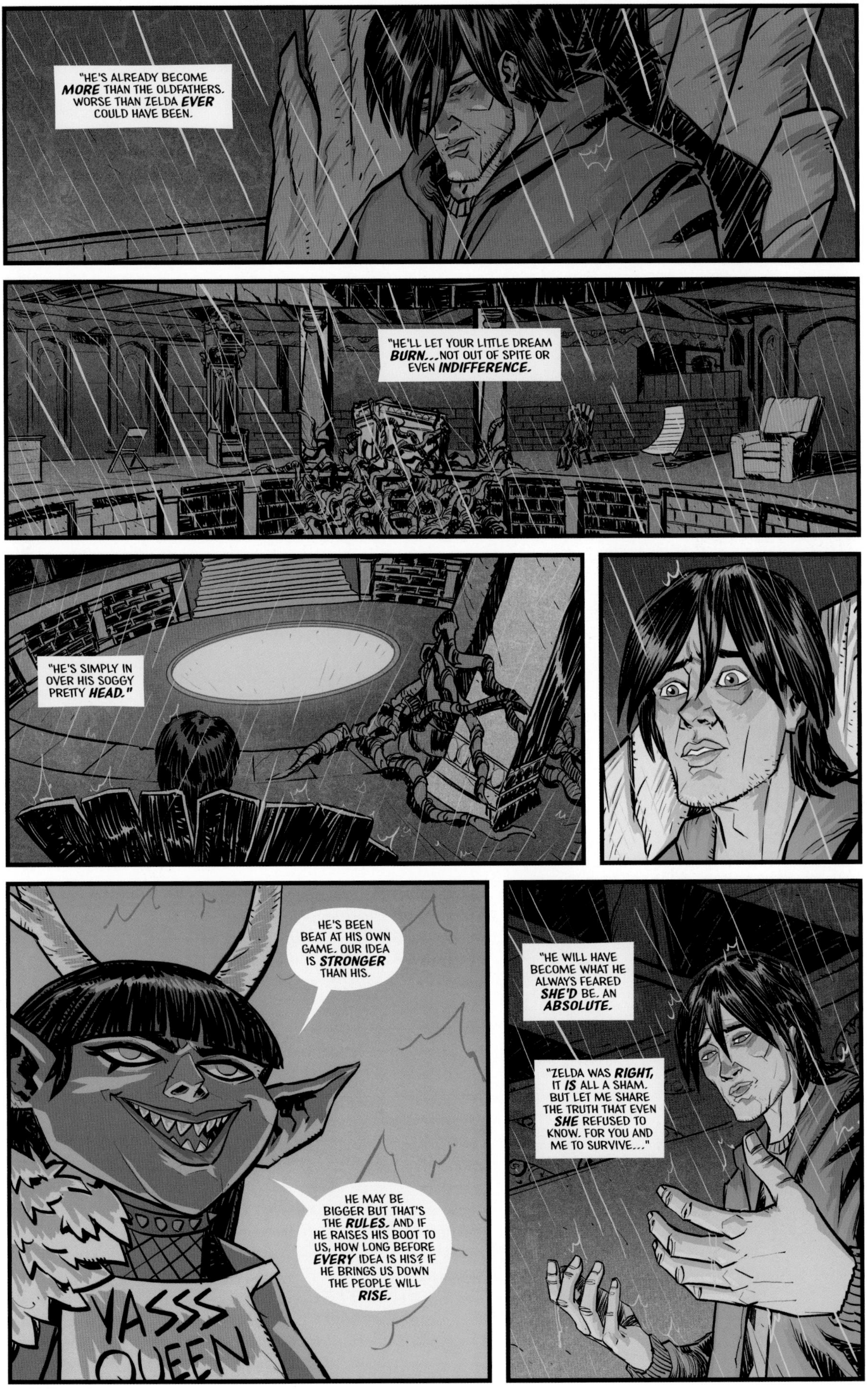
"HE'S ALREADY BECOME MORE THAN THE OLDFATHERS. WORSE THAN ZELDA EVER COULD HAVE BEEN.
"HE'LL LET YOUR LITTLE DREAM BURN... NOT OUT OF SPITE OR EVEN INDIFFERENCE.
"HE'S SIMPLY IN OVER HIS SOGGY PRETTY HEAD."
HE'S BEEN BEAT AT HIS OWN GAME. OUR IDEA IS STRONGER THAN HIS.
HE MAY BE BIGGER BUT THAT'S THE RULES. AND IF HE RAISES HIS BOOT TO US, HOW LONG BEFORE EVERY IDEA IS HIS? IF HE BRINGS US DOWN THE PEOPLE WILL RISE.
YASSS QUEEN
"HE WILL HAVE BECOME WHAT HE ALWAYS FEARED SHE'D BE. AN ABSOLUTE.
"ZELDA WAS RIGHT, IT IS ALL A SHAM. BUT LET ME SHARE THE TRUTH THAT EVEN SHE REFUSED TO KNOW. FOR YOU AND ME TO SURVIVE..."

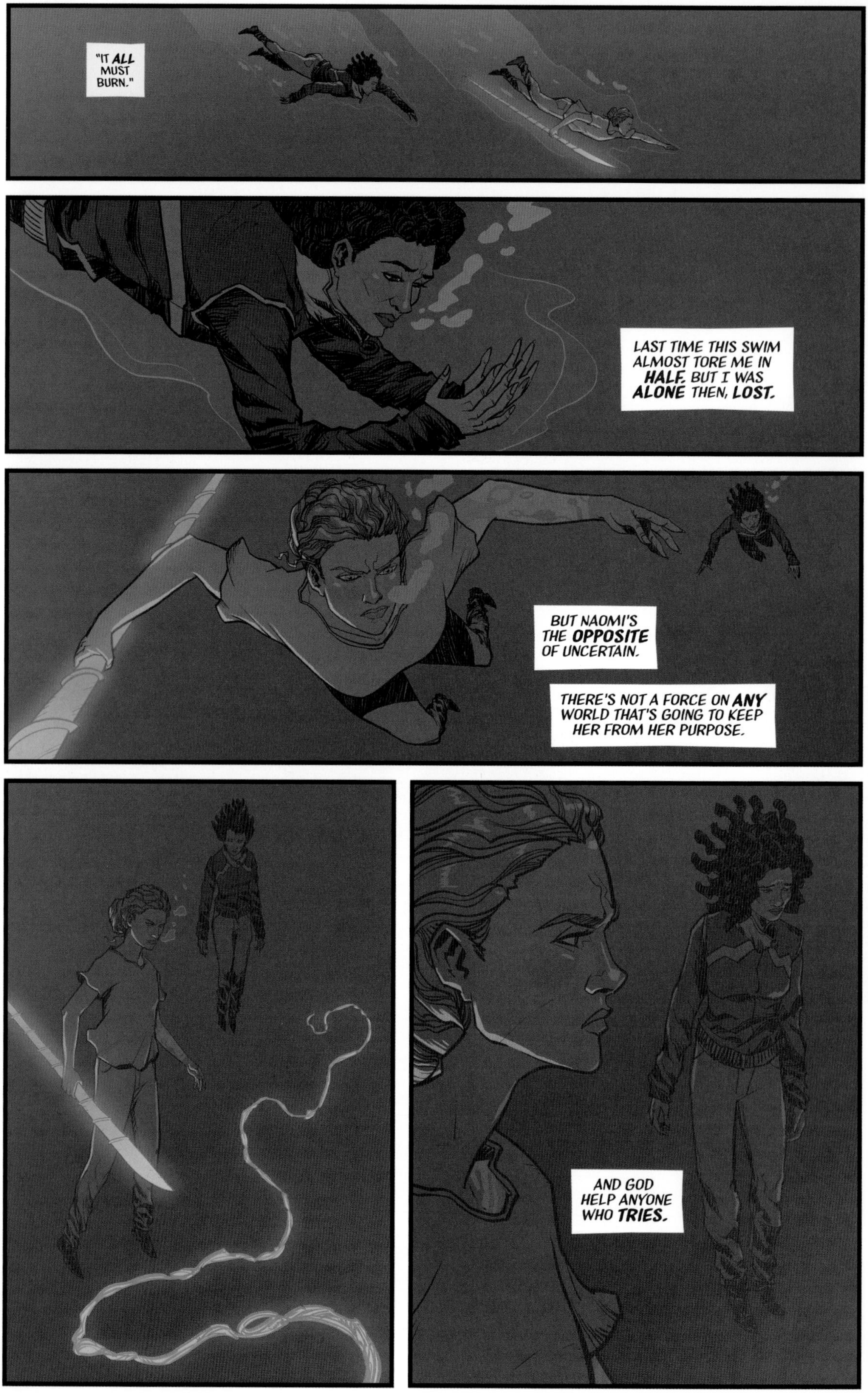
"IT ALL MUST BURN."
LAST TIME THIS SWIM ALMOST TORE ME IN HALF. BUT I WAS ALONE THEN, LOST.
BUT NAOMI'S THE OPPOSITE OF UNCERTAIN.
THERE'S NOT A FORCE ON ANY WORLD THAT'S GOING TO KEEP HER FROM HER PURPOSE.
AND GOD HELP ANYONE WHO TRIES.

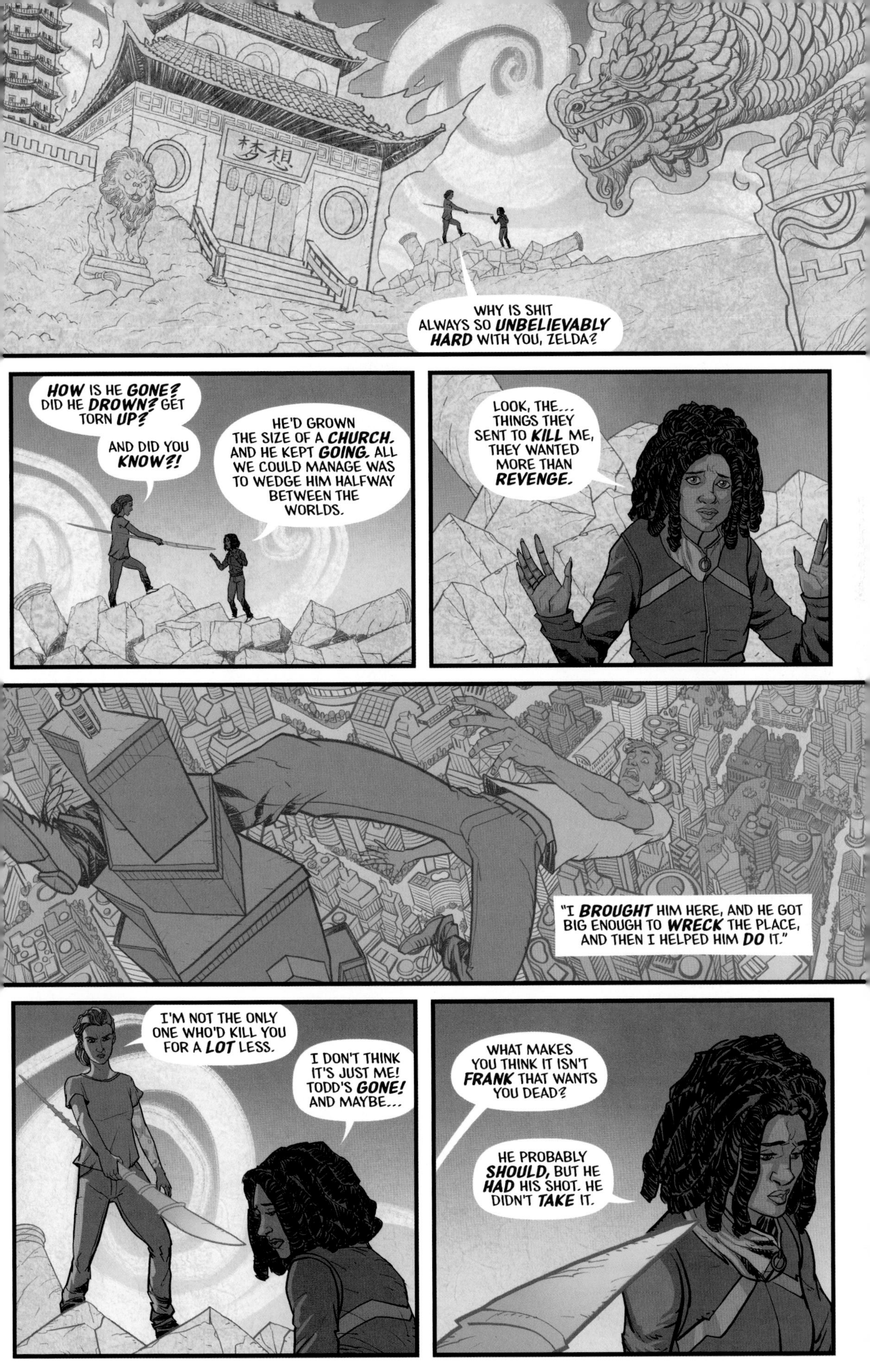

梦想
WHY IS SHIT ALWAYS SO UNBELIEVABLY HARD WITH YOU, ZELDA?
HOW IS HE GONE? DID HE DROWN? GET TORN UP?
AND DID YOU KNOW?!
HE'D GROWN THE SIZE OF A CHURCH. AND HE KEPT GOING. ALL WE COULD MANAGE WAS TO WEDGE HIM HALFWAY BETWEEN THE WORLDS.
LOOK, THE... THINGS THEY SENT TO KILL ME, THEY WANTED MORE THAN REVENGE.
"I BROUGHT HIM HERE, AND HE GOT BIG ENOUGH TO WRECK THE PLACE, AND THEN I HELPED HIM DO IT."
I'M NOT THE ONLY ONE WHO'D KILL YOU FOR A LOT LESS.
I DON'T THINK IT'S JUST ME! TODD'S GONE! AND MAYBE...
WHAT MAKES YOU THINK IT ISN'T FRANK THAT WANTS YOU DEAD?
HE PROBABLY SHOULD, BUT HE HAD HIS SHOT. HE DIDN'T TAKE IT.

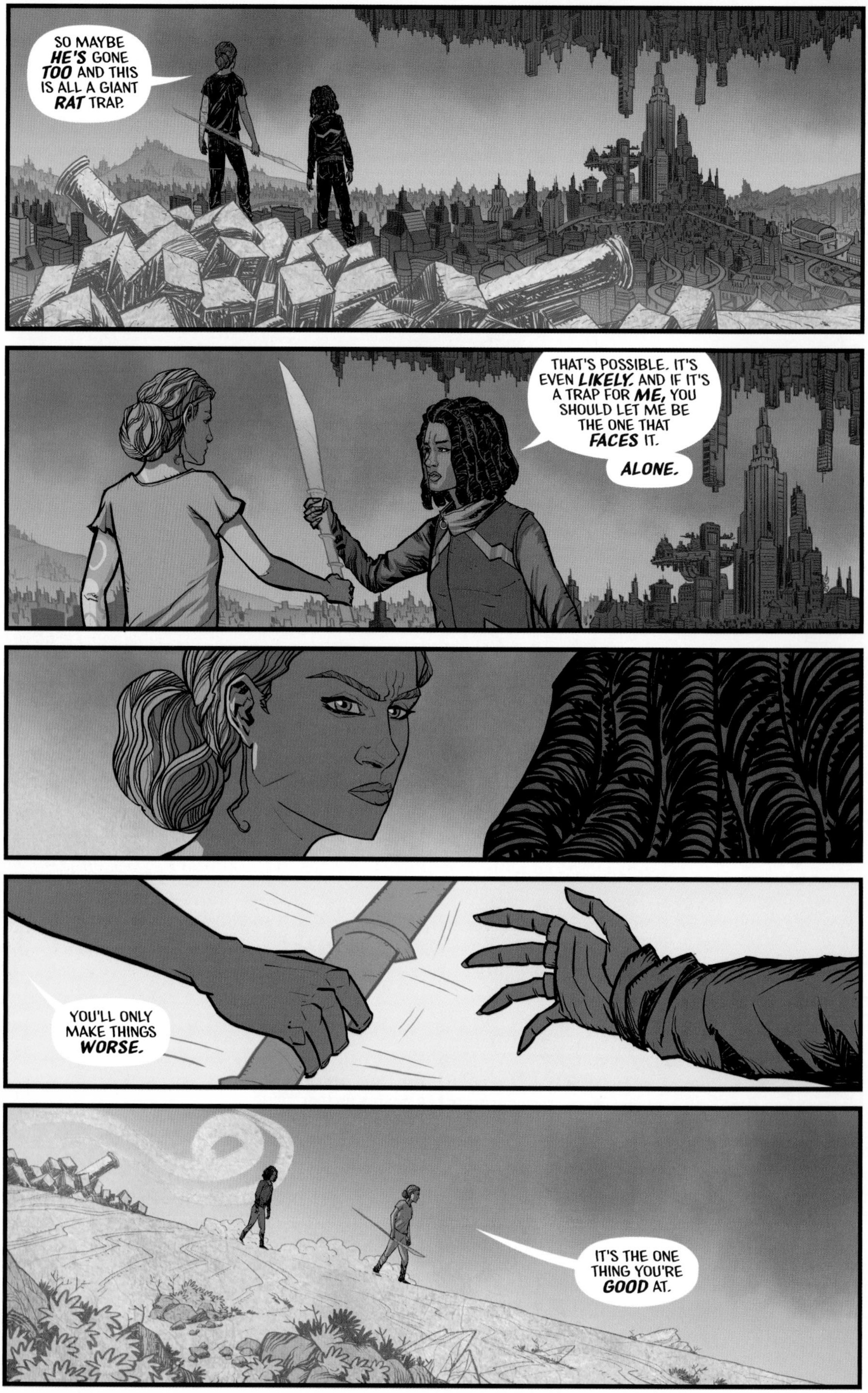
SO MAYBE HE'S GONE TOO AND THIS IS ALL A GIANT RAT TRAP.
THAT'S POSSIBLE. IT'S EVEN LIKELY. AND IF IT'S A TRAP FOR ME, YOU SHOULD LET ME BE THE ONE THAT FACES IT.
ALONE.
YOU'LL ONLY MAKE THINGS WORSE.
IT'S THE ONE THING YOU'RE GOOD AT.

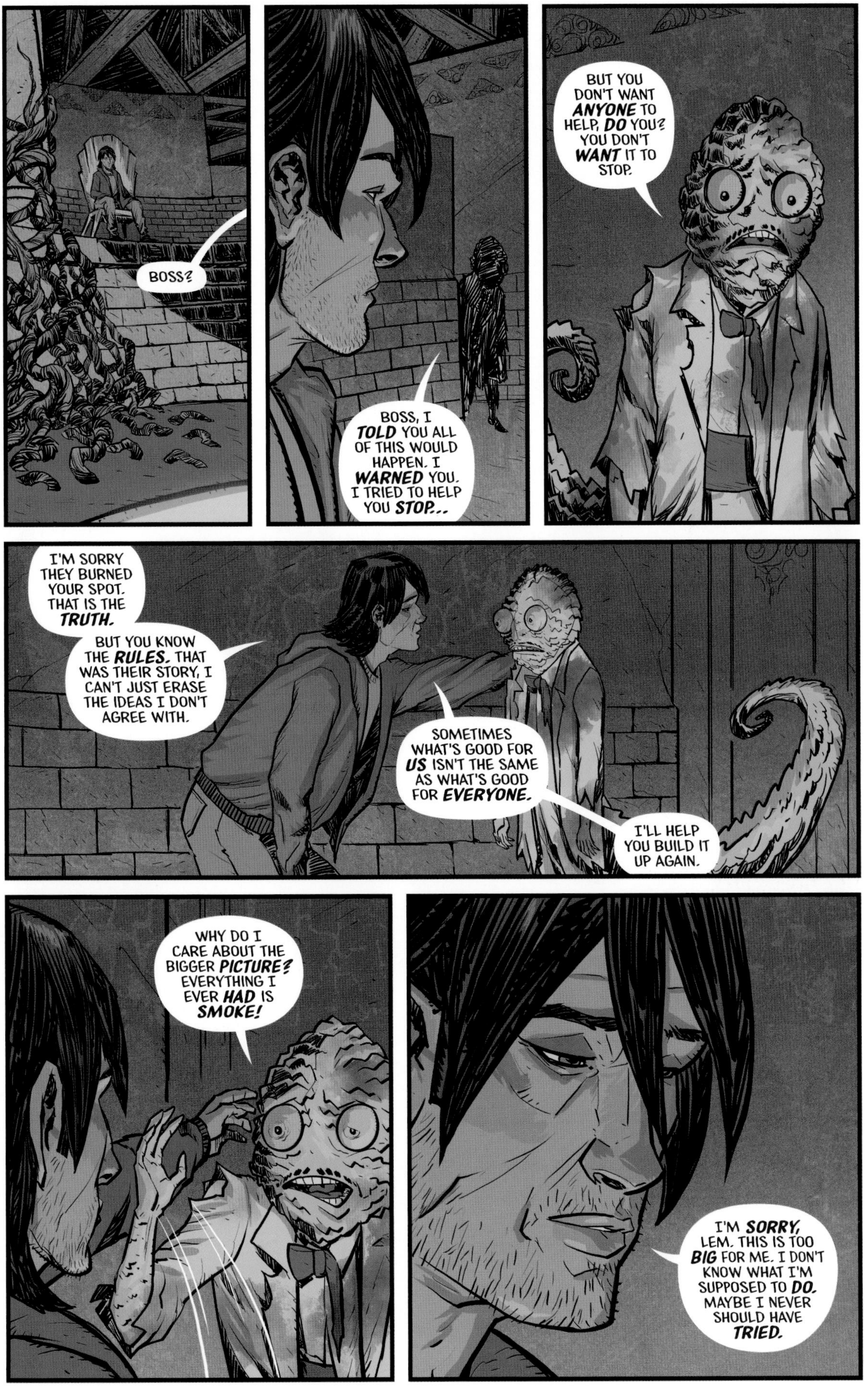
BOSS?
BOSS, I TOLD YOU ALL OF THIS WOULD HAPPEN. I WARNED YOU. I TRIED TO HELP YOU STOP...
BUT YOU DON'T WANT ANYONE TO HELP, DO YOU? YOU DON'T WANT IT TO STOP.
I'M SORRY THEY BURNED YOUR SPOT. THAT IS THE TRUTH.
BUT YOU KNOW THE RULES. THAT WAS THEIR STORY, I CAN'T JUST ERASE THE IDEAS I DON'T AGREE WITH.
SOMETIMES WHAT'S GOOD FOR US ISN'T THE SAME AS WHAT'S GOOD FOR EVERYONE.
I'LL HELP YOU BUILD IT UP AGAIN.
WHY DO I CARE ABOUT THE BIGGER PICTURE? EVERYTHING I EVER HAD IS SMOKE!
I'M SORRY, LEM. THIS IS TOO BIG FOR ME. I DON'T KNOW WHAT I'M SUPPOSED TO DO. MAYBE I NEVER SHOULD HAVE TRIED.

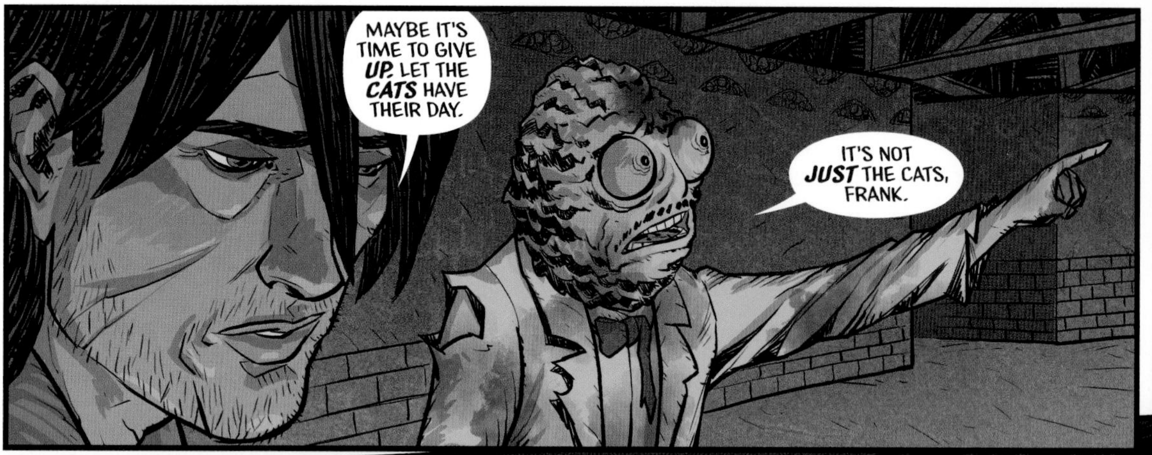
MAYBE IT'S TIME TO GIVE UP. LET THE CATS HAVE THEIR DAY.
IT'S NOT JUST THE CATS, FRANK.

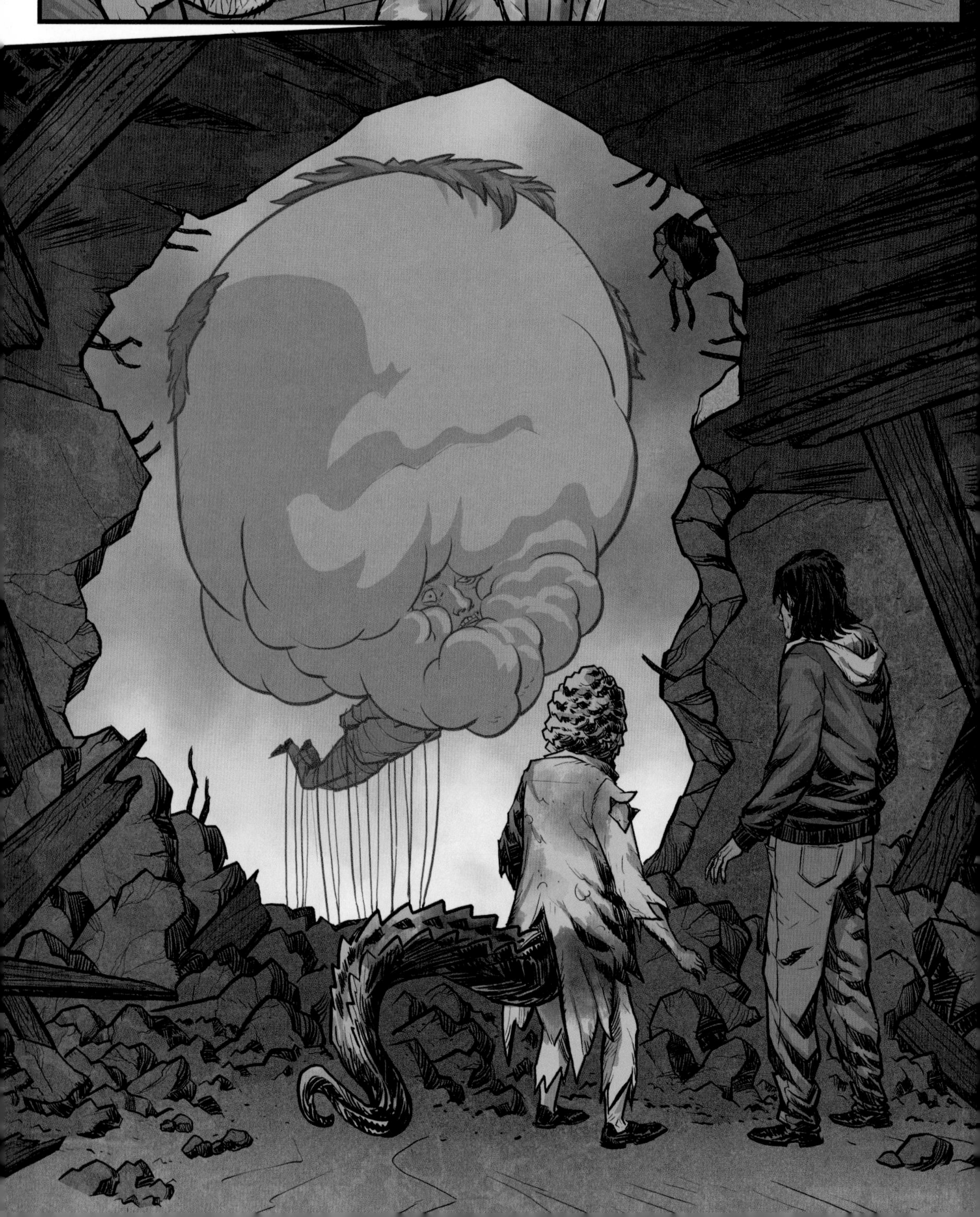

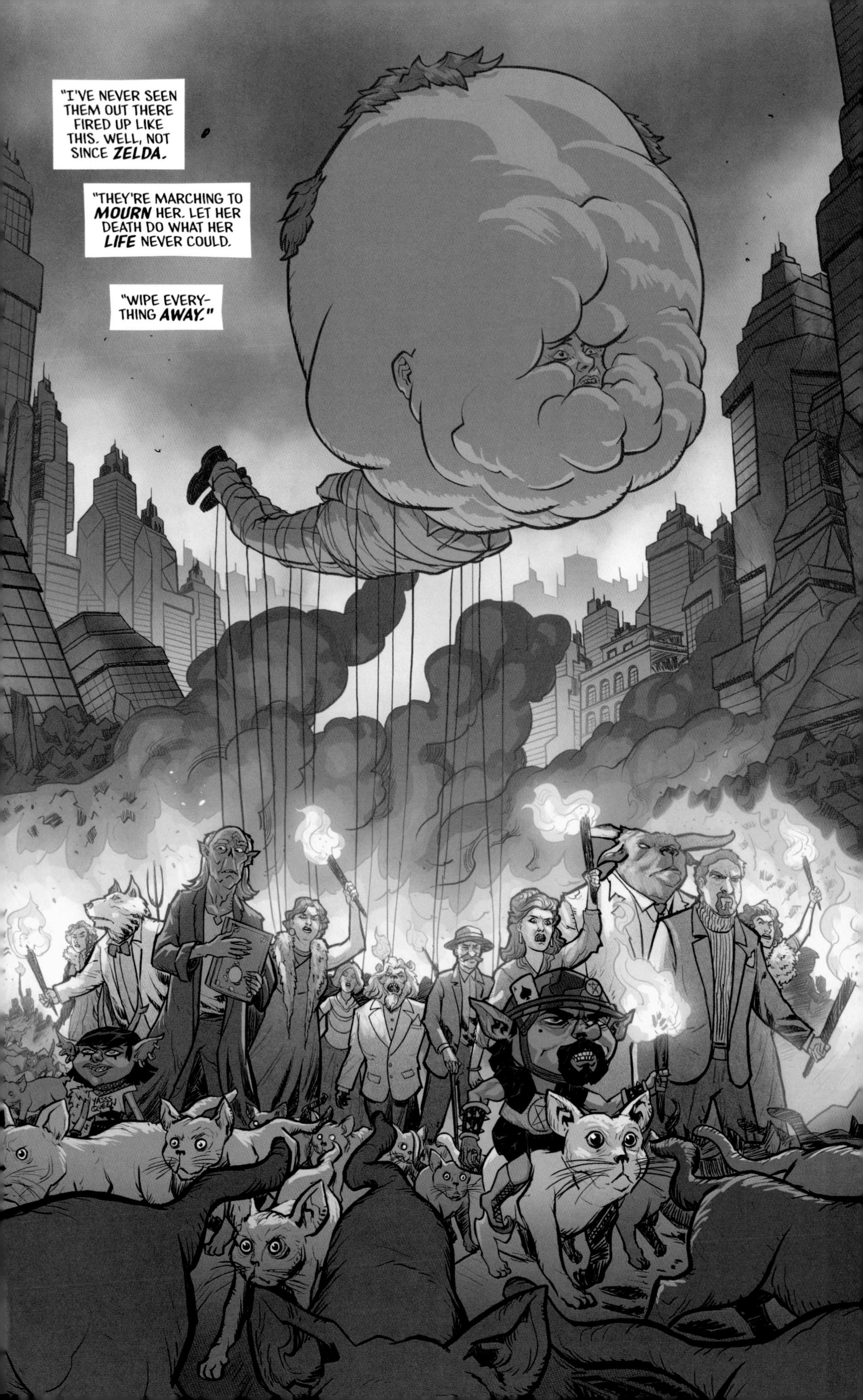
"I'VE NEVER SEEN THEM OUT THERE FIRED UP LIKE THIS. WELL, NOT SINCE ZELDA.
"THEY'RE MARCHING TO MOURN HER. LET HER DEATH DO WHAT HER LIFE NEVER COULD.
"WIPE EVERY-THING AWAY."
YASSS QUEEN

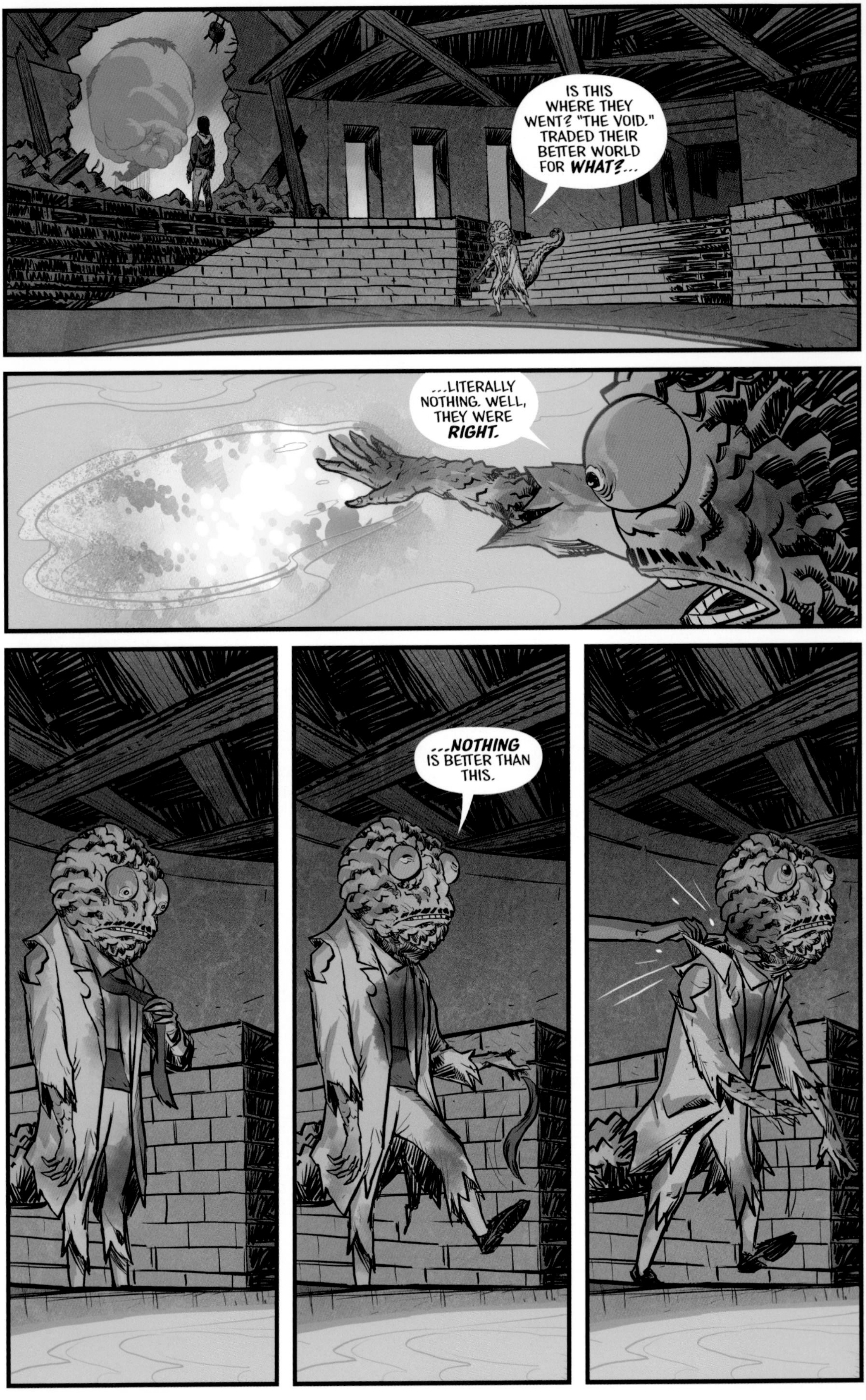
IS THIS WHERE THEY WENT? "THE VOID." TRADED THEIR BETTER WORLD FOR WHAT?...
...LITERALLY NOTHING. WELL, THEY WERE RIGHT.
...NOTHING IS BETTER THAN THIS.

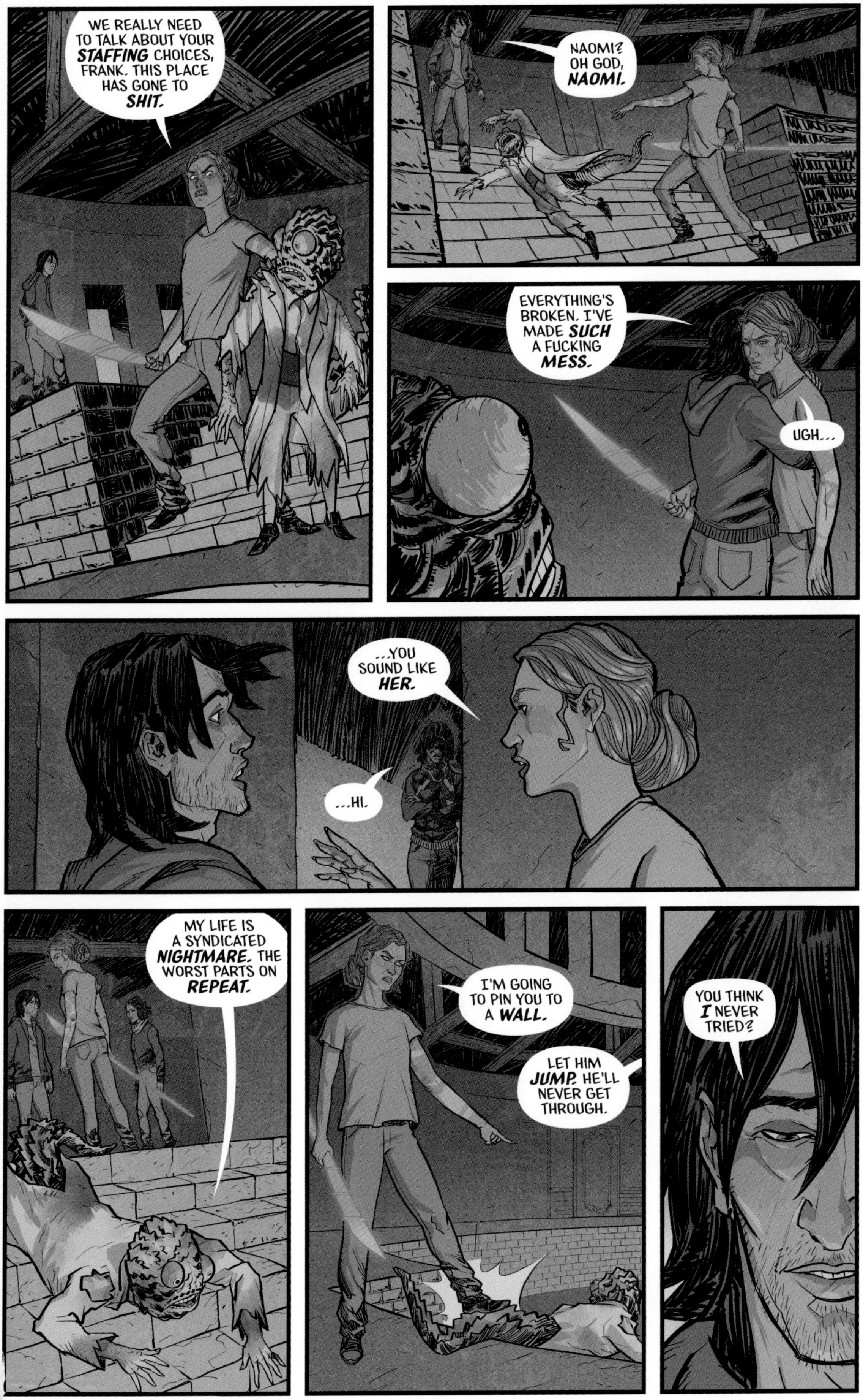
WE REALLY NEED TO TALK ABOUT YOUR STAFFING CHOICES, FRANK. THIS PLACE HAS GONE TO SHIT.
NAOMI? OH GOD, NAOMI.
EVERYTHING'S BROKEN. I'VE MADE SUCH A FUCKING MESS.
UGH...
...YOU SOUND LIKE HER.
...HI.
MY LIFE IS A SYNDICATED NIGHTMARE. THE WORST PARTS ON REPEAT.
I'M GOING TO PIN YOU TO A WALL.
LET HIM JUMP. HE'LL NEVER GET THROUGH.
YOU THINK I NEVER TRIED?

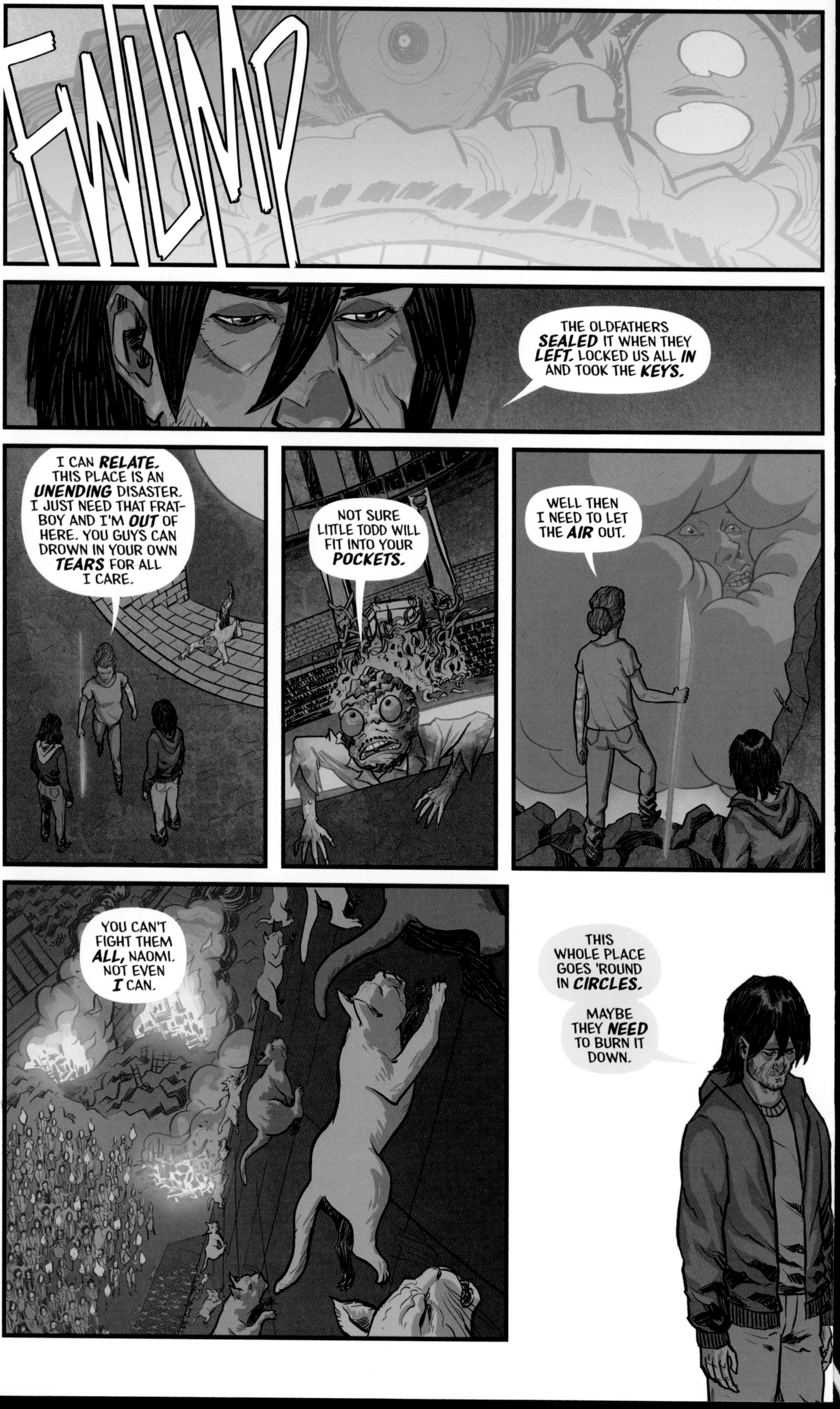
FWUMP
THE OLDFATHERS SEALED IT WHEN THEY LEFT. LOCKED US ALL IN AND TOOK THE KEYS.
I CAN RELATE. THIS PLACE IS AN UNENDING DISASTER. I JUST NEED THAT FRAT-BOY AND I'M OUT OF HERE. YOU GUYS CAN DROWN IN YOUR OWN TEARS FOR ALL I CARE.
NOT SURE LITTLE TODD WILL FIT INTO YOUR POCKETS.
WELL THEN I NEED TO LET THE AIR OUT.
YOU CAN'T FIGHT THEM ALL, NAOMI. NOT EVEN I CAN.
THIS WHOLE PLACE GOES 'ROUND IN CIRCLES.
MAYBE THEY NEED TO BURN IT DOWN.

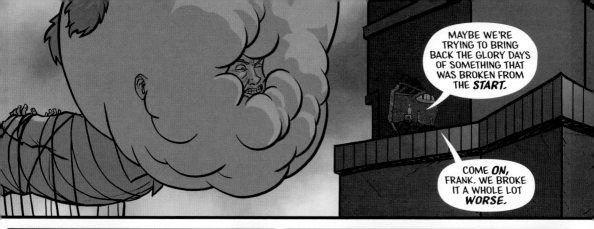

MAYBE WE'RE TRYING TO BRING BACK THE GLORY DAYS OF SOMETHING THAT WAS BROKEN FROM THE *START.*

COME *ON,* FRANK. WE BROKE IT A WHOLE LOT *WORSE.*

DID WE? OR DID THEY TIP IT OVER AND *RUN* BEFORE IT *FELL?*

MAYBE WE *DIDN'T* DRIVE THE OLDFATHERS AWAY. MAYBE WE JUST GAVE THEM AN *OUT.*

NO. *NO* ONE GETS OFF THAT EASY.

NO ONE JUST GETS TO *FORGET.*

WELL THEY ARE *GONE,* AND WHERE THEY'VE GONE WE *CANNOT* FOLLOW.

TRAVELING THROUGH WORLDS...YOU JUST NEED A GOOD ENOUGH *REASON,* RIGHT?

YOU'VE GOT THAT *LOOK* IN YOUR EYES, THAT *SAVIOR* LOOK...

THEY NEED ME DEAD OUT THERE, TO TAKE *OVER.* BUT IF WE TAKE *THAT* AWAY FROM THEM...YOU GET A BLANK SLATE. A FAIR *FIGHT.*

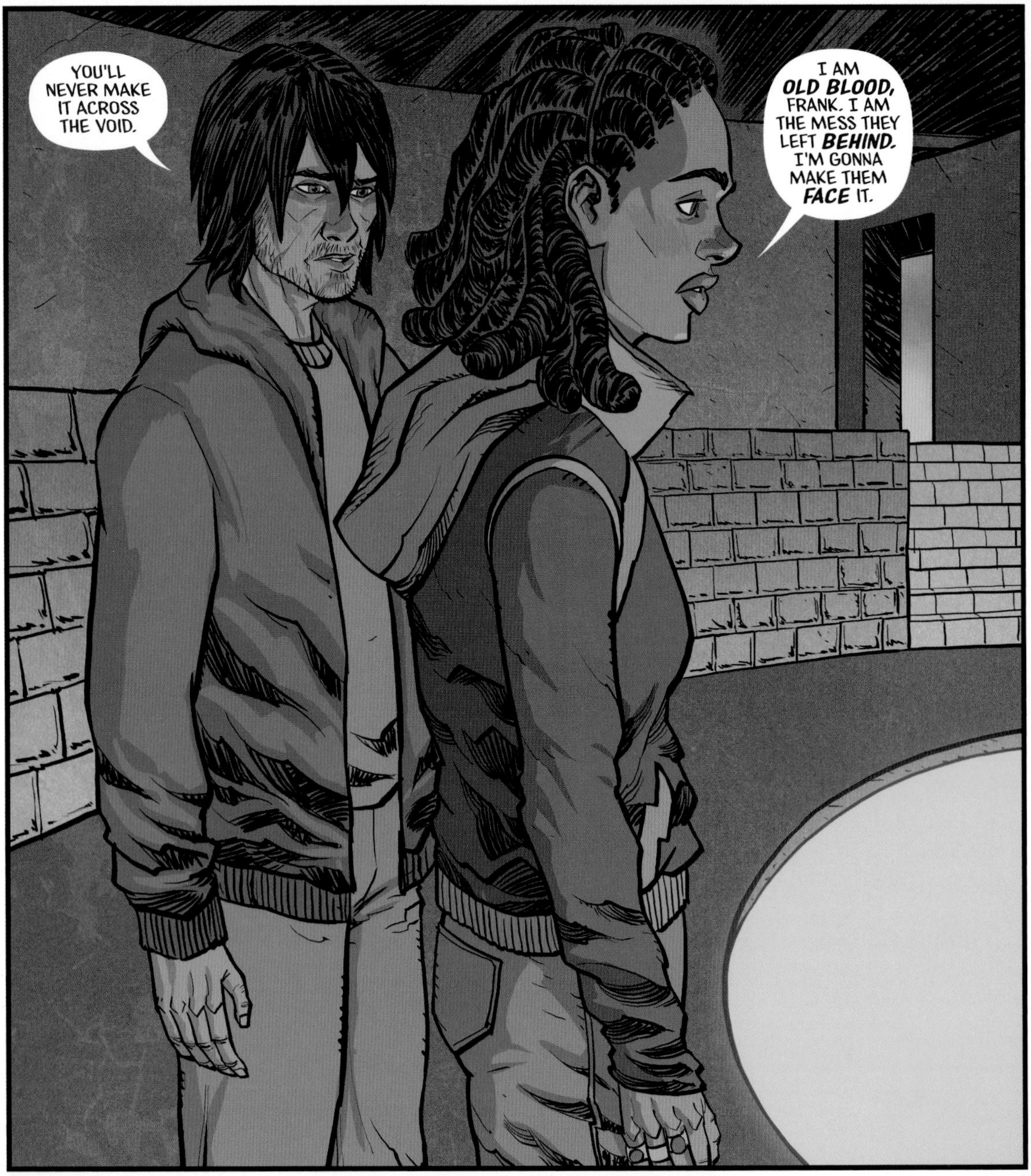
YOU'LL NEVER MAKE IT ACROSS THE VOID.
I AM OLD BLOOD, FRANK. I AM THE MESS THEY LEFT BEHIND. I'M GONNA MAKE THEM FACE IT.

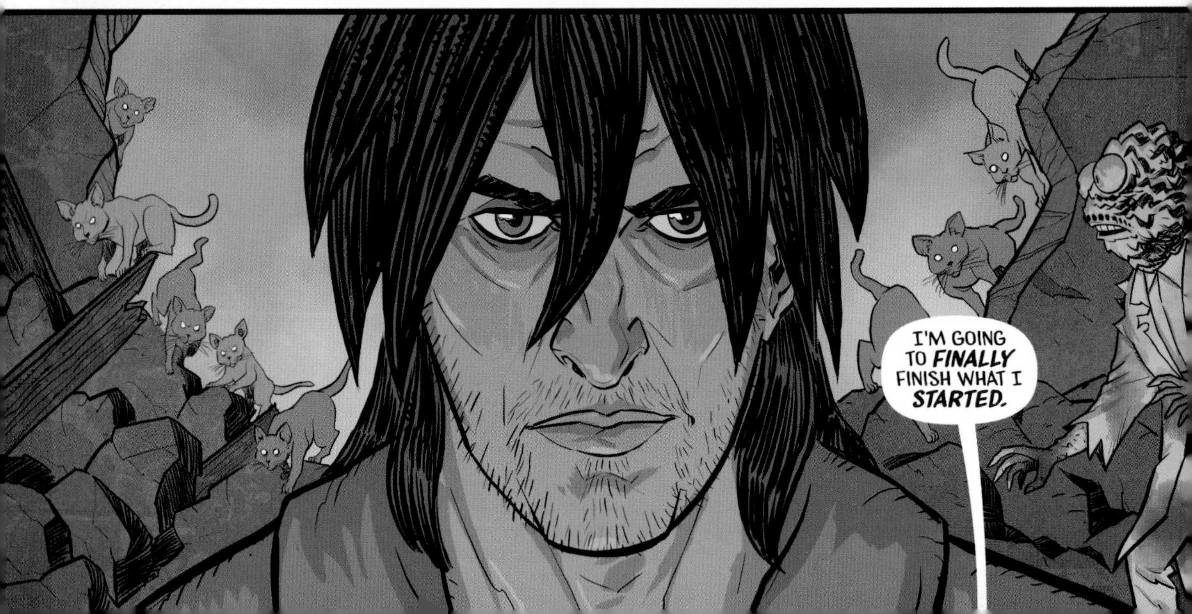
I'M GOING TO FINALLY FINISH WHAT I STARTED.

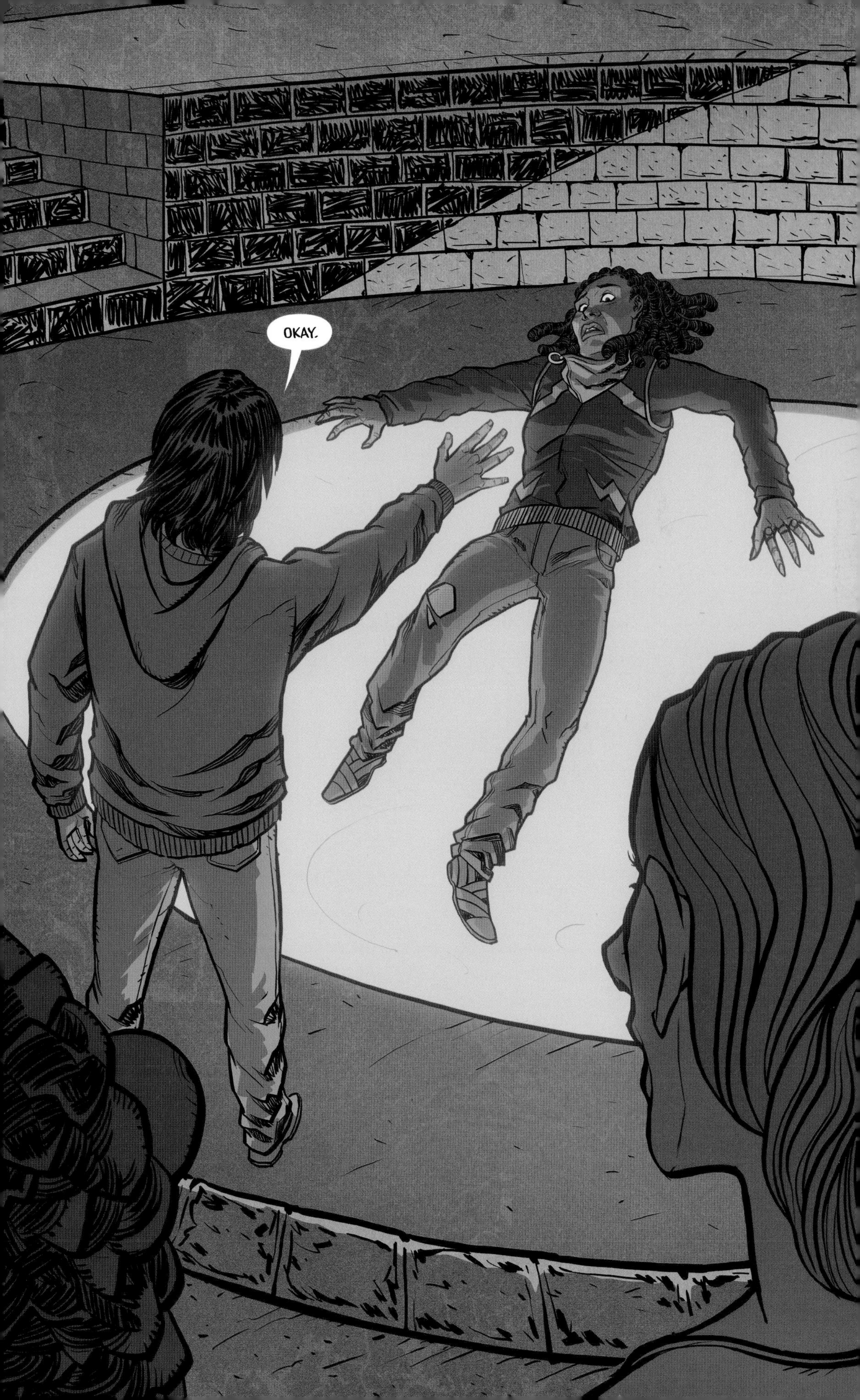
OKAY.

Chapter 10

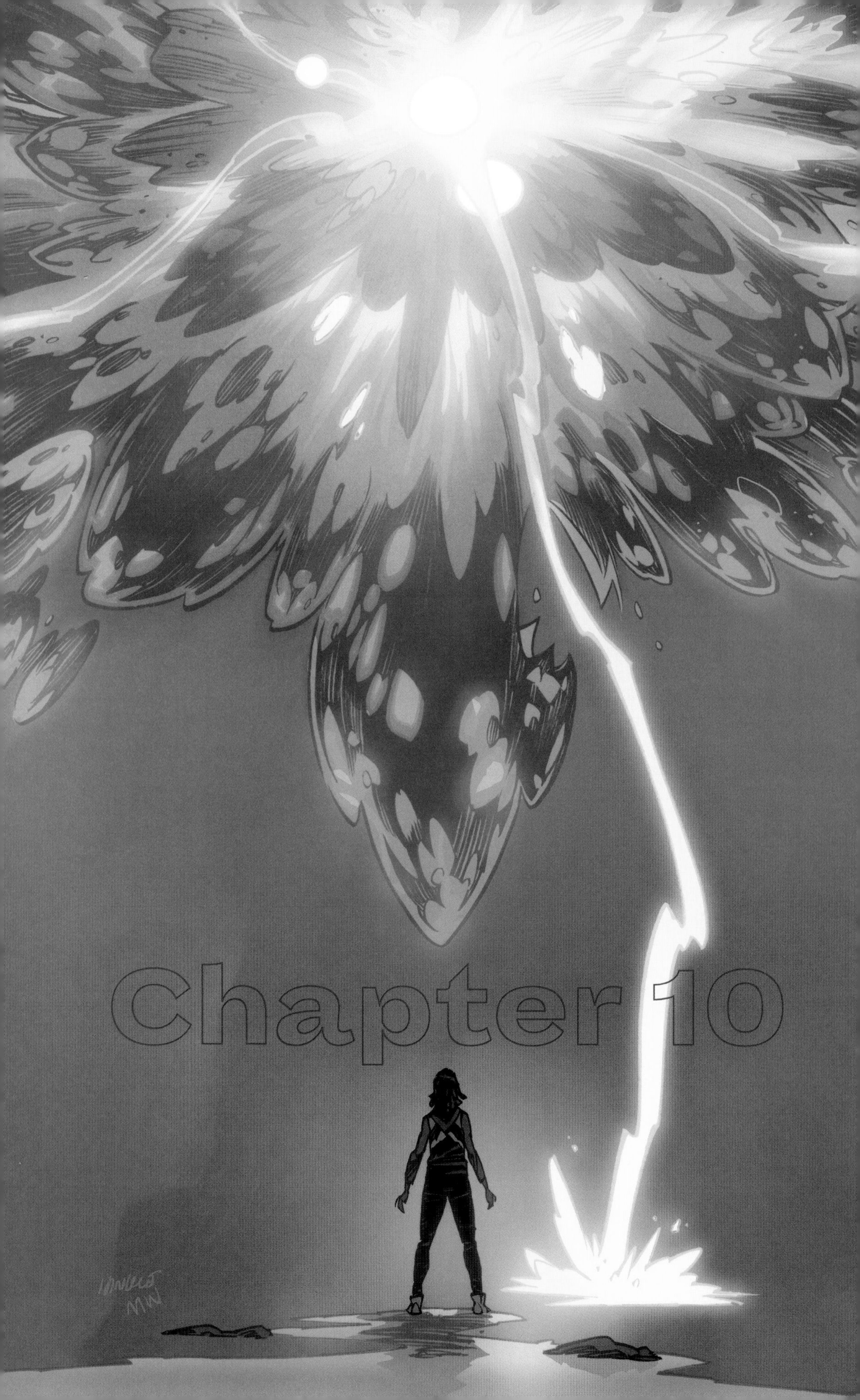

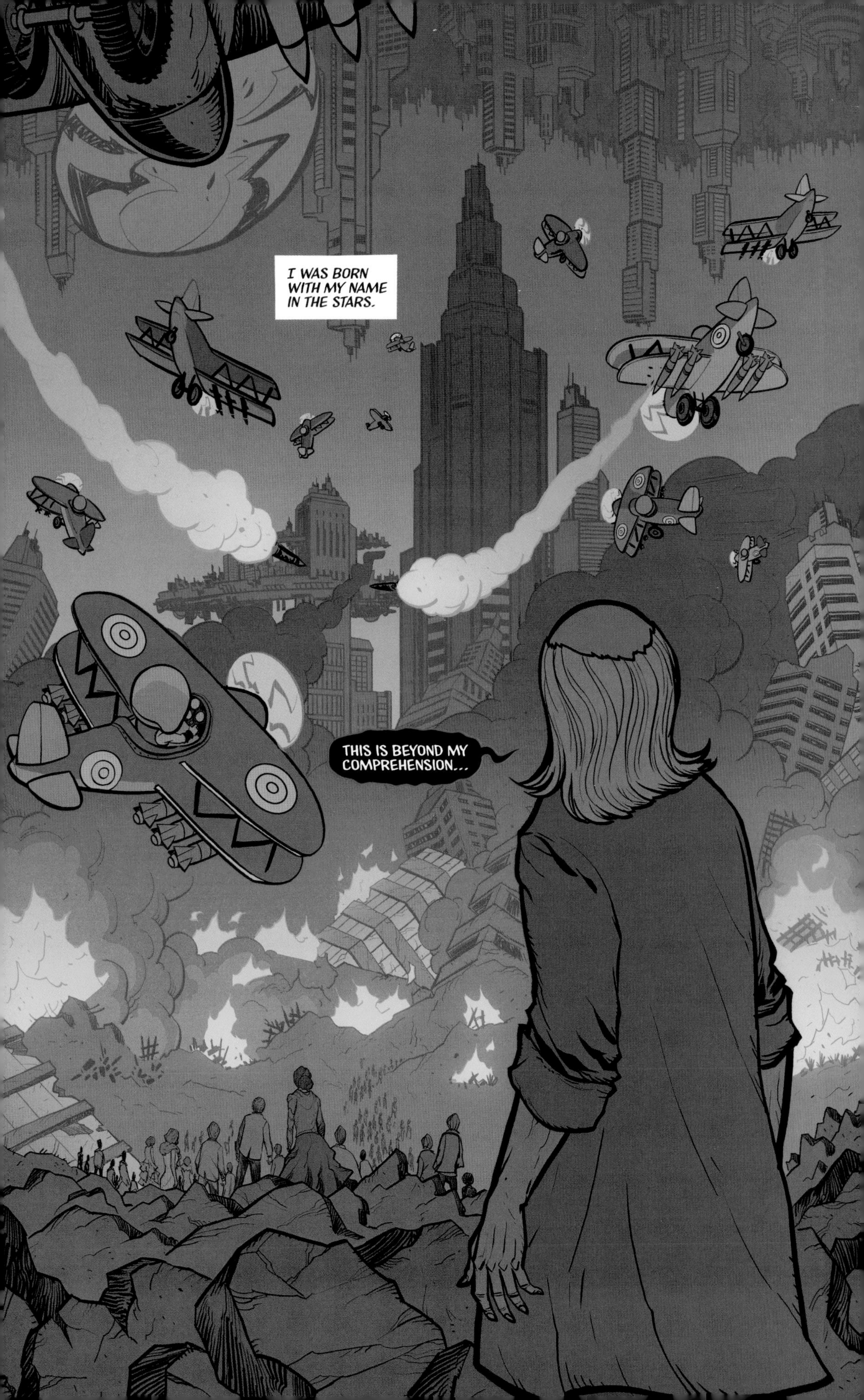
I WAS BORN WITH MY NAME IN THE STARS.
THIS IS BEYOND MY COMPREHENSION...

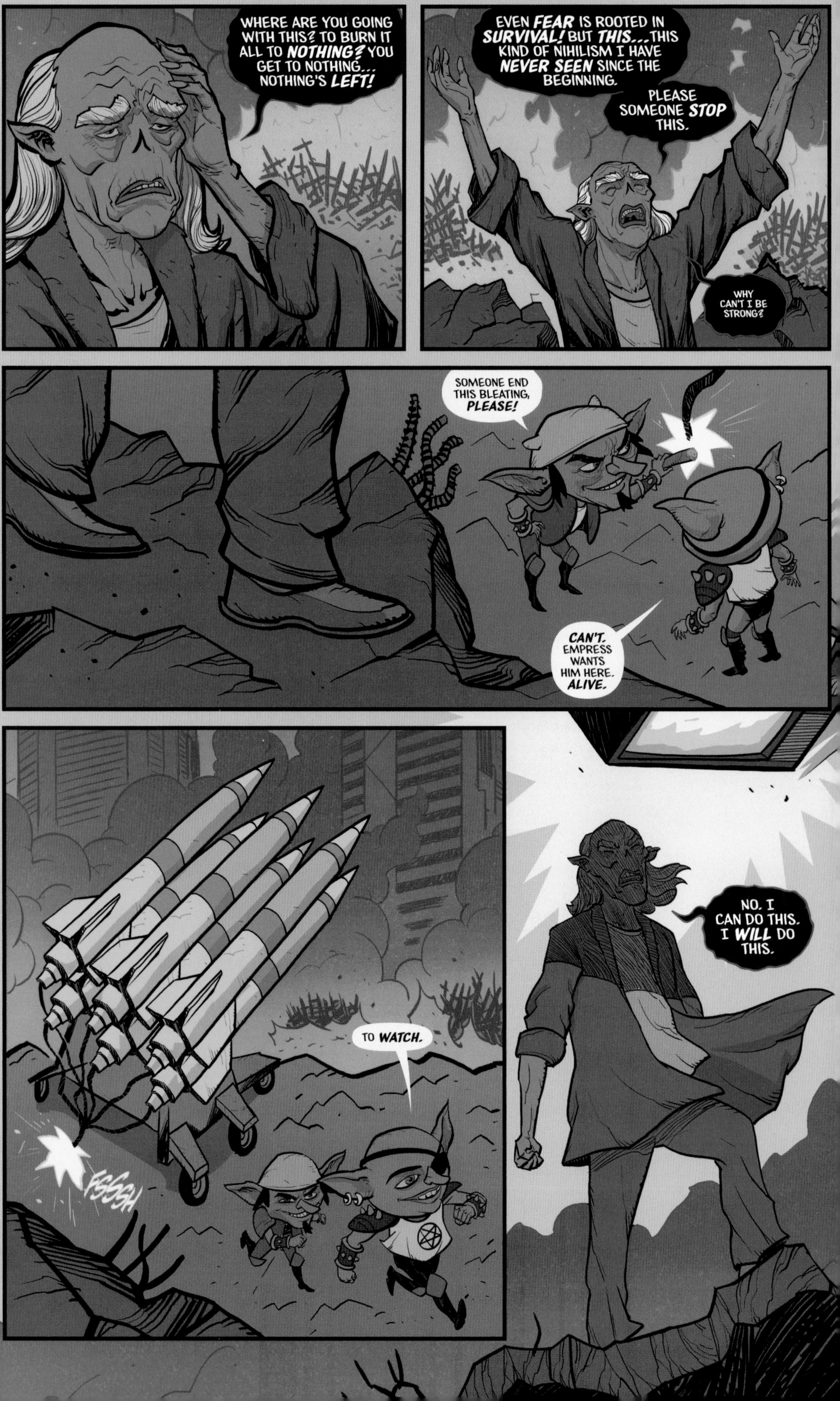
WHERE ARE YOU GOING WITH THIS? TO BURN IT ALL TO NOTHING? YOU GET TO NOTHING... NOTHING'S LEFT!
EVEN FEAR IS ROOTED IN SURVIVAL! BUT THIS...THIS KIND OF NIHILISM I HAVE NEVER SEEN SINCE THE BEGINNING.
PLEASE SOMEONE STOP THIS.
WHY CAN'T I BE STRONG?
SOMEONE END THIS BLEATING, PLEASE!
CAN'T. EMPRESS WANTS HIM HERE. ALIVE.
TO WATCH.
FSSSH
NO. I CAN DO THIS. I WILL DO THIS.

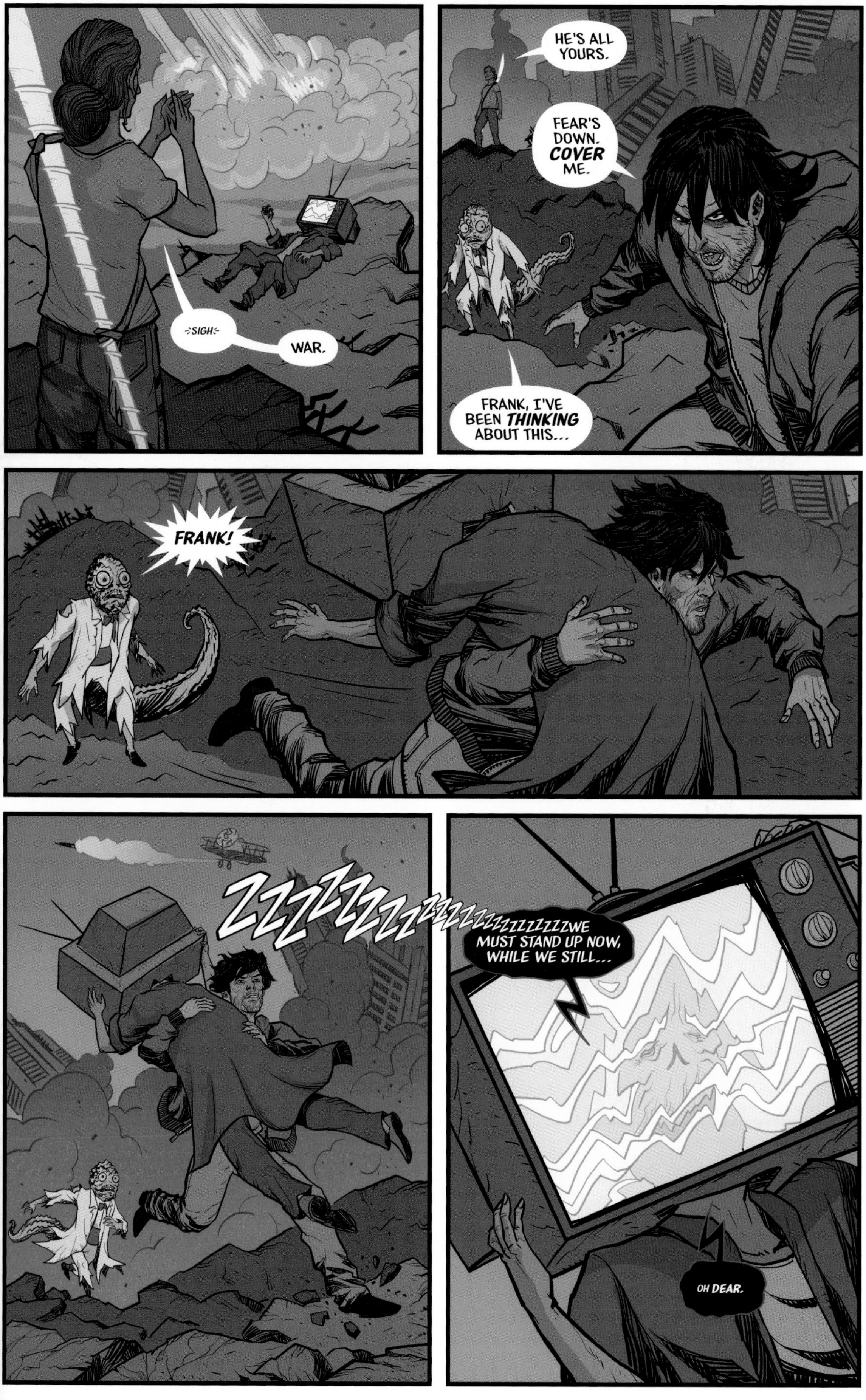

~SIGH~
WAR.
HE'S ALL YOURS.
FEAR'S DOWN. COVER ME.
FRANK, I'VE BEEN THINKING ABOUT THIS...
FRANK!
ZZZZZZZZZZZZZZZZZZZZZZZZZWE MUST STAND UP NOW, WHILE WE STILL...
OH DEAR.

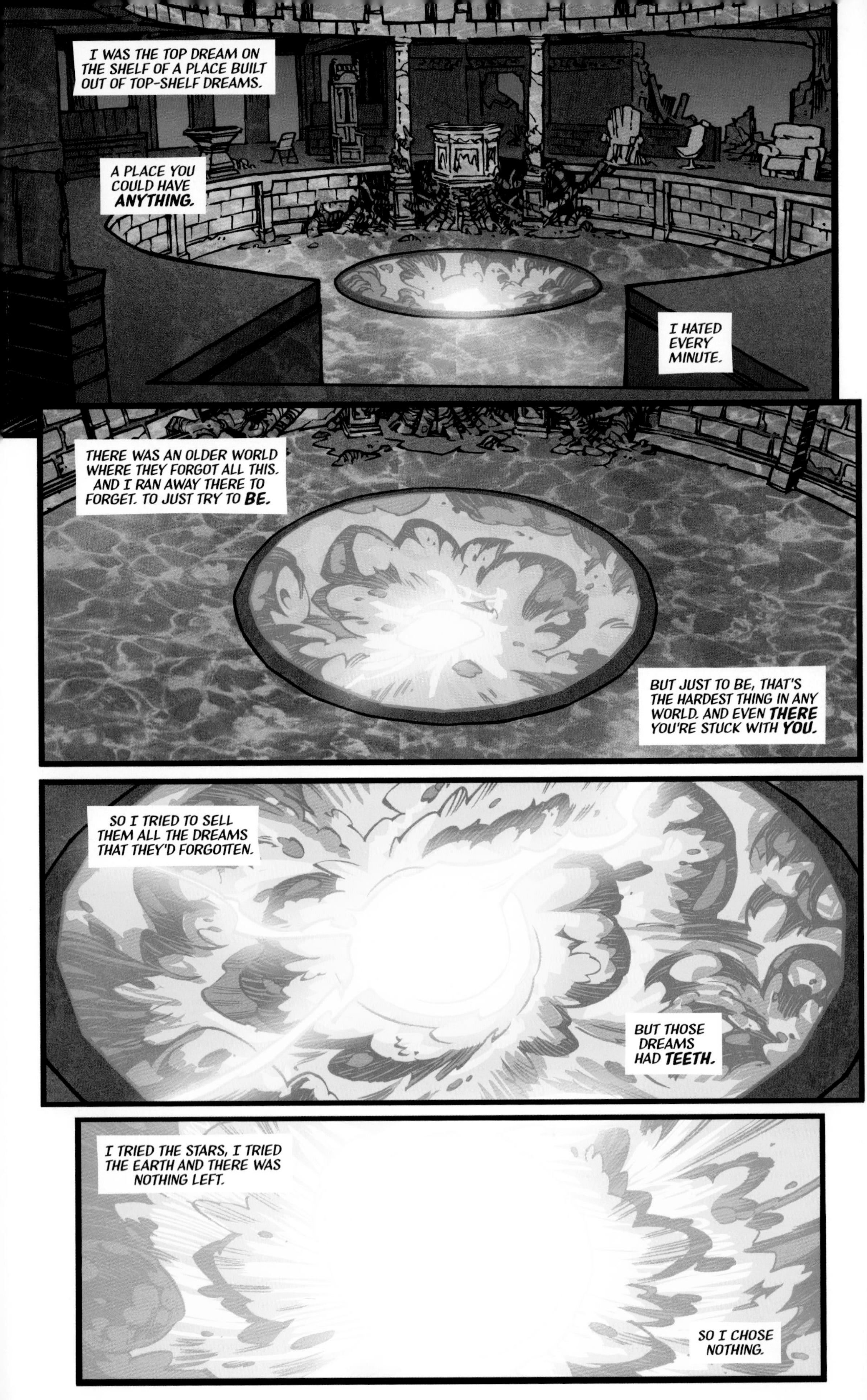
I WAS THE TOP DREAM ON THE SHELF OF A PLACE BUILT OUT OF TOP-SHELF DREAMS.
A PLACE YOU COULD HAVE ANYTHING.
I HATED EVERY MINUTE.
THERE WAS AN OLDER WORLD WHERE THEY FORGOT ALL THIS. AND I RAN AWAY THERE TO FORGET. TO JUST TRY TO BE.
BUT JUST TO BE, THAT'S THE HARDEST THING IN ANY WORLD. AND EVEN THERE YOU'RE STUCK WITH YOU.
SO I TRIED TO SELL THEM ALL THE DREAMS THAT THEY'D FORGOTTEN.
BUT THOSE DREAMS HAD TEETH.
I TRIED THE STARS, I TRIED THE EARTH AND THERE WAS NOTHING LEFT.
SO I CHOSE NOTHING.

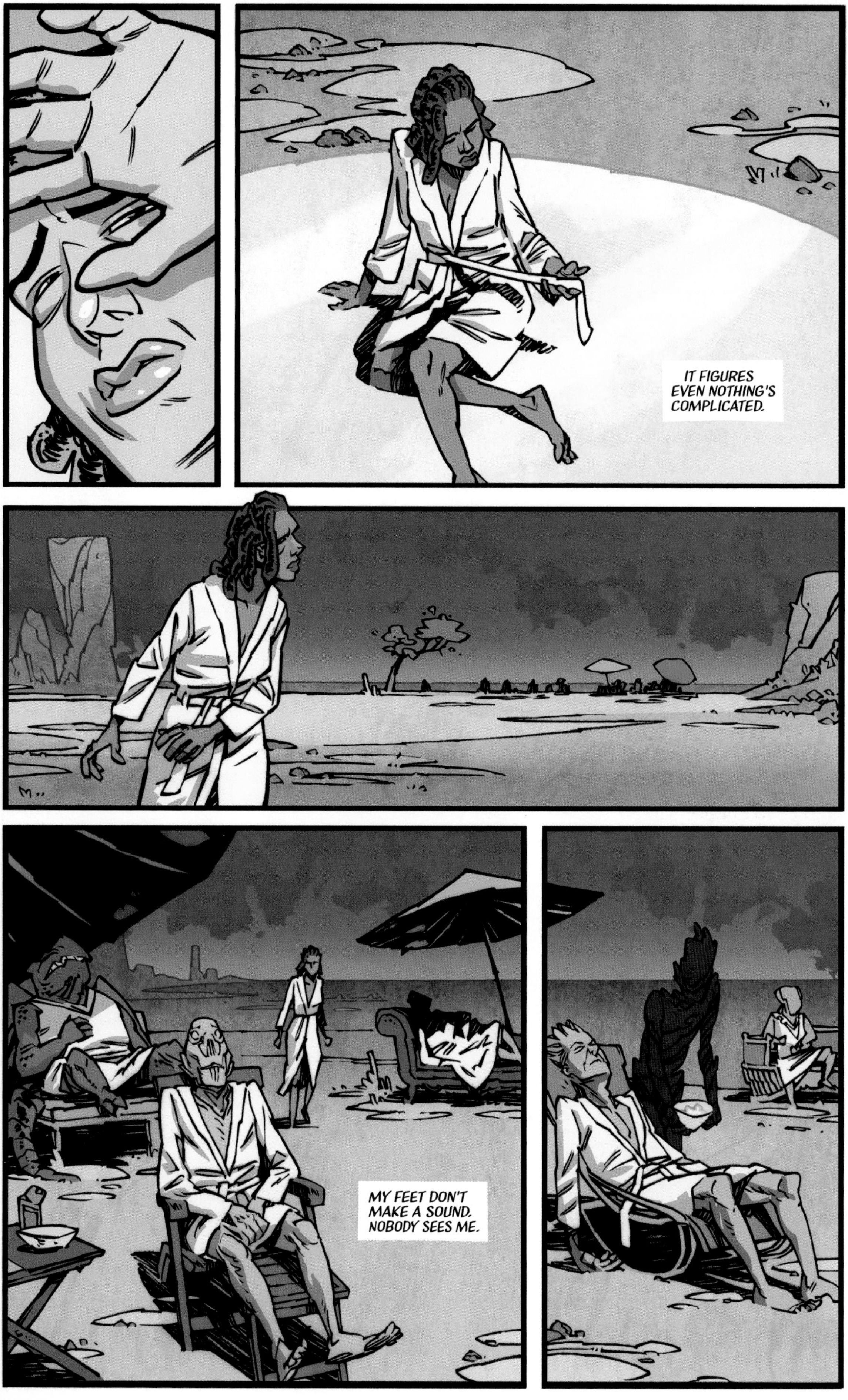
IT FIGURES EVEN NOTHING'S COMPLICATED.
MY FEET DON'T MAKE A SOUND. NOBODY SEES ME.

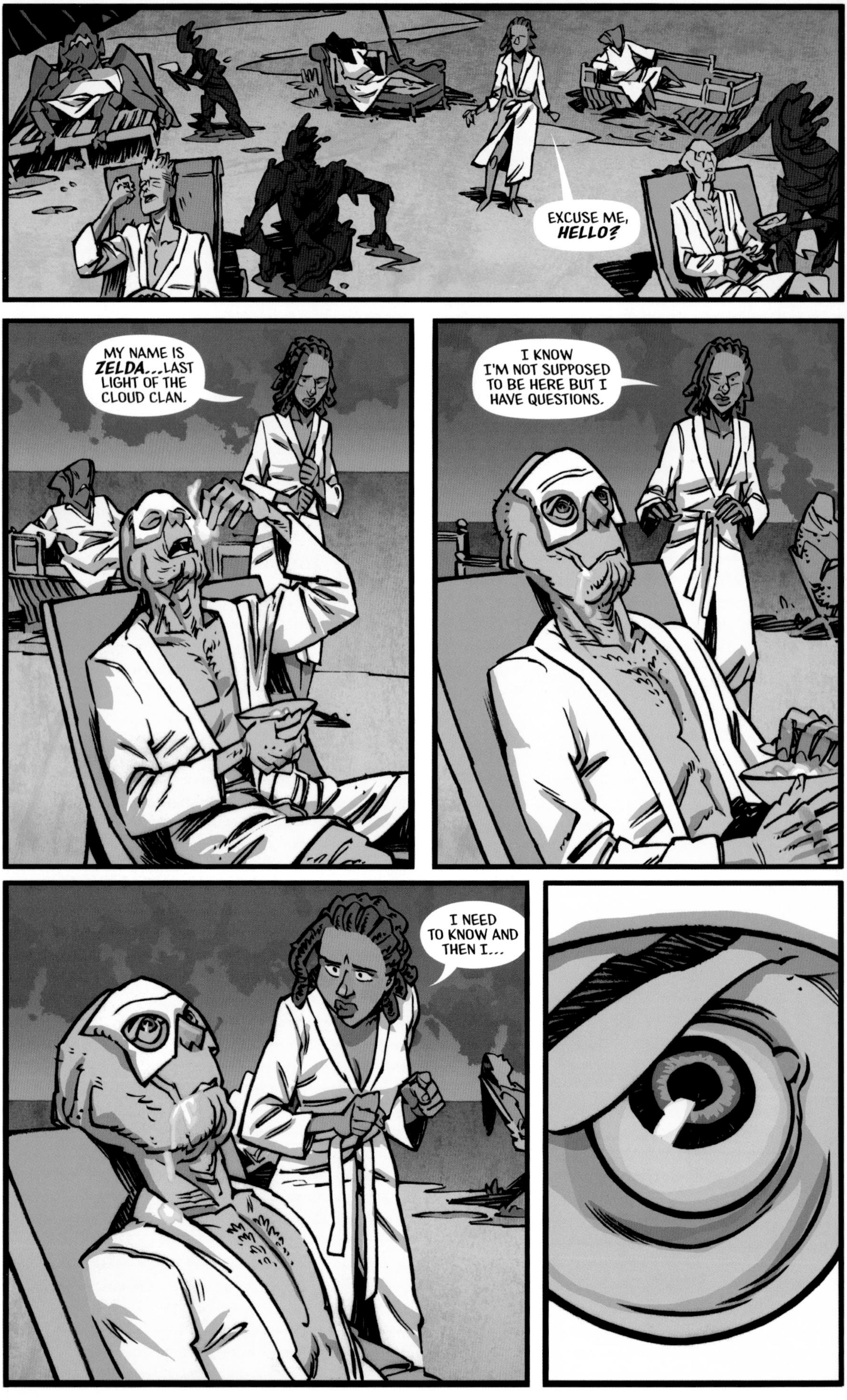
EXCUSE ME, HELLO?
MY NAME IS ZELDA...LAST LIGHT OF THE CLOUD CLAN.
I KNOW I'M NOT SUPPOSED TO BE HERE BUT I HAVE QUESTIONS.
I NEED TO KNOW AND THEN I...

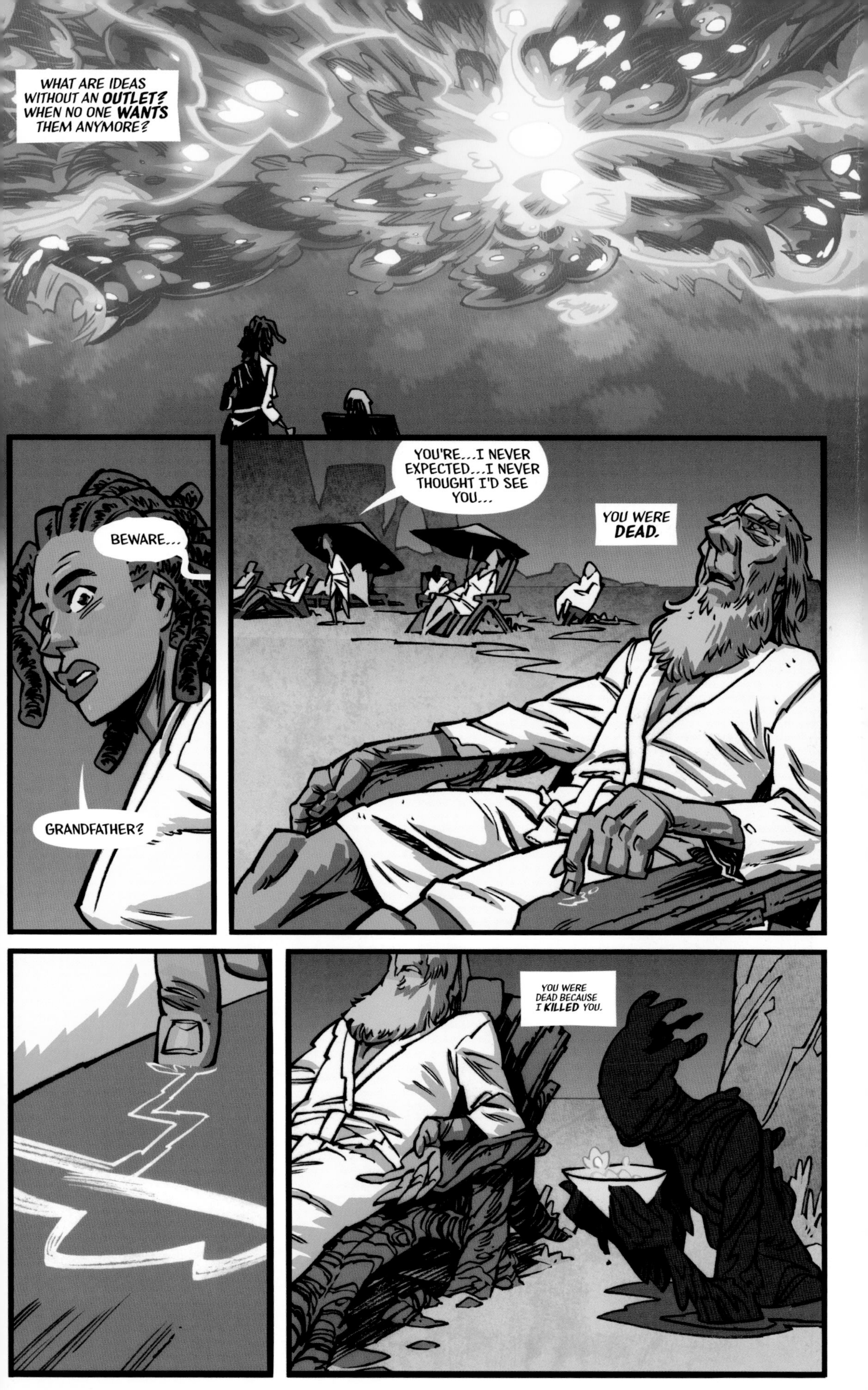
WHAT ARE IDEAS WITHOUT AN OUTLET? WHEN NO ONE WANTS THEM ANYMORE?
BEWARE...
GRANDFATHER?
YOU'RE...I NEVER EXPECTED...I NEVER THOUGHT I'D SEE YOU...
YOU WERE DEAD.
YOU WERE DEAD BECAUSE I KILLED YOU.

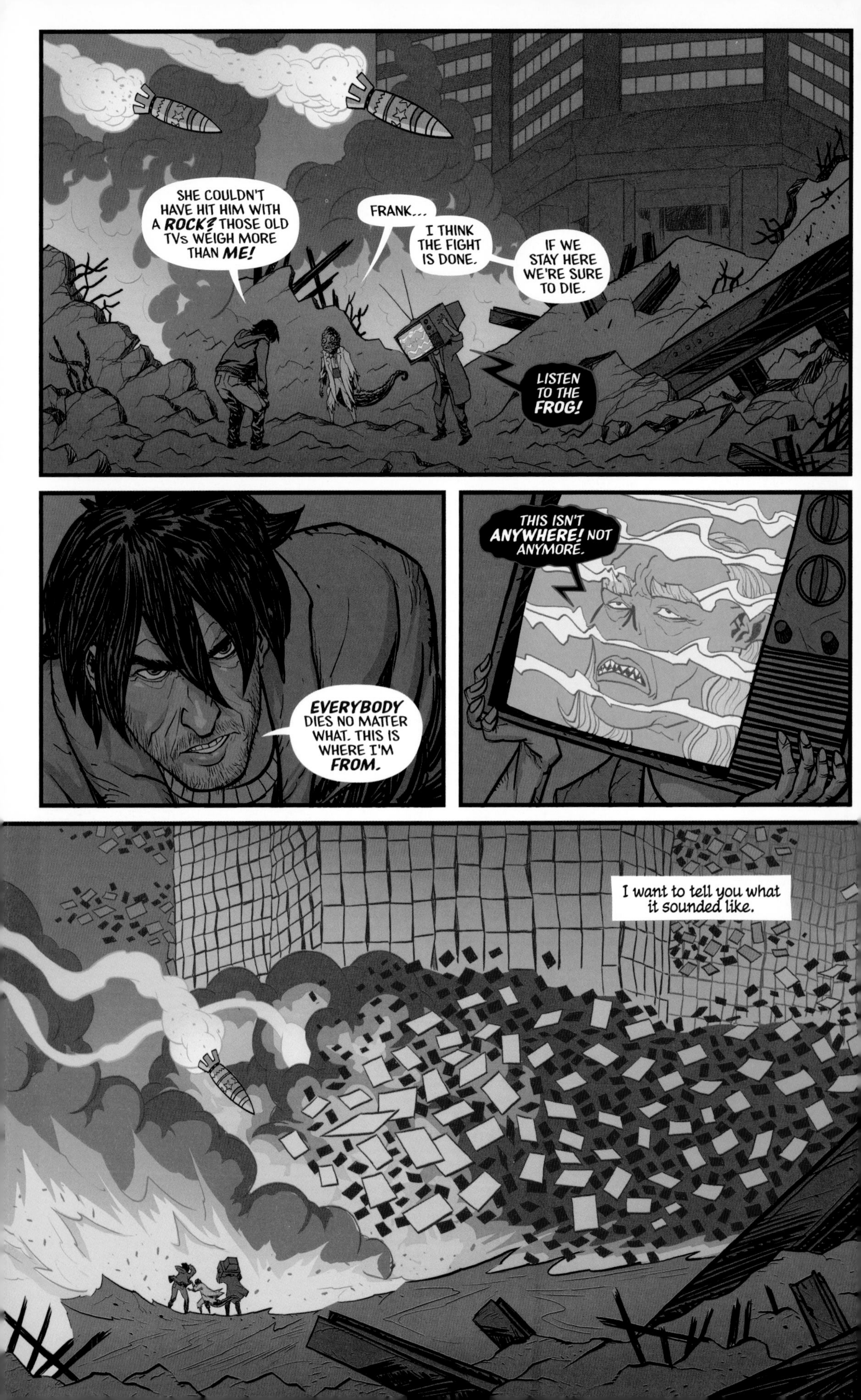

SHE COULDN'T HAVE HIT HIM WITH A ROCK? THOSE OLD TVs WEIGH MORE THAN ME!
FRANK...
I THINK THE FIGHT IS DONE.
IF WE STAY HERE WE'RE SURE TO DIE.
LISTEN TO THE FROG!
EVERYBODY DIES NO MATTER WHAT. THIS IS WHERE I'M FROM.
THIS ISN'T ANYWHERE! NOT ANYMORE.
I want to tell you what it sounded like.

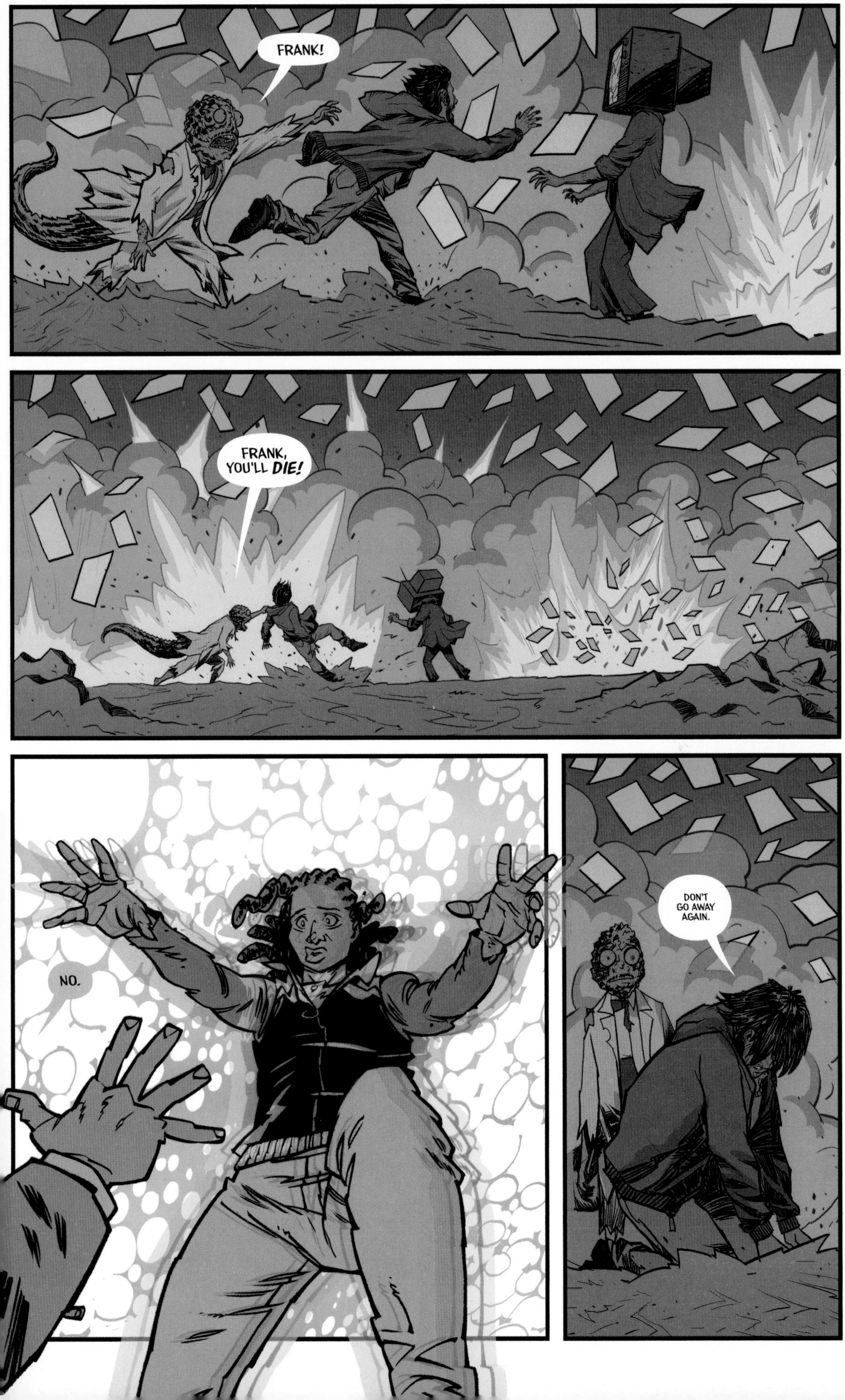
FRANK!
FRANK, YOU'LL DIE!
NO.
DON'T GO AWAY AGAIN.

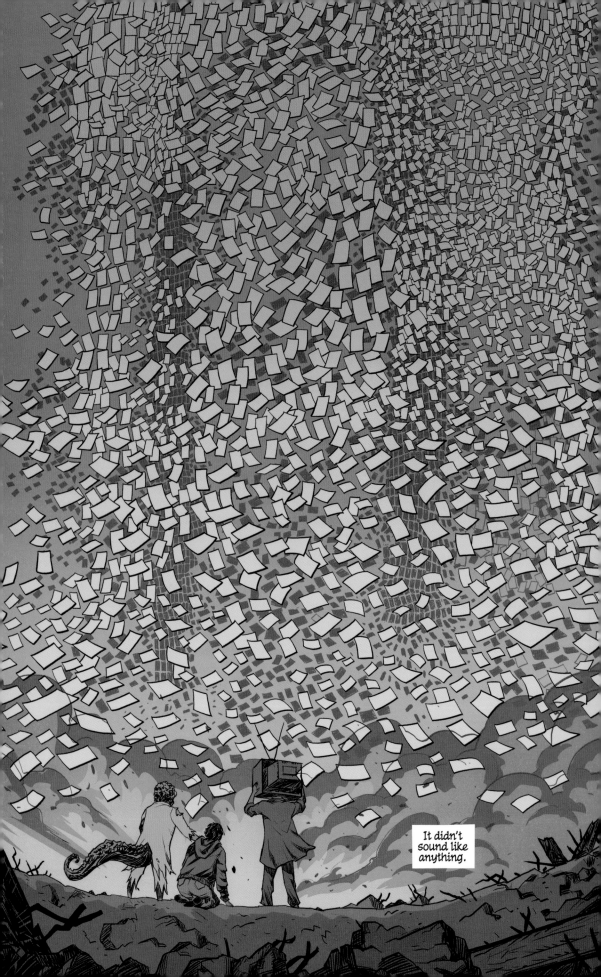

It didn't sound like anything.

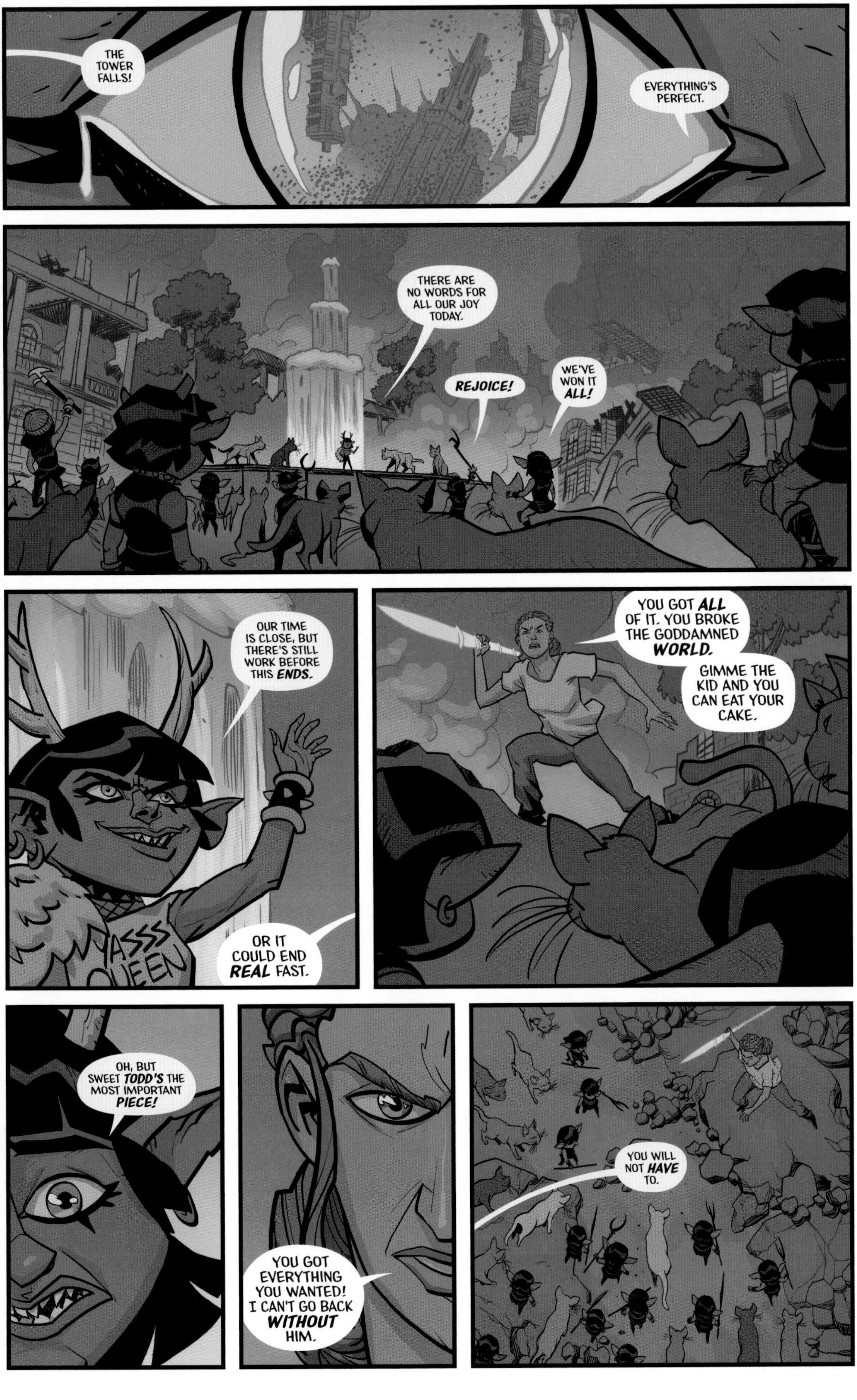
THE TOWER FALLS!
EVERYTHING'S PERFECT.
THERE ARE NO WORDS FOR ALL OUR JOY TODAY.
REJOICE!
WE'VE WON IT ALL!
OUR TIME IS CLOSE, BUT THERE'S STILL WORK BEFORE THIS ENDS.
OR IT COULD END REAL FAST.
YASSS QUEEN
YOU GOT ALL OF IT. YOU BROKE THE GODDAMNED WORLD.
GIMME THE KID AND YOU CAN EAT YOUR CAKE.
OH, BUT SWEET TODD'S THE MOST IMPORTANT PIECE!
YOU GOT EVERYTHING YOU WANTED! I CAN'T GO BACK WITHOUT HIM.
YOU WILL NOT HAVE TO.

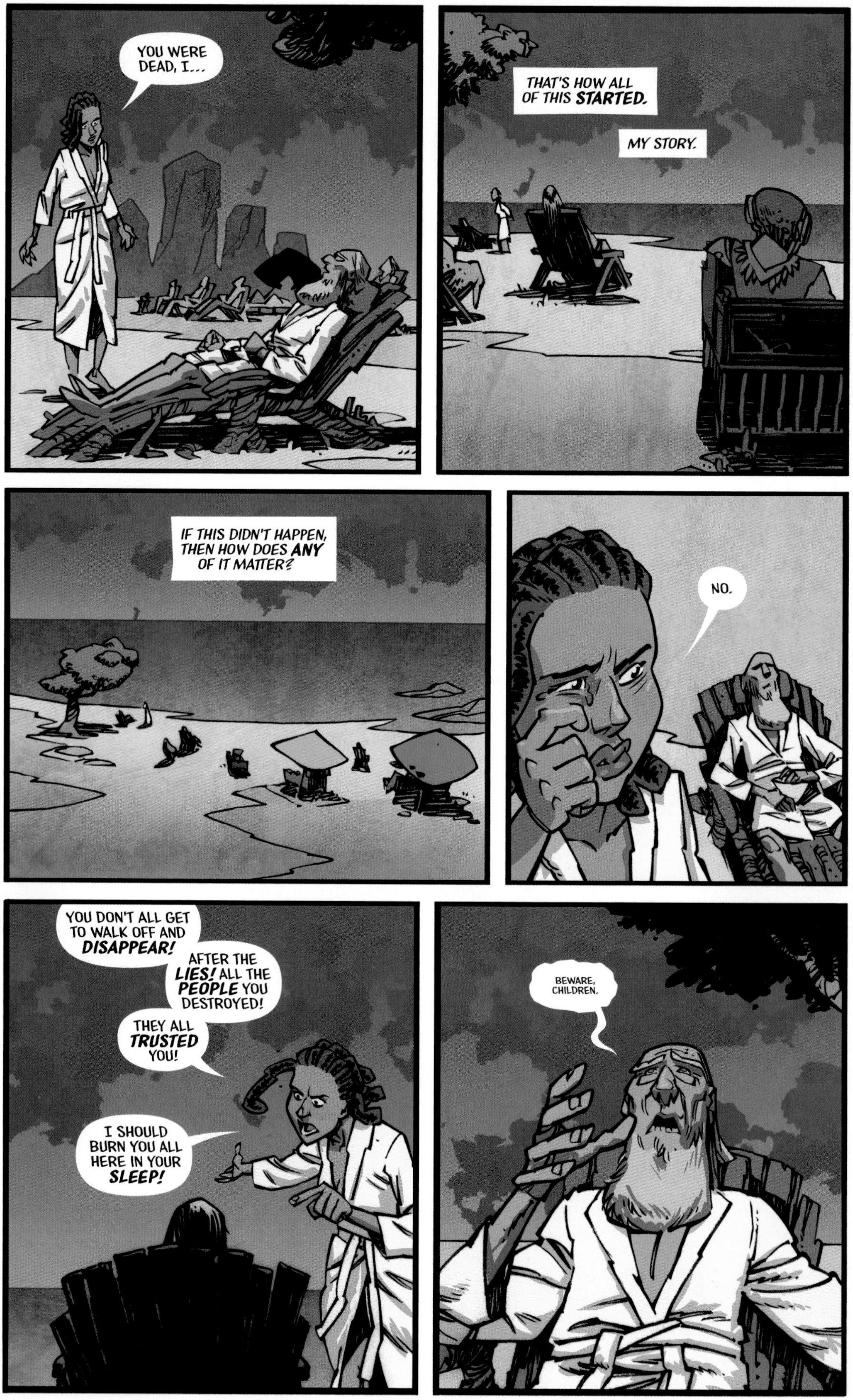
YOU WERE DEAD, I...
THAT'S HOW ALL OF THIS STARTED.
MY STORY.
IF THIS DIDN'T HAPPEN, THEN HOW DOES ANY OF IT MATTER?
NO.
YOU DON'T ALL GET TO WALK OFF AND DISAPPEAR!
AFTER THE LIES! ALL THE PEOPLE YOU DESTROYED!
THEY ALL TRUSTED YOU!
I SHOULD BURN YOU ALL HERE IN YOUR SLEEP!
BEWARE, CHILDREN.

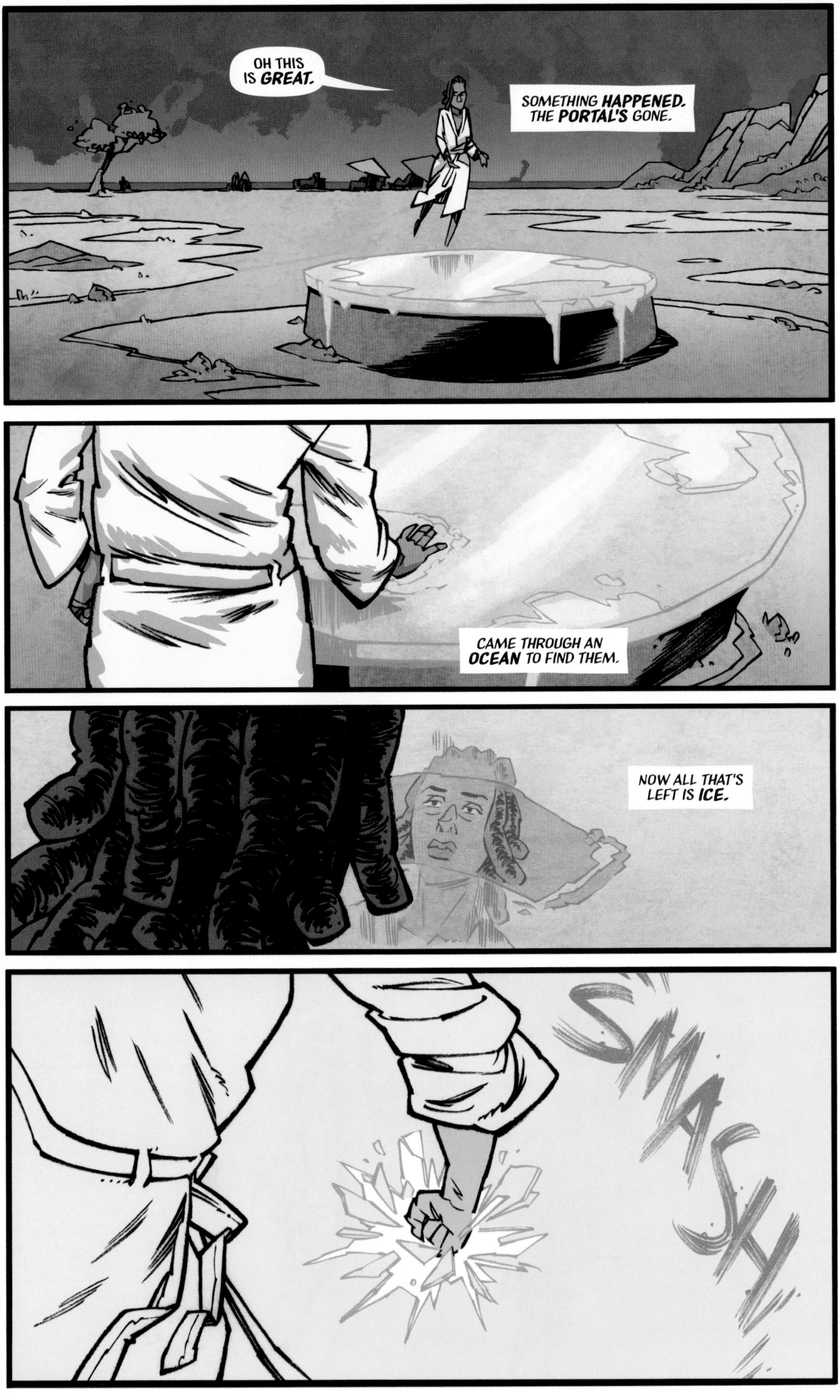
OH THIS IS GREAT.
SOMETHING HAPPENED. THE PORTAL'S GONE.
CAME THROUGH AN OCEAN TO FIND THEM.
NOW ALL THAT'S LEFT IS ICE.
SMASH!

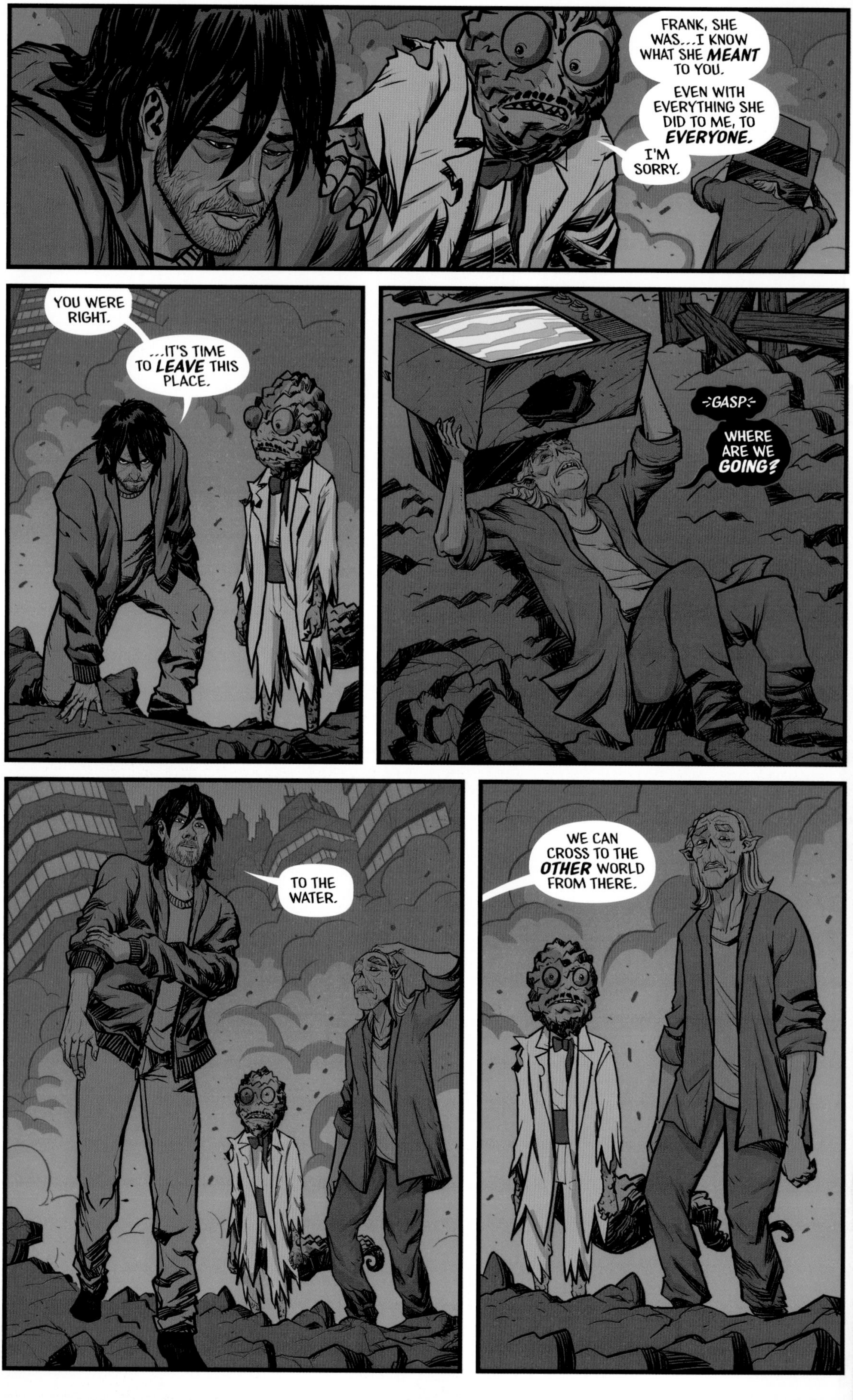

FRANK, SHE WAS...I KNOW WHAT SHE MEANT TO YOU.
EVEN WITH EVERYTHING SHE DID TO ME, TO EVERYONE.
I'M SORRY.
YOU WERE RIGHT.
...IT'S TIME TO LEAVE THIS PLACE.
GASP
WHERE ARE WE GOING?
TO THE WATER.
WE CAN CROSS TO THE OTHER WORLD FROM THERE.

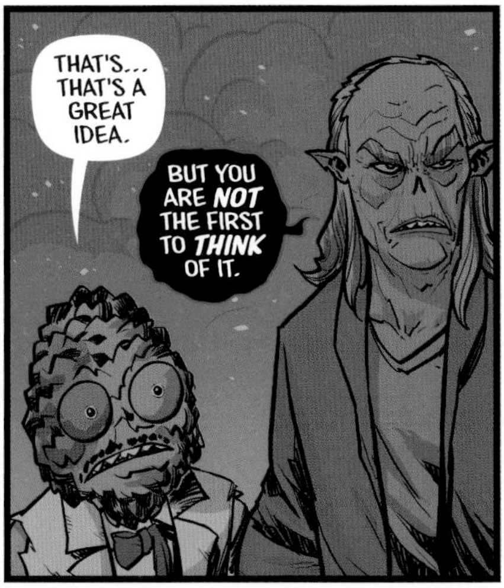
THAT'S... THAT'S A GREAT IDEA.
BUT YOU ARE **NOT** THE FIRST TO **THINK** OF IT.

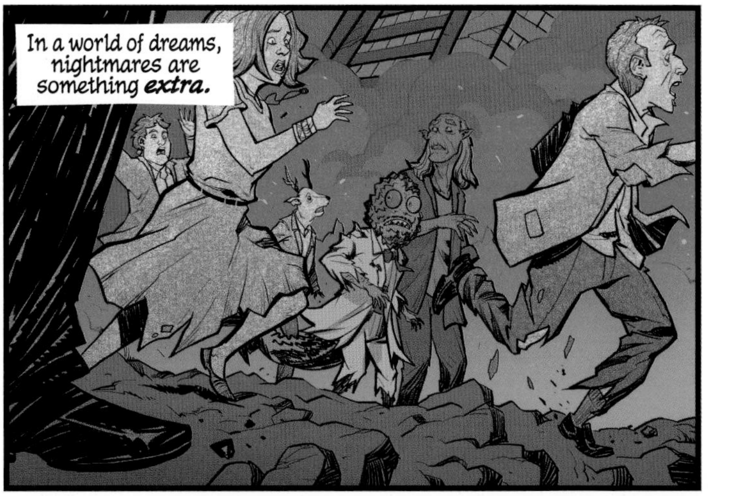
In a world of dreams, nightmares are something **extra.**

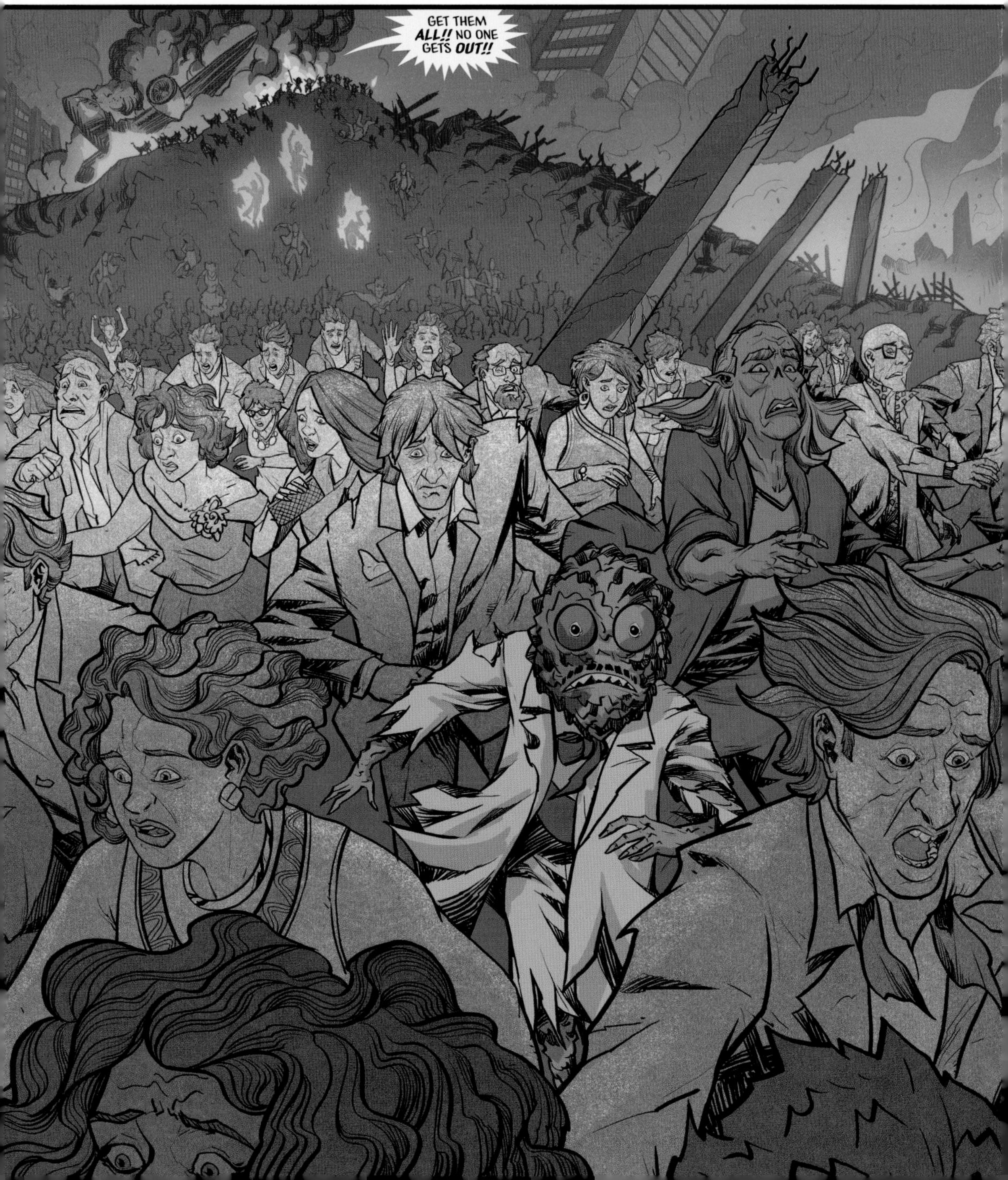
GET THEM **ALL!!** NO ONE GETS **OUT!!**

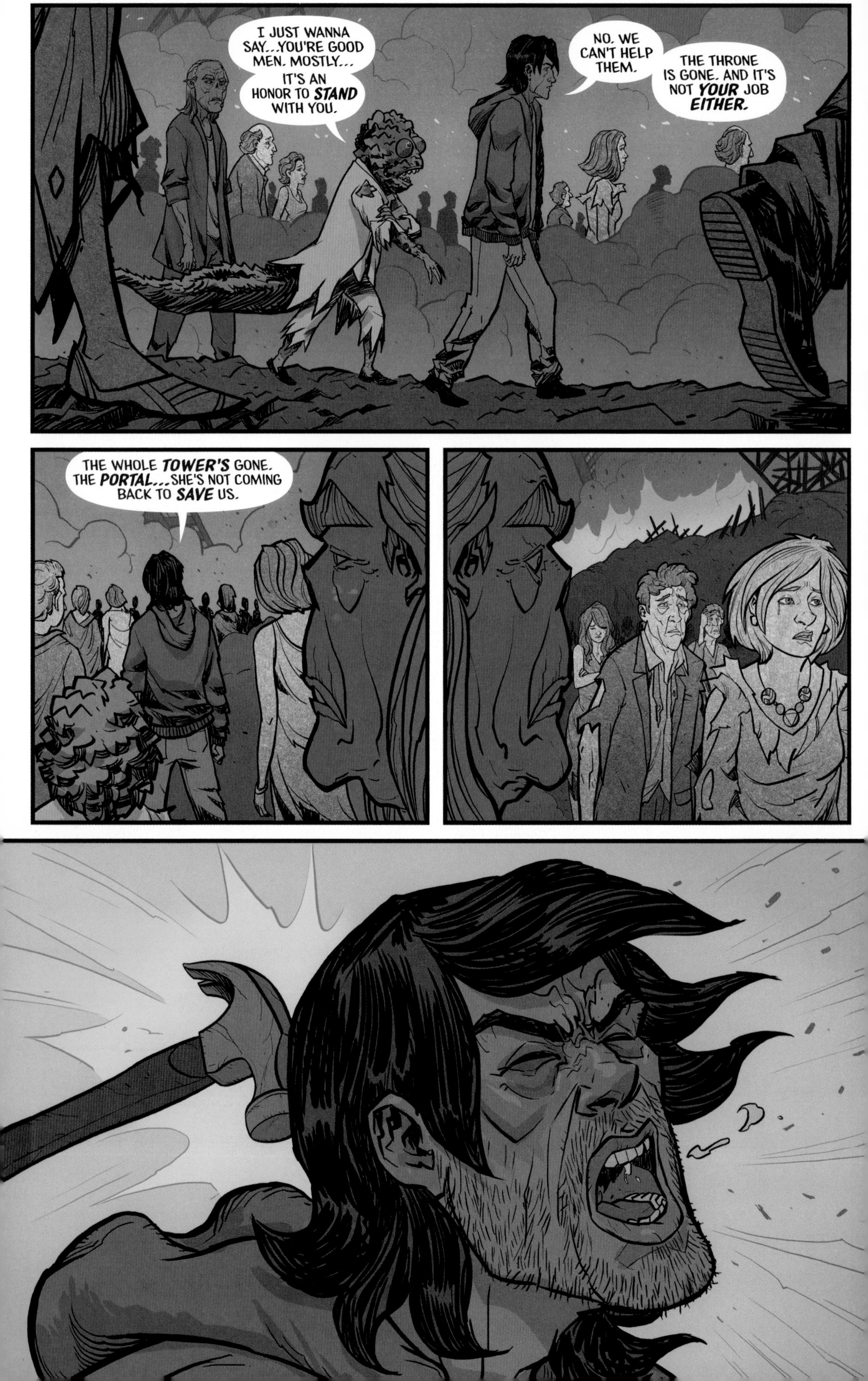

I JUST WANNA SAY... YOU'RE GOOD MEN. MOSTLY...
IT'S AN HONOR TO **STAND** WITH YOU.
NO. WE CAN'T HELP THEM.
THE THRONE IS GONE. AND IT'S NOT **YOUR** JOB **EITHER.**
THE WHOLE **TOWER'S** GONE. THE **PORTAL...** SHE'S NOT COMING BACK TO **SAVE** US.

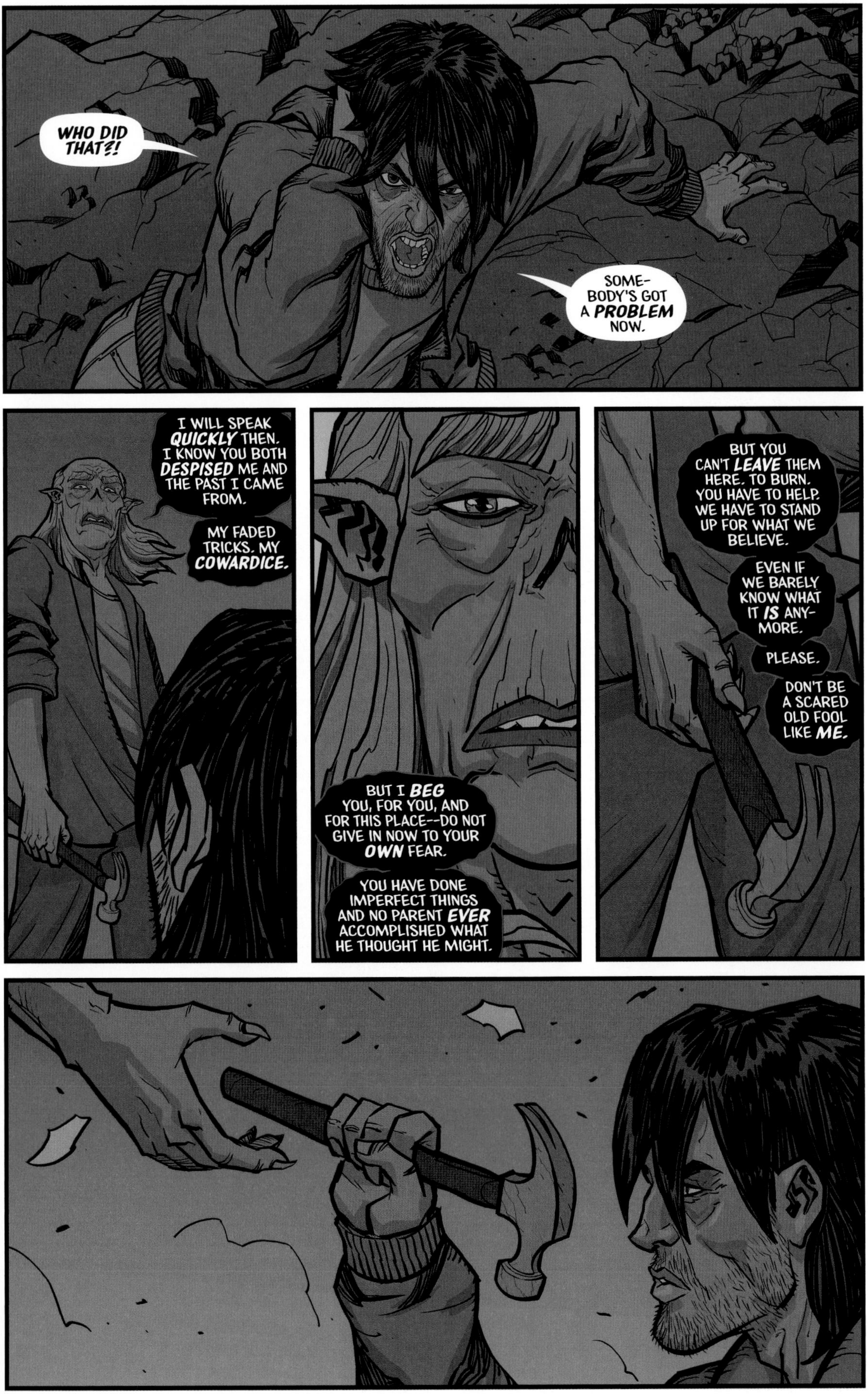
WHO DID THAT?!
SOME-BODY'S GOT A PROBLEM NOW.
I WILL SPEAK QUICKLY THEN. I KNOW YOU BOTH DESPISED ME AND THE PAST I CAME FROM.
MY FADED TRICKS. MY COWARDICE.
BUT I BEG YOU, FOR YOU, AND FOR THIS PLACE--DO NOT GIVE IN NOW TO YOUR OWN FEAR.
YOU HAVE DONE IMPERFECT THINGS AND NO PARENT EVER ACCOMPLISHED WHAT HE THOUGHT HE MIGHT.
BUT YOU CAN'T LEAVE THEM HERE. TO BURN. YOU HAVE TO HELP. WE HAVE TO STAND UP FOR WHAT WE BELIEVE.
EVEN IF WE BARELY KNOW WHAT IT IS ANY-MORE.
PLEASE.
DON'T BE A SCARED OLD FOOL LIKE ME.

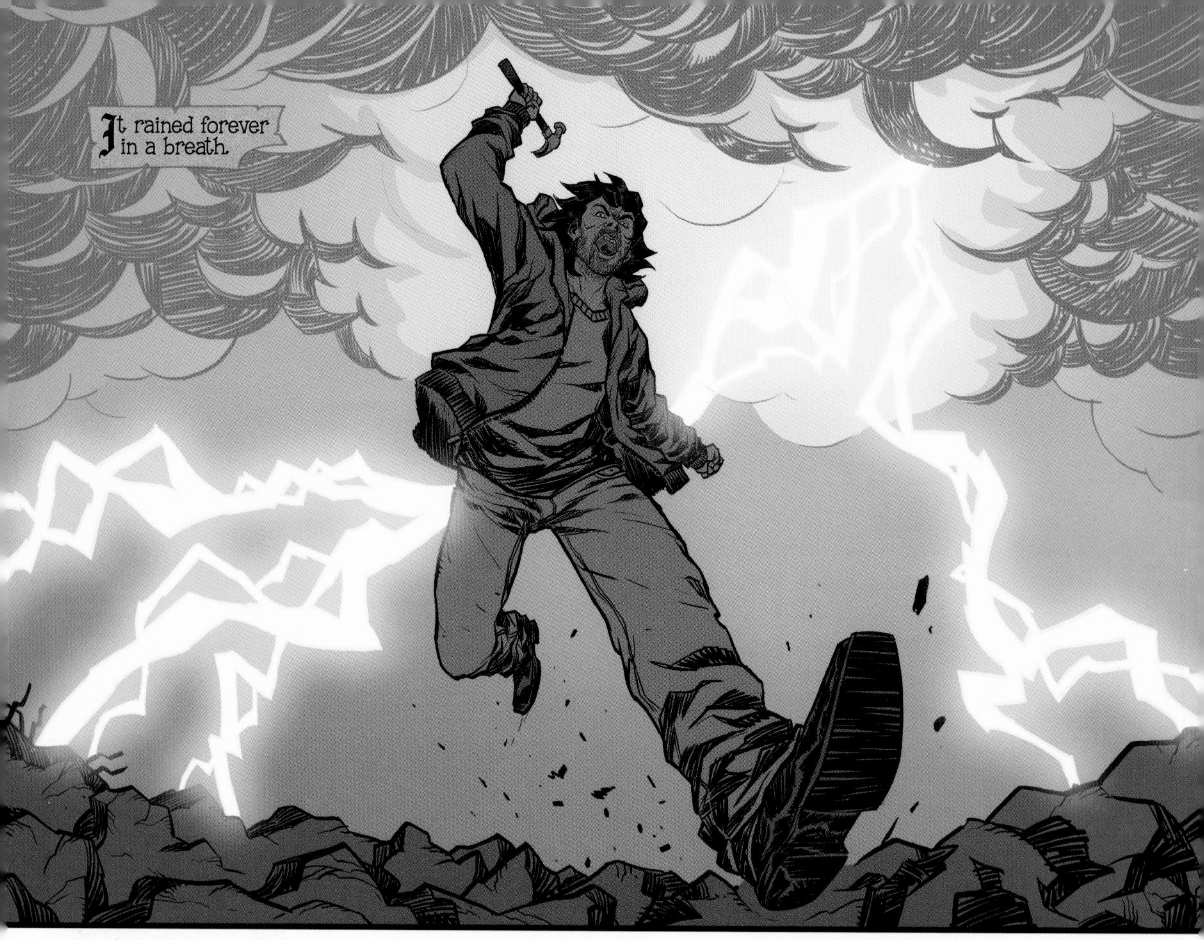
It rained forever in a breath.

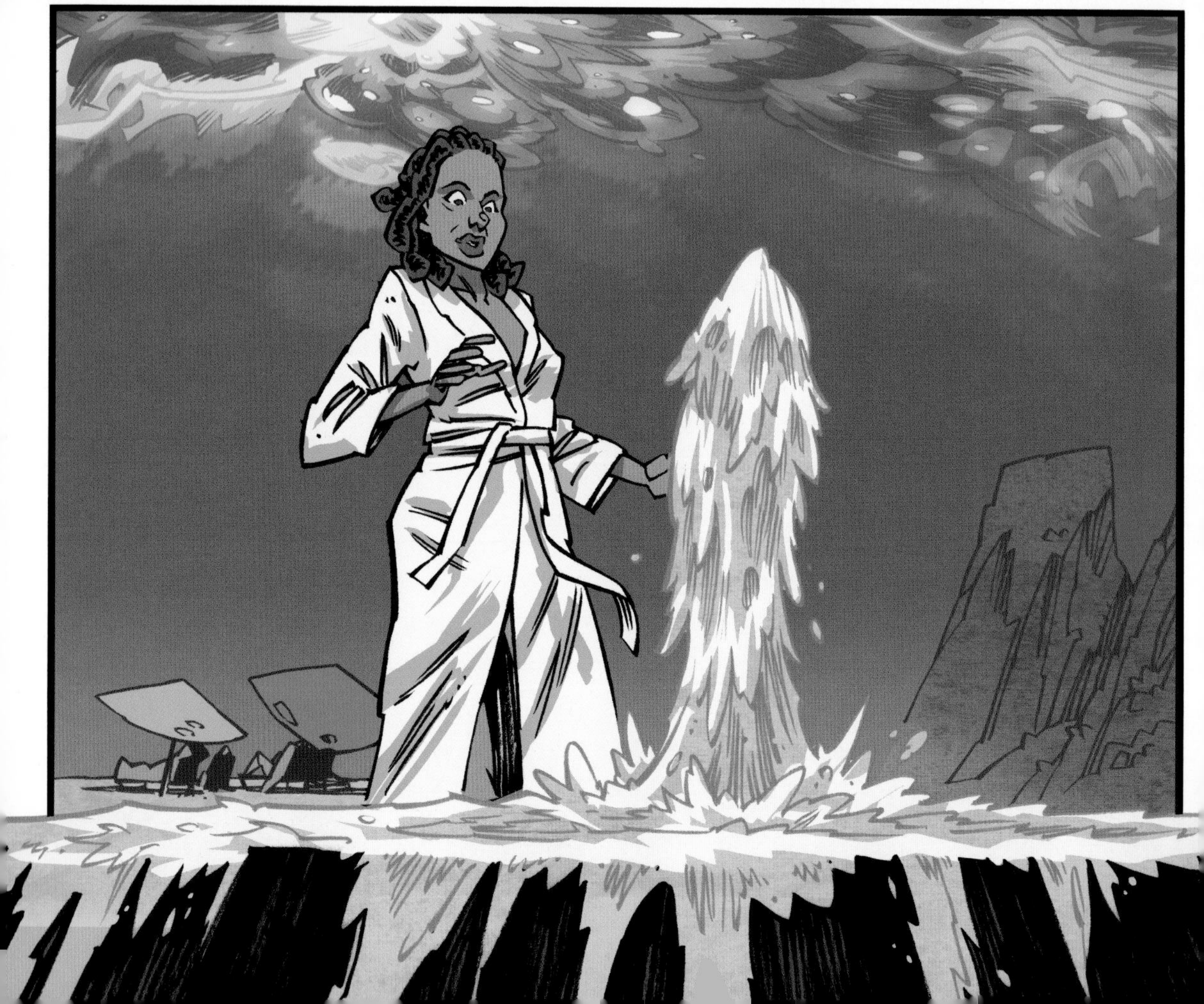

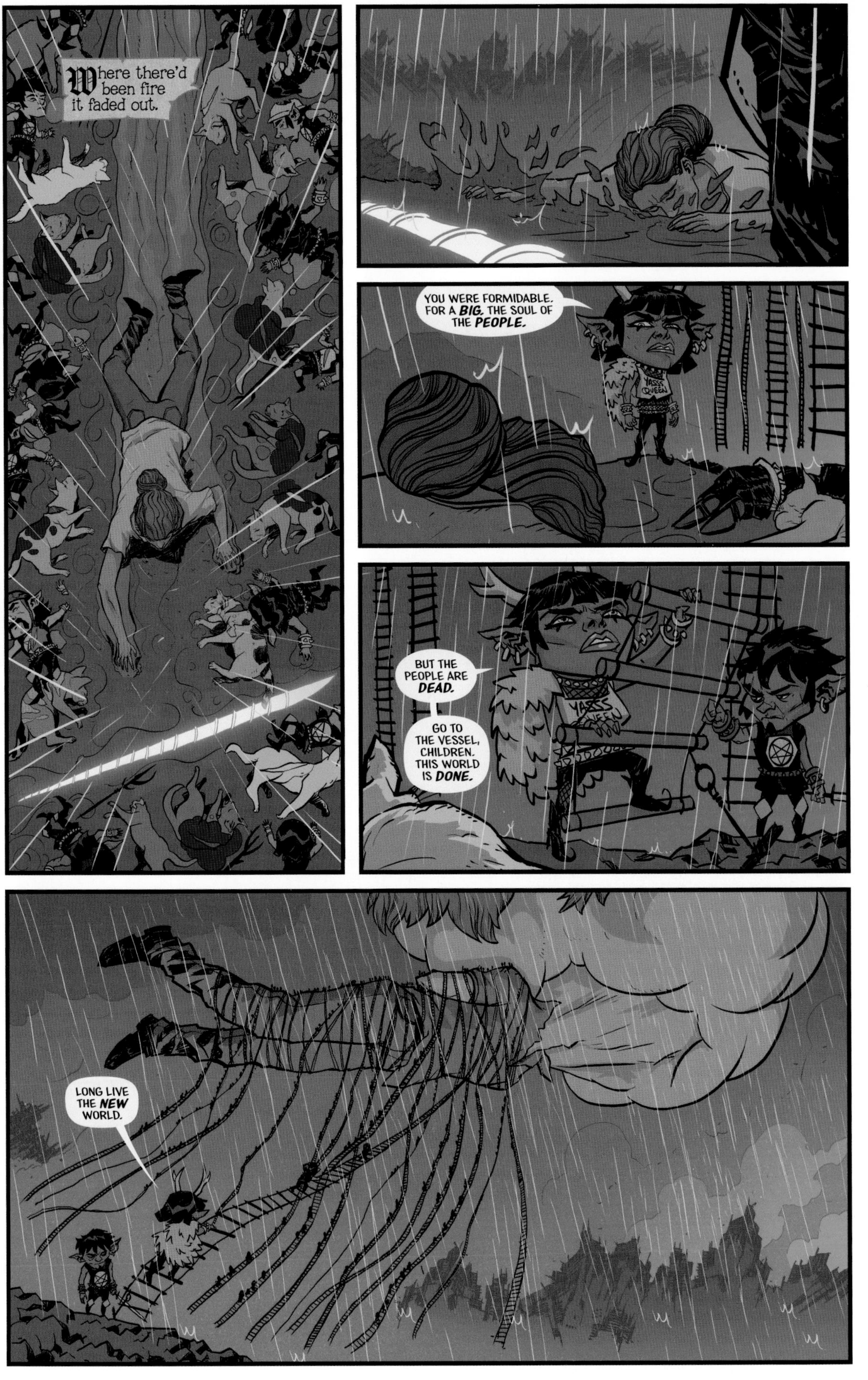
Where there'd been fire it faded out.
YOU WERE FORMIDABLE. FOR A BIG. THE SOUL OF THE PEOPLE.
YASSS QUEEN
BUT THE PEOPLE ARE DEAD.
GO TO THE VESSEL, CHILDREN. THIS WORLD IS DONE.
LONG LIVE THE NEW WORLD.

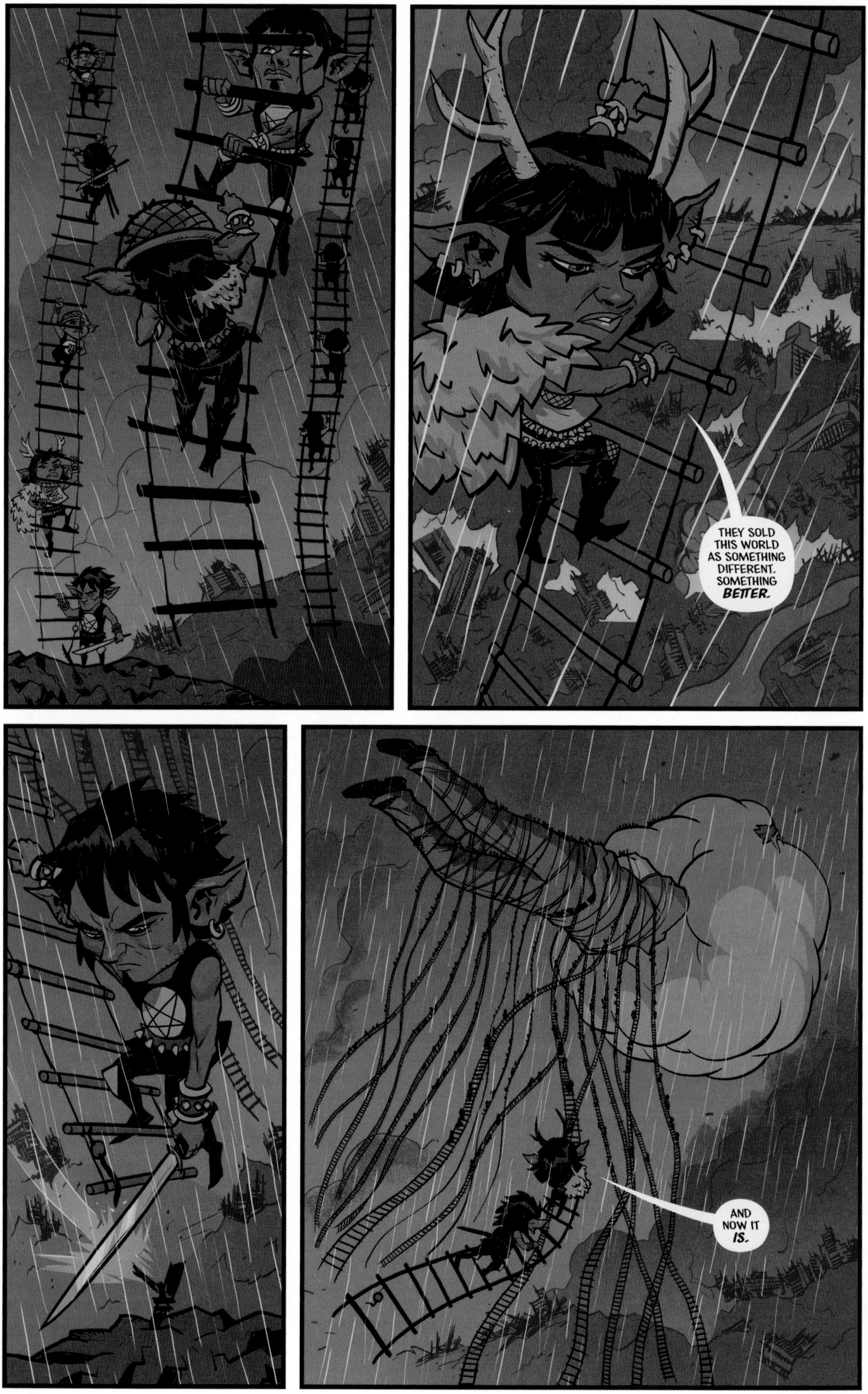
THEY SOLD THIS WORLD AS SOMETHING DIFFERENT. SOMETHING *BETTER.*
AND NOW IT *IS.*

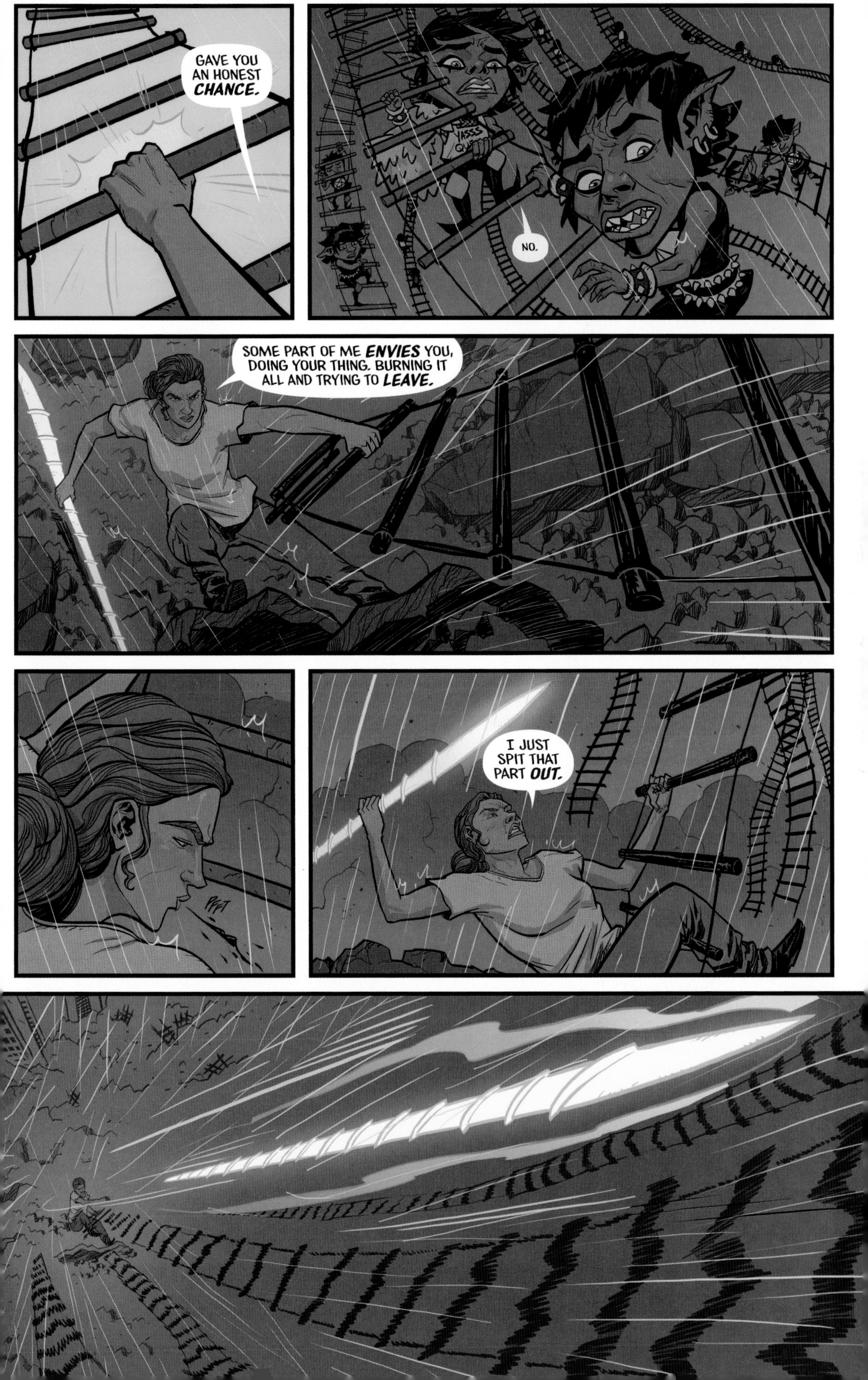
GAVE YOU AN HONEST CHANCE.
NO.
SOME PART OF ME ENVIES YOU, DOING YOUR THING. BURNING IT ALL AND TRYING TO LEAVE.
I JUST SPIT THAT PART OUT.

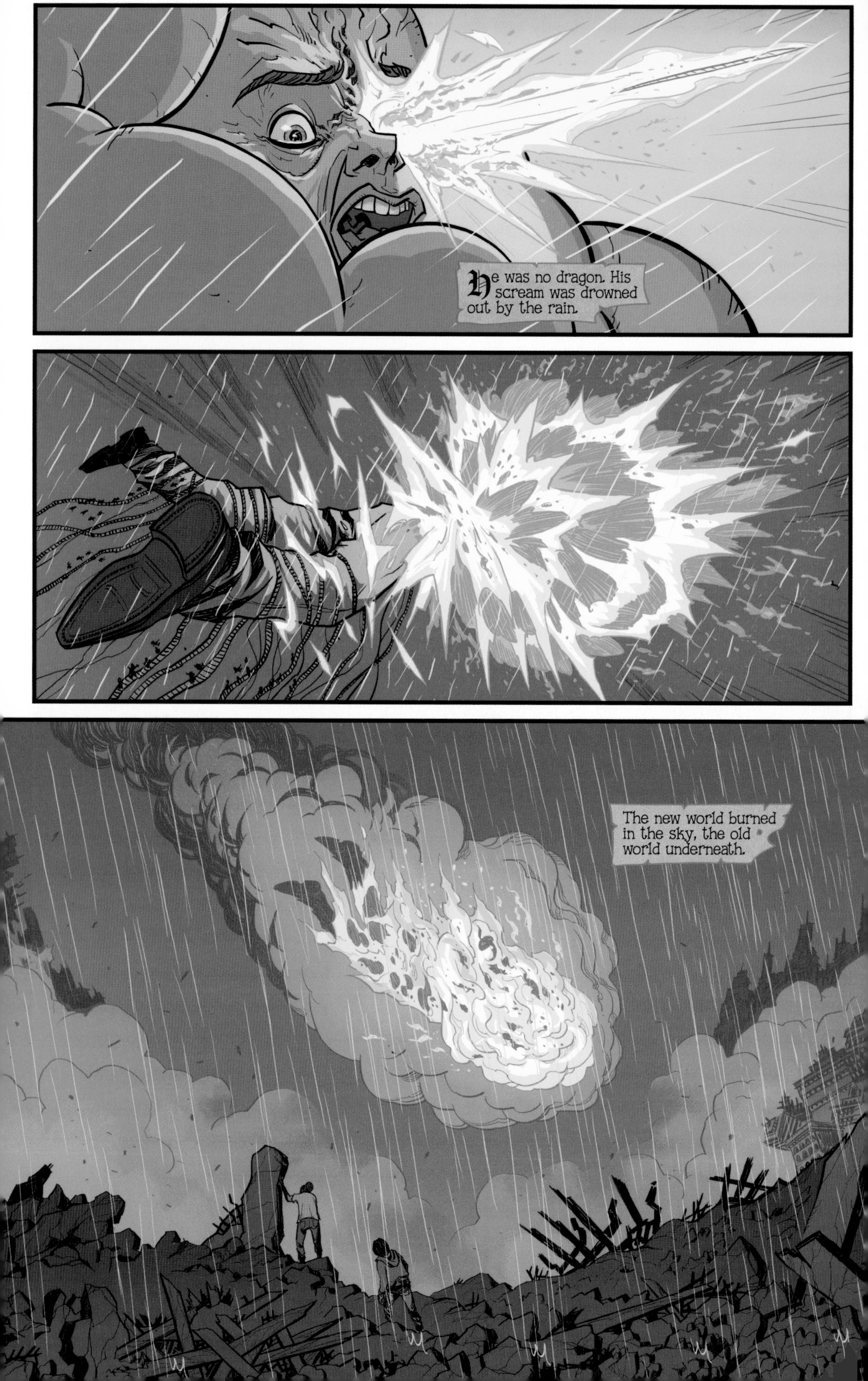
He was no dragon. His scream was drowned out by the rain.
The new world burned in the sky, the old world underneath.

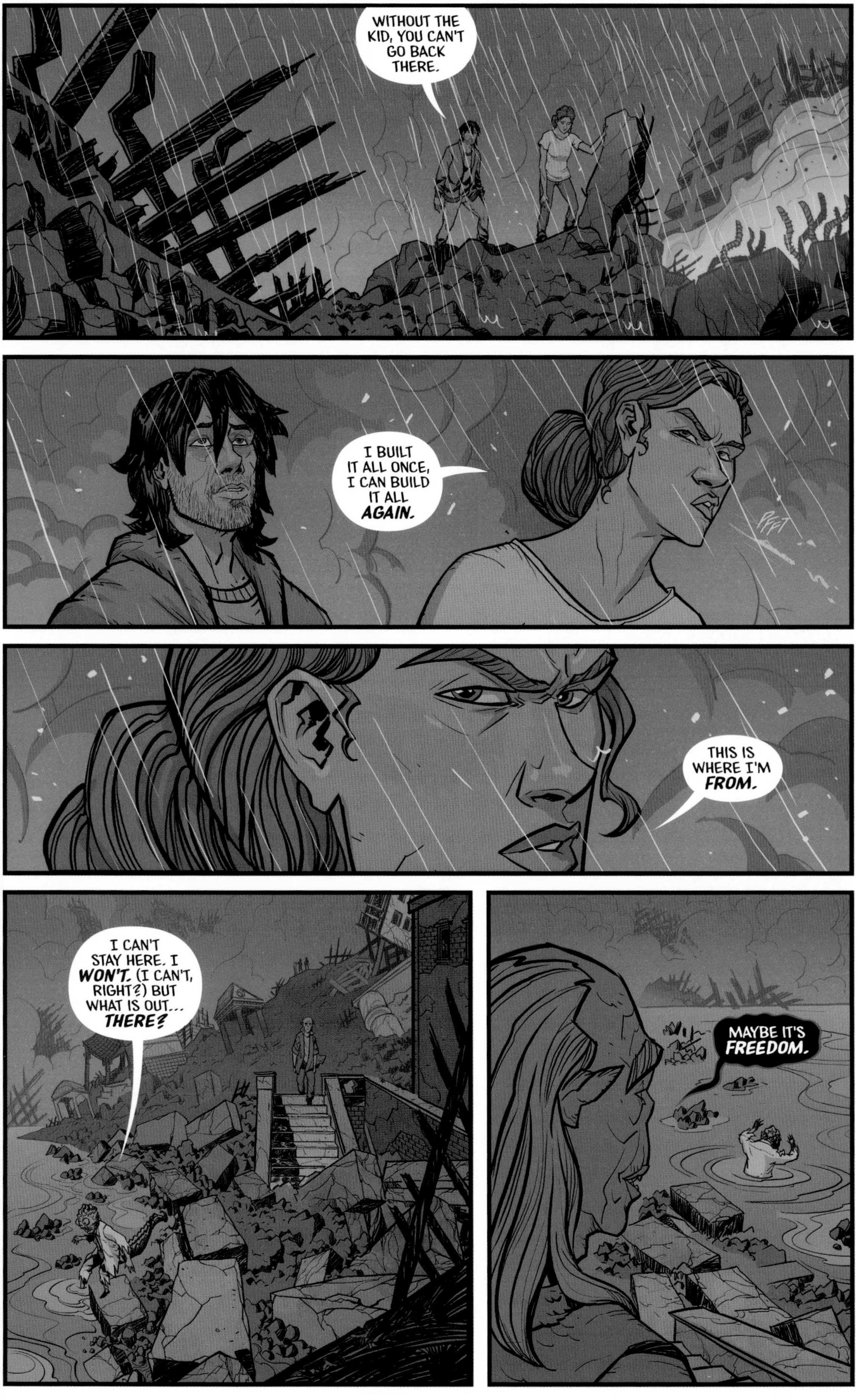
WITHOUT THE KID, YOU CAN'T GO BACK THERE.
I BUILT IT ALL ONCE, I CAN BUILD IT ALL AGAIN.
PFFT
THIS IS WHERE I'M FROM.
I CAN'T STAY HERE. I WON'T. (I CAN'T, RIGHT?) BUT WHAT IS OUT... THERE?
MAYBE IT'S FREEDOM.

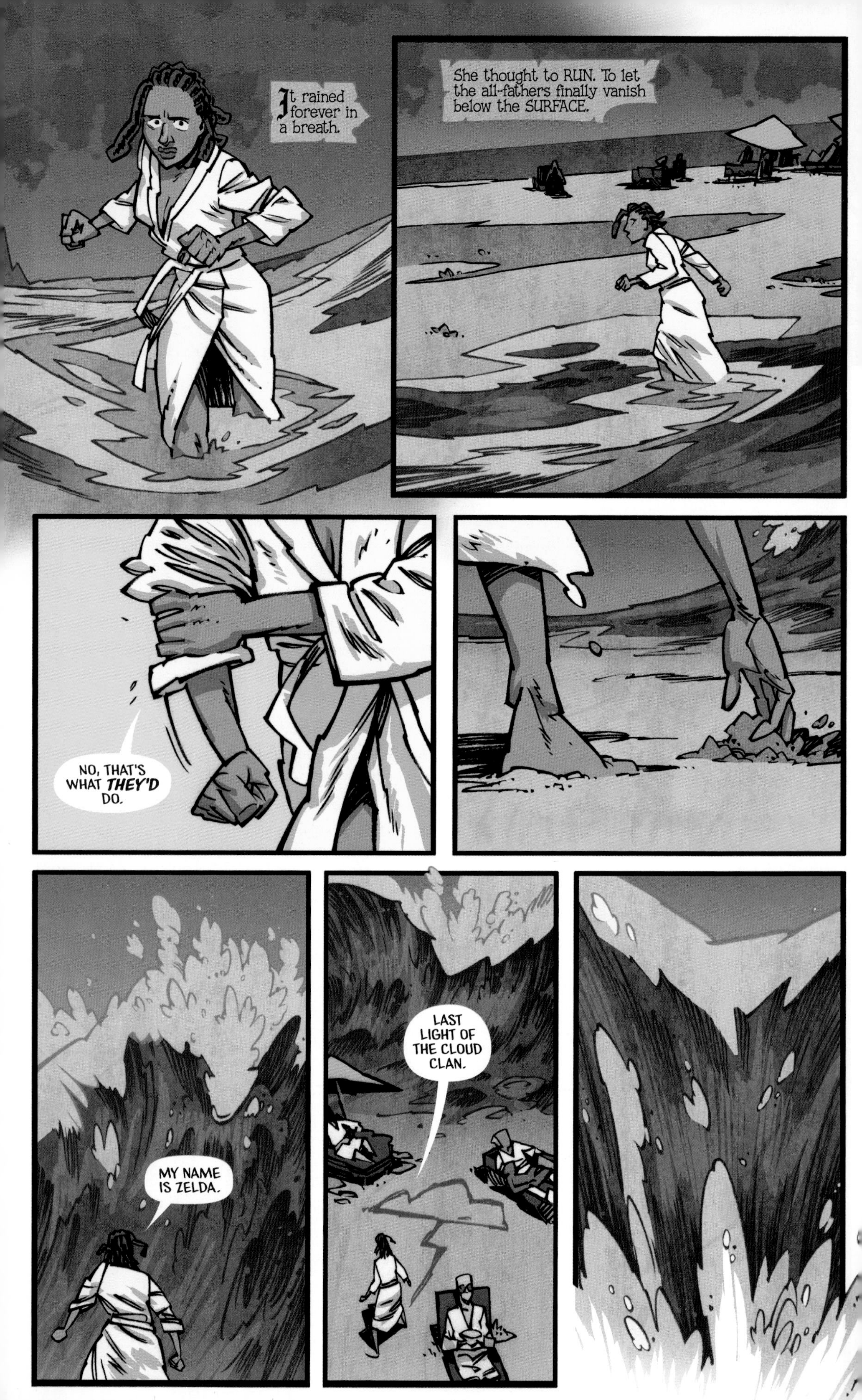
It rained forever in a breath.
She thought to RUN. To let the all-fathers finally vanish below the SURFACE.
NO, THAT'S WHAT THEY'D DO.
MY NAME IS ZELDA.
LAST LIGHT OF THE CLOUD CLAN.

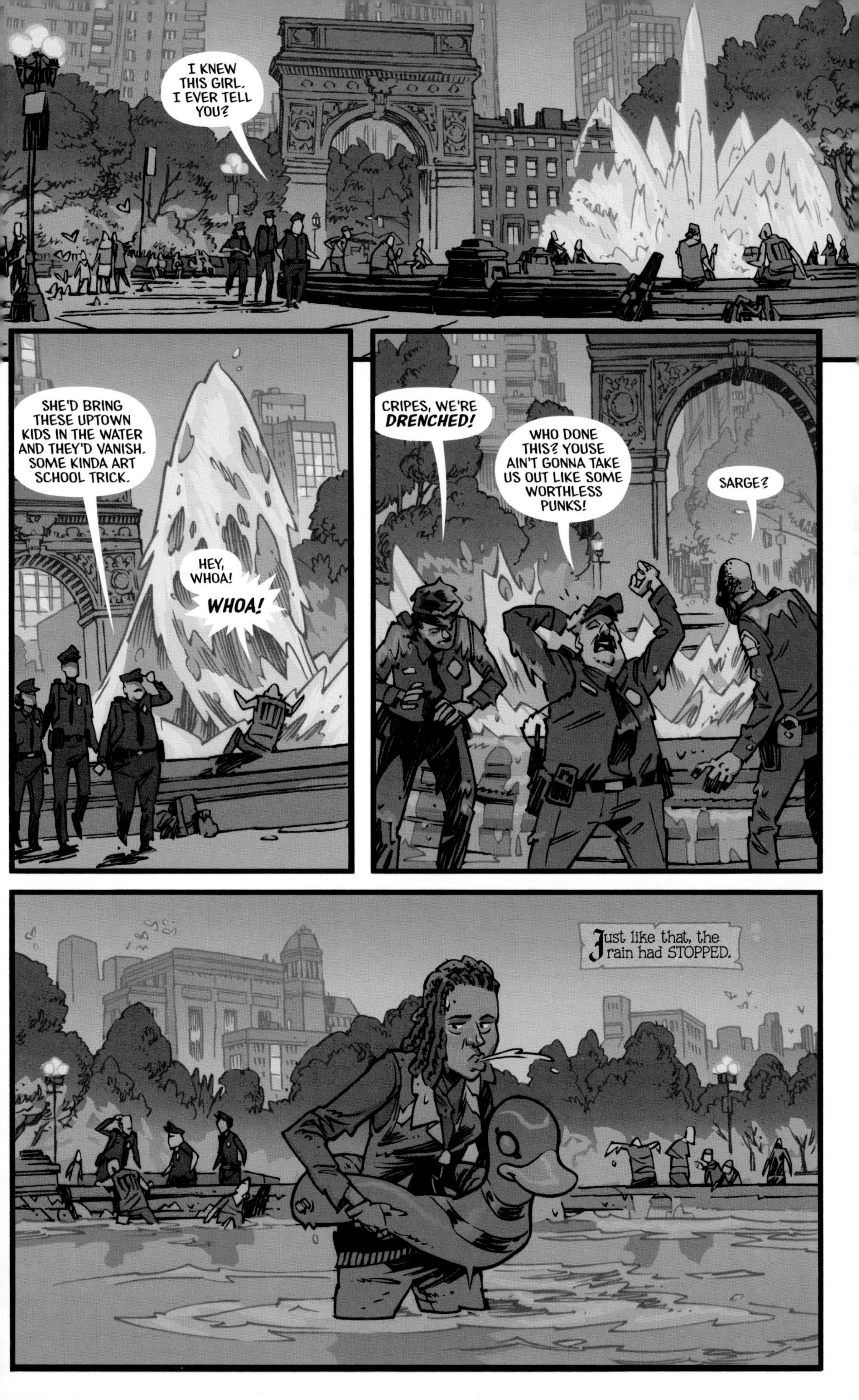
I KNEW THIS GIRL. I EVER TELL YOU?
SHE'D BRING THESE UPTOWN KIDS IN THE WATER AND THEY'D VANISH. SOME KINDA ART SCHOOL TRICK.
HEY, WHOA!
WHOA!
CRIPES, WE'RE DRENCHED!
WHO DONE THIS? YOUSE AIN'T GONNA TAKE US OUT LIKE SOME WORTHLESS PUNKS!
SARGE?
Just like that, the rain had STOPPED.

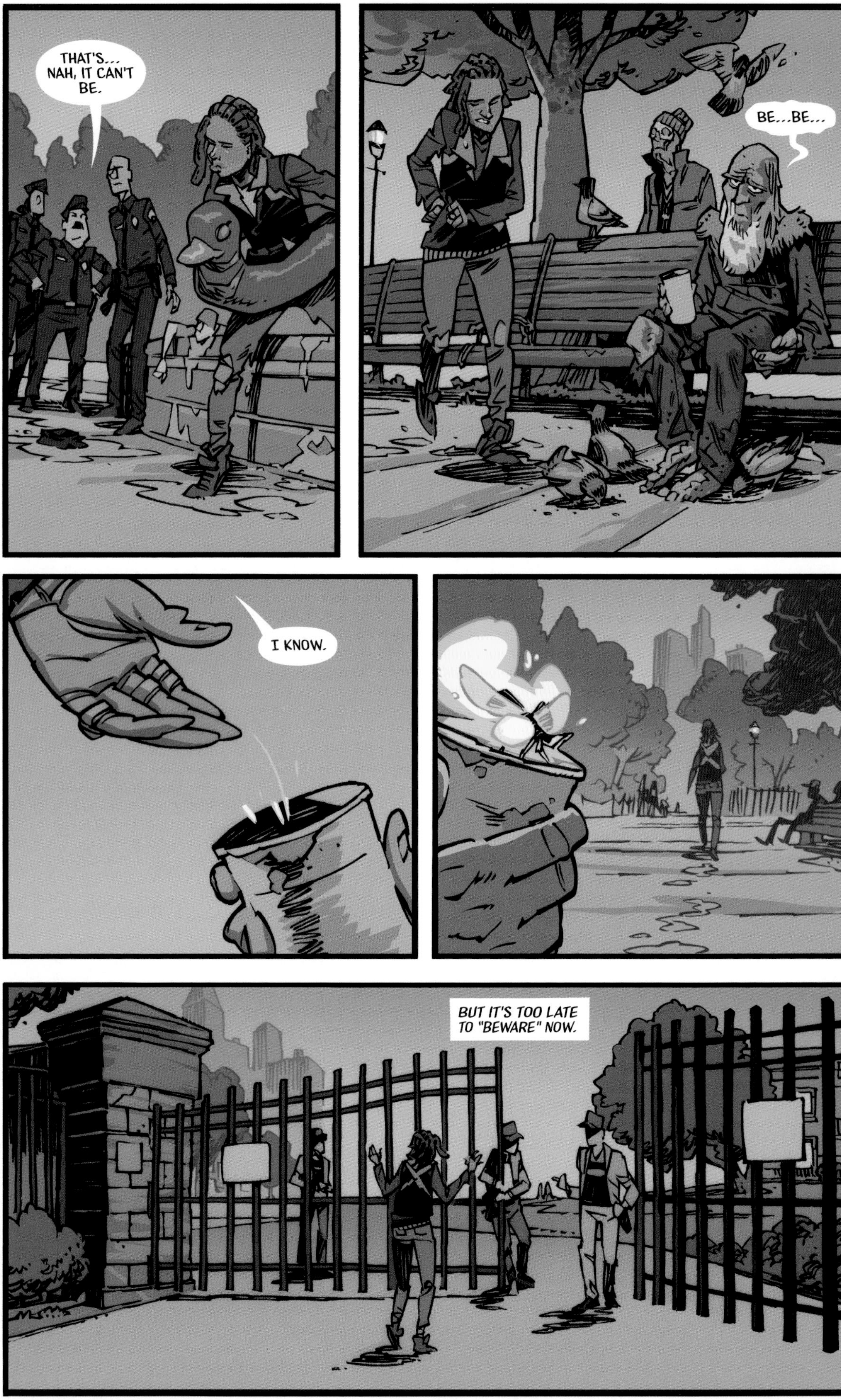
THAT'S... NAH, IT CAN'T BE.
BE...BE...
I KNOW.
BUT IT'S TOO LATE TO "BEWARE" NOW.

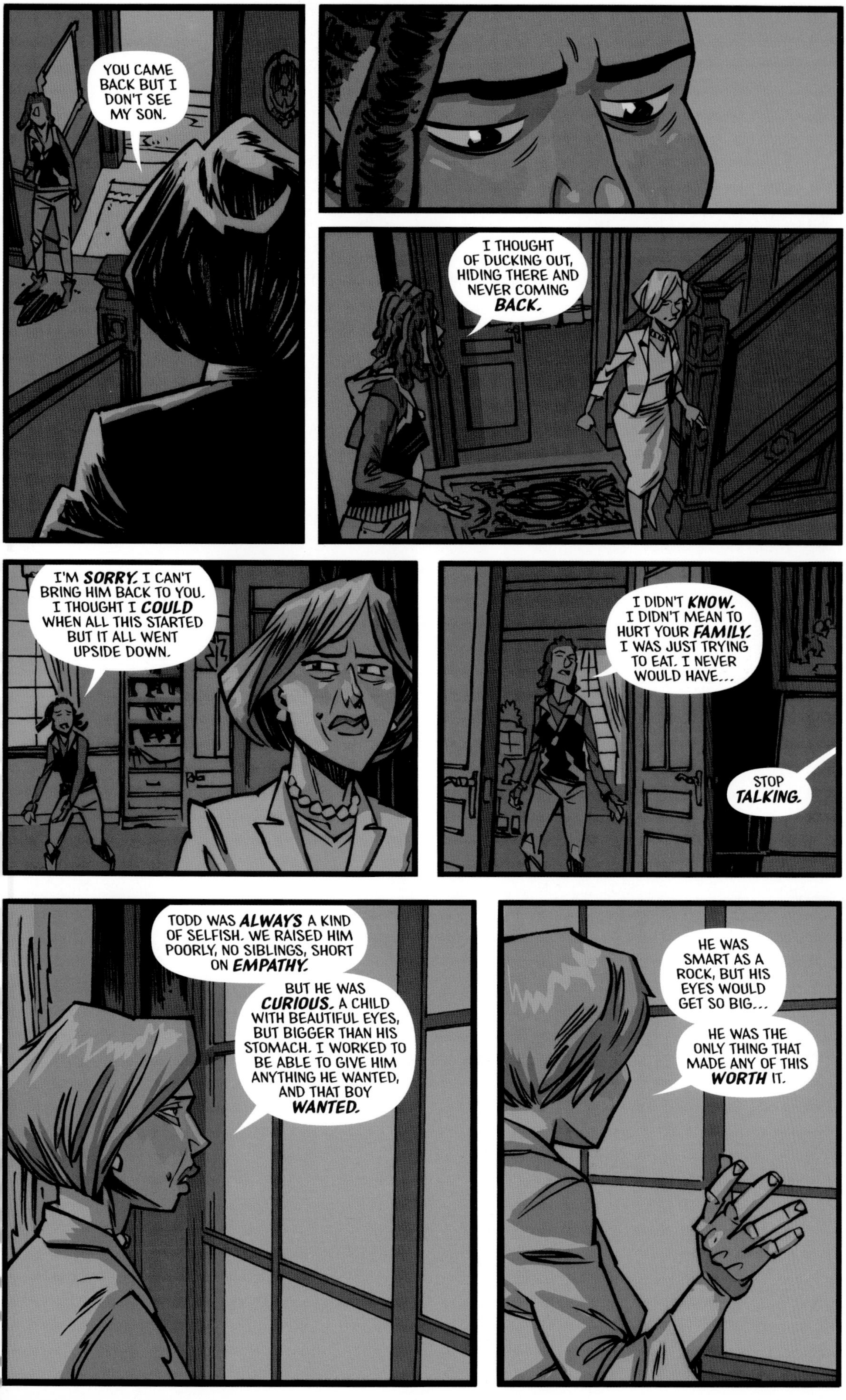

YOU CAME BACK BUT I DON'T SEE MY SON.
I THOUGHT OF DUCKING OUT, HIDING THERE AND NEVER COMING BACK.
I'M SORRY. I CAN'T BRING HIM BACK TO YOU. I THOUGHT I COULD WHEN ALL THIS STARTED BUT IT ALL WENT UPSIDE DOWN.
I DIDN'T KNOW. I DIDN'T MEAN TO HURT YOUR FAMILY. I WAS JUST TRYING TO EAT. I NEVER WOULD HAVE...
STOP TALKING.
TODD WAS ALWAYS A KIND OF SELFISH. WE RAISED HIM POORLY, NO SIBLINGS, SHORT ON EMPATHY.
BUT HE WAS CURIOUS. A CHILD WITH BEAUTIFUL EYES, BUT BIGGER THAN HIS STOMACH. I WORKED TO BE ABLE TO GIVE HIM ANYTHING HE WANTED, AND THAT BOY WANTED.
HE WAS SMART AS A ROCK, BUT HIS EYES WOULD GET SO BIG...
HE WAS THE ONLY THING THAT MADE ANY OF THIS WORTH IT.

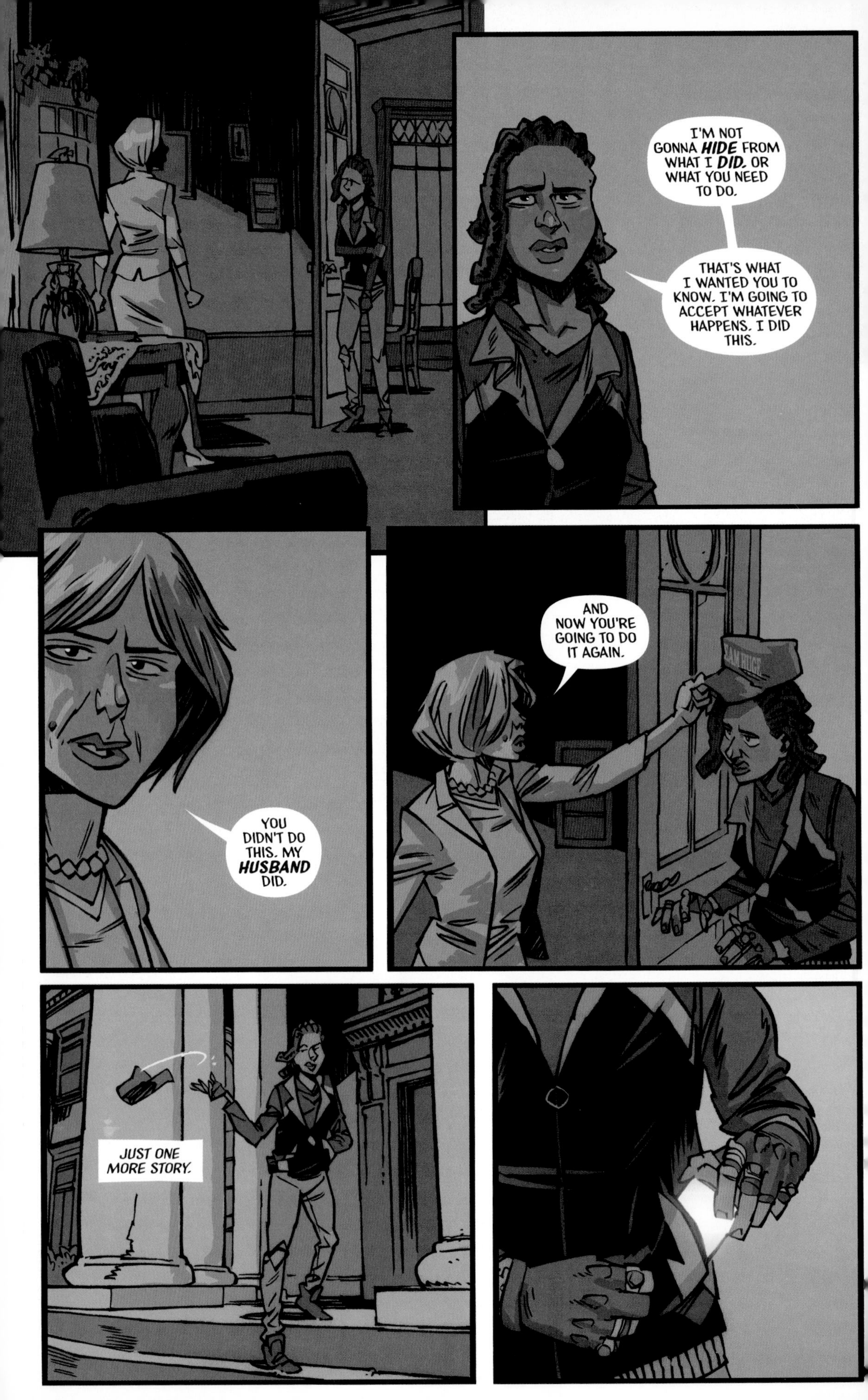
I'M NOT GONNA HIDE FROM WHAT I DID. OR WHAT YOU NEED TO DO.
THAT'S WHAT I WANTED YOU TO KNOW. I'M GOING TO ACCEPT WHATEVER HAPPENS. I DID THIS.
YOU DIDN'T DO THIS. MY HUSBAND DID.
AND NOW YOU'RE GOING TO DO IT AGAIN.
JUST ONE MORE STORY.

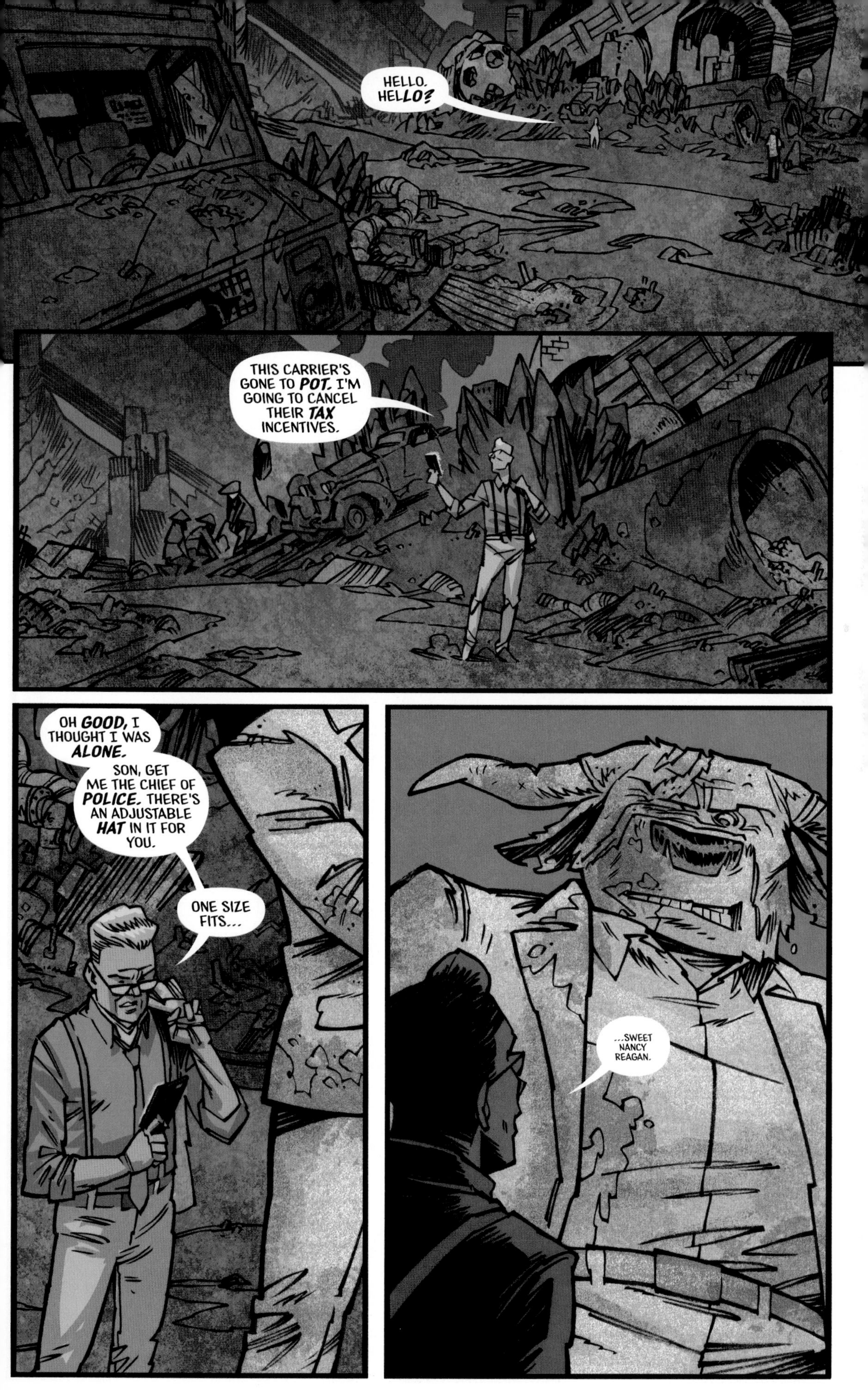
HELLO.
HELLO?
THIS CARRIER'S GONE TO POT. I'M GOING TO CANCEL THEIR TAX INCENTIVES.
OH GOOD, I THOUGHT I WAS ALONE.
SON, GET ME THE CHIEF OF POLICE. THERE'S AN ADJUSTABLE HAT IN IT FOR YOU.
ONE SIZE FITS...
...SWEET NANCY REAGAN.

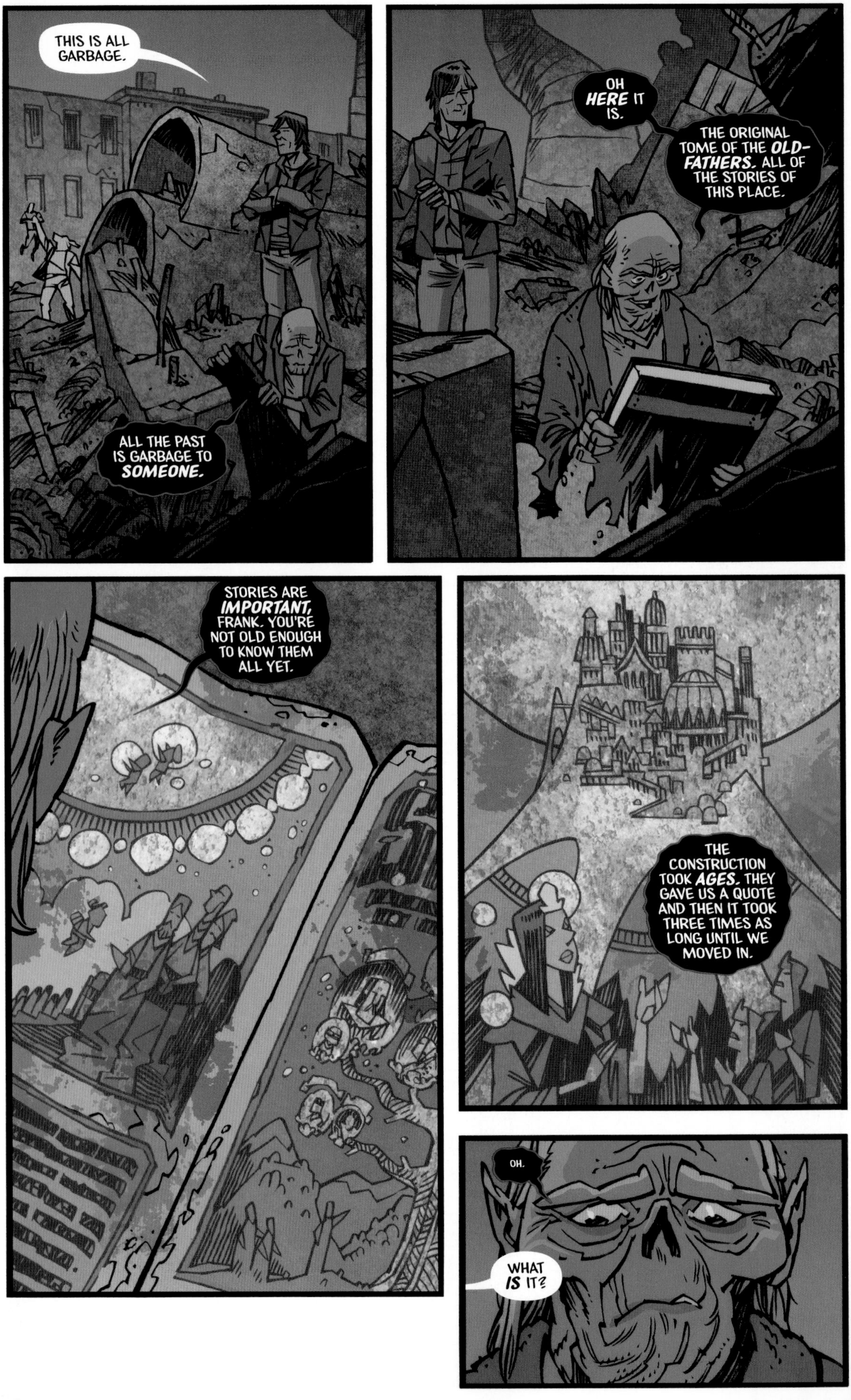

THIS IS ALL GARBAGE.
ALL THE PAST IS GARBAGE TO SOMEONE.
OH HERE IT IS.
THE ORIGINAL TOME OF THE OLD-FATHERS. ALL OF THE STORIES OF THIS PLACE.
STORIES ARE IMPORTANT, FRANK. YOU'RE NOT OLD ENOUGH TO KNOW THEM ALL YET.
THE CONSTRUCTION TOOK AGES. THEY GAVE US A QUOTE AND THEN IT TOOK THREE TIMES AS LONG UNTIL WE MOVED IN.
OH.
WHAT IS IT?

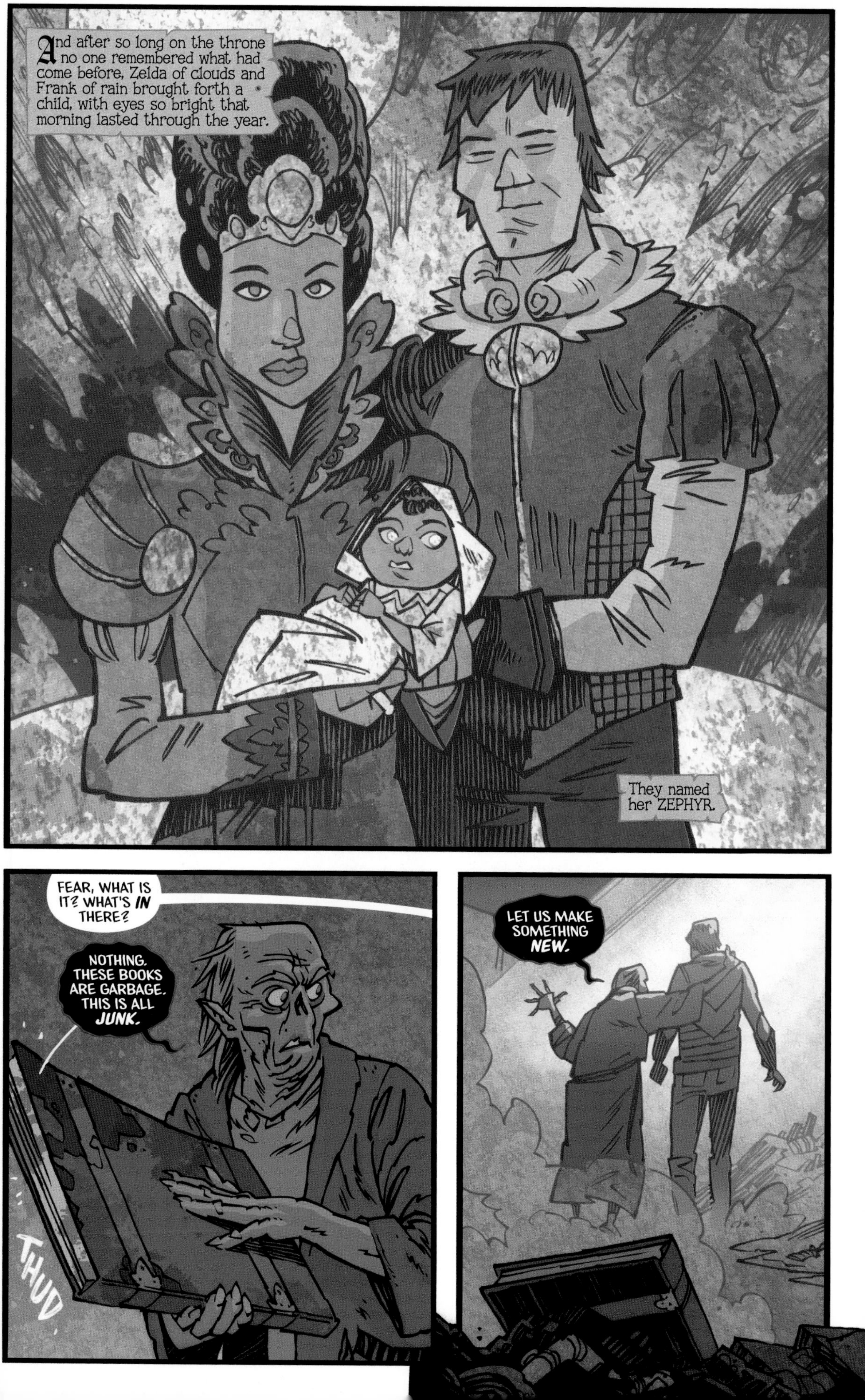
And after so long on the throne no one remembered what had come before, Zelda of clouds and Frank of rain brought forth a child, with eyes so bright that morning lasted through the year.
They named her ZEPHYR.
FEAR, WHAT IS IT? WHAT'S *IN* THERE?
NOTHING. THESE BOOKS ARE GARBAGE. THIS IS ALL *JUNK*.
THUD
LET US MAKE SOMETHING *NEW*.

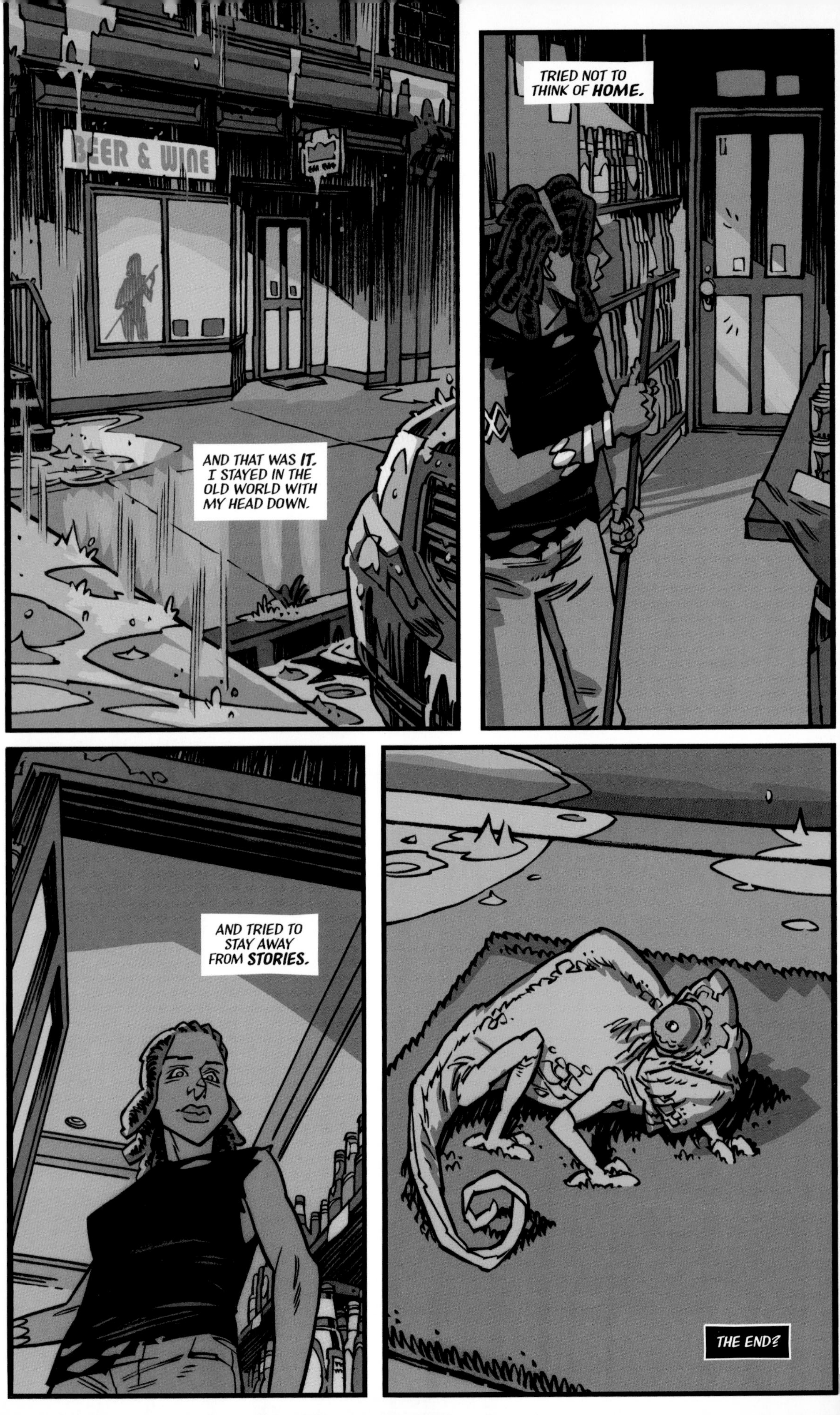
BEER & WINE
AND THAT WAS IT. I STAYED IN THE OLD WORLD WITH MY HEAD DOWN.
TRIED NOT TO THINK OF HOME.
AND TRIED TO STAY AWAY FROM STORIES.
THE END?

BLACK CLOUD, VOL. 2: NO RETURN. First printing. August 2018. Published by Image Comics, Inc. Office of publication: 2701 NW Vaughn St., Suite 780, Portland, OR 97210. Copyright © 2018 Againdemon, LLC, Jason Latour, and Greg Hinkle. All rights reserved. Contains material originally published in single magazine form as BLACK CLOUD #6-10. "Black Cloud," its logos, and the likenesses of all characters herein are trademarks of Againdemon, LLC, Jason Latour, and Greg Hinkle, unless otherwise noted. "Image" and the Image Comics logos are registered trademarks of Image Comics, Inc. No part of this publication may be reproduced or transmitted, in any form or by any means (except short excerpts for journalistic or review purposes) without the express written permission of Againdemon, LLC, Jason Latour, Greg Hinkle, or Image Comics, Inc. All names, characters, events, and locales in this publication are entirely fictional. Any resemblance to actual persons (living or dead), events, or places, without satirical intent, is coincidental. Printed in the USA. For more information regarding the CPSIA on this printed material call: 203-595-3636 and provide reference #RICH−810857.
Contact: Law Offices of Harris M. Miller II, P.C. (rightsinquiries@gmail.com). ISBN: 978-1-5343-0669-1.